Sex and Vanity

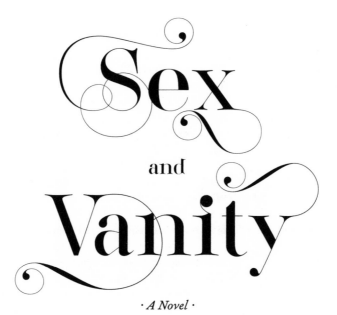

Sex
and
Vanity

· *A Novel* ·

Kevin Kwan

Doubleday
Canada

Doubleday Canada and colophon are registered trademarks of
Penguin Random House Canada Limited

Library and Archives Canada Cataloguing in Publication

Title: Sex and vanity / Kevin Kwan.
Names: Kwan, Kevin, author.
Identifiers: Canadiana (print) 20200206516 | Canadiana (ebook) 20200206532
| ISBN 9780385695404 (hardcover) | ISBN 9780385695435 (EPUB)
Classification: LCC PS3611.W36 S49 2020 | DDC 813/.6—dc23

This is a work of fiction. Names, characters, places, and incidents either are the
product of the author's imagination or are used fictitiously. Any resemblance
to actual persons, living or dead, events, or locales is entirely coincidental.

Jacket design by John Fontana
Jacket illustration by Clément Dezelus

Printed and bound in the USA

Published in Canada by Doubleday Canada,
a division of Penguin Random House Canada Limited

www.penguinrandomhouse.ca

10 9 8 7 6 5 4 3 2

Penguin
Random House
DOUBLEDAY CANADA

For Capri, the island that feeds my soul,
and for New York, the city that took me in,
nurtured me, and changed me forever

Sex and Vanity

From: Isabel Chiu
To: lucietangchurchill@gmail.com
Subject: la dolce vita

Lucie!!!

I'm sooooo happy you're coming to my wedding in Capri! Do you know, apart from my family, you're the person I've known the longest who will be there? I can hardly believe we've been friends since I was 13 and you were 7—you were the *only* kid I ever babysat, although I would hardly consider it babysitting since you had to endure repeated viewings of *Roswell* and hearing me moan nonstop about my obsessions. (Remember Nikolai? Ran into him at Erewhon the other day. He's in LA working as a location scout for Lawrence Bender, and he's totally unrecognizable now!)

Anyway, after getting approval from my mom's fortune teller, we've chosen an auspicious day in July to celebrate our nuptials, and Capri, where Dolfi spent every summer of his youth and where his family has deep roots, will be absolutely magical at that time. It's so special to me that you're joining us, and of course I remember your cousin Charlotte and look forward to seeing her too. I can't wait for all of us to be on the island together and for you to meet my friends!

My calligrapher is behind schedule because she was a bit unprepared for the sheer number of guests, but the formal invitations should be done by the end of the month. Be on the lookout for yours!

xoxo,
Issie

To: Lucie Tang Churchill & Guest

999 FIFTH AVENUE, APT. 12B
NEW YORK, NY 10028

Mr. and Mrs. Christopher Chiu

request the pleasure of your company
at the marriage of their daughter

Isabel

~ to ~

Mr. Adolfo Michelangelo De Vecchi

son of Conte Andrea De Vecchi
and Contessa Laudomia De Vecchi

at the Villa Lysis
on Saturday, 20th July 2013
at five o'clock
and afterward at
Villa Jovis
Capri, Italy

❧

RSVP
ISABEL CHIU
875 NIMES ROAD
LOS ANGELES, CA 90077

The trail was lit by tall flickering torches, but Charlotte Barclay still felt like she could have fallen a thousand times on the pathway. She knew she had broken the cardinal rule that every seasoned magazine editor like herself always adhered to: dress sensibly, not frivolously, when traveling. Staring down at the tattered hemline of her party dress and cursing her decision to wear stilettos borrowed from Olivia Lavistock at the last minute, she felt like she had been stumbling through the woods for hours, although it had been only about fifteen minutes, and when the villa finally came into view, its Ionic columns illuminated in high relief against the dark liquid night, she breathed a sigh of relief.

Patting down her fastidious blond bob—a style that had not altered since her days at Miss Porter's—Charlotte climbed up the uneven marble steps and entered the terrace overlooking the Bay of Naples, feeling disoriented yet again. The graceful veranda that was empty an hour ago had been transformed in the blink of an eye into yet another banquet space where a lavish midnight buffet was set up, and wedding guests lured from the ballroom were grazing like chic gazelles at the long tables laden with delectable treats.

Charlotte glanced around nervously, feeling as if every single one of those damned Italian *principessas* and *contessas* was scrutinizing her every move. How could the most exquisite wedding she'd ever witnessed have morphed so quickly into a living nightmare? She saw Auden Beebe pile a heap of lobster ravioli onto his plate, and for a moment she wanted to rush over to him for help. *No, he's the wrong person. He won't quite understand.* The Ortiz sisters were just coming up the stairs. *Absolutely not them.*

When she spotted Olivia perched at one of the high-top bistro tables along the wall, she could finally feel the tension in her shoulders ease. Olivia would know what to do. Olivia would be cool; she was an avant-garde filmmaker. Olivia was English, but she wasn't like the other English here. She lived in LA and had gone to school in Paris, so she'd probably seen some shit in her time. Olivia would help her out of this unthinkable mess.

Charlotte marched up alongside her, covertly grabbing her elbow. Olivia immediately caught Charlotte's look and misread it. "Sure, call me a hypocrite. But after watching you inhaling pasta, focaccia, biscotti, and every possible variation of gluten for the past week, what did you think would happen? This white truffle and caviar pizza is better than wild muddy sex in a Scottish dale with Sam Heughan. You ought to write about it in your magazine."

Charlotte tried to speak but found that her throat was too parched.

"I'm talking about the pizza, not the muddy Scottish sex," Olivia clarified, although Charlotte clearly hadn't been listening to a word she had said. She simply leaned against Olivia, trying to catch her breath.

"Are you okay?" Olivia asked, registering the shell-shocked expression on Charlotte's face for the first time.

"I'm okay . . . but Lucie . . . God help the girl!" Charlotte gasped, reaching for a flute of prosecco. Charlotte gulped down the drink, and then, slumping against the stone balustrade, started to hyper-ventilate.

"What happened to Lucie? Should I get help?" Olivia asked.

"She doesn't need any help, she's fine. Actually, she's not fine. Oh, my poor Lucie. Everything's ruined! Abso-*fucking*-lutely ruined!"

Olivia frowned, not sure what to make of this outburst. She hadn't known Charlotte Barclay very long, but they had become thick as thieves over the past week, and Olivia would never have imagined that this unflappably poised woman in her mid-forties would suddenly, apparently, lose it. "Charlotte, how many glasses of champagne did you have at dinner?" Olivia delicately inquired.

Straightening up and brushing off the stray twigs caught on her Oscar de la Renta gown, Charlotte said furtively, "Olivia, can I trust you? Can I count on your help?"

"Of course you can."

Charlotte continued. "You know I'm only at this wedding as a favor to Lucie's family. I'm just the plus-one here, and my only job was to keep an eye on my young cousin. But I've failed in my duty. Utterly, epically failed. We should never have come to this wedding. We should never have come to Capri. Jesus Christ, her mother's going to lose her shit when she finds out! And my grandmother's going to skin me alive!"

Charlotte buried her face in her hands, and Olivia could see that she was legitimately anguished. "Find out what? And *where* is Lucie now?"

"I don't know. I don't want to know. I don't know how I'll ever look her in the face again."

"Charlotte, please stop being so cryptic. I can't help you if you don't tell me what's happened."

Looking her dead in the eye, Charlotte said, "You've got to promise you'll never tell a soul."

"I promise."

"Swear on it. On your mother's grave."

"Mother still lives and breathes, but I'll swear on her life."

Charlotte exhaled. "When did you last see Lucie?"

"I'm not sure . . . on the dance floor with the bridal party? She was dancing with Sandro, and I thought they looked like such a lovely pair—him with those long Botticelli curls, and Lucie in that gossamer dress, dancing amid all those candles. It looked so gorgeous, I almost wanted to take a picture to remember it for a future scene."

"Yes, they were dancing. But after the fireworks, I noticed that Lucie had disappeared. I heard that some of the young ones had gone up to Villa Jovis again, so I went up to the ruins looking for her."

"You trekked all the way up the hill again? In my Viviers?" Olivia reflexively peered at Charlotte's feet, wondering how obliterated her shoes were.

"This fellow in a golf cart drove me up. Anyway, when I got up there, would you believe what I found? A whole bunch of kids smoking weed in the chapel. It looked like a drug den in Tangier!"

Olivia rolled her eyes. "Charlotte, *please* don't tell me you are upset because Lucie was doing that. All the kids have been smoking every night behind the pool. That kid whose family owns Ecuador brought a whole trunk bursting to the brim with goodies, so I'm told."

"Olivia! Do you really think I'm that much of a square? I went to Smith,[*] remember? Lucie's nineteen years old, and I couldn't care less if she wants to get baked as a Pop-Tart. Let me finish! I went through the great hall, and then I climbed up to the watchtower, but I couldn't find Lucie anywhere. I was wandering around those godforsaken ruins lit only by lanterns, and just when I thought I was completely lost, I found a passage leading outside to the cliff walk— that precarious path right by Tiberius's Leap."

"Dear God, please don't tell me Lucie fell!"

---

[*] Smith College in Northampton, Massachusetts, is considered one of the finest women's liberal arts colleges in America, with notable alumnae like Gloria Steinem, Barbara Bush, and Julia Child. Not that this has stopped the nearby men's fraternities from coining the saying "Smith to bed, Mount Holyoke to wed, and Amherst girls to talk to."

"No, it's nothing like that! I went out to the edge and saw some steps leading down to a little grotto, so I went down and that's . . ." Charlotte paused for a moment, steeling herself. "That's when I saw them."

"Who is *them*? What were they doing?"

"Olivia, I couldn't believe it. I just couldn't believe my eyes," Charlotte moaned.

"Let me guess . . . were they doing bumps?"

"Noooo!" Charlotte said dismissively.

"Sacrificing goats?"

"Olivia, it was . . . unspeakable!"

"Oh, come on, nothing is that unspeakable."

Charlotte shook her head vehemently. "I'm so mortified. Lucie, my poor little cousin, has ruined herself. She's absolutely ruined her life!"

Olivia wanted to shake her. "Charlotte Barclay! Tell. Me. What. You. Saw!"

Looking around again as if she had been caught committing the most cardinal sin, Charlotte leaned toward Olivia's ear and began to whisper.

Olivia's eyes widened. "Who? Whaaaat?! What the fuck?"

"What the fuck is right. I was so alarmed, I couldn't help myself. I blurted out, '*Stop it!*' "

Olivia threw her head back and let out a shriek that sounded like murder.

Capri

· 2013 ·

Dearest Lucie and Charlotte,

Our wedding weekend is almost here, and we thought it would be helpful to give you a quick rundown of the festivities so you can better plan your travel schedule (and your outfits!):

Tuesday, July 16
5:00 p.m.
Welcome cocktails at the Gardens of Augustus
hosted by Marchesa Marella Finzi-Contini (Dolfi's aunt!)
Dress: Informal

Wednesday, July 17
1:30 p.m.
Lunch at Da Luigi Beach Club
hosted by Isabel Chiu
Dress: Beach chic

9:00 p.m.
Dinner at Ristorante Le Grottelle
hosted by Dolfi De Vecchi
Dress: Informal

Thursday, July 18
10:00 a.m.
Hike the historic "Passatiello" path from Anacapri to Capri
led by Auden Beebe
Dress: Walking shoes or hiking boots

9:00 p.m.
Dinner at Il Riccio
hosted by Constantine and Rebecca Chiu (my big brother & his wife!)
Dress: Cocktail

Friday, July 19

11:00 a.m.

Excursion to Villa Lachowski in Positano

led by Mordecai von Ephrussi

Dress: Informal

7:30 p.m.

Sunset music recital and banquet
at the monastery of Certosa di San Giacomo

hosted by the Conte and Contessa De Vecchi

Dress: Formal

Saturday, July 20

5:00 p.m.

WEDDING CEREMONY

Villa Lysis

WEDDING RECEPTION

Villa Jovis

Dress: Formal

Sunday, July 21

2:00 p.m.

Farewell lunch onboard the super yacht *Bravo Olympia*

Dress: Resort chic

Please choose to arrive on the day that's most convenient for you, and our wedding coordinator, Gillian (gillian@devecchichiuwedding.com), will contact you to coordinate your VIP transfers and arrival to Capri. Of course, we hope you'll be able to make it to all the events, beginning on Tuesday. We are so honored that you're able to take the time out of your busy life, and we can't wait to share every special moment of our wedding week on the enchanted island with you!

xoxo,
Issie & Dolfi

I

≋

Anacapri

ISOLA DI CAPRI, ITALY, 2013

The midmorning haze cleared a few miles outside of Naples, and from the helicopter, Capri suddenly appeared like a glistening rock, as if the gods had cast a giant emerald down into the middle of the sea. Lucie (92nd Street Y Nursery School / Brearley / Brown, Class of '16) glanced down at the deep blue waters, wondering how warm it was and how soon she could jump in. She loved the feel of ocean water on her skin.

Turning to her cousin Charlotte (Rippowam / Miss Porter's / Smith), she asked excitedly, "What's the first thing you want to do?"

"There's this restaurant, Michel'angelo, which has a spaghetti with fresh Campania tomatoes and burrata that's supposed to be out of this world."

"Yummy!"

"How about you?"

"I'd like to swim in the Blue Grotto."

"Can you swim in it?"

"I don't see why not."

"Hmm . . . isn't it very deep?"

"I've swum in the Atlantic and the Caribbean. I think I can handle swimming in a little cave on an island," Lucie said lightly. She hoped Charlotte wouldn't be fretting over her safety throughout their trip like her mother would. Thankfully, Charlotte was already distracted by the view out her window.

"Quite stunning, isn't it?" Charlotte remarked, marveling at the dramatic peaks of the island swathed in clouds.

"You know, Emperor Tiberius thought it was the most beautiful place in the world, so he moved the capital of the Roman Empire here in the first century A.D. Issie's wedding is going to take place at the ruins of his palace," Lucie said.

Charlotte smiled. "This is why I love traveling with you. I can always sit back and rest assured that you've done all the homework. You're like my personal Wikipedia and Yelp all rolled into one! Remember that trip to Quebec one Christmas where you mapped out the whole itinerary based on where we'd find the best hot chocolate?"

"I was actually trying to find the best poutine for Freddie," Lucie corrected.

"Ugh, Freddie and his poutine! I weep for your brother when he loses that teenage metabolism. Jesus, is that where we're landing?" Charlotte pointed out the window at the helipad atop a majestic hotel with arched terraces.

"Looks like it."

"That's not where we're staying, though?"

"No, we're at the Bertolucci. I think this is the place where all the celebrities like Mariah Carey and Julia Roberts stay," Lucie remarked.

"Then I'm glad we're not staying here! Hotels that cater to celebrities are generally always awful. If you're not famous, they treat you like pond scum," Charlotte commented as the AgustaWestland AW109 made a dramatic swooping turn before landing on the rooftop of the hotel.

Several attendants rushed out to assist with their luggage, while a lady in a stylishly retro white shift dress came out to greet them. Checking their names off a list on her iPad, she said, "You must be Signorinas Churchill and Barclay? Welcome to Anacapri! Please enjoy our welcome refreshment." A crisply attired waiter presented them with ice-cold Bellinis in tall Venetian glasses, while another waiter bore a platter of fresh strawberries dipped in white chocolate.

"Thank you! But you do know we aren't staying here?" Charlotte said cautiously as she reached for a strawberry.

"Yes, of course. As wedding guests of Ms. Chiu, you are naturally our guests too. Your hotel is in Capri town, and we will send your luggage ahead to the hotel."

"But is it safe?" Charlotte fretted.

"Don't worry, signora, your luggage will be very safe with us. Meanwhile, we have arranged your transportation downstairs," the lady graciously explained as she escorted them down to the lobby, where a magnificently restored candy-apple-red 1950s Fiat cabriolet taxi awaited them in the driveway.

"*Buongiorno!* I take you to Capri—just ten minutes away," the driver said with a flourish as he opened the door for them.

Making herself comfortable in the car, Lucie commented, "Well, if that was the pond-scum treatment, I want to know how Julia Roberts gets treated when she arrives."

"Well, maybe they googled me and saw who I was," Charlotte remarked with nary a hint of irony. As one of the senior editors at *Amuse Bouche* magazine, Charlotte behaved with a distinct entitlement that came from being an employee of the influential magazine and its even more influential parent company, Barón Snotté Publications. Now she turned her attention toward the handsome cream-and-yellow-striped linen awning of the vintage convertible. "Wouldn't it be wonderful if all our taxis in the city* looked like

---

* Charlotte, like many native New Yorkers, called Manhattan "the city," since to them it's the only city that matters. (Charlotte was born at Lenox Hill Hospital, which, for New Yorkers of her generation in the 10021 zip code, was really the only acceptable place to be born.)

this? So much better than those ridiculous 'Taxis of Tomorrow' that already look so worn out."

"I don't think this linen roof would survive one week in the city," Lucie said, laughing while fingering the fabric and letting her hand dangle out into the breeze. As the taxi made a hairpin turn around the steep curve, she exclaimed, "Oh, wow! Check out the view on your left!"

Charlotte caught a quick glimpse of the cliffside plunging down to the sea hundreds of feet below and gasped, "Sweet Jesus, I'm going to get vertigo! I'm purposely not looking!" She searched around for something to grip on to but found nothing except a chilled bottle of champagne with a jade-green ribbon around it. Tied to the ribbon was a card embossed with their names. "Oh, look, this champagne's for us! Your friend's being rather generous, isn't she? Two first-class plane tickets, the helicopter transfer from Rome to Capri, this gorgeous car, champagne—and you're not even one of her bridesmaids!"

"Issie's always been tremendously generous. She was my neighbor back when we lived at 788 Park, remember? She used to pass along her hand-me-downs. She wore many of her outfits only once or twice, and that's how I got that little—"

"That little white Chanel purse when you were in the third grade!" exclaimed Charlotte, finishing Lucie's sentence. "That's right. I had forgotten—I thought you knew Isabel from Brown."

"Not really—she was so many years ahead of me. But she's always been like the big sister I never had."

"Well, you are being quite spoiled by your big sis, aren't you? A week of grand parties culminating in a wedding that I bet will put Kate and William's to shame," Charlotte remarked in a tone that sounded excited and disapproving at the same time. "How much did you say her father was spending on the whole affair?"

"Issie didn't say. She's much too polite to ever tell me anything like that, but I'm sure the wedding will be *everything*!" Lucie said, still not quite believing her luck. Not only was this the first wedding she'd been invited to *as a grown-up,* rather than just one of the kids dragged by default to some family wedding, but this was also the first real trip she'd been on without her mother and brother.

When Lucie first received the ornate hand-engraved invitation, her heart sank when she caught sight of the date: *July 20.* Though she was nineteen and could of course do as she pleased, Lucie, being the dutiful daughter that she was, still deferred to her mother. The third weekend in July was reserved for her mother's annual fund-raising summer gala for the Animal Rescue Fund of Long Island, of which she was president of the board, and she relied heavily on Lucie's help at the event. It was only after UN-level negotiations that her mother finally relented—Lucie could attend the wedding, with the caveat that her older cousin Charlotte would accompany her. Her brother, Freddie, nicknamed their forty-four-year-old cousin "Madam Buzz-kill" behind her back, but Lucie felt that she could handle her cousin well enough, and any little annoyance would be worth it.

Lucie might have grown up in the same prewar Rosario Candela–designed building as her friend, but Isabel's life was several notches more glamorous. For starters, her father was a diplomat who, according to the building's elevator men, hailed from one of Asia's most successful business dynasties, so the Chiu family occupied the sprawling eighteen-room duplex penthouse, while the Churchills lived in a classic seven on the tenth floor.* Likewise, the doormen whispered that whenever the Chius went away, it was always via Teterboro Airport, which was a dead giveaway that the family flew only private.

With her striking beauty, effervescent charm, and academic drive, Isabel was easily one of the most popular students at the Lycée Fran-

---

* New York real estate speak for a prewar apartment that consists of seven rooms: a formal living room, a dining room, a separate kitchen, three full bedrooms, and a maid's room. In 2018, the average median price for a classic seven was $4.6 million.

çais. When she turned eighteen, she made her debut at Le Bal* in Paris and graced the cover of *Taiwan Tatler,* and by the time she graduated from Brown, she had more than thirty thousand followers on Instagram. Nowadays she worked in Los Angeles for a film production company, and Lucie mainly kept in touch by following her on social media, admiring the places she got to travel to—London for the Frieze Art Fair, Park City for Sundance, Bahia for a party at Caetano Veloso's—and the cool friends who surrounded her wherever she went.

Charlotte interrupted her reverie. "Tell me the name of Isabel's fiancé again? The count?"

"Dolfi. His full name is Adolfo De Vecchi. I don't think he's a count—that's his father."

"And he plays polo?"

"Yes, he's got a nine-goal handicap. His whole family has been into polo for generations."

"The polo-playing son of an Italian count marries a Taiwanese heiress. My, Lucie, you're really running with the international ooh-la-las these days," Charlotte teased.

Soon they arrived at the town of Capri, which was built high on the mountain overlooking the harbor. Waiting by the bustling taxi stand on Via Roma was an Italian man in his twenties wearing a short-sleeved white shirt and white trousers that appeared at least two sizes too tight. "Welcome to Capri! I am Paolo, from the Bertolucci. Please allow me to escort you to the hotel. It is just a short walk away," the man said.

They strolled into the main public square, where a gleaming white clock tower stood opposite from the historic Cathedral of Santo Stefano. Four competing outdoor cafés lining the square bustled

---

* Le Bal des Débutantes, held in Paris every November, is a ball introducing debutantes from around the world. Previous debutantes have included girls from European aristocracy, the children of celebrities, and girls whose parents simply have insane amounts of money.

with chic patrons sipping their cappuccinos, chatting, and people-watching from their bistro tables.

"This is the piazzetta. We call it 'the living room of Capri,' " Paolo noted.

"You would never find a living room like this in America—everyone is so nattily dressed here!" remarked Charlotte.

As they walked beyond the piazzetta and down Via Vittorio Emanuele, Charlotte's discerning eye did a quick assessment and she found herself quietly impressed. Capri seemed to embody the most marvelous blend of historic and modern, high and low, simplicity and decadence. Here they were, strolling along a cobblestone street where a humble tobacco kiosk neighbored a sleek boutique selling hand-sewn driving moccasins, and a shop glittering with the most lust-worthy jewels stood just a few paces down from the rustic gelateria, where the scent of freshly baked cones wafted into the air. "How charming! How charming!" Charlotte kept saying at every turn. "Can you even believe this place exists?"

"It's glorious," Lucie replied, relieved that everything met with her cousin's approval so far. All the same, she couldn't imagine how anyone—even her extremely jaded cousin—could find fault with this island. She loved seeing the clusters of Italian children running up and down the street laughing wildly, the old grandmas resting their tired feet on the steps of designer boutiques, the impeccably dressed couples walking along hand in hand, bronzed and glowing from their hours under the sun. And no matter where you turned, there was the view—of undulating hills dotted with white villas, ancient fortress ruins commanding every ridgetop, and the sea sparkling in the golden sun.

Charlotte made a dead stop outside a sandal shop, seemingly transfixed.

"We are famous for our sandals, signora. Beyoncé, Sarah Jessica Parker, all the famous stars buy sandals in Capri," Paolo said proudly.

"If I had Beyoncé's budget, I'd take that tangerine pair over there. And the gold ones. And the ones with those cute little pom-poms. Hell, I'd take every single pair in the window!" Charlotte gushed.

"You're welcome to buy me the ones with the pink suede tassels," Lucie remarked.

"That's *so* you! You know, we should get a pair for your mother. Don't you think she'd like those braided leather sandals? Let's make a note of this place, please!"

Lucie suddenly caught a glimpse of her reflection in the window and let out a shriek. "Charlotte! How could you let me walk through town looking like this? I look like a cocker spaniel!"

"You do not! You look like you've just been on a joyride along the Amalfi Coast, which you have," Charlotte said with a reassuring smile. She knew Lucie had always been self-conscious about her natural curls and spent half her life straightening her hair. The lucky girl had no idea how ravishing she looked with her long, lustrous locks loose and wild, coupled with that improbably perfect blend of Eastern and Western features. Perhaps that was a good thing—she would have to spend less time fending off all the boys on this trip.

Paolo guided them down a twisting narrow lane, and before long, they arrived at the Hotel Bertolucci, a charming white modernist villa bursting with purple bougainvillea vines along every wall. Stepping into the breezy lobby and taking in the plush white sofas, Solimene ceramics, and gleaming blue-and-white majolica tiles, Charlotte registered her approval. "This is exactly as I imagined! How marvelous is this place? Now I feel like we're truly on holiday!" They were shown into a tiny elevator, which took them two levels up, and were led down a hallway smartly carpeted in a cream-and-navy-striped sisal.

"We go first to your room, and then I will take your friend to her room," Paolo said to Charlotte.

"She's my cousin," Charlotte corrected.

"Oh? Your cousin?" Paolo glanced reflexively at Lucie in surprise, but Lucie simply smiled. She knew that within the next few seconds, Charlotte would automatically launch into the explanation she had always given since Lucie was a little girl.

"Yes, her father was my uncle," Charlotte replied, adding, "Her mother is Chinese, but her father is American."

So is Mom. She was born in Seattle, Lucie wanted to say, but of course she didn't.

They arrived at the first room and watched as Paolo twisted a heavy, gold-tasseled key and opened the door. The ladies entered the room, and as soon as Paolo drew open the curtains to let in more light, the smiles evaporated from their faces. Lucie glanced at Charlotte in dismay.

"What is that out there?" Charlotte asked, peering out the window.

"It is a cat," Paolo replied, gesturing at the calico sunning itself on a low stone wall.

"I know 'it is a cat,' " Charlotte said, mimicking his accent. "That's not what I meant. Can we see the other room?"

"Of course, it is just two doors down."

Paolo opened the door to Lucie's room, and the ladies peered in. "You like, signorina?"

Before Lucie could reply, Charlotte cut in. "Mr. Paolo, there's been a huge mistake. We need to see the manager. Pronto!"

II

Hotel Bertolucci

CAPRI, ITALY

The hostess tried to show Lucie and Charlotte to a table in the middle of the lunchroom, but Charlotte was having none of it. "We'll sit *here*, if you don't mind," she huffed, shoving her yellow canvas tote bag firmly onto a table by the window as if she were planting the first flag on the South Pole.

The hostess backed away with a shrug as Charlotte continued to fume. "We specifically reserved rooms with ocean views, and now they are telling us we can't have them because some other guests extended their stay? What a sham!"

"Don't you think they really *are* booked up because of the wedding?" Lucie wondered.

"Well, that's not our problem. Those people who overstayed should be moved into the rooms that they've pawned off on us. Why should we have to suffer and take the rooms facing that damn cat licking its balls in an alley? And why aren't the cats on this island neutered?"

Lucie noticed a few people in the dining room look up in their direction and thought she'd better try harder to placate her cousin. "As far as alleys go, it's a very nice one."

"There's no such thing as a nice alley, Lucie. Hobos hang out in alleys, and people go into alleys to do three things: vomit, do drug deals, or get stabbed."

"Charlotte, I somehow don't think that's going to happen here. And the manager did say he would move us the minute another room became available."

"Just you watch—he's going to move us on the very last day." Charlotte took a bite of focaccia from the basket on the table and immediately spat it out discreetly into her napkin. "Ew! This focaccia is soggy. It's clearly been sitting out all morning."

Lucie sighed. It was only the first day of their trip, and Charlotte was already kicking up a fuss about everything. She wondered if Charlotte was partly upset because when she imperiously announced to the manager that she was "the produce editor at *Amuse Bouche*—one of America's leading food and lifestyle magazines," he gave her a blank stare, and it had zero effect on their room situation.

"Ma'am! Signora! Over here! Can we have some fresh focaccia please? I want it warm and toasty, do you hear? Warm and toasty! And bring me some *olio d'oliva* and *balsamico*,"* Charlotte ordered. Turning back to Lucie, she said, "I can't believe you're not more upset. I mean, this is your holiday more than mine."

"I *am* disappointed, but there's not much more we can do, is there?" Lucie was always conscious of being born into privilege, and it had been drummed into her from an early age by her mother to "always be grateful and never complain." She was well aware that her room in this five-star hotel, even with the less-than-perfect view,

---

* Pretentious Italian for "olive oil" and "balsamic vinegar," which, by the way, only Americans use to dip their bread in. Italians would never be caught dead doing anything like that, preferring to eat their bread plain.

was far nicer than what most people on the planet would ever be able to enjoy, so she was loath to grumble.

Charlotte, however, had a different take on the situation. "It's an absolute sin to be paying such an outrageous rate for a room that looks nothing like the ones shown on their website. I mean, we haven't even talked about the decor!"

"What do you mean?"

"It's absolutely hideous. It looks like a Versace dress exploded all over my room."

Lucie laughed. "Well, I kind of like the giant gold octopus headboard."

Charlotte continued to rant. "It's your first time on Capri, one of the most beautiful places in the world. I'll be fine, really, but it's totally unfair that you should be deprived of a room with a decent view."

Suddenly, they heard a voice behind them. "Miss, excuse me, miss."

Lucie and Charlotte turned around to see an Asian lady in her fifties smiling at them. She was wearing a fuchsia sarong wrap dress and an enormous black-and-white-striped hat.

"Yes?" Charlotte asked.

"My son and I have rooms that look out at the sea and the Faraglioni rocks. We should swap rooms!" The lady gestured at the youth—a boy of twenty—sitting across from her.

Charlotte paused, momentarily caught off guard by the offer. Who was this curious woman with the flying-saucer hat, too much eye shadow, and quasi-English accent? And why would she give up her own rooms? "Um . . . that's very kind of you to offer, but we'll manage, thank you."

"Don't just manage. If you're so unhappy with your rooms, you should take ours."

Charlotte smiled stiffly. "We're not unhappy."

"Oh? You've been complaining nonstop for the past ten minutes."

Charlotte felt put out by the woman's statement. "Well, I'm sorry if we've disturbed you . . ."

"You haven't disturbed me, not really. But if it matters to you and your friend so much to see the sea, I want you to have our rooms. Actually, they are suites—deluxe suites—and they each have a nice living room, a bathroom with a huge Jacuzzi, and adjoining balconies. The view is amazing, I can assure you."

"Then it really wouldn't be fair," Lucie spoke up. She noticed the boy gazing at her with an intensity that she found a little disconcerting. Unlike his dramatically outfitted mother, he was dressed in khaki denim shorts, a black tank top, and Birkenstocks. But the simple nature of his outfit did nothing to camouflage the fact that he was strikingly, almost unbearably handsome. Their eyes caught for a moment, and Lucie felt a strange, almost electrical charge. She quickly averted her eyes back to his mother, who seemed relentless in her campaign.

"Fair or not doesn't matter to me. We have been to Capri before, and we come from Hong Kong, where our flat overlooks the harbor. And we have a house in Sydney, in Watsons Bay, where we can see whales do backflips, and another beachfront house in Hawaii, in Lanikai. We get to see the ocean till we're sick of it, so this is nothing to us."

Charlotte let out a little gasp. The woman turned her attention to Lucie, and she could feel her giving her the once-over. "Are you here for Isabel Chiu's wedding?"

"We are," Lucie answered.

"So are we! How do you know Isabel?"

"She's a friend from childhood."

"Oh, you are from Taipei?" The woman looked surprised.

"No, I'm from New York. I knew Isabel when she lived in New York."

"Ah, New York, I see. I love New York! Isabel's mother and I are cousins. I'm Rosemary Zao [Maryknoll Convent School / University of Sydney / Central Saint Martins], and this is my son George [Diocesan Boys' School / Geelong Grammar / UC Berkeley, Class of '15]. We should all be friends, and you really should take our rooms!"

"May I ask what the rate is for your deluxe suite?" Charlotte asked, not wanting to be stuck with an exorbitant bill at the end of their stay.

Rosemary waved her hand dismissively. "*Hiyah,* don't worry about the money. It's my treat!"

"No, no, that would be much too generous of you," Charlotte said.

While the two older ladies continued their pantomime of protestations, Lucie noticed George beginning to fold and twist the paper napkin on his table with a Zen-like calmness. Within a few moments, he had fashioned the napkin into a long-stemmed rose. He held the origami rose up and tilted it toward Lucie, as if offering it to her, before placing the flower on the brim of his mother's hat while she was turned around talking to Charlotte.

Weirdo, Lucie thought. Confused by his gesture, she pretended like she hadn't seen him.

Meanwhile, Rosemary's voice had gone up several decibels. "No, no, it's your first time in Capri, you should have a view of the sea. You must see the sunrise, and the sunset, and, oh—the seagulls! They are so cute; they come flying right up to my balcony and try to steal my toast! Come on, I know you'll love it. You *must* take our rooms!" Lucie saw that everyone was staring openly at them now.

"We simply cannot impose," Charlotte said firmly.

Rosemary gave them an exasperated look before turning to her son. "Why won't they take our rooms? George, *nei tung keoi dei gong la. Keoi dei wui teng nei ge.*"*

Up till this point, George had sat as silent as the Sphinx, but now he looked straight at Charlotte and Lucie and spoke up in a soft drawl that was vaguely reminiscent of an Australian surfer. "There's nothing to say. Of course you must take our rooms. We insist."

---

* Cantonese for "You go talk to them. They will listen to you."

"Well, let me insist that we won't!" Charlotte scoffed.

George turned to his mother as if he hadn't even heard Charlotte. "Let's just speak to the manager and he'll handle it."

"Yes, yes! Ettore can get housekeeping to pack up all our bags and move everything!" Rosemary said excitedly.

This was too much for Charlotte. She stood up from the table and said, "You're very kind, but we really cannot trouble you like this. Have a nice day. Lucie, come."

≋

III

Poolside at the Bertolucci

CAPRI, ITALY

Charlotte and Lucie left the dining room and found a table under the loggia by the pool. As they sat down, Lucie looked at her cousin and started to giggle. She couldn't help it—she always seemed to giggle whenever she felt uncomfortable.

Charlotte shook her head in annoyance. "Jesus! What a crazy lady! What was her deal? Was she trying to impress us with her parade of oceanfront properties? Does she think we are some sort of charity cases that are going to bow down in gratitude just to spend a night in her 'deluxe suite'?"

"I think she was just doing the 'Chinese auntie' thing."

"Well, she's not your auntie, and she's certainly not mine."

"That's not what I meant. She's just being a bit of a showoff but trying to be generous at the same time. I've met a bunch of Mom's relatives who are just like that. You should see these ladies fighting over the bill at lunch. It's like watching an opera."

"What do you mean? They don't want to pay their fair share?"

"No, Charlotte, they're all fighting to pick up *the whole check*! They screech at each other, play tug-of-war over the bill, or try to bribe the waiter not to let anyone else pay. Apparently it's considered good manners to make a big show of it," Lucie tried to explain.

"I'll never understand that sort of behavior. To me, this woman crossed a line. And what do you make of that son of hers?"

"I'm not sure. He barely spoke," Lucie said with restraint. The truth was she had an instant aversion to really attractive guys, ever since her eighth-grade boyfriend, Ryan Frick—who looked like a young Jared Leto—two-timed her with Maggie Hoover, a Spence girl who was known to everyone in their generation because she could put her entire fist in her mouth.

"Well, I thought he seemed like an arrogant snot! Who is he to insist that we take their rooms? My God, this hotel is turning out to be a nightmare. First they give us the wrong rooms, and then we have to deal with these sort of people. I should have listened to Giles, my travel editor, and just shelled out the money for the Punta Tragara. This would never have happened there. Penny wise, pound foolish, as they say. Shall I call them up and see if they have any ocean-view rooms available? I don't care what we have to pay anymore. I'll call up Diane at the family office and sell some bonds if I have to."

Just as Lucie was about to answer, she saw someone familiar in the distance. "Look at that man coming down those steps. Isn't that Auden Beebe?"

Charlotte peered at the tall man in his forties with a perfectly groomed beard and shoulder-length blond hair walking through the archway of the lobby out onto the terrace. "It sure is! Auden! Auden!"

Auden Beebe (City and Country / Saint Ann's / Amherst[*]) turned and approached them. "Hullo," he said warmly, although it was clear that he recognized the ladies without quite being able to place them. As a celebrated yoga master, life coach, motivational speaker, and self-help author (his bestseller, *The Preppie Guru*, had been on the *New York Times* bestseller list for the past two years), he

* Dropped out his junior year to go to shaman school in Peru.

was accustomed to meeting thousands of people who felt that they knew him intimately.

"Auden, it's Charlotte Barclay and Lucie Churchill. We were at your workshop at Canyon Ranch last spring? In Lenox?" Charlotte said effusively.

"Yes, of course, the cousins!" Auden said, breaking into a wide smile. "What brings you to Capri?"

"We're here for a wedding," Lucie answered.

"Ah. Let me guess . . . Dolfi De Vecchi's?"

"Yes!" Lucie and Charlotte said in unison.

"Dolfi has been coming to my workshops for years, and Isabel more recently. I'm officiating the wedding."

"What serendipity!" Charlotte was clearly enraptured by the trifecta of Auden's fame, his family's listing in *The Social Register,* and his resemblance to Alexander Skarsgård.

"Mr. Beebe, is it true you're opening a Preppie Guru Lounge in East Hampton?" Lucie asked.

"Please call me Auden, and yes, next summer. It's going to be a pop-up on Newtown Lane, right next door to James Perse. We're going to start small at first and offer an Ayurvedic juice bar, qigong, puppy yoga, breath work meditation, and maybe some sound healing. See what the community responds to."

"Excuse my ignorance, but what is puppy yoga?" Charlotte inquired.

"It's a yoga session in a room filled with puppies. They'll be frolicking around your mat and licking you in the face while you're in downward dog."

"How adorable! My family summers in East Hampton, and I'm going to be at puppy yoga every day," Lucie said.

"Terrific! In the meantime, I'll be leading yoga every morning down by the pool here, minus the puppies."

Just then, two ladies in their sixties dressed in smartly tailored linen pantsuits stopped by their table on their way to the garden. One of them smiled wryly at Charlotte. "You poor things! We saw what happened in the dining room. I'm sorry you were put in that situation. What an atrocious lack of manners!"

"She's been like that all week," added the other lady. "She overheard us talking about how much we loved the orchids at this flower shop next to the church, and the next thing you know we came back to our suite and found it filled with orchids. Dozens of pots, compliments of Rosemary Zao! Now it looks like we're having a wake!"

"I do hope you and your friend can get your rooms sorted out to your satisfaction," the first lady said to Charlotte sympathetically.

"Thank you. Lucie is actually my cousin. My mother and her father were brother and sister," Charlotte said.

"Oh, how nice," the ladies said in unison. They nodded at Auden before walking on, and his curiosity was piqued. "May I ask what happened in the dining room that so scandalized the unflappable Ortiz sisters of Manila?"

Lucie and Charlotte hesitated for a split second, and Auden immediately picked up on it. "Apologies, I'm being too nosy."

"No, you're fine," Charlotte said, before breathlessly recounting what had just transpired with Rosemary Zao in the dining room. ". . . she kept insisting, and she was making such a spectacle of it, we felt so uncomfortable that we had to seek refuge here."

"Actually, I think she was trying to be nice—it just came out in a peculiar way," Lucie interjected.

"Peculiar is an understatement! She was trying much too hard, and I can't figure out what her angle is," Charlotte said.

"What if there was no angle? I think, coming from New York, you have a natural instinct to look for a motive in everything . . . I do the same thing myself," Auden offered. "Having gotten to know Mrs. Zao, I think her offer was likely made in a pure spirit. She's only known me for a few days, but she's already invited me to do a workshop in Hong Kong and even told me she'd arrange the space to host it and invite all her friends. And yesterday, she spontaneously ordered pineapple and coconut sorbets for everyone lying around the pool. I thought it was a lovely gesture."

Charlotte let out a deep sigh. "Well, I guess I've made a mistake. You think I've been too suspicious and judgmental?"

"Charlotte, Auden's not saying that . . . ," Lucie began.

"Not at all," Auden insisted.

"Yes, I'm afraid my weakness is that I'm too uptight and proper. I believe too much in decorum. Everyone says it."

Lucie wanted to roll her eyes but kept herself in check. She knew this game of her cousin's all too well—Charlotte was the queen of guilt trips, and now she was looking her straight in the eye. "Lucie, everything I do, I do with the best of intentions. I'm here out of your generosity, and my only interest is in safeguarding your good name."

"My good name? You sound as if we're living in the Edwardian age!" Lucie laughed.

"Lucie, you are a *Churchill,* don't ever forget that. Your name and standing are everything, and wherever you go, you are representing the family."

There it was, the "family" reminder that Charlotte never failed to invoke. Charlotte was inordinately proud of their storied roots—all that lore about being *Mayflower* descendants who married into one of Britain's most aristocratic families and kept the roof over their castle repaired thanks to their great-great-great-grandfather's Wall Street fortune. Lucie tried to brush it off, but then she realized Charlotte was still going on about it.

"Your mother specifically wanted me to look out for you, but maybe I've been too overzealous in my attempts to protect you. Would you like me to obligate you to these strangers? Would you like me to see if the Zaos want to be turned out of their rooms?"

Lucie sighed in resignation. "No, I wouldn't want you to do that."

Auden observed the stalemate between the two cousins and decided to make an offer. "Ladies, might I make a suggestion? Since I know the Zaos a bit better, I am happy to act as your intermediary. I'll see if they are truly willing to trade their rooms, and if the offer still stands, I will make sure they aren't going to be inconvenienced."

"Well, apart from that, I do want to be sure there are no *expectations* implicit in their offer," Charlotte said.

Auden paused for a split second, catching her drift. "Yes, yes, of course. And if the Zaos have changed their minds, I can promise you there will be no awkwardness."

Charlotte gave Lucie a circumspect look before turning to the man. "Auden, you are a godsend!"

IV

The Gardens of Augustus

CAPRI, ITALY

The Gardens of Augustus were once part of the estate of the German munitions heir Friedrich Alfred Krupp, who created a series of expansive terraces perched high on a cliff that afforded incredible views of the island and the sea. Here, pathways lined with lush beds of pink geraniums and dahlias wound around towering Italian cypresses on meticulously manicured lawns.

Arriving at the garden gates, Charlotte whispered urgently to Lucie, "Are we at the wrong party?"

"I don't think so," Lucie said, glancing again at the invitation on her phone as they joined the clusters of guests lining up to enter the park.

Charlotte surveyed the assembled group of men and women dressed as though they had been invited to cocktails at Buckingham Palace. "You said tonight was going to be casual!"

"I swear that's what the invitation says. *Welcome cocktails. Informal,*" Lucie insisted.

"Well, everyone here is obviously illiterate. On what planet is this considered 'informal'?" Charlotte grumbled as she eyed the lady ahead of them in a pearl-gray cocktail dress, her ruby-and-diamond pendant drop earrings sparkling in the late-afternoon sun. Charlotte was wearing her favorite sleeveless navy linen dress from Max Mara, which she thought she had smartened up with a brown pashmina embroidered with blue flowers draped around her shoulders, but among this crowd she might as well be dressed for the farmers' market. Lucie at least looked dressier in her calf-length ice-blue Stella McCartney dress, and she had the advantages of her improbably photogenic features and youth.

"Lucie, no one has seen us yet. Should we rush back to the hotel and change?"

"I think it's too late for that. Look up, Charlotte!"

Charlotte raised her head and saw a drone hovering right above them. "Jesus Christ! Are we under surveillance?"

"No, it's Issie's film team. She told me there were going to be drones documenting every moment of the weekend. Now that we've been caught on video, it's going to look really silly if we come back in ten minutes wearing different outfits," Lucie said.

Entering the gardens, they saw that the whole place had been decorated to look like a Moroccan fantasy. Hundreds of colorful Moorish lamps hung from every tree, precious Berber carpets had been laid out on the grass, and artfully arranged on them were poufs and lounge chairs upholstered in iridescent silks. In the middle of the garden rose a twelve-foot pyramid of Venetian glass flutes, obviously beckoning to be overflowing with champagne. A team of videographers dressed entirely in black circled the party, some of them holding state-of-the-art video cameras, while others piloted the fleet of drones that hovered in the sky.

Suddenly, they heard a call from through the trees. "Lucie! Lucie!"

Lucie looked up and saw Isabel and Dolfi waving from the terrace above them. "Too late now," she muttered to her cousin as she rushed up the steps toward her friends.

"You made it!" Isabel (Taipei American School / Lycée Français / Brown) said excitedly, giving her a big hug. "I'm so happy you're here! Isn't Capri beautiful? Aren't these gardens beautiful?"

"Not half as beautiful as you look tonight," Lucie replied, admiring Isabel's pleated lavender Tibi dress, which she wore with matching gold cuff bracelets and a chunky gold-and-diamond chain belt.

"Aww! Thank you. Dolfi, didn't I tell you that Lucie is the sweetest person I know? I used to call her my little angel. She's never had a bad thing to say about anyone—unlike me!" Isabel cackled.

Dolfi (Rome International School / Le Rosey / Brown) turned to Lucie and said in an accent that seemed to meld British boarding school with Italian Casanova, "Just the other day I told Isabel that it has been much too long since we've seen you. This college thing is really such a nuisance—you should just drop out and come sailing with us to Fiji."

"That sounds like an awesome idea!" Lucie said.

"I'm not sure your mother would agree," Charlotte cut in.

Dolfi reached for Charlotte's hand and gave it a gallant kiss. "And you must be the enforcer?"

"I'd like to think I'm more like the voice of reason," Charlotte said, completely disarmed by Dolfi. She studied the strapping young Italian aristocrat with shoulder-length hair and the Nate Archibald–perfect amount of stubble standing next to his chic bride-to-be. With her statuesque figure, jet-black hair pulled into a high ponytail, and impossibly long, thick eyelashes, she looked like one of the contestants on *Dancing with the Stars*, Charlotte's guilty pleasure. In fact, they both did.

They chatted for a few moments, when Isabel suddenly rolled her eyes. "Oh God, here comes my mother's friend Mordecai! I promise I'm doing you a favor—you should get out of here now while you still can. Go check out the view from the top terrace before the sun sets!"

They wandered up the stairs to the high terrace, as Charlotte gushed all the way. "Why didn't you tell me that Dolfi was such a tall drink of water? I would have dressed up more! Did you see his nose? That's the kind of nose plastic surgeons couldn't create for all the money in the world. That perfect patrician profile comes only to people born to Roman families that have spent *at least* fifteen generations drinking water straight out of their ancient aqueducts! You should follow Isabel's example and bring someone like that home! Not now, of course. In a decade would be perfect."

Lucie laughed lightly. She wasn't used to hearing her cousin gush over anyone like that. Arriving at the top deck, they were mesmerized by the panoramic views of the Gulf of Salerno stretching to the horizon as far as the eye could see. A woman in her early forties with a mass of pre-Raphaelite curls leaned against the green metal railing in front of them, taking pictures with her camera. Turning around, she grinned at them. "Oh, good, I'm glad I'm not the only one who didn't get the memo about wearing our tiaras tonight."

Lucie smiled, thinking that the lady looked very cool in her black jumpsuit, black ankle boots, and black denim jacket. She wondered if her outfit was designed by Rick Owens. "Is that a Leica?" she asked, pointing at her silver-and-black camera.

"My grandfather's, from the thirties," the woman replied in a husky British accent that Charlotte and Lucie both immediately registered as posh.

"I've always wanted a Leica. I've just begun using an old Nikon from the seventies that my uncle gave me."

"Where is it?"

"I left it back home. I guess I'm so used to my phone that I didn't think to take it with me," Lucie said a little sheepishly.

"That's the problem with smartphones. No one thinks to use a real camera anymore. Capri would have been the perfect place for your Nikon—you can't take a bad picture on this island. It's like India. Anywhere you point, you get an amazing shot." The woman handed Lucie her camera. "Here, try it out."

Lucie held up the camera's viewfinder to her eye and looked out at the ocean. In the near distance below them, an enormous, sleek yacht idled in the calm bay, and she could just make out a few figures standing on the top deck and the name of the boat: *Odin.*

Charlotte, having nothing to do, stuck out her hand at the woman. "I'm Charlotte Barclay, and this is my cousin Lucie Churchill."

"I'm Olivia Lavistock [Willcocks / Lycée Français / American School of Paris / La Fémis]. You're New Yorkers, I assume?"

"Yes. Is it that obvious?" Charlotte asked.

"I could spot you two from a mile away. The way you dress, the way you walk."

Charlotte gave her a once-over. "And let me guess, you're from London?"

"You're partly correct. I grew up in London, but I'm American and live in LA these days."

Charlotte tried again. "Then I'm guessing you work in entertainment?"

"Guilty as charged. I make films."

"Anything we might have seen?" Lucie asked, putting down the camera.

"Probably not. I directed a short that won an award at Venice many years ago, and I worked in Paris for a while for Claire Denis and Eugène Green. Everything I'm working on right now is in development. Speaking of which, I saw you both at the hotel earlier today at lunch. It was like a scene straight out of a Merchant Ivory film! What happened? Did Madame Zao succeed in convincing you to take her rooms?"

Charlotte paused for a moment before answering. "As a matter of fact, she did, and we are very grateful."

"Lucky you! So, how is the view?"

"It's okay," Charlotte said.

"It's pretty incredible," Lucie said, talking over her.

"Well, I wish I had complained about my room in front of Madame Zao! Isn't she a character? I love it! There aren't enough characters these days, especially among the rich. Everybody with money has become so cookie-cutter—they dress the same, collect the same ten artists, stay at the same hotels around the world, and even eat at the same restaurants. They all want to be miserable and dissatisfied in the same place."

"Do you really think that's true?" Lucie asked.

"Why don't we do a little experiment? What neighborhood do you live in?"

"The Upper East Side."

"Oh, that's too easy. On the Upper East Side, the only places the rich will eat at are Swifty's, Orsay, Café Boulud, Elio's, and Sette Mezzo. Lunch at Sant Ambroeus or Via Quadronno, and if you're vegetarian you go to Candle 79. Going downtown means only going as far south as Doubles. Am I right or am I right?

Lucie gasped. "How on earth did you know?"

"I cheated. My father lives on Ninety-First between Lex and Third. His wife only ever wants to eat at Swifty's."

"How boring. This is why I live in Gramercy Park—the best food is all downtown. The real downtown!" Charlotte sniffed.*

"I wouldn't disagree, but my point is there's so little originality among the one percent crowd these days. I wish we still lived in the time when the heiress Millicent Rogers would marry an Austrian count and announce that for her honeymoon, she was going to Africa to discover a new breed of monkey! Now, the man who built these gardens was quite the character. Krupp, in his time the richest man in Germany. Do you know how he spent his dosh?"

"How?" Charlotte asked.

"He liked to host lavish orgies, usually with thirty or forty young men. Local fishermen. He probably shagged them right here on this terrace."

Charlotte's jaw dropped as Lucie tried to stifle a giggle.

Olivia continued her story. "You know he was married with two

---

* Gramercy Park is *not* the real downtown, but for Charlotte downtown meant going only as far south as Buvette on Grove Street or occasionally to Tribeca back when Chanterelle was still around.

daughters when he started coming to Capri, but his wife back in Germany suddenly began receiving anonymous letters and compromising photos."

"What happened?" Charlotte asked, finding herself strangely curious about this sordid tale.

"What always happens. The press found out, and it became a huge scandal in Germany, of course. So he committed suicide, and his wife ended up in the loony bin."

"How shocking," Charlotte said, shaking her head.

"Actually, it's quite a tame story by Capri standards. This has always been an island of sybaritic pleasures, and people have been coming here since ancient times to indulge in whatever got their rocks off. Krupp wasn't the first. Do you want to know what Emperor Tiberius used to do with virgins up at his palace?"

Lucie, who was getting uncomfortable with where the conversation seemed to be heading, spotted waiters entering the lower terrace with silver platters of cocktails and canapés. "Why don't I get us some drinks?" she said, making a beeline for the steps. As she wandered through the lower garden, she suddenly passed by George Zao standing stock-still in front of a clump of trees, staring at something.

"Oh, hello," she said, trying to be polite, although she wondered, *Why is he always staring like that?*

"Lenin," he said, turning to her.

"Pardon me?"

"It's a statue of Lenin."

"Oh, wow. I guess it is, isn't it?" Lucie said, noticing for the first time the white marble bas-relief depicting Lenin in profile that was partially hidden by foliage.

"Don't you find it odd?"

"Odd?"

"That there would be a statue of him here."

"There are lots of statues here."

"Yes, but why one of the most famous communists, on an island devoted to conspicuous consumption?"

"Is that what you think of Capri?"

"Just look around you," George said with a half smile, before walking off.

Lucie frowned, not knowing what to make of their encounter but feeling strangely annoyed. Was he somehow criticizing her? Was she being unobservant or obtuse, or, worse, being labeled a conspicuous consumer herself?

Lucie went up to the waiter standing beside a small circular fountain filled with lotus flowers and grabbed three flutes of champagne off his silver tray. As she walked carefully up the steps trying not to spill any of the bubbly, she came upon Rosemary Zao dressed in a shimmering gold caftan festooned with peacock feathers. She thought it was funny how different mother and son looked—he was way underdressed in a brown linen shirt and awful mustard-colored jeans that were too tight on him, looking like he had stumbled into the wrong party in the wrong decade, whereas his mom's outfit was a party unto itself.

"Ah, Lucie! How pretty you look in blue! Do you like your room? Isn't it nice?" Rosemary asked excitedly.

"Yes, it's very nice. Thanks again, Mrs. Zao. It's such a treat to be able to enjoy the view."

"I'm so glad. I told you the suite was amazing, didn't I? Now, let me ask you something. You are hapa,* yes?"

"Um, yeah." Lucie nodded, caught off guard. It wasn't very often that she was asked that question so directly.

"Which side is the Chinese side?"

"My mother is Chinese."

"How nice. My husband, Emerson, was hapa too—his grandfather was Australian. That makes George one-eighth Aussie, although he looks Chinese, don't you think? But that's why he's so

---

* Hawaiian for "half," the word has come to mean a person of mixed Asian and other racial heritage. These days, "hapa" has generally become the most accepted word to use among hapas.

handsome. He's like Bruce Lee. You know Bruce Lee's mother was half German?"*

"I didn't, actually," Lucie replied politely, although her mind was reeling. Did Mrs. Zao actually just say that her son was handsome *because he was one-eighth Aussie?*

"I think you and George have a lot in common. You two should be friends."

Lucie could feel her jaw tighten in annoyance. What was this woman talking about? She had nothing in common with her son.

"You could be a good influence on George. He's too serious for his age. He worries too much."

"What does he worry about?" Lucie asked, before regretting it instantly. Why did she ask a question when she could have just made a quick exit?

"Everything! The icebergs melting, world poverty, penguins, you name it. I don't know why, but this son of mine feels the weight of the world on his shoulders. Ever since his father died four years ago, he feels like he's responsible for me. But I tell him, 'Don't worry about me! Go out and have fun!' When I was his age, I was going dancing every night. My goodness, the times I had at Disco Disco or the Club 97 in Lan Kwai Fong!"

"Well, I do think our generation feels more burdened than yours. I mean, climate change, poverty, and penguins are all real concerns."

"Yes, but there needs to be balance. You know, the middle way. Look, I'm not asking you to be his girlfriend or anything. But maybe you could . . . you know . . . be nice to him."

Lucie felt too awkward to say anything, but it didn't matter because Rosemary wouldn't stop talking.

"You know, I had to drag George to this wedding. He didn't

---

* Actually, she's wrong about Bruce Lee's mother being half German, but it was an oft-repeated myth. Bruce's mother, Grace Ho Oi-yee, stated that her father was Chinese and her mother was English, and when Bruce himself was once asked if he thought of himself as Chinese or North American, he replied, "I think of myself as a human being, because under the sky, we are but one family, it just so happens that we look different."

want to come. He said he didn't want to witness a massive waste of money."

"Well, I'm not sure how much your son is going to like me, Mrs. Zao. You see, I don't think this wedding is going to be a massive waste at all. Isabel is my dear friend, and she does everything with intention and heart. I think it's all going to be wonderful!" Lucie turned abruptly and headed quickly up the stairs. She was spilling champagne along the way and knew she was behaving rudely, but she didn't care. She was beginning to think that Charlotte had been right all along, and she was regretting the decision to accept the Zaos' rooms. Rosemary's words kept ringing in her ears. *Maybe you could . . . you know . . . be nice to him.* What the hell did she mean by that?

V

Da Luigi Beach Club

CAPRI, ITALY

"Valentino used to live in that villa. This is the street where all the oldest, most historic houses are," Isabel said, pointing up the hill as she strolled with Lucie along Via Tragara. One side of the street consisted of high stone walls, imposing hedges, and ornate gates, giving only tantalizing glimpses into the worlds hidden beyond them. The other side had lower walls where one could admire the beautiful gardens and terraces of villas that looked out to the sea.

"This is my favorite street so far. I thought Via Camerelle was lovely, but then it just keeps getting more beautiful the farther along you go, doesn't it?" Lucie remarked, trailing her fingers over the hibiscus bushes along the wall.

"That's the thing about this island—it reveals its secrets slowly. I've been here probably half a dozen times and I still feel like I'm discovering a whole different island every time I come," Isabel said.

"I'm so glad you texted me this morning," Lucie said as she strolled happily along the sun-dappled lane with her friend, breathing in the scent of orange blossom that seemed to follow them everywhere.

"Of course! I need to have some alone time with you, before the onslaught!" The two of them had met on the terrace of the Grand Hotel Quisisana and caught up over a breakfast of croissants, truffled scrambled eggs, and cappuccinos, and now they were heading to the beach club to meet up with some of Isabel's friends.

"It's such a treat to have this time with you, right before your wedding. Are you sure there isn't anything I can do to help?" Lucie inquired.

"Everything's being taken care of. Gillian's managing an army of staffers precisely so I don't have to stress out and can actually enjoy my own wedding. But you are very nice to offer," Isabel replied, thinking for the hundredth time how well brought up Lucie was. She'd always had a soft spot for Lucie and felt very protective over her ever since she babysat her during the time of Lucie's father's death. Lucie had been only eight years old, but she was so stoic through it all, an absolute rock for her devastated mother. She didn't cry once at the memorial service and brought the standing-room-only crowd at the church to tears when she went up to the altar and gave an a cappella rendition of Sting's "Fields of Gold."

Shaking off the memory of those days, Isabel continued. "You know, Dolfi and I thought that fewer people would come if we had a destination wedding, and we could do something very intimate. But we made the mistake of picking Capri. Everybody wanted to come!"

"How many guests are you having?"

"The head count as of yesterday was four hundred and eight."

"Four hundred and eight!" Lucie squealed.

"I know, crazy, right? This is why every hotel is booked up in town. But if the wedding had been in Taipei, I would have been forced to invite over a thousand guests, easily. So I'm taking consolation in that."

They reached a fork in the road, where Lucie noticed a small ceramic plaque affixed to the stone wall with the words DA LUIGI BEACH CLUB painted on it. Isabel steered them onto the lower road, which quickly became a steep pathway that wound all the way down the hill. Halfway down the pathway, they rounded a corner and Lucie gasped audibly, stopping dead in her tracks. Before her was the most astonishing view. Three towering rock formations jutted out of the sea, just off the island's coast, and in front of the rocks was a private bay where the beach club was situated. The waters all around the shoreline shimmered from the lightest hint of turquoise to the most intense shade of azure blue, beckoning all to come bathe at the foot of the rocks.

"This is the most beautiful place I've seen in all my life!" Lucie said, as she took in the landscape. "These are the famous Faraglioni rocks, aren't they?"

"Yes. Legend has it these were the rocks on which the sirens would meet, where they would sing their songs to bewitch sailors," Isabel informed her.

"I believe it! The rocks look totally enchanted. I'd jump off a ship and swim straight for them!"

"You see the one that's farthest away?"

"That's the home of a species of blue lizard* found only on that rock," Lucie said with a smile.

Isabel laughed. "I forgot who I was with. Of course you'd already know far more about this island than I do!"

"Not really, I just read the whole Fodor's guidebook on the plane."

They arrived at the club and checked in with the hostess standing by the entrance to a rustic, whitewashed building where the restaurant was. Deck chairs with bright blue cushions and matching blue umbrellas were placed all along the different sections of rocks leading down to the sea. Isabel made a beeline for her friends, who were clustered around the highest point overlooking the water, sunning themselves. There were about a dozen girls from around the globe, all from different eras of Isabel's life—some from her college years,

---

* *Podarcis sicula coerulea*, the famous blue lizard of the Faraglioni that scientists believe developed its distinct color to camouflage itself with the surrounding waters and blue sky.

some from her work, a few from her time in Taiwan. Isabel made sure to introduce Lucie to everyone.

"Where's Dolfi?" Lucie asked.

"The guys chartered a boat and went fishing this morning," Isabel announced.

"Thank God we're rid of them for a while," said Amelia (Taipei American School / Northwestern / NYU Stern), Isabel's friend from Taipei who was also the maid of honor.

Isabel quickly removed her Missoni cover-up, while Lucie stripped off her shorts and unzipped her light cotton hoodie. Underneath was her new blue-and-white-striped plunge V-neck one-piece swimsuit. She had thought that it looked sort of retro cool when she bought it at a little boutique in Nolita, but now, standing among these older and more sophisticated women, she wondered if it looked a little childish. All of them were sporting swimsuits far more fashionable and revealing—Isabel in a lime-green-and-purple Emilio Pucci bikini, Amelia in a plunging Eres one-piece, Daniella (Gan Israel Kindergarten / Wilbur Avenue Elementary / Portola / Taft / Beverly Hills High / Cal State Northridge) from Los Angeles in a black Norma Kamali with asymmetrical cutouts, Sophie (Woollahra Preschool / Queenwood / Brown) from Australia in a barely there red Valentino bikini, and one of the Italian girls, Talitha (British School of Milan / ICS / Saint Ann's / Le Rosey / Parsons), was even topless.

Feeling suddenly self-conscious, Lucie wandered down the steps to the concrete platform at the edge of the water. At last, she was here. She loved nothing more than swimming in the sea. From where she was standing, the glacially clear water appeared like it could be freezing. How cold would it actually be? *Only one way to find out,* she thought. Taking a deep breath, she plunged in.

"How is it?" Isabel shouted down at her.

"Heaven!" Lucie shouted back. "It's the perfect temperature!" This being July, the Mediterranean had been warming nicely throughout the past few months, and Lucie loved gliding through these waters. Most of her summers had been spent swimming in the frigid ocean off Long Island, and this seemed tropical by comparison. She swam out quickly to the farthest point, where a rope and buoy indicated the outer perimeter of where the current was safe, and flipped onto her back.

This was absolute bliss. The sea was so buoyant that she could simply float along without much effort at all, and she stretched out languorously, staring at the Faraglioni rocks looming above her. One of the enormous rocks had formed an arch perfectly through its middle, and she wondered whether she could swim all the way out there and through the arch. A small boat suddenly came speeding through it, leaving a violent wake and making Lucie think better of her notion.

As she bobbed along quietly, she began to hear the *splish-splash* of an approaching swimmer. "Lucie! Lucie in the sky with diamonds!" a voice said, and she turned to see Auden Beebe bobbing along next to her. "Or should I say, Lucie afloat in the ocean blue. You are quite the little mermaid!"

"What do you mean?"

"Well, you seemed to glide over the water in record time. Took me twice as long just to catch up," Auden said, catching his breath as he hung on to a buoy.

"I swam varsity at Brearley."

"Obviously! I've never seen anyone execute the trudgen more perfectly."

"Thanks. I take it you were on a swim team too?"

"Until I dropped out, yes. Are you on your college team now?"

"No. It's not really the sort of thing one does at Brown."

"Ah yes. I recently heard someone call it 'an excellent school for people who want to read a lot and have feelings.' "

"Haven't heard that one," Lucie said, rolling her eyes.

"So . . . what does one do at Brown?"

"Well, mostly I read a lot and have feelings."

"Ha!"

"Sorry, hope that didn't come across as rude."

"Lucie, don't ever apologize for a perfect comeback. Besides, I'm in the business of having feelings, remember? I remember how excited you were last year to start college. So tell me, what was the thing you loved the most in your first year?"

"Hmm . . . probably my painting class."

"What sort of things did you paint?"

"Mostly abstract stuff. I've been painting on unprimed canvases, and I love the feel of that."

"Do you know the work of Morris Louis? He did his best work on unprimed canvases."

"Of course! I love his veil paintings. I did a few earlier this summer inspired by him, and also by Helen Frankenthaler's work."

"That sounds marvelous. I'd love to see them sometime."

"I have a few photos on my phone, but you can always see the real thing when you're out in East Hampton next."

"Let's do both. Have you been around to any of the art galleries in Capri yet?"

"Not yet, but I'm hoping to."

"Isabel's got us all on quite a schedule with all the fetes, hasn't she?"

"I'm loving it. The only thing I really want to do that's not on the schedule is go swimming in the Blue Grotto."

"That one's going to be tricky. They don't allow swimming in there anymore, but what they do now is row you into the grotto in a little boat."

"Well, if I'm in a little boat, can't I just jump in for a few minutes?"

"Spoken like a true rebel."

"Have you been to the grotto?"

"Yes, many years ago."

"And was it as spectacular as everyone says it is?"

"It was incredible. You really ought to go, especially since you are a mermaid. Also, make sure you don't miss Villa San Michele."

"That's Axel Munthe's house, isn't it? I hear the art is amazing."

"It's more antiquities than paintings, but I think you'll love it.

The house and gardens are so beautifully situated, I'm sure it will inspire you. So, tell me, why did you choose Brown instead of going to RISD?* I mean, it's literally across the street in Providence."

"Oh, you know, I'm trying to balance things out by being a biology major.† I don't think my mom would be too happy if I had just gone straight to art school."

"Has she told you that?"

"Not in so many words, but I know she'd want me to do something more practical."

"I think the most impractical thing one can do is not follow your passions."

Lucie considered his words as she lay floating, looking up at the cloudless sky. After a few moments, she turned to Auden. "I think I've left the others long enough."

"See you back on dry land," Auden murmured, his eyes closed as he treaded water meditatively.

Lucie arrived back at the shore just as the girls were getting up for lunch. She quickly toweled herself off, put on her clothes, and joined the girls upstairs at the restaurant, where they were seated at a long table on the outdoor deck overlooking the bay.

"You were out there with Auden for quite a while. I'm so jealous!" Isabel declared.

"Why?" Lucie wondered.

"Don't you think he's amazing? Every time I talk to him, I feel like I've had a decade's worth of therapy."

"He's an interesting guy," Lucie volunteered.

"He never gives anyone that much one-on-one time. Do you know how much he charges for his private coaching sessions?"

---

* Rhode Island School of Design, which, incidentally is where three members of the Talking Heads—David Byrne, Tina Weymouth, and Chris Frantz—first met.

† Even though Emma Watson majored in English literature, Duncan Sheik studied semiotics, and JFK Jr. chose American studies, biology is tied with economics as the most popular major at Brown University.

"Well, we weren't having a session. We were talking about swimming."

"Yeah, you sure swam out far! Let's hope you've built up an appetite!" Isabel said, as a battalion of waiters arrived right on cue with the food.

Before long, the table was laid out family style with the most delectable array of dishes. There was *insalata caprese*—the island's namesake salad of sliced buffalo mozzarella, tomatoes, and sweet basil—deep-fried zucchini flowers stuffed with ricotta, sesame-crusted tuna over a bed of arugula and cherry tomatoes, fresh langoustines, risotto with squid and shrimp, gnocchi with radicchio and caciocavallo cheese, linguini with clams, and what turned out to be Lucie's favorite—spaghetti with pistachio pesto, clams, lemon, and basil.

"Oh my God! I think I'm going into a pasta-induced coma!" Isabel sighed, finally surrendering her fork.

"I've eaten at some great restaurants, but this is one of the best Italian meals I've ever had in my life!" declared Daniella.

"Does the food taste better because we're sitting here surrounded by this incredible view, or is the food really that good?" Isabel wondered.

"I think it's definitely both. Atmosphere is everything. I mean, look at the water! And the rocks! And up there is my dream house," Sophie said, pointing up at the beautiful white-columned villa perched high on the edge of the cliff.

"Isn't it spectacular? I've been eyeing it all morning," Daniella said.

"I wonder how prices are here compared with Sydney. You can't get anything on the water anymore for less than ten million," Sophie said casually.

"I bet it's pricier than Sydney. Capri is one of the most expensive property markets in the world because they stopped allowing people to build anything new on the whole island back in the sixties. There's so little inventory, you basically have to wait for someone to die," Daniella replied.

"Daniella, you're such a property goddess! I bet the first thing you did when you got here was head straight to the property agent!" Isabel teased.

"No, the first place I headed to was Il Laboratorio, the boutique. Then I went to the property agent!"

"How do you even get up to that villa? I don't think there's a road anywhere near it," Talitha wondered.

"Can you imagine the view from up there?" Daniella said.

"Ladies, stop looking up there. You're missing quite a view down here. Delicious dude alert!" Amelia suddenly declared. All the heads at the table swiveled to where she was pointing.

Lucie's eyes widened. Walking toward the water's edge was George Zao, wearing nothing but a white Speedo.

"Stop it! That's my cousin George!" Isabel shrieked.

"OMG! That slice of chiseled heaven is your cousin?" Amelia gasped.

Isabel gave Amelia a look of disbelief. "Second cousin, actually. You think he's cute?"

"Um, yeah! He's a total snack! You could cut diamonds on that jawline. And check out that six-pack on him."

"More like *twelve*-pack!" Talitha gawked.

"You know, for so long he was just this scrawny kid, I hadn't really noticed his transformation. What can I say, he's got great genes," Isabel deadpanned, flicking her hair for effect.

The girls watched as George climbed up to a high rock, stretched out his arms, and executed a perfect dive into the sea.

Amelia clapped her hands. "I'll give that ten points!"

Isabel turned to Lucie. "I think you and George are at the same hotel. Have you met him yet?"

"Um, we've crossed paths," Lucie said, feeling her face flush. She hadn't told Isabel about switching rooms with the Zaos yet, and now she didn't think she was ever going to.

"He's maybe a year ahead of you, I think. Goes to Berkeley," Isabel continued.

"Does he? He doesn't say much," Lucie said, feeling a mix of emotions begin to well up inside.

"He's very quiet, isn't he? He's always been that way," Isabel said, watching her cousin as he swam back to shore. He padded over to the outdoor showers directly opposite from where they were sitting on the terrace and began rinsing himself off.

Amelia stared brazenly at him. "Yes, definitely a ten!"

"I'd give him a nine, minus one point for the Speedo. I'm not a huge fan of them—you can practically tell his religion, even from up here," Daniella commented.

"Speedos are disgusting! They remind me of my fat uncles or Don Johnson on *Miami Vice*,"* Talitha chimed in.

Sophie giggled. "In Australia, all the lifeguards on the beach wear them. We call them budgie smugglers."

"More like a falcon smuggler in his case," Amelia said.

Lucie stole a quick glance at George and then looked away. She felt so embarrassed for him, and at the same time she felt something else, something unexpected that took her by surprise. Anger. What in the world possessed him to wear that ghastly Speedo? Why would he want to put himself on display like that? To open his body up to assessment, to ridicule? And then to show off to the whole world with that attention-seeking dive. Obviously, he thought he was God's gift! Why was she even surprised that George Zao was just like his crazy mother?

---

* Don Johnson, to my knowledge, never wore a Speedo on television. Talitha is obviously confusing him with David Hasselhoff on *Baywatch*.

VI

Da Costanzo

CAPRI, ITALY

Olivia insisted on taking Charlotte and Lucie shopping for sandals when they had mentioned it the previous evening, but at the appointed time after lunch, only Lucie appeared in the hotel lobby.

"It's just going to be me," Lucie said as she got out of the elevator.

Olivia raised an eyebrow. "That bad, huh?"

"She can't even get out of bed. I've never in my life seen Charlotte hungover until today."

"Should we even be going out when she's like this?"

"Yes, she urged me to go. She said she just wants to sleep."

"Poor Charlotte! Now I feel awful. I should have stopped her," Olivia said with a little laugh.

"How much did she have to drink last night?" Lucie asked. She had been seated at Isabel's table during dinner at Le Grottelle, a restaurant set partially inside a cave at one end and on a hillside terrace with sea views at the other, so she had no idea what Charlotte and Olivia had been up to at their end of the party.

"Oh, I can't remember. You know when wine is that good, it just tastes like candy and you lose track of how many you've had."

"I only had a few sips."

"*A few sips?* Lucie, they served two Château Lafites *and* a Haut-Brion last night! It was brought in specially from the De Vecchi cellars. Don't tell me you only had a few sips!"

"Well, I don't have much of a tolerance. Unfortunately I inherited the Asian flush gene from my mom," Lucie joked.

"I see," Olivia murmured, not understanding what Lucie meant and thinking that Charlotte had been right when she said last night that Lucie was "a good kid." Her own college years in Paris had been quite a different story.

The two of them walked out of the hotel and Lucie, by habit, started veering left toward Via Ignazio Cerio.

"Where do you think you're going?" Olivia asked.

"Aren't we heading to Via Camerelle?" Lucie asked, referring to Capri's most famous shopping street.

"Hell no! You can't walk through town before five, are you crazy? We'll be trampled to death by tourists! Locals and those of us in the know avoid town at all costs between the hours of ten and five, when all the hydrofoils from Sorrento and Naples arrive and spit out thousands of day-trippers."

"Really?"

"Lucie, trust me, don't even *think* of being seen in town until after five, when the last boat has left for the day. That's when the island becomes magic again and all the bright young things come out from hiding and head to the piazzetta for drinks."

"I had no idea," Lucie said, amused by Olivia's insistence.

"Well, learn from me, kiddo. I've been coming to Capri every summer for years."

"But aren't we going to miss all the sandal shops if we avoid town?"

"Not at all. Because there is only one sandal shop you need to go to, and I'm going to take you there via the back route, where we can avoid the huddled masses and their snot-nosed, sticky-fingered *enfants*." Olivia expertly guided Lucie through a maze of back lanes snaking behind the hotels. The quiet little streets seemed a world away from the rest of Capri, even though they were only a few blocks away from the main square.

They found themselves in the heart of a neighborhood where the walls rose up high on both sides, making Lucie feel as if she were deep within a remote medieval hill town. The patina of glitz so ubiquitous throughout the rest of Capri had vanished. Here, the white walls were gray with dirt and the windows didn't gleam. There wasn't a single luxury hotel or designer boutique anywhere in sight, but instead they passed a tailor, a little grocery stall with crates of fresh produce stacked outside, and a trio of boys playing soccer along a wall.

Lucie found the rustic modesty rather charming and beautiful in its own way. "How did I miss this whole neighborhood?"

"You think the locals all shop at Prada? This is the real 'hood, where the shops cater to people who actually have to live here year-round. Look at that old tailor working away in there . . . isn't he absolutely adorable? And these little tykes trying to kill each other over a ball. Christ, this one's going to break his neck!" Olivia observed, carefully sidestepping a laughing boy as he slammed his body full force against the wall trying to defend the ball.

As they walked by a hair salon with faded posters of models in the window that, judging by the hairstyles, hadn't been changed since the mid-1980s, Olivia continued her monologue: "The true beauty of this island is in its people and all these authentic areas off the beaten path. Think of all the tourists who only come to Capri for one day and rush around trying to see everything on the tourist map but miss all this. Or the ones who arrive at Marina Grande, take a boat out to see the Blue Grotto, and don't even realize that the town of Capri is actually on top of the mountain and not part of the harbor below. I think they should actually ban day-trippers and require all visitors to spend at least three nights on the island. There should also be a fashion assessment before they can get off the boat—no tacky tourists. Now *stop*!"

Lucie stopped dead in her tracks, suddenly alarmed.

"Take a deep breath!" Olivia ordered.

Lucie relaxed and inhaled deeply.

"Tell me, what do you smell?"

"I don't really smell . . . anything," Lucie lied politely. The odor of cat piss was so strong, it made her eyes water.

"You're smelling the real Capri here. *La vera Italia!*" Olivia announced, before marching on. Turning down an impossibly narrow lane, they descended a flight of stone steps and found themselves in front of a tiny, unpretentious shop that looked like it had been carved into the rock face of the hill centuries ago.

"This is Da Costanzo, my favorite sandal maker."

Lucie stepped into the shop and felt like she had been transported into Aladdin's cave. Thousands of leather cords, buckles, and gemstones in every color imaginable hung along the walls of the shop, and arrayed all over the floor and on shelves were the most stylish sandals Lucie had ever seen.

"*Buongiorno,* Antonio! *Buongiorno,* Alvina! *Come stai?* This is my friend Lucie from New York. Tell her what she absolutely needs to have this season." Turning to Lucie, Olivia said, "Now, Antonio's been making all these sandals by hand for decades. His father, Costanzo, who was the original sandal maker, touched the feet of Jackie Kennedy, Sophia Loren, and Clark Gable. Imagine that!"

"Oh, wow," Lucie said. She tried to picture one of those legendary icons standing in the same little space she was in, but all she could think of was poor Costanzo having to handle thousands upon thousands of sweaty, stinky feet every day.

"Everyone is wanting the rose-gold leather this year," Antonio said, reaching over from the stool where he sat making the sandals every day and handing Lucie a sandal with two simple cords of shiny leather crisscrossing the big toe and wrapping around the ankle.

"Try it on. Feel how soft the leather is," Antonio's wife, Alvina, said with a warm smile. Lucie slipped a pair on and was amazed by how comfortable they were.

"So chic! So sexy! So minimalist! It's the Donald Judd of sandals! You could wear this to the beach and head straight to cocktails!" Olivia pronounced. "Antonio, I want one, please. But could you do me a pair on the black leather sole?"

"Of course," Antonio replied.

Olivia suddenly caught sight of a man in a white linen jacket with a waxed mustache on the other side of the street holding a big golf umbrella over an elderly woman swathed in a bejeweled headscarf. A few paces behind them walked two security guards in dark suits and sunglasses.

"Oh, it's Mordecai! I have to have a word with him about tomorrow's excursion!" Olivia dashed out of the shop before Lucie could say anything.

Lucie took her time leisurely trying on different styles, chatting about New York with Alvina, and getting her foot measured by Antonio. In the end, she chose two pairs of sandals for herself: one in the rose gold, but done in a dramatic gladiator style with the leather cords wrapping all the way up her calves, and a classic T-strap in pale pink suede accessorized with two matching suede tassels. Antonio would custom-make them to fit her feet perfectly and have them delivered to the hotel. She also bought tan leather flip-flops for her brother, Freddie, and a faux-leopard-print pair for her mother.

Thirty minutes had passed, and Olivia had still not returned. Deciding not to wait any longer, Lucie paid for her purchases and walked out onto Via Roma. It was half past four, and the street was wall-to-wall packed with tourists dashing about in a frenzy doing last-minute shopping, catching buses, or heading for the *funicolare* that would take them down the mountain to catch the last ferries.

About fifty Japanese came marching along, trying valiantly to maintain an orderly line behind their tour group leader, who was holding up a stick with a yellow rubber duck on the end of it. Lucie was jostled along with the crowd for a few minutes before she darted quickly into the vestibule of a vintage jewelry shop for a moment's respite.

She was a little annoyed that Olivia had abandoned her and wondered if she would be able to find her way to the hotel along the back lanes again. The crowd thinned out for a moment, and Lucie managed to make it to the piazzetta without incident, where she found the last available table at the Gran Caffè. She sat down gratefully, placing her shopping bag on the wicker seat next to her and poring over the leather-bound menu.

A silver-haired waiter in a dapper white blazer approached the table and said with a bow, *"Konnichi wa!"*

Lucie stared at him in confusion for a few moments before realizing he was greeting her in Japanese.

"Er . . . *Ni hao ma?*" he tried again.

"I'm sorry, I don't speak Chinese," she said, turning up the volume on her American accent.

"Ah, *Americana!* Easy peasy. Let me guess, you want Diet Coke with ice?"

Lucie forced a smile. "Actually, I think I'll try the *granita al limone.*"

"Lemon granita! Perfect for this hot day," the waiter said jovially.

The sun was just cresting over the mountaintop directly in Lucie's sight line, so she put on her sunglasses. In her short white Erdem shirt dress with the cute Bresson lace sleeves and her dark glasses on, she somehow felt very European and grown-up at the moment. This is what she loved doing the most whenever she traveled to Europe—sitting at an outdoor café, watching the world go by. Whenever they visited Paris, she always insisted on dragging her mother and Freddie to an outdoor table at La Palette, her favorite café in Saint-Germain, and she wished that they could be here with her right now.

Lucie glanced covertly at the people seated around her. She loved checking people out and making up stories in her mind about them. On her left was a young, attractive Italian couple, looking longingly into each other's eyes—on their honeymoon, possibly? To her right were two smartly dressed men: an American guy with dark blond hair in a blue-striped T-shirt and navy blazer talking to an Asian guy with a goatee wearing a pair of round 1930s retro-style sunglasses. They looked like they worked in fashion and were here on business. She overheard the Asian guy saying, "I need to remember to get sandals made for Alexandra and Jackie," and she wondered if it was because he noticed her shopping bag from Da Costanzo. Behind her were two middle-aged women smoking and having an intense discussion in German while a humongous Great Dane sat quietly at their heels. Were they sisters rehashing an old family feud?

Within a few minutes, the waiter returned and placed a large glass bowl on her table containing a mountain of slushy lemon granita, accompanied by a single thin slice of cantaloupe wedged onto the rim of the glass. Lucie smiled in delight at the dessert before her. It reminded her of the desserts she loved getting at Serendipity when she was a kid, although this presentation looked decidedly more elegant.

She sat at her table sipping the granita contentedly from the straw. It was deliciously icy, and the freshly squeezed lemon juice was so refreshingly tart as it went down her throat. She was wondering if she should take a nibble of the cantaloupe now or save it for after she finished the granita when out of the corner of her eye, she saw a tall, elderly white-haired man enter the piazzetta, wobble slightly, and then stumble against the table where the Italian couple was seated. The Italian man sprang up from his chair and helped the man to his feet. The old man stood for a split second, took a step forward, and then went crashing down again, his head landing right on Lucie's dessert, breaking the glass bowl and splashing lemon granita all over her.

Lucie found herself glued to her chair, unable to move. It seemed as if time had stopped. No one did a thing. The Italian couple stared helplessly at the old man, the Germans just sat there, and the waiters stood like statues. All around them were dozens of glamorous-looking people, frozen at their tables and gawking. She heard the American beside her say, "I think he's dying," and then somewhere behind her, a lady with a British accent cried, "We. Simply. Must!"

The man's eyes rolled back, she heard a rattle deep in his throat, and his face turned blue, but all she could see was red—the red blood vessels in the whites of his eyes, the red gushing from his head onto the white tablecloth. She finally stood up, and then she felt the ground beneath her spin and everything went black.

Lucie had no idea how long she had been unconscious, maybe it was just seconds, but when she came to, she felt something warm and soft cradling her neck. She looked up and saw George Zao looking down at her and realized that his hands were cushioning her head.

"You okay?" he asked.

She nodded, and then she turned and saw a waiter hovering over the old man, who was now lying on the ground in front of her. The waiter was pounding on the man's chest repeatedly as the Great Dane started whimpering.

"Just stay here. Don't try to get up," George said, jumping up and heading toward the man on the ground. "Stop hitting him like that." He pushed the waiter aside. "Someone call a doctor!" he shouted, as he bent down, lifted the man's chin, and gave him two quick rescue breaths.

Lucie got up from the ground slowly and began backing away from the scene. George was now frantically pumping the man's chest and yelling, "Fucking call a doctor!" Something within her told her that she couldn't look anymore. She couldn't stand there and watch this man die. She turned around and started walking away. The minute she rounded the corner, out of sight of the piazzetta, she started to run.

≋

VII

Arco Naturale

CAPRI, ITALY

George found Lucie sitting on a stone bench, staring out at the Arco Naturale, a gigantic natural limestone arch that rose out of the mountainside 650 feet above the sea.*

"Are you all right?" he asked.

Lucie fixed her eyes out on the view, purposely not looking at him. She knew there were bloodstains on his shirt, and she couldn't bear to see them. "How did you know I was here?"

"I didn't. After leaving the piazzetta, I just felt like coming here."

Lucie could feel her jaw tighten. Why was he always showing up where she least wanted him to be? She got up from the bench and leaned against the green iron fence that faced the sea, hoping he would get the message.

George inhaled, as if about to say something.

"Please . . . don't speak! Please don't tell me what happened to that man. I don't want to know," Lucie blurted in a choked voice.

---

* One of Capri's most spectacular natural wonders, the arch is actually the remnant of a cave that collapsed millions of years ago during the Paleolithic age.

George walked up to the fence and stood near her. Just beyond the fence, the arch towered over them, rising so unexpectedly and improbably out of the cliff it looked like it could have been placed there by aliens. Through the arch was a perfect view of the sea hundreds of feet below, the water glowing in lustrous shades of aquamarine.

They took in the otherworldly view in silence, and after a while, George spoke. "The first time I came here, when I was about twelve, I was so blown away by the sight of this arch that I thought it had to be a vortex. Like maybe some sort of gateway to a parallel universe. I wanted to leap through the arch and be transported somewhere else in time."

"I wouldn't mind being somewhere else in time right about now," Lucie said numbly.

"Follow me." George moved suddenly, and Lucie thought for a second that he was actually going to hop over the fence. Instead, he began heading toward the trail that led down the mountainside. She debated whether she wanted to follow him and then thought, *What the hell.*

Lucie walked a few paces behind George as they headed along a steep paved trail and then down a long set of steps that wound along the thickly forested part of the island.

"Pablo Neruda would hike this trail every day when he lived on the island," George said.

Lucie said nothing, but she was surprised by this bit of trivia coming from George. He didn't seem like the type to read poetry. At the bottom of the steps, they rounded a corner and she found herself standing at the mouth of a cavern. She realized with an unexpected jolt that they were at the Grotta di Matermania. It was one of the places she had put on her must-see list—a natural cavern that was one of the most ancient archaeological treasures of the island.[*]

---

[*] Over the centuries, there have been many theories about the cave, which was most certainly a sacred space in ancient times, with some archaeologists believing that it was

"You wanted to go somewhere back in time, so here we are," George said.

Lucie wandered into the cavern, where walls and stairways had been carved out of the limestone to create different levels and spaces within. This was once a nymphaeum for the ancient Romans, she thought, placing her hand against the cavern walls, strangely warm to the touch, and wondering what mystical rituals these ruins must have witnessed through the ages. She could feel a strange energy pulsating throughout the cave, the same energy she felt when she had visited other ancient sites like Stonehenge and the Mayan temples at Tulum.

At the back of the cavern rose a natural formation that resembled an altar, no doubt the focal point of ceremonies when the cavern was itself a temple. Lucie climbed up to stand in front of the altar and closed her eyes. She wasn't religious by any means—her mother's family was Buddhist and her father's was nominally Episcopalian—but something compelled her to say a silent prayer for the man in the piazzetta.

When she opened her eyes, George was nowhere in sight. She wandered out of the cavern, but he wasn't there either. Should she head back up the steps, or keep going down the trail? She decided to explore a little further, feeling a bit annoyed with herself as she wandered along a path that seemed to be taking her farther and farther down the hill. Where would this lead to? Why in the world was she even looking for George? Hadn't she told him she wanted to be alone? There was something about George—something in the way he spoke, his mannerisms, and his whole vibe—that she found so unsettling, and yet here she was thinking about him again.

It dawned on her that she had never really known an Asian guy before. Asian women, like her mother, Isabel, and so many of her

---

used in ancient Mithraic rituals (google that), while others think that it was a temple dedicated to Cybele, the goddess of wild nature and fertility. Whatever the truth might be, many teenage locals believe it's the best place to get stoned, or laid, or preferably both. Wild nature and fertility indeed.

classmates, had naturally always been part of her life, and at Brearley there had even been three other half-Asian girls in her year. But somehow she had lived her whole life hardly ever interacting with an Asian boy. Freddie didn't count at all—in striking contrast to her, he took after their father in appearance and behaved like the quintessential WASP, right down to his smelly old Sperrys. Strangers meeting them never thought they were related, and someone even mistook Freddie for her boyfriend once. She had met some of her male Chinese cousins from Seattle and Hong Kong when she was younger, but they barely made an impression. Of course, it didn't help that she had gone to an all-girls school like Brearley and lived her whole life on the Upper East Side. Sure, there were a few Asians here and there at the private schools around her neighborhood, but most of the Asian boys in the city went to Stuyvesant,* or so she heard. Plus, the guys she had known were all Asian Americans, and George was nothing like them. He was a Chinese boy from Hong Kong who had spent a few years in Australia. So what exactly did that make him? He didn't seem Australian, despite his quasi-Aussie accent. He was much more Chinese in his ways. He sounded strange, he moved strange, he dressed strange. He probably smelled strange too.

Just when she decided to turn around and retrace her steps to the Arco Naturale, Lucie suddenly caught sight of something through the trees. Down the hill was the most spectacular house perched on top of a little peninsula that jutted out into the sea. The red house was rectangular in shape, but its entire back facade comprised reverse pyramidal steps leading from the ground all the way up to the roof, which was a huge flat patio. It was the coolest house Lucie had ever laid eyes on, and, feeling compelled to get a closer look, she kept on the pathway until she came to a set of steps leading to the

* Consistently ranked one of the best public schools in New York City, Stuyvesant excels in math and science and counts among its alumni Thelonious Monk, Tim Robbins, Ron Silver, Lucy Liu, and many world-renowned mathematicians and scientists you've never ever heard of.

house. There was no gate, but painted on the top step was the word PRIVATO.

"Private property," a voice behind her said, startling her. She turned to see George standing on the pathway just above her.

"Don't sneak up on me like that! Where did you go?"

"I thought you needed some alone time, so I went exploring a bit further."

"This house is quite incredible."

"It's Casa Malaparte, one of the greatest houses ever built. Wanna take a closer look?"

"You just said it was private property."

"I don't think there's any harm walking a bit farther to get a better look." George began walking down the steps, and Lucie followed a bit skeptically. When they reached the house, a man suddenly popped his head out a window and called down to them.

"'*Sera, Giorgio! Come va?*"

"*Va bene, Niccolò. Possiamo dare un'occhiata?*" George replied.

"*Certo!*"

Lucie looked at George in surprise. "Wait a minute, you speak Italian? You know him?"

"I do. He's the caretaker. I was here yesterday looking around."

"Why?"

"Why not? I'm thinking of doing a project inspired by the house."

"Project?"

"I study sustainable environmental design at UC Berkeley."

"Oh," Lucie said. She was beginning to see him in a whole new light.

They climbed up the steps to the flat white roof, which was like a viewing deck for the most glorious panoramic views of the Gulf of Sorrento. Lucie walked as close to the edge of the roof as she dared to and looked out, taking a deep breath. The sun was beginning to set, making the calm sea shimmer in the most seductive shades of gold. She was feeling so much lighter all of a sudden, and she felt almost guilty about it.

George was sitting on the top step of the roof, gazing up at the island and the seagulls that circled endlessly around the jagged peaks. Lucie sat down next to him, finally feeling like she had to say something.

"I'm so ashamed," she began. "I don't know why I ran away."

"You don't need to explain."

Lucie sighed deeply. "I took a CPR class back in high school. I even got an A, believe it or not. But today . . . I dunno . . . I could've done something. I *should've* done something! I was having the loveliest time just sitting in that café, and then suddenly out of nowhere this terrible thing happened. I just . . . froze. And then I couldn't face it, and my body just took over."

"It was a traumatic sight. I wanted to run too. I wanted so much not to be there, but no one was doing anything."

"I don't know how I'm ever going to walk through the piazzetta again."

"You left your shopping bag at the café."

"I know. I was going to head back there eventually and get it. I also skipped out on my bill."

"I tried to pay for you, but the waiters wouldn't let me. They waived it."

"They did?"

"I did get your bag for you. But . . ." George paused, giving her a sheepish look. "I'm sorry, I threw the bag away."

"What? Why did you do that?"

George turned away from her. "I didn't want you to have to see it. It was all splattered with blood, even inside. There was blood on the sandals."

Lucie said nothing for a moment. She thought of how trivial those sandals had suddenly become to her. In the course of one afternoon, everything had changed. In the blink of an eye, someone had died. Someone's father, someone's husband, someone's friend. People would be shocked and grieving. She didn't even know the old man, and she was grieving for him. If only she had done something, if only she had started giving him CPR sooner, he might have survived. How was she going to sit through the dinner tonight at the Michelin-starred restaurant that everyone else was so excited about? How would she be able to enjoy Isabel's wedding? How could she begin to enjoy anything ever again?

George peered into her eyes with that same intensity that used to freak her out, but she somehow found it soothing now. It was as if he could read every single thing going through her mind.

"Can I tell you a story, if I promise it has a happy ending?" he asked.

"Sure, I guess." She stood up, and they began walking along the roof toward the water.

"Once upon a time, there was a girl who sat in a café on the square in Capri, enjoying an afternoon drink . . ."

Lucie froze in alarm. She was about to cut George off, when he said, "I know you didn't want me to say anything, but I think you need to know the old man in the piazzetta is okay. We managed to revive him."

Lucie stared at George wide-eyed as he went on with his story.

"While I was doing CPR on him, the doctor arrived. He was this young guy in board shorts carrying a black leather case, and he had a defibrillator inside. He gave the man a shock with the machine, and he started to breathe again."

Lucie didn't know what was happening to her. She began hyperventilating uncontrollably, and then her entire body started to heave with sobs. She leaned on George, weeping into his shoulder in relief.

George put his arm around her and continued to speak in a soft, steady voice: "The old man was British, and his wife arrived at the piazzetta right as we revived him. She had been down the street shopping at Ferragamo. By the time I left, he was sitting up in a chair, getting treated by the doctor while his wife scolded him for running off . . ."

Marina Grande

CAPRI, ITALY

Charlotte was the first to arrive at the designated meeting place by the cathedral steps, where she found a man with a flamboyant, Daliesque mustache pacing impatiently. Baron Mordecai von Ephrussí (Wetherby / Dragon / Harrow / Magdalen College, Oxford), as he introduced himself, was an acclaimed author, art historian, antiquities consultant, and, currently, fellow at the American Academy in Rome, where he was—as he told anyone who mattered—working on "the definitive biography of Luchino Visconti." The Baron claimed to descend from a long line of Franco-Prussian Jewish aristocrats, even though he was born and raised in England. He had a grand title, but was living off an even grander overdraft, and depended on the good graces of his friends, usually grand ladies of a certain age and status who enjoyed his wit, title, gossip, and expertise on pre-Napoleonic Limoges, not necessarily in that order.

Sizing up his outfit of white-and-blue-striped seersucker trousers, crisp white button-down shirt conspicuously monogrammed with the initials M V E just above his left midriff, navy polka-dot cravat tied around his throat, and Cleverley wing-tips, Charlotte knew exactly how to engage with him. After a quick greeting and exchanging polite chitchat about the gorgeous weather, they did what everyone else in their crowd did and segued into the name game, with Mordecai launching the first volley:

"And what do you do, Ms. Barclay?"

"I'm an editor at *Amuse Bouche*."

"Ah, *Amuse Bouche*. Superb magazine, superb." *Not as good as* Bon Appétit, *but perhaps I can sell her on my idea of writing about Empress Josephine's obsession with* îles flottante.

"Thank you," Charlotte responded. *I'm not going to ask him what he does. It'll drive him nuts, and he'll tell me within two minutes.*

"You must live in New York, then. Tell me, are you by any chance related to Theodore and Annafred Barclay?" Mordecai asked.

Charlotte smiled. *There it was. It only took him thirty seconds to ask.* "Yes, Teddy's my cousin."

Mordecai smiled back. "What a small world! Such a lovely couple. When I'm not slaving away on my book at the American Academy in Rome, I'm the historical consultant for the Prince's Trust International." *She's a Barclay. Of course, only a Barclay can afford to look this unfashionable in Capri.*

So I'm wrong. He told me what he does in under a minute. "The Prince's Trust. Yes, Teddy's been so involved with helping Charles, and of course Camilla and Annafred go way back."

"I saw them at a dinner just last month at the Serpentine Gallery." *How dare you call their royal highnesses by their first names!*

"Did you? I spent a lovely weekend at Highgrove with Teddy and their royal highnesses earlier this summer." *Eat your heart out, Mordecai.*

"Highgrove is lovely in the summertime, isn't it? Now, even lovelier is Pemberley. My cousins, the D'Arcys, keep it up rather well." *Try to top that, Ms. Barclay!*

"So I've heard. How do you know Isabel and Dolfi?" *He was probably their decorator.*

"I have been great friends of her parents, for ages. Many years ago, I had the pleasure of working with Geoffrey Bennison on the Chius' first house on the Bishops Avenue."

I'm too good at this. "I loved Bennison's work. He redid some rooms for my grandmother back in the late seventies."

"He did?" *Who the fuck is her grandmother and why don't I know about those rooms?*

At this point, Lucie arrived at the church steps, rescuing Charlotte from further interrogation.

"Thank you so much for going back and getting my sunblock, Lucie. I would have looked like a Maine lobster without it. Mordecai, this is my cousin Lucie Churchill."

"Hello," Lucie said.

"Enchanted." *Hmm. What a pretty Eurasian.* "Tell me, how exactly are you two related?"

Before Lucie could answer, Charlotte jumped in. "Lucie is the daughter of Reggie Churchill, my mother's brother." *Try that on for size.*

"Ah yes, Reginald Churchill." *How intriguing. And good lord, this means Charlotte's a Churchill and a Barclay. Must be swimming in pots of money.*

Lucie couldn't help but frown. She knew Charlotte dropped her father's name only when she was trying to impress people. She was wondering what the story was with this Mordecai fellow, and she soon understood.

"Now, I think we are just waiting for Mr. Beebe, Ms. Lavistock, and the Ortiz sisters, and then I can call ahead to let the Sultanah know we are ready. She will meet us down at Marina Grande, and then we will all proceed together to Positano to tour the villa."

"The Sultanah?"

"Yes! Today, we have the honor of my great friend the Sultanah of Penang joining us on our little outing."

"What is a sultanah?" Lucie asked.

"My dear, she is Malay royalty of the highest order. She is the royal consort to the Sultan of Penang. She is the queen! Now, we are already in breach of royal protocol by keeping her waiting, but if Mr. Beebe had the decency to be more punctual . . ."

At that moment, Auden Beebe appeared at the foot of the steps with Olivia and the Ortiz sisters, holding an umbrella over the ladies so gallantly that Mordecai could no longer complain.

"So sorry we're late. It's all my fault—I forgot my Leica and had to rush back to my room," Olivia said breathlessly.

The party made its way to the *funicolare* for the short journey down the mountain, and then Mordecai led them to the pier where they were to be picked up for their excursion. They stood along the empty dock for a few minutes, and Olivia, tiring of the sweltering sun, glared at Mordecai. "I thought you said the royal Shahtoosh was meeting us here?"

"I sent the *Sultanah* a text as soon as we arrived at Marina Grande. She'll be along in a few minutes. Her majesty must always be the last to arrive, you understand," Mordecai officiously explained.

"Should I call her 'Your Majesty' too?" Lucie asked.

"First of all, protocol dictates that you should never speak to the Sultanah unless she speaks to you first. You may address her as 'Your Majesty' the first time you greet her and, subsequently, 'ma'am.' "

Olivia looked at Auden and Charlotte, rolling her eyes.

"I take it you have a history with Monsieur le Baron?" Charlotte whispered to Olivia.

"If he's really a baron, then I'm Marie fucking Antoinette. Yes, Mordecai and I go way back. He made my life hell at first when I worked at the Fondation Pierre Bergé one summer, but then his attitude changed the minute he found out who I was related to," Olivia whispered back.

Just then, a large black Mercedes pulled up to the pier, and two bodyguards dressed in dark sunglasses and black suits emerged. The taller one marched down the dock and gave the group a quick once-over before tapping his earpiece and muttering, *"Kami bersedia untuk ratu!"**

The other bodyguard opened the back door of the limousine, and a small, chubby woman in her late seventies wearing a flowing Pucci caftan and matching Pucci hijab emerged. As she walked toward the dock, Lucie could already see the massive canary diamonds sparkling from her head scarf, and she quickly recognized her as the lady in the bejeweled headdress who had walked past the sandal shop the other day.

"Let's form a line to receive her. Now, the Malays prostrate themselves to the knees and bow their heads all the way to the floor when they meet their Sultanah, but I think a bow or a curtsy will suffice here," Mordecai said in a jittery voice.

"For fuck's sake, Mordecai, I wouldn't curtsy even if she were the Dowager Countess of Grantham," Olivia quipped.

Ignoring her comment, Mordecai bowed deeply and was about to address the Sultanah when she breezed right past him and hugged the Ortiz sisters excitedly. "Paloma! Mercedes! I didn't know you were coming! When did you arrive?"

"Sunday. We were in Paris first," Paloma (Saint Scholastica / Ravenhill Academy / Universidad Complutense de Madrid) said.

"For our fittings, you know," Mercedes (Saint Scholastica / Ravenhill Academy / University of Hawaii) added.

"You know these ladies?" Mordecai said in surprise.

"Know them? Of course! Mordecai, these girls own about five thousand of the Philippines' seven thousand islands. I am nothing compared to them!" the Sultanah (privately tutored till the age of ten / Cheltenham Ladies' College) exclaimed.

"Oh, come on, you are royalty. We are commoners," Paloma said.

"We are just housewives!" Mercedes added.

"Uh-huh, sure!" The Sultanah rolled her eyes, turned to Morde-

* "Ready for the queen!" in Malay.

cai again. "Talk about Paris, these girls and I used to go to all the shows together . . . Scherrer, Féraud, and my favorite . . . Jacqueline de Ribes. How I wish I could still fit into her dresses!"

"And remember, we used to hang out at Régine's!" Paloma said excitedly.

"These girls really know how to party!" the Sultanah said with a loud cackle. "Now, Mordecai, please introduce me to all these lovely people."

Mordecai quickly made introductions all around, and Lucie found that the Sultanah couldn't have been more down-to-earth and friendly. Lucie found herself transfixed by this beautiful woman with huge eyes that were further accentuated with heavy Elizabeth Taylor–style eye shadow.

"It's so nice to have you youngsters around. Thank you for joining us dinosaurs on this adventure!" the Sultanah said to Lucie and Charlotte with a warm smile, before turning to Mordecai. "So where's *Queen Mary*?"

"*Queen Mary*?" Mordecai cocked his head.

The Sultanah gestured at the empty dock, her kiwi-fruit-sized emerald ring flashing in the sun. "The big boat you were telling me all about?"

"Ah, yes! Har har, very funny. The yacht should be arriving at any minute, Your Majesty." He turned to the rest of the group and announced, "My dear friends the Murphys, who own Villa Lachowski, have the most stunning yacht that they are so graciously sending here just for the Sultanah. It was decorated by Alberto Pinto, and it's one of the ten biggest yachts in the world."

Right as he uttered those words, a pair of black rubber dinghies sped into the harbor and pulled up alongside their dock.

"Meester Epussy?" the boatman in the first dinghy asked in thickly accented English.

"You mean *Baron* von Ephrussí? Yes, that's me," Mordecai said in his most snotty tone, snapping to attention.

"Okay, how many?" the boatman asked gruffly.

"Er . . . are we supposed to get on these little boats? Are they going to take us to the yacht?" Mordecai asked, confused.

"No yacht. We go to villa now."

"In these rubber dinghies? You must be joking!"

"No joke. We go now, okay?" the boatman insisted, clearly annoyed.

"Please call your boss, or whoever manages the Murphys' fleet. There's been some mistake. They were supposed to send the big yacht, not a tiny dinghy!"

"Mordecai, these aren't dinghies. These are Goldfish Rib Boats. They are high-performance speedboats and really quite expensive," Auden explained, highly amused by the situation.

"Goldfish, catfish, angelfish, I don't care what they are. Her Majesty cannot ride all the way to Positano on this bloody *thing*!"

"Actually, I would love to ride on this thing! It looks like such fun!" the Sultanah chimed in.

Mordecai's jaw dropped, not quite sure what to say.

"The queen has spoken! Let's get on with it. *Andiamo!*" snapped Olivia. "Your Majesty, allow me to help you aboard."

The Sultanah got into the first boat with one bodyguard, Mordecai, Olivia, and Charlotte, while Lucie, the Ortiz sisters, Auden, and the other bodyguard rode in the second boat. Because of the way the Goldfish was designed, there were no proper seats. Instead, there were upright patrol seats that resembled back braces for the passengers to lean against while gripping the handlebars in front of them for support. The Sultanah, who stood right behind the boatman, said to him, "I've seen these before at a military inspection parade. My army uses them for tactical missions. I hear they go very fast."

"Yes, very fast," the boatman replied, as he piloted slowly out of the marina.

"Let's see how fast it can go! I have a need for speed!" the Sultanah gleefully declared.

"Okay. Hold on tight!" the boatman said as he revved up the engine and the Goldfish took off like a rocket.

"Jesus Mary!" Mordecai shrieked, almost falling off the back. He gripped on to his handlebar tightly, not quite believing how fast the boat was going. As soon as they were out on the open sea, the boat began bouncing on top of the waves so violently that it seemed like a roller coaster ride gone out of control. Mordecai held on for dear life as the boat zipped across the Bay of Naples at what seemed like warp speed.

"Slow down! Slow the fuck down!" Mordecai screamed, but between the wind and the roar of the engine, it was impossible for the boatman to hear him. His knuckles were white from gripping, and he didn't know how much longer he could hold on before he was flung out of the boat. Mordecai watched helplessly as the Sultanah kept getting jolted several inches into the air every time the Goldfish hit wave after wave. One big wave and she would be tossed like a rag doll into the Mediterranean. Why weren't they given life jackets? Suddenly, the headline that would surely go viral around the world flashed before his eyes:

SULTANAH OF PENANG DROWNS
OFF THE AMALFI COAST:
BARON VON EPHRUSSÍ TO BLAME

IX

Villa Lachowski

POSITANO, ITALY

Lucie closed her eyes and savored the mist from the waves against her face as the boat sped along. She had a sudden, vivid flashback to the times her father took her sailing in his catboat. They would drive down to the little dock on a hidden inlet off Springy Banks Road and sail out of Three Mile Harbor into Gardiners Bay, and Lucie would sit at the bow, tightly holding the leather strap nailed into the deck, as he had taught her to do. Out on the bay, rogue waves would crash against the bow, splashing her all over, but she would laugh and laugh, just like her father did.

Her father was always happiest on the water, and he would bound barefoot along the edge of the wooden boat like the nimblest acrobat, expertly maneuvering the sail and the rudder, always in those scuffed chinos and his faded orange anorak. Lucie wondered whatever happened to that anorak. Was it still hanging in the closet in the mudroom at East Hampton? She would have to look for it when she was back. As they rounded the bay, the village of Positano came into view, rising into the cloudless blue sky like an apparition. Lucie stared up in awe at the gleaming white buildings hugging a vertiginous cliff like an enchanted wonderland straight out of a Tolkien novel. No wonder everyone called it the jewel of the Amalfi Coast.

Beyond Positano's crescent beach, the Villa Lachowski commanded its own rocky promontory, and Mordecai's boat was the first to arrive at the villa's private dock. A cluster of men in topaz-blue polo shirts and crisp white shorts stood ready to assist the arriving guests, and the Sultanah was the first to climb out of the Goldfish, giggling like a schoolgirl. "That was amazing! I haven't had this much fun since I went with my granddaughter to Burning Man!"

"I'm g-g-glad you enjoyed that, Your Ma-Majesty," Mordecai stammered as he wobbled out of the boat, trying to steady himself on dry land.

"What a beautiful day for a boat ride! Did we lose the others?" the Sultanah wondered.

"I think the others took the scenic, arrive-alive route," Charlotte remarked, looking rather green herself.

Soon, the second Goldfish could be seen approaching at a leisurely speed from around the cove, and its passengers alighted on the dock looking more relaxed and far less windblown than the early arrivals. Mordecai did a quick head count of his flock, genuinely relieved that the whippet-thin Ortiz sisters hadn't been blown off-deck.

"Excellent, excellent, we've all made it here in one piece, more or less. Now, if everyone's ready, we shall be received by Tom and Geraldine Murphy, the owners of this magnificent villa," Mordecai said, as a tall gentleman dressed entirely in black came strolling down the dock toward them.

"That's the estate manager," Mordecai told everyone. "Ah, Stephane! *Comment allez vous?* Are Tom and Gerri up at the villa?" Mordecai was a bit perplexed that his friends hadn't appeared at the dock to greet their royal guest.

"Monsieur Murphy is in London, and Madame Murphy sends her regrets. She was called away to Sardinia on urgent business this morning," replied Stephane with a courtly bow.

"What a pity! Sardinia—she must have taken the yacht, then?" Mordecai inquired.

"No, she took the Wally."

Mordecai looked puzzled. "So . . . why didn't you send us the yacht?"

"Monsieur le Baron, you insisted that your group *had* to be picked up at eleven fifteen sharp and back in Capri by three p.m. The Goldfish were the quickest way to get you all here. The yacht would have taken an hour each way," Stephane patiently explained, clearly accustomed to his persnickety guest.

"Brilliant move, Mordecai," Olivia remarked.

Ignoring her, Mordecai silently cursed himself for insisting on the time restriction. They missed their opportunity on the yacht, and now they would miss seeing the main salon, where there was a fabulous framed photograph of him posing with Geraldine Murphy and Princess Diana that he was dying for the group to stumble upon.

"Now, I have to go into town, but Allegra is ready to give your party the tour," Stephane offered.

"That won't be necessary—I can lead the tour. After all, I know this place like the back of my hand," Mordecai declared, feeling a bit more himself again. He led the group to the staircase carved out of the rocky side of the cliff, and they began the leisurely climb up. The property consisted of six pristine white villas situated on a series of spectacular terraces that cascaded down to the sea, and each terrace was a distinct wonderland devoted to the indulgent whims of its privileged owners.

On the first terrace, they encountered a manicured lawn where a row of four-poster Balinese beds faced the sea, with white linen canopies artfully draped above each bed.

"This is where Geraldine gets her shiatsu massage every afternoon," Mordecai noted. "The lower level of this villa is a state-of-the-art spa where the Murphys maintain a battalion of therapists."

"Their personal Aman resort!" Charlotte commented.

Paloma Ortiz shook her head in dismay. "I look at those sun beds and all I can think of is melanoma."

Arriving at the next terrace above, the group passed a magnificent koi pond that meandered along the curves of the cliff. Water lilies floated on the surface, while hundreds of exotic carp undulated hypnotically in the waters below.

"These are Tom's prized koi. He has a full-time marine biologist who makes sure that these koi are fat and healthy. See the white-and-orange one over there with the head that looks like a deformed tangerine? A representative for the imperial family of Japan offered the Murphys 1.5 million dollars for that fish," Mordecai proudly announced.

"I sure hope it doesn't get picked off by a seagull," Olivia commented.

The Sultanah peered down at the fish, looking unimpressed. "My grandfather loved koi and kept them in gigantic urns back at the old palace, but I prefer golden arowanas."

Undeterred by the crowd's lack of enthusiasm for the decorative koi, Mordecai stood on the steps in front of a pair of massive carved bronze doors, cleared his throat, and raised his voice: "Your Majesty, ladies, and gentlemen, we are about to enter one of the greatest houses on the Mediterranean coast still remaining in private hands. In fact, it can be argued that along with La Leopolda in Villefranche-sur-Mer, once the residence of my dear friend Lily Safra, and the Château de l'Horizon in Vallauris, once owned by Prince Aly Khan, who was a dear friend of my father's, Villa Lachowski is arguably the finest historic waterfront villa in the world. The original structure was built in 1928 by a local family, and it was far more modest—a beach bungalow, really. But when the legendary director Francesco Lachowski acquired it in 1957, he greatly expanded the property. With his discerning eye and access to some of the finest artisans working on his film productions, he was able to create his private Xanadu here."

"Didn't Graham Greene stay here?" Auden asked.

"Yes, the villa is indeed famous because some of the most legendary people visited—Greene, Callas, Nureyev, von Karajan, they were all guests here."

Olivia murmured into Charlotte's ear, "I wish we had some tequila. We could take a shot every time Mordecai says the word 'legendary.' "

"I'd be drunk already," Charlotte replied.

Entering the grand foyer, Mordecai continued. "Now, as we proceed through this imposing threshold into the drawing room, I want you to note the peculiar architectural homages to Sir John Soane that are evident throughout . . ."

Lucie admired her surroundings but did not have much interest in the "peculiar architectural homages to Sir John Soane." She wished that Mordecai would allow them to enjoy the place without his commentary, as her eyes wandered from the de Chirico painting commanding the mantelpiece to the grid of Agnes Martin drawings along a wall and the enormous Cy Twombly canvas casually propped up on a long wooden bench.

"The art's not too shabby, is it?" Auden commented.

"Not too shabby at all!" Lucie said, still astonished that she was standing just inches away from a Twombly.

"Didn't you promise to show me some of your artwork?" Auden asked.

"Oh, sure. When we get back to the hotel this afternoon, I can show you some pictures on my iPad."

"It's a date!" Auden said.

As they proceeded from the drawing room into the library, Mordecai began methodically pointing out all the most expensive first editions and rare manuscripts in the Murphys' collection. Lucie's mind drifted for a moment until she noticed Paloma, the sister with the pixie-cut hair and more dramatically plucked eyebrows, mouthing something to her.

"Pardon me?" Lucie said.

"I said you have a neck like a swan." Paloma smiled.

"Really?"

"Yes, it's long like Audrey Hepburn's. So beautiful!"

"Er . . . thank you," Lucie said, as always feeling a bit awkward whenever someone paid her a compliment.

"You must get it from your mother?"

"Hmm, I guess. I've never thought about it, but yes, my mother does have quite a long neck."

"Where is she from?" Paloma continued to probe.

"Seattle."

"I meant is she Chinese, Japanese, Korean?"

"Oh, sorry. Yes, she's of Chinese ancestry, but she's third-generation Asian American. Her grandfather was one of the very first Chinese students to graduate from Yale with a medical degree," Lucie added, not wishing these ladies to think her mother was fresh off the boat.

"How interesting," Paloma said, clearly not as curious about Lucie's family history as she was with her 23andMe results.

Mercedes jumped into the conversation. "And your father, what is his ancestry?"

"English, Scottish, and Swedish," Lucie replied as patiently as she could. Why was it that only other Asians interrogated her about her background?

"You must thank your mother for your beautiful features, then. I thank mine every morning when I look in the mirror. It's because of my Chinese blood that I haven't needed a face-lift yet!"* Mercedes giggled.

"You're part Chinese?" Lucie asked.

"Yes, of course. My sister and I are *torna atrás*—we have Chinese, Spanish, and Filipino blood. You know, most Filipinos have mixed blood. We are all *mestizos,* like you."

"I had no idea."

"Now, tell me, dear, how long have you been modeling?"

* She's lying, of course. She had a face-lift and neck-lift back in 2000.

Lucie laughed out loud at the preposterousness of the idea. "Me? I've never modeled."

Mercedes gave Paloma a look before turning back to Lucie. "Really? All this time we thought you were that girl in the new Chanel perfume ads."

"I swear it isn't me."

"It sure looks like you! Now, why don't you model? Our cousin Kris owns the top talent agency in Manila, and she would recruit you in a heartbeat!"

"We should also recruit that one coming down the stairs," Paloma said, gesturing.

Lucie turned around and saw George Zao bounding down the marble steps, followed by his mother. It was the first time she had seen him since Casa Malaparte. Before she could help herself, she found herself smiling at him and then almost immediately wanted to kick herself. Why did she grin at him like that? She felt like a total idiot.

"Rosemary, George, what a surprise!" Auden said cheerily as he clapped George heartily on the back.

Mordecai gave the late arrivals a quick once-over. Who on earth was this woman, and what possessed her to think she could join his group wearing those flamingo-pink sweatpants? "Madame, I don't seem to recall you signing up for my tour?" he said haughtily.

Olivia was about to spring to their defense, but Rosemary gave Mordecai a confused look. "We didn't sign up for anything—we were here for breakfast."

"You're friends with the Murphys?" Olivia asked, almost smirking.

"Yes, old friends. Tom and my husband owned a company together."

Mordecai's interest was instantly piqued. "Oh, really? Which one?"

"I can't remember . . . was it the oil company? The refineries? No, it was the shipping company. Yes, they owned a fleet of tankers together, the largest fleet in the Pacific."

Mordecai did an abrupt one-eighty and he smiled at Rosemary solicitously. "Well, Mrs. Chao—"

"It's *Zao*," Rosemary corrected.

"Yes, Mrs. Zao, I was just at the start of my historical tour. Geraldine might have told you that I was the one who found this villa for them. You are most welcome to join us . . ."

"Oh, we don't need a tour. We've stayed here many times; this is like a second home for us. Gerri insisted that I try her new float tank after breakfast, and now I'm going down for a Thai massage on the beach," Rosemary declared before padding off with the ease of a longtime houseguest. George followed after her, and as he passed Lucie, he murmured in that low, quiet voice, *"Hey."*

"Hey," Lucie said, feeling the sudden rush of blood to her cheeks.

X

The High Garden at Villa Lachowski

CAPRI, ITALY

The group had just finished Mordecai's encyclopedic tour of every precious nook and cranny of the remarkable property, and for their patience they were rewarded with a sumptuous lunch held on the enchanting terra-cotta-tiled terrace, where wisteria vines wrapped around every column and the most arresting view of Positano stretched out before them like a perfectly retouched postcard.

"I'm having sensory overload. I'm not sure where to look—at the breathtaking view, at these adorable hand-painted majolica plates, or at this glorious feast!" Charlotte said as she sat down in her cushioned wicker chair, assessing the meal on the table with approval. Along with a chilled lobster and saffron bisque and a classic Caesar salad featuring cured Amalfi anchovies, the Murphys' chef also brought out huge platters of strozzapreti tossed in a creamy sea urchin sauce and a delectably light mortadella, pistachio, and lemon pizza.

Tucking into her pasta, Mercedes whispered rather loudly to everyone on her side of the table, "I now know more than I ever imagined about neoclassical Piedmontese furniture."

"It could have been worse," Paloma said with a slight giggle.

"Really? I couldn't possibly see how," Olivia interjected.

"That Mrs. Zao could have come along on the tour," Mercedes whispered.

"Are you not a fan?" Charlotte said with a slight smirk.

Paloma pursed her lips for a moment, before replying, "She is perfectly lovely. I just wouldn't want to be on a two-hour tour with her, that's all."

Mercedes waved her hand in front of her sister's face dismissively. "Oh, Paloma, stop being so polite. We just weren't impressed by the way Mrs. Zao bragged about her husband's companies. Not impressed at all!"

"Was it really bragging? She was asked the question by Mordecai, and she simply gave him an answer," Olivia countered.

"It was the manner in which she said it. Did she have to boast that it was the largest fleet of tankers on the planet? I mean, our family founded businesses in the Philippines that go back to the eighteen hundreds, but we never would have mentioned it quite like that. My mother would have given us a tight slap!" Mercedes said.

"Mother could have taught that woman a thing or two about subtlety! Her style is just a bit too *Hong Kong* for my taste," Paloma sniffed.

"How do you define 'too Hong Kong'?" Charlotte asked as she tore off a slice of the pizza and carefully removed every bit of mortadella and cheese with her knife and fork.

Paloma pondered for a moment. "There's a certain showy quality. The colors they choose to wear, and how they don't mind being seen dripping in jewels at all hours of the day."

"You call it showy, I call it flair. I suppose I have a penchant for extravagant, eccentric style. Mrs. Zao reminds me of Anna Piaggi or the Marchesa Casati," Olivia said.

"Well, you should have seen the rubies she wore to go swimming yesterday. My jeweler would have had a heart attack!"

"And that son of hers, the silent one. No doubt he's handsome, but have you ever heard him speak? It's quite odd," Mercedes mused.

"I think he's just a little full of himself," Charlotte commented.

"You know, I read somewhere that beautiful men lack a conscience," Mercedes interjected.

"Oh, what rubbish! He's perfectly nice to me. I just don't think he's one for small talk," Olivia said.

Lucie soaked in the ladies' banter but said nothing. She couldn't help but notice the Sultanah seated at the other end of the table, being fawned over by Mordecai. Even though she was wearing a blindingly colorful caftan and dripping in jewels, the Ortiz sisters didn't seem to disapprove of her.

. . .

After lunch, the group dispersed to pursue various pampering distractions. The Sultanah and the Ortiz sisters treated themselves to the warm goat's milk and honey manicures being offered in the spa (with Mordecai tagging along, of course), Auden went for a dip in the waters off the villa's private beach, and Charlotte, Olivia, and Lucie decided to take advantage of the sun beds on the lower terrace. The Balinese beds were situated at the perfect vantage point under an allée of tall umbrella pines, allowing the harsh afternoon sun to filter gently down to them while the crosswinds blew a cool sea breeze.

Lying on her belly and staring out at the azure waters from her plush silk mattress, Charlotte let out a deep sigh. "This is absolute bliss!"

"I've always found billionaires to be a miserable lot, but once in a while I think it might not be *that* bad to have enough cash to afford a place like this," Olivia said with her eyes closed as she savored the sunlight on her face.

"You know, I almost married one with a place not too different from this," Charlotte murmured lazily.

Lucie stared at her cousin curiously. "Really?"

"Yes. Raphaël. His parents had a villa in Cap-Ferrat, and we spent a few heavenly weeks there the summer after I graduated from Smith."

"That was your hot summer romance, wasn't it? We've all had at least one," Olivia remarked.

"What happened?" Lucie asked, having a hard time imagining Charlotte engaged in a hot summer romance with anyone.

"My parents happened. Raphaël proposed and wanted me to move to London with him, where he was about to start a job at Rothschild's. But Mom and Dad didn't approve. And neither did Granny. They all thought I was much too young and he was a little too, shall we say . . . exotic."

"Where was he from?" Lucie asked.

"He was born in Paris, to an extremely wealthy and aristocratic family."

"So what was wrong with that?" Lucie pressed on.

"Do you really need me to spell it out for you? *They were Jewish.*" Charlotte mouthed the last part.

"Oh," Lucie said quietly, her face clouding over. "Did your parents really object because of that?"

Charlotte sighed. "There were many reasons, but that was certainly a factor. It remained unsaid, but I know my parents. And I think you're old enough now, Lucie, to realize how Granny can be sometimes. She used to refer to Jews as 'the visitors.' I was so confused whenever she said that until I realized what she meant when I took her shopping for cosmetics at Bergdorf's one day. She whispered to me, 'Time to change my regimen. The *visitors* have all discovered La Prairie!' "

"Oh dear God," Olivia huffed contemptuously, while Lucie remained silent. Unlike her cousin, she had learned from a very early age precisely how her grandmother could be, and she preferred to block those memories out.

"What happened to Raphaël?" Olivia inquired.

"You know, the usual. Married some other blonde, had a bunch of kids, got divorced, got fat."

Olivia snorted. "They all get fat, don't they?"

"But when he was younger, boy, let me tell you . . . he was really something."

Olivia raised an eyebrow. "How something was he?"

"Remember that guy in *Sixteen Candles* that Molly Ringwald was obsessed with?"

"Do I? I was obsessed with him too! God, what was his name? And what ever happened to him?"*

"I'm not sure, but Raphaël looked just like him, only handsomer."

"Was he a good kisser? French boys are the best kissers, I find."

Charlotte turned onto her back and glanced at her cousin. "Lucie, would you be a darling and go fetch us some drinks. An Arnold Palmer, maybe? I'm dying of thirst."

"Me too. Get them to put some vodka in mine," Olivia said.

Lucie rolled her eyes. "Okay, I get the hint."

She got up from her bed, left the terrace, and relayed the drink orders to a passing spa attendant. She wished to explore more of the grounds but wanted to avoid running into George again at all costs. Since he was probably with his mother getting a Thai massage down by the beach, Lucie thought it best to head upward. She wandered into a beautiful greenhouse constructed of stained-glass windows where a profusion of orchids was being cultivated, and then found another terrace where built-in sofas along the walls were scattered with colorful kilim pillows. Every corner of the property seemed to reveal a stunning new surprise, and she felt as though she were exploring some sort of Alice in Wonderland dreamscape. *It's all too beautiful,* she thought. *I don't think I could live in a place this beautiful all year long.*

Following signs to the High Garden, she climbed the staircase behind the old villa and came to a glade of ancient tropical palms that created a lush, verdant grove. As she entered, she came upon a

---

* His name was Michael Schoeffling, and after retiring from acting in 1991, he started a business producing handcrafted furniture (if you believe Wikipedia).

marble fountain gurgling next to a carved Etruscan bench. She sat down for a moment in this serene spot, enveloped in the greenery and the chorus of cicadas making their midsummer mating calls, trying to make sense of her thoughts.

All through lunch, it felt like her mind had been doing Cirque du Soleil–size contortions over George and his mother. Why were the others being so mercilessly critical? The Ortiz sisters were such hypocrites. They didn't care for Mrs. Zao's "showy" style, but weren't they being showy in their own way? Every time she saw the sisters, they were immaculately outfitted from head to toe, and even the Sultanah confirmed that the sisters dressed in couture. Yes, their black pearl earrings, delicate cashmere cardigans, and Chanel kitten heels looked subtler than Rosemary's spangled chiffon caftans, but it was a look that still screamed of money, the sort of money that was far snobbier than the Zaos'. The sisters might live in Manila, but they were so interchangeable with all the women she had grown up around, the ones who populated the Upper East Side. And it was so apropos of Charlotte to align with those sisters. In a few decades, she would be just like them. She would be exactly like them all.

At the same time, Lucie felt terribly annoyed with herself. Ever since she had been with George at Casa Malaparte, she hadn't been able to stop obsessing over her actions. She was mortified that she had allowed herself to sob in his arms like that. She had never cried so dramatically like that in front of anyone, even her mother, and she wondered what he must think of her now.

After her fit of tears on the rooftop had subsided, she had pulled away from him quickly, embarrassed, and they had walked back to the hotel in silence, George maintaining a respectful few paces behind her. He always seemed to be behind her. When did he first see her on the piazzetta? How was he right there when she fainted? Had he been sitting behind her the whole time? He probably saved her from cracking her skull on the ground. Just like he had saved that man's life when everyone else just stood there staring as they sucked on their Aperol spritzes. His quick heroism, tirelessly giving the man mouth-to-mouth, was what made the difference between him living and dying.

The palm grove opened onto a hilltop garden overgrown with wild barley and poppies. From this summit, the panoramic views of Positano and the sea beyond were breathtaking to behold, but Lucie found her eyes focusing on something else: the figure of a man standing on the precipice of a crumbling stone wall. Lucie cursed herself silently. Six villas, seven terraces, and thirty acres of grounds, but of course she would run into George. Lucie's first instinct was to turn around and head back down to the lower terrace. The last thing she wanted to do was face him again, risk speaking again.

She was about to flee when George glanced around, his face inscrutably in half shadow. Against the deep blue sky and the intense white of the midafternoon sun, his skin glowed like alabaster. Inexplicably, she found herself walking slowly through the swaying barley toward him. He jumped down from the wall, and all of a sudden she imagined it was still yesterday, and she was still lying on the cold volcanic cobblestone of the piazzetta, George leaning over her, his mouth pressed against hers, blowing into her urgently, breathing in that warm breath of life.

Before she knew what was happening, she felt her lips pressing against his.

"Lucie! Lucie, are you there?"

Charlotte emerged through the palm grove just as Lucie jolted away from George.

"Lucie! I've been trying to find you for ages! Mordecai wants us down at the dock immediately. He says we have to go *right now* if we want to take the yacht back to Capri!"

≈≈≈

XI

Hotel Bertolucci

CAPRI, ITALY

"When did you paint these?" Auden asked.

"Over the past two years. This one's the most recent, it's not really finished. I worked on it until I had to leave for Italy," Lucie replied, pointing to an image of overlapping swaths of deep purple.

They were sitting in the salon of the hotel. Auden leaned forward from his armchair and stared at the iPad in astonishment. When Lucie had first told him about her paintings while they were swimming in the cove at Da Luigi, he thought he'd be seeing the pleasant abstract paintings to be expected of a nineteen-year-old—the sort of faux Franz Kline pieces one could find at Restoration Hardware that would go perfectly with your new curved velvet sofa and your fiddle-leaf fig plant.

Auden had led plenty of creativity workshops in his time and witnessed the artwork that came out of them from his artistically frustrated clients; most of it ranged from amateurishly angsty to downright awful. He would never have called himself an art expert, but the work flashing before his eyes seemed precociously accomplished. In looking at the canvases soaked in restrained monochromatic *al nero di seppia* tones, brushstrokes infused with a Dionysian physicality, he sensed an unresolved Lacanian tension that juxtaposed the lyrical gestures of early Helen Frankenthaler, the bold symbology of post–Los Angeles Judy Chicago, and the visceral fury of pre-Madonna Basquiat.*

"Lucie, I'm absolutely floored by this work. I'm so impressed."

"Really?" Lucie looked up at him blankly.

"You've only been painting for a year?"

"No, I've been doing art since I was very young, and I took art classes all through high school."

"Your work is . . . dare I say . . . sui generis. It's original, sophisticated, and fresh, and more importantly, I feel that you are channeling your soul into these paintings. I can't wait to see the real canvases. Why, I'd love to buy one of your works and hang it at the new studio in East Hampton!"

Lucie's eyes widened. "You're kidding, right?"

"I never kid about stuff like this. You already know what I think— you should be in art school and not wasting time studying semiotics or whatever at Brown. You have a true gift, and I think you could really be at the forefront of a new generation of artists. Think about it."

"Thank you. I will." Lucie nodded politely, not wanting to challenge him. She didn't want to prolong this little vernissage any longer; she just wanted to get back to her room.

As Lucie strode across the lobby toward the elevator, Auden stared after her, even more intrigued than before. Seeing these paintings was like witnessing the work of a girl possessed. The girl who had just been seated before him with the perfect posture and her hair in a tight ponytail, so composed as she swiped through her artwork, did not for one second resemble someone who would be able to cre-

---

* This line is just one example of the kind of bullshit Auden learned to write in his Deconstructing Art of the Postwar Era course at Amherst. If he hadn't dropped out, he might have had a whole other career as a critic for *Artforum*.

ate those canvases. Where was the real Lucie Churchill hiding? Or better yet, why?

Auden could not have known that even before Lucie had boarded the Murphys' super yacht, cruised back to Capri while being held hostage to another design tour by Mordecai, crammed into a taxi with the Ortiz sisters, waded through the wall of tourists on the walk back to the hotel, and placidly sat there presenting her artwork and pretending to listen politely, her mind was somewhere else entirely, and it was playing this over and over on a constant loop:

Did he kiss me or did I kiss him? Fuck, I think I kissed him first. Why did I kiss him? Why oh why oh why? Did it really happen? How much did Charlotte see? Why did she show up at that very moment? Where is George now? What is he thinking right now? What must he think of me now? Did he kiss me or did I kiss him?

Returning to her room at long last, Lucie closed the door behind her, fastened the security latch, and transformed into the girl whom Auden Beebe had sensed in the paintings. As she lay on her bed with her phone, she became a girl possessed as she searched desperately for anything and everything she could find about George Zao online.

First up was his Instagram account, which was easy to locate because he had liked Isabel's first post from Capri. His account name was @zaoist, and Lucie immediately recognized the image that he used as his avatar—the rocks arranged in a spiral pattern was unmistakably a photo of *Spiral Jetty*, a sculpture created in the middle of a lake in Utah by the artist Robert Smithson. She had read all about it in her art history class last semester.

Curiously, there wasn't a single photo of himself or any other person on George's account. Did he not have a single friend? Actually, that wasn't true. He had 4,349 followers! That was 3,000+ more than she had. How in the world did he have so many followers when he was following only 332 people? He obviously wasn't very active on the app, since there were only eighty-eight posts. Scrolling through his feed, she saw that it consisted of perfectly composed architecture, food, and travel images. If all he did was post photos from other travel and design sites, why was he getting so many likes? Lucie started to scrutinize the images in his posts more closely:

A chapel in Ronchamp. *Okay, it's that chapel designed by that famous architect.**

Char siew bao in a bamboo steamer. *Yum.*

Dominique de Menil's house in Houston. *Is that an Yves Klein on the wall?*

The swimming pool at the Amangiri resort. *Take me there.*

A vintage Airstream trailer in Marfa. *Cool.*

Zion National Park at sunset. *Wow.*

Spam sushi. *Yuck.*

A copy of *Learning from Las Vegas* on an empty desk. *What's this book?* Lucie quickly googled it: "*Learning from Las Vegas* created a healthy controversy upon its appearance in 1972, calling for architects to be more receptive to the tastes and values of 'common' people and less immodest in their erections of 'heroic,' self-aggrandizing monuments." *George sure is an architecture geek.*

A wooden shack in the middle of the desert. *Whatever.*

A bacon cheeseburger between two doughnuts. *Yuck. Why are guys into gross foods?*

A humpback whale breaching in Sydney Harbor. *So cool.*

The Faraglioni rocks. *Been there.*

A blue lizard. *How cute. Is it that species that's found only on that rock?*

The stairs at Casa Malaparte. *Of course.*

The silhouette of a figure standing on the roof at Casa Malaparte.

Lucie gasped as she realized it was a photo of her. She zoomed in on the image. Yes, it was definitely her, taken yesterday right before she had her meltdown on the roof. For a moment, she got annoyed.

---

* This architectural masterpiece by Le Corbusier was formally named the Chapelle Notre-Dame du Haut.

Why did he take her picture like that without her consent? What a creep! Was he one of those guys who went around taking pictures of girls when he knew they weren't looking? As Lucie stared at the picture longer, she began to calm down. It *was* a beautiful shot. And with the sun against her, turning her figure into a black silhouette against the golden light, it wasn't as if she was recognizable. It could have been anyone. She made a quick screen grab of the photo, and it dawned on her that all the perfectly composed pictures on his Instagram weren't reposts from other accounts. Every single picture had been taken by him. George had a good eye, and she found herself grudgingly impressed.

Shifting from Instagram to Twitter, Lucie found twenty-three George Zaos, but after some detective work she realized that none of those accounts was his. It made sense that George wouldn't be on Twitter. Since he hardly spoke, why would he ever want to tweet? She went next to Facebook, where she located him quickly since they were both "friends" with Isabel and Dolfi. However, his account was set to the highest privacy settings, so it didn't give much away. She couldn't see how many friends he had; she couldn't see any of his posts. What she could see was his Facebook profile pic and his banner photo, which was a black-and-white image of a gorilla sitting on a beach. Standing nonchalantly off to the side was a man with a surfboard, looking out at the waves and completely ignoring the gorilla. Was it meant to be funny?

George's profile picture was another black-and-white shot of him grinning into the camera. It looked like one of those pictures purposefully chosen to be casual, as if he just put up whatever random photo was available. It wasn't perfectly composed and he didn't look too posed or too cute in it. In fact, he looked a few years younger— his face rounder and less chiseled—and he was wearing a nondescript black T-shirt and a cap. She tried to make out the logo on the cap but it was blocked by a pair of Ray-Ban Wayfarers tucked over the brim.

Frustrated that she wasn't finding much on his social media, Lucie tried googling his name. There were hundreds of other George Zaos, of course, but only one decent hit—a headline from the *Daily Telegraph* in Australia in 2009:

MOSMAN SURFER GEORGE ZAO EARNS
SPOT AT WORLD JUNIOR TITLES IN TAIWAN

To the right of the headline was a small picture of George at around fifteen in a wetsuit, standing against a backdrop with Surfing NSW and Quiksilver logos. His hair was down to his chin, and there appeared to be blond streaks in the front. Lucie clicked on the story excitedly but came up against a paywall that revealed only a short excerpt:

> . . . Mosman surfer George Zao has secured after taking a break from his HSC studies to compete at a surf event in Victoria. Whether he wins or not, George will be a contender for . . .

To read the rest of the article, she would have to pay twenty-eight dollars a year for full digital access. Lucie tossed her phone to the side with a groan. How had she wasted so much time? She had spent the past hour searching online and had learned nothing new about George Zao except that he was a good photographer, liked disgusting high-calorie foods and gorillas, and had been a champion surfer when he was younger. Where were the silly random tweets, photos of ex-girlfriends, or posts about whatever he happened to be passionate about?

There was a quick series of knocks on the door, which Lucie immediately recognized as Charlotte. "Lucie? Are you there? Can you help me?"

Lucie climbed out of the bed reluctantly, undid the security latch, and opened her door.

"Lucie! Why aren't you dressed yet? The concert starts in twenty minutes!" Charlotte exclaimed.

"I fell asleep," Lucie lied.

"Can you help me with the hooks? This dress is absolutely impossible," Charlotte said as she fussed with the fasteners along the back of her vintage silk brocade cocktail dress.

"You look very pretty in it, though," Lucie said, making fast work of the hooks.

"Thank you, dear. Mainbocher. It was our grandmother's, you know. There's a picture of her somewhere wearing the dress at El Morocco, sitting in a booth with William Holden."

"Who's William Holden?"

Charlotte shook her head with a sigh. "Millennials! The first thing I'm going to do when we get back to New York is sit you down and make you watch *The World of Suzie Wong*. Now quick, quick. Get ready. You haven't even done your hair!"

"I'm just going to put it in a French twist. It'll take me two seconds."

"Chop, chop! Get to it! We don't want to be late!"

"It's not going to start on time, Charlotte, and we're going to be so unfashionably early as always. We're in Italy, remember?" Lucie said.

"Well, Olivia and the Ortiz sisters said they would be in the lobby at six forty-five sharp, and I haven't been brought up to keep anyone waiting. Now, are you sure you don't want me to help you with your hair?"

"I'll be fine," Lucie said as she herded Charlotte toward the door. After her cousin had left the room, Lucie plopped down on the sofa with a sigh. A memory began to surface, and for a moment she was transported to a beautiful beachfront house in Hobe Sound.

She was six years old, squinting in pain as the sour-faced Irish maid pinched her right shoulder to steady her, while with her other hand she brushed Lucie's hair forcefully, stinging her scalp each time with the hard wire brush. Lucie sat there quietly, her eyes brimming with tears. She knew better than to make a sound.

"It's no use, ma'am. I've given it a hundred strokes and it's still frizzing up like a French poodle."

"Good God, you're right, it is just like a French poodle." Lucie's grandmother laughed dryly. "Lucie, did you not wear your swimming cap like I told you to before going into the pool? Did you get chlorine in your hair?"

"I wore it, Granny."

"Ugh, what impossible hair! I've never seen anything like it. Okay, change of plan, Oonagh. Why don't we use some coconut oil to slick it down and get rid of the frizz that way? It'll give it some gloss. Then we can give her braids on either side, and she can wear my Lacroix dragon jacket like it's a robe. If we can't make her look like the other girls, let's give her the china doll look. Lucie, remember how we used to play china doll? You're going to be my precious little Chinese empress at the party tonight!"

Lucie stirred herself from the memory, wondering how she was ever going to face George tonight. He probably thought she was a total freak. Why in the world did she kiss him? She didn't even like him. What came over her to make her lunge at him like that back at the villa? Over and over, she was doing nothing but making bad decisions and embarrassing herself. Ignoring him, crying on him, kissing him. What would her grandmother think if she saw her behaving like this? Maybe she had Stendhal syndrome, being surrounded by so much beauty at that spectacular villa overlooking Positano. She had heard of people arriving in Paris or Rome for the first time and bursting into tears uncontrollably, overpowered by the exquisiteness of everything. No, she blamed Charlotte and Olivia. It was all that kissing talk between them after lunch that stirred her up and confused her.

Just then, she heard a strange shuffling sound on the floor. She looked down and saw that a little envelope had been slid under the door. Jumping off the sofa, she rushed to the door and opened it, peering out to see who was there.

The hallway was empty.

Lucie tore open the envelope and found a folded sheet of beautiful Italian parchment paper. Unfolding it, she let out a quick gasp. Written on it in prep school cursive was one line:

In one kiss, you'll know all I haven't said.

—Pablo Neruda

XII

Certosa di San Giacomo

CAPRI, ITALY

As luck or Murphy's Law would have it, the one time that Lucie and Charlotte were a few minutes late in Italy was the one time the event started early. From Via Pizzolungo, the Certosa di San Giacomo looked smaller than it did when one actually passed through the narrow iron gates and entered the monastery. Here, the cousins discovered that they had to walk for what seemed like miles through a complex of ancient buildings, passing magnificent cloisters and expansive gardens that overlooked the sea. Arriving at the chapel at long last, they found the space packed and the concert about to commence.

"I'm sorry, I tried to save seats for you, but the Queen of Sheba wasn't having it," Olivia told Charlotte in a hushed voice, darting her eyes at the elderly Italian lady with the enormous shellacked beehive festooned with emeralds seated next to her.

Charlotte forced a smile. "That's perfectly fine. There are a few seats left at the back, I believe, otherwise we can just stand."

Seeing how cross Charlotte was, Lucie apologized again. "I'm sorry, I shouldn't have washed my hair. I don't know what I was thinking."

"What *were* you thinking, Lucie? You know your hair takes ages to dry, and I told you we were already going to be late. And no one can even tell that you washed your hair when it's put up."

"I just wanted to get the sea out of my hair," Lucie lied. She hadn't washed her hair at all; she had spent the past thirty minutes trying to calm herself after receiving the mysterious Neruda poem, trying on six different outfits in a panic and finally settling on the long black gown with a bandeau top—the one her mom called her "Rita Hayworth dress"—that made her feel more sophisticated and grown-up. She had worn it at the Frick Young Fellows Ball,* where Bill Cunningham had complimented the dress and taken her picture, and she felt that she needed this armor against George, even though she was sure he wouldn't notice—he dressed in such a nondescript way and would probably be oblivious to her sartorial efforts.

As they took their seats in the back row, Charlotte wondered out loud, "Where did all these people suddenly come from? I hardly recognize anyone."

"I think many of them arrived just in time for the wedding tomorrow," Lucie surmised, using the excuse to stand up and scan the room. She was trying to spot George but couldn't locate him anywhere in the crowd.

Conte Andrea De Vecchi, a tall, imposing man in his sixties, and his wife, Contessa Laudomia, a striking strawberry blonde dressed in an emerald-green gown that Lucie recognized from Valentino's spring collection, approached the altar in front of where the orchestra of musicians had been set up. Looking very distinguished in a dark velvet dinner jacket, the Conte tapped on the microphone with

---

* The annual Young Fellows Ball at the Frick Collection is one of the highlights of the New York social season, partly because it is one of the few charitable events that manages to draw a chic "under-forty" crowd, or rather people who claim to be under forty.

his finger and addressed the crowd in charmingly accented English: "Your Majesties, Highnesses, Holinesses, Excellencies, ladies, and gentlemen, my wife and I are so honored that you have all come tonight from different corners of the earth to celebrate the nuptials of our son Adolfo to *la bella* Isabel. We are here in one of the oldest buildings in Capri, and to me the most beautiful. It was built in 1371 on the orders of Count Giacomo Arcucci on land donated by my ancestor Queen Giovanna D'Angiò of Napoli as a sanctuary for the Carthusian monks. Tonight, as we take sanctuary together in this sacred place, we are very lucky to have with us the maestro Niccolo Miulli leading the Orchestra Sinfonica di Roma, who will be accompanying the incomparable Dame Kiri Te Kanawa!"

The crowd gasped in surprise as the celebrated diva took the stage in a billowing cape of orange shantung silk over an iridescent violet ball gown. The orchestra began to play, and as Kiri bellowed out the first notes of "Chi il bel sogno di Doretta" from Puccini's opera *La rondine,* Mordecai could be heard letting out a moan of ecstasy so loud it sounded slightly obscene.

Even from the back row, Lucie was transfixed by Kiri's incredible voice. She couldn't believe that anyone could hit those high notes with such clarity, and as she sat there in the chapel, lulled by the ethereal beauty of Kiri's next aria, "Bailero," from *Chants d'Auvergne,* she found herself staring up at the vaulted arches of the chapel. The ceilings and walls had once been completely covered by a fresco, much like the Sistine Chapel, but now only a few colorful fragments from the original painting remained on the white plaster ceiling, punctuating the starkness in a random way that reminded her of jigsaw puzzle pieces.

Why did her life suddenly seem like a jigsaw puzzle that had been overturned? She had always gone through the world with such certainty, such methodical precision, like a perfectly sung aria, and now in just a few days it seemed like everything had become so confusing. Messy. And more than anything she hated messy. Was George actually the one who slipped the poem under her door? It *had* to be him, right? After all, he was the only person who had mentioned Neruda to her. What exactly was he trying to say with that line?

Lucie was a bundle of conflicting emotions. On one hand she was willing to admit that she found herself intrigued by George, but on the other hand she was repelled by her own interest. He was the absolute antithesis of the type of guy she liked. She sat there, fixating on all the things she couldn't stand about him. He was a mama's boy. A pretty boy. A surfer/jock. A tank-top-and-Birkenstock-wearing slob. A self-righteous eco-warrior. A brooding weirdo who took himself much too seriously.

Kiri capped off the concert with her most enduring song, "O mio babbino caro," and the audience murmured in approval. As the swoon-inducing aria filled the chapel, Lucie found her eyes wandering to the fresco under the dome of the chapel, where some artist centuries ago had painted the typical scene of God and Jesus with saints, angels, and cherubs, their limbs all tangled up together in the clouds. At the apex of the fresco, Jesus floated above the clouds partially swathed in teal-colored robes that had been pulled down to his waist, exposing his muscular torso. Lucie stared at this decidedly hunky Jesus, counting the muscles in his six-pack, following the line of shading that accentuated his pecs, thinking, *What beautiful nipples. God, what is wrong with me? I'm going to hell for thinking of Jesus's nipples in a monastery!*

As Kiri sang the last notes of the aria, her voice effortlessly trailing off into a delicate whisper, Mordecai was the first to jump out of his seat. *"Brava! Bravissima!"* he shouted, clapping wildly as the rest of the audience rose to give the legendary soprano a rapturous standing ovation. After a few minutes, as the guests began to disperse outside for cocktails, Lucie and Charlotte headed toward Olivia, who was standing in the middle of the chapel chatting with Dolfi's parents.

Through the crowd, Lucie caught sight of George at last. He was standing near the altar speaking to the conductor, and as he stretched his arms out, gesturing enthusiastically, Lucie was surprised at what a commanding presence he cut tonight. In his cream linen suit, crisp white band-collar shirt, and suede oxfords, there was a distinct air of sophistication about him. *Thank God I wore the Tom Ford,* she thought.

As Lucie got closer to George, she racked her brain thinking of what she might say. Was there some subtle reference she could make about the poem? Should she compliment him on his outfit, maybe say something like, "I didn't realize you cleaned up so well." Ugh, no, that was terrible. Maybe she ought to quickly google a poem of Neruda's and recite a line to him as a greeting. It would be very enigmatic. Yes, that's what she would do. As Charlotte and Olivia began oohing and ahhing over each other's outfits, Lucie got out her phone and quickly typed: Pablo Neruda poem.

The first thing that popped up was this:

I want to eat the sunbeam flaring in your lovely body,

Hell no, Lucie thought. As she scrolled through the next poem, she felt a gentle tap on her shoulder. *Oh God, it's him.* She braced herself and turned around, taken aback to see Auden smiling at her.

"So what do you think of Diefenbach's paintings?"

"Um, who?" Lucie put her phone away quickly.

"Karl Diefenbach. The paintings in the refectory?"

"Oh, I haven't seen them. We got here a bit late."

"Here, come with me," Auden said, taking her by the arm and whisking her down the corridor before she could protest. "You really must see them."

They entered the refectory—a large, serene space where the austere white walls were hung with massive oil paintings by Diefenbach. The paintings were uniformly dark and moody, depicting the island from different vantage points. There were dramatic cliff-top landscapes, stormy seascapes, and even nighttime views of a grotto seemingly lit by candlelight. Lucie studied the canvases intently, quietly moved.

"What do you think?" Auden asked.

"I love them."

"I knew you would," Auden said with a little laugh.

"This isn't what I was expecting. What are they even doing hanging in a monastery?"

"I believe Diefenbach spent his final years living on the island."

"They're like nothing I've ever seen. So haunting . . . surreal almost," Lucie said as she stared at a particularly dramatic painting of the Faraglioni glimmering in the moonlight. She remembered being at Da Luigi and standing in the same spot that Diefenbach had, gazing out at the mystical rocks. Turning to Auden, she said, "I wonder why he chose to paint everything so dark, when to me Capri is all about the light."

"I would venture to ask the same thing about your paintings. Diefenbach was a symbolist. I feel like painting was for him a way to explore the inner landscape, rather than the outer one, don't you think?"

Lucie smiled, revealing nothing.

Suddenly, the sound of a familiar piano composition could be heard echoing through the chamber.

"The Goldberg Variations, my favorite!" Lucie exclaimed. They wandered back into the chapel and found it empty except for Isabel, Dolfi, and a few others clustered toward the front of the altar where the grand piano was. Isabel turned to beckon Lucie to join them, and that's when she saw George seated at the piano. Lucie stepped closer to the piano and watched in astonishment. George's fingers were gliding over the piano keys with such apparent effortlessness, such grace and fluidity, it didn't even look like he was actually playing. She noticed for the first time George's long, elegantly tapered fingers and saw that his eyes were closed as he swayed slowly back and forth, completely lost in the music that he was creating.

She knew then exactly what she wanted to say to George. She was going to say, "I wonder if Neruda could play Bach as well as you can." Now she just needed to get one second alone with him. She would seize the moment after he finished playing, and maybe she could use the excuse of showing him the Diefenbachs in the refectory. But just as he was finishing the piece, Gillian, the hyperefficient wedding coordinator, marched into the chapel with a panicked look and whispered something urgently into Isabel's ear.

"Oh, shit! Sorry," Isabel said to Gillian before turning to the rest of the group. "We need to get to the banquet. Apparently Dolfi's grandmother started making a toast, not realizing that we weren't even there!"

The group dashed quickly toward the central cloister where the banquet was being held, and when Lucie first caught sight of the space, she gasped in delight. The vast courtyard was filled with round tables covered in silver brocade and groaning with immense antique silver candelabras that looked like they had come straight from the Vatican. Over each table were suspended silver orbs of varying sizes, each containing candles floating on water. The water and flickering candles within the translucent silver cast a rippling, gossamer light over the entire space, making the already enchanting cloister look even more luminous and otherworldly.

Lucie quickly got to her assigned table, crossing her fingers that George would be seated there too. Instead, she found herself between an Italian youth with long blond hair who didn't speak a word of English and, if the engraved place card next to her chair was correct, BARON MORDECAI VON EPHRUSSÍ. Her heart sank, and to make things worse, from where she was sitting she had the perfect view of George two tables away taking his seat between Sophie, Isabel's beautiful Australian friend, and some equally stunning Asian woman named Astrid. One of the wedding's black-clad videographers was not so discreetly documenting the scene of the photogenic trio greeting one another as if they were longtime friends meeting up at the front row of New York Fashion Week.

Mordecai, who had been chatting with some English duchess at the next table, returned to his seat rather reluctantly and raised an eyebrow at Lucie. "Where have you been, young lady? Up to some mischief, I hope?"

"Not quite. We were at an impromptu piano concert given by George Zao."

"Really? And what was our strapping young Narcissus playing?"

"The aria from the Goldberg Variations."

"How predictable!" Mordecai grumbled.

"He played it quite beautifully, actually."

"I'm sure he did. But just once I wish someone would bust out Schoenberg or John Cage when they sit down at a piano. There's nothing more trite than playing the Goldberg Variations, except perhaps 'Für Elise.' "

Not wishing to challenge him, Lucie tried to change the topic. As the waiters began ladling the steaming *zuppa di pesce* into her bowl, she held up her spoon. "I think this is the heaviest spoon I've ever come across."

"Ah yes, the famous De Vecchi silver. Forged in Firenze in the seventeenth century, I believe. They had it flown in from the family vaults yesterday."

Admiring the immense silver candelabra at the center of the table, Lucie said, "It's all so grand, I'm not sure how the wedding banquet tomorrow is going to top this!"

"Well, since the Chius are picking up the bill for the entire wedding week, the De Vecchis obviously had to do something impressive for tonight. They couldn't let those gauche Asians steal their thunder, could they?"

Lucie said nothing but thought that Isabel was anything but gauche.

Mordecai mistook Lucie's silence for anger and began backpedaling furiously. "I do hope you weren't offended by what I just said. I didn't mean anything by it. I love the Asians! Some of my dearest friends are Asians, like the Chius and the Sultanah of Penang."

"No worries, I wasn't offended at all." Lucie smiled, amused that he was flustered.

"I'm so relieved. I just think it's fascinating to witness all this—a Chinese girl of immense fortune marrying into one of the oldest families in Europe, splashing her money around on one of the most decadent weddings the world has ever seen. It's like Henry James all over again, *avec le Chinois.* I can see all the old Roman and Neapolitan families sneering in the corners. But there's a new world order in place, and Old Europa better get used to it. I forget you're partly Chinese, you see. I'm actually quite color blind—I don't *ever* think of people in terms of their skin tone. I think of you as a New Yorker."

Lucie nodded diffidently. Just when she thought Mordecai could do no worse, he piped up again. "Tell me, dear, what do you consider yourself?"

"I'm not sure what you mean."

"When you look in the mirror, do you feel more Asian or more Caucasian?"

"Well, I'm equal parts both . . ."

"But do you lean toward a particular side? It's rather marvelous that you could pass for either."

Lucie gritted her teeth, finally angry. "You know, I've never tried to pass for anything. I feel like I'm just me."

"Very well put, young lady. Very well put. Now, tell me, are you out?"

"I'm assuming you're referring to the cotillion and not the closet?"

"Har har! Yes, indeed."

"I decided not to take part in all that debutante stuff, although my grandmother wanted me to."

"This would be your Churchill grandmother? Tell me, how exactly are you all related to the English Churchills?"

Lucie reached for the crystal goblet in front of her. She wasn't much of a drinker, but if she had to endure this inquisition for another three courses, she might as well get completely shitfaced. She gulped down the entire glass of wine, and the rest of the evening soon blurred at the edges. She was feeling super chill for a while, and then events started happening as though everything was in fast-forward, going so fast until there was nothing but flashes of moments . . .

. . . tasting an incredibly tender rack of lamb that, in the words of Baron von Ephrussí, went "improbably well with the Musigny."[*]

. . . trying to use Google Translate to converse with the golden-haired Italian youth seated to her left. His name was Sandro, and he was Dolfi's seventeen-year-old cousin from Como. He liked drum and bass. And Reese Witherspoon.

. . . watching a dish of delicious-looking zabaglione with Venetian white peaches being placed in front of her, but not recalling if she actually ate it.

. . . feeling a hand on her shoulder and Isabel saying to her, "Let's ditch this joint!"

. . . taking a tender to an immense, futuristic yacht moored just off Marina Piccola, where Isabel's girlfriends had arranged the "Couture Costume Bachelorette Party."

. . . putting on a gold Jean Paul Gaultier bustier top, Azzedine Alaïa cheetah-print leggings, and electric-blue eye shadow.

. . . gobbling down four red velvet cupcakes in a row before realizing that they were infused with cannabis.

. . . going to the karaoke lounge and the girls all wanting to sing 1980s hits.

. . . belting out Whitney Houston's "I Wanna Dance with Somebody" with Isabel and Daniella.

. . . staring at the Italian paratroopers storming the yacht by helicopter as the girls screamed and screamed.

. . . realizing that the absurdly over-tanned paratrooper in the shaggy wig was Dolfi when he stripped off all his clothes and did a cannonball off the top deck of the yacht.

---

[*] A 1988 Domaine Comte Georges de Vogüé Musigny Cuvée Vieilles Vignes, to be exact, put away in the year of Dolfi's birth precisely for this occasion.

. . . seeing another guy colliding midair with one of the drones as he tried to do a somersault into the sea.

. . . getting blindfolded and being forced to play Pin the Tail on the Donkey with someone dressed in a furry donkey costume.

. . . hearing Isabel shouting, "No, guys, leave her alone! Don't touch my little angel! Lucie has immunity tonight!"

At some point, she remembered stumbling belowdecks vomiting red velvet into the pristine white toilet with a sleek automatic lid that kept trying to decapitate her, and curling up in a big circular bed with an immense white fur throw thinking how warm and cuddly it was but how sad that it had to be made of so many cute dead animals, and all of a sudden she was back in the chapel again, where a choir of Italian boys dressed in white robes stood in front of her singing Crowded House's "Don't Dream It's Over" a cappella, and as she sat there listening to their angelic voices, she looked up at the fresco on the ceiling again, staring skyward at Jesus, and suddenly his bare pink torso transformed into the golden-brown perfection of George's chest, and there she was too, floating above the clouds next to George in his blindingly white Speedo, as he turned to her, saying, "You have a freedom within, Lucie, you have a freedom without."

Lucie found herself saying, "I'm ready!"

Stretching out his arms Christ-like, George grabbed her hand, and together they plunged headlong out of the heavens and into the deep, unknown depths of the sea.

Hey now, hey now, don't dream it's over.

XIII

Villa Lysis

CAPRI, ITALY

"I'm surprised you're even alive," Charlotte remarked when Lucie appeared at the hotel's poolside café just as she and Olivia were finishing lunch. "How hungover are you?"

"Actually, I feel fine," Lucie said, downplaying it by a mile.

Olivia peered at Lucie's bloodshot eyes and chuckled.

"This is completely unlike you, Lucie! Disappearing like that without telling us and partying all night on a yacht? I had to find out where you were from Mordecai, of all people, and you know what loose lips that man has," Charlotte chided as she took the last bite of her *parmigiana di melanzane*.

"Charlotte, there's nothing scandalous for him to say. It was Issie's bachelorette party. It was my duty to attend."

"Well, clearly her duty did not involve thinking of your well-being. You are so much younger than her other friends, and I wasn't born yesterday—I'm sure you all did not spend the night on board a super yacht playing Cards Against Humanity," Charlotte quipped.

Olivia leaned in toward Lucie. "I heard a rumor that there were mountains of pure Colombian cocaine and Isabel's friends hired male strippers dressed as ninjas?"

"*Ninjas?* There were no drugs, just fashion, and the 'male strippers' turned out to be Dolfi and his crew," Lucie said, trying to sound blasé but quietly alarmed that she couldn't recall anything about the evening past a certain point. Her roommate at Brown would come back to the room on weekends after getting completely trashed, claiming to not remember a thing, but Lucie never believed it was possible. Now she believed.

"What do you mean 'fashion'?" Charlotte probed suspiciously.

"There were all these fun couture designer costumes waiting for us on the yacht, and we each picked an outfit. I wore a vintage bustier that had been designed for Madonna's 'Blond Ambition' tour, and we all sang karaoke and ate cupcakes," Lucie explained.

Charlotte gave her a dubious look. "Thankfully you appear to have all your limbs, or I would not know what to say to your mother! Now, Olivia and I are off to the hair salon. You clearly forgot about *your* one p.m. appointment."

"Oh, shoot!" Lucie sighed, rolling her eyes.

"Well, get some food into your system and take a hot bath. You don't have all day, you know. We have to leave for the wedding by four o'clock at the latest, and it's already almost one thirty. God knows how long our appointments will take with these Italian stylists! If you are dressed and ready by the time we get back, I might just help you with your updo," Charlotte said in a gentler tone as she got up from the table.

Olivia leaned over and patted Lucie on the shoulder. "Tomato juice with a raw egg. It will fix you right up. I'll order you one on our way out."

Lucie slumped into her chair and put her sunglasses on, feeling the first twinges of a headache. Several squealing German kids sprinted through the garden and did cannonballs into the pool, the sound of their splashes causing her to have a flashback to the night before. She was in the pool on the yacht . . . the smaller one on the top deck . . . and were someone's toes getting sucked? It wasn't hers . . . thank God not hers. And then suddenly she recalled seeing George last night. He was definitely on the yacht. Was he the one in the donkey costume? Yes, it *was* him. The hair on the nape of his neck was a little wet from being in that furry mask for so long, and she knew that because her fingers were caressing his head as they were dancing, right before she had to rush into the bathroom to throw up. Yes, that's what happened. How mortifying. Did he see her throw up? Did she say something idiotic to him that she might regret for the rest of her life?

It was a question she was still pondering three hours later when she arrived at the gates of Villa Lysis for the event that everyone had been anticipating and speculating endlessly about—the wedding ceremony! From the lovely beach club lunch and divine dinner held in an ancient grotto to the exclusive Villa Lachowski excursion and the grand banquet in a fourteenth-century monastery, each event had been more spectacular than the last. How on earth was Isabel going to top all that?

Isabel did not disappoint.

Villa Lysis was arguably the most advantageously situated house in all of Capri. Perched on the easternmost edge of the island, high up on the mountain, the secluded villa was an homage to Louis Seize and classical Greek architecture, boasting Ionic columns decorated with filaments of gold mosaic tiles and marble steps spanning the entire front facade and leading down to a circular garden of towering trees that framed a commanding view of the sea, the dramatic cliffs, and Marina Grande in the distance.

Today, it looked as though God had sprinkled millions of seeds from the heavens onto the estate, as the villa appeared to be in full bloom. Flowers burst from the ground to the rooftop, from every corner and crevice; boughs of white and pink delphiniums draped over the grand portico, while camellias and stephanotis wound up each column and millions of rose petals blanketed the terrace in front of the house, creating an ombré pattern so that the petals gradually intensified from white to blush to the most intense magenta in the middle, where they formed the shape of a blooming lotus flower. On this decadent carpet of flowers were hundreds of gold Hepplewhite chairs meticulously arranged into a spiral pattern, ending in the very center at the lotus.

"It's like a giant mandala made out of rose petals! Can you imagine how many flowers it must have taken to cover this whole garden? Are there any roses left on the planet anymore, or did they all sacrifice themselves for this?" Olivia said, shaking her head in disbelief.

"It's just *beyond*! The flowers alone must have cost Isabel's family several million," Charlotte surmised.

"The Chius own the biggest plastics manufacturer in Taiwan—I wouldn't worry too much about it," Olivia quipped.

"I'm kicking myself for not thinking to cover this wedding for *Amuse Bouche*. I wonder who has the scoop. Is someone from *Vogue* or *Harper's Bazaar* here? Or *Town & Country* or maybe even *Elle Decor*?" Charlotte wondered, thinking like a competitive magazine editor as she observed the army of black-clad videographers piloting the UFO-like drones that circled over the villa, capturing every moment of the event from different vantage points.

"Isabel is much too private to have any media covering her big day. Didn't you see in the orientation letter that they requested no one post any pictures on social media?" Lucie reminded her cousin.

Rosemary Zao suddenly appeared next to them in a gold lamé ball gown with immense ruffled sleeves and said, "Lucie, let's take a selfie and I'll put it on WeChat!"

"Um . . . Mrs. Zao, I'd be happy to take a picture with you, but I don't think we're supposed to post anything," Lucie replied.

"Nonsense! I just won't tag our location, and no one will know we're at Isabel's wedding. You look so pretty in that dress. Lanvin, right?" Rosemary asked, admiring Lucie's deep scarlet gown, which had a tea-length skirt of translucent pleated panels that created the most beautiful rippling effect as she moved.

"Um, no, it's Morgane Le Fay."

"Huuuuh? I've never heard of that designer. Is he French?"

"No, *she's* Argentinean but based in New York—her real name is Liliana Casabal, and she's got a great boutique in SoHo."

"You know all the coolest designers. If I had a daughter, I'd want her to dress just like you!" Rosemary praised.

Charlotte, who looked rather regal in her buttercup point d'esprit lace Oscar de la Renta gown and a four-strand pearl choker borrowed from her mother, gave Rosemary a mischievous look. "And who designed *your* dress? Alexis Carrington?"

Rosemary let out a loud gasp and slapped Charlotte on the arm excitedly. "*Hiyah,* how did you know? This is vintage Nolan Miller! I bought it at a charity auction and they said that Joan Collins actually wore the dress on *Dynasty*! I think it was the episode when Blake tried to choke her to death."*

"The famous choking gown! That is just too fabulous for words. You win the grand prize for most original outfit, Mrs. Zao!" Olivia remarked.

"No, no, you should win the prize too," Rosemary said rather unconvincingly as she tried to decipher Olivia's asymmetrical, deconstructed black Comme des Garçons dress that looked like it had been savaged by pinking shears. After Rosemary had made all of them pose for what seemed like ten dozen pictures, Lucie asked as casually as possible, "Where's George?"

"Oh, didn't you know? He's one of the groomsmen. Dolfi asked him to step in at the last minute because his friend Colby, the one from Dallas, had to go to the hospital when he broke his cock."

---

* Actually, Alexis wears a white spangled cocktail dress in the famous "Blake chokes Alexis" season finale, not the gold ruffled gown worn by Rosemary. Both dresses are fabulous, but nowhere near as fabulous as the pink taffeta ball gown Alexis wears to her daughter Amanda's wedding to the Prince of Moldavia, where (spoiler alert!) rebels storm into the cathedral in a coup attempt, spraying bullets from uzis that manage to kill everyone at the wedding except the cast of *Dynasty*.

"His whaaat?" Charlotte's eyes widened, not sure she had heard right.

"You know, his cock. His pee-pee, his birdie. Yes, apparently Colby took too much Viagra at the party on the boat last night and his cock got so swollen it got trapped in a donkey costume with some girl? I don't really know the whole story, but apparently they had to fly him to the hospital in Naples to drain the blood from his cock."[*]

Lucie held her hand to her mouth, looking like she was shocked but actually trying to stop herself from having a laughing fit. She knew if she looked at Charlotte she would totally lose it.

"I do hope the boy doesn't have a hard time recovering," Olivia said with an absolute straight face.

"Who's recovering? Is Isabel okay?" Mercedes Ortiz asked, suddenly appearing alongside the foursome with her sister.

"Isabel's fine," Rosemary assured her. "It's this schoolmate of Dolfi's from Texas who had to get his big co—"

"My goodness, you ladies look incredible!" Charlotte loudly cut her off. For as long as she lived she did not ever again want to hear Rosemary utter the word that, if it had to be used, should be used only in reference to roosters.

"Yes, what terribly chic ball gowns!" Olivia echoed, admiring the sisters dressed in complementing shades of lilac silk festooned with intricate beading and ostrich feathers.

"Let me guess . . . Elie Saab?" Rosemary asked.

"Valentino!" Mercedes and Paloma said in unison, appearing offended that Rosemary would even dare mention any other couturier.

Olivia turned to Lucie covertly. "Are you ever going to tell me what *really* happened on that yacht?"

Before Lucie could formulate a response, she was quite literally saved by the bell. A line of groomsmen in dove-gray linen suits, led

---

[*] Unfortunately this potential side effect does not appear anywhere on the warning label for Viagra.

by George, came scattering out of the villa ringing antique Tibetan bells, indicating to the guests that it was time to take their seats. As Lucie observed George guiding several elderly guests, she found herself desperately trying to recall one thing: *If he wasn't the one in the donkey suit last night, was he even at the party? Or did I dream that too?*

After everyone was seated around the spiral, a woman in a silvery halter-neck gown appeared at the edge of the balcony overlooking the garden. She held up a violin and began playing the first few notes of a melody as Dolfi appeared at the side of the garden with his parents. Suddenly the sounds of a full orchestra filled the air, accompanying the violinist in Ennio Morricone's love theme from *Cinema Paradiso,* as the three of them began a slow, regal march toward the assembled guests, the Contessa already tearing up as she walked alongside her son, who was dashingly outfitted in a bespoke tuxedo from Battistoni. They arrived at the lotus bloom in the middle of the spiral, where Auden Beebe, striking in a midnight-blue silk jacquard sherwani, was waiting to greet them.

There was a moment of silence as the Conte and Contessa took their seats, and then the first chords of a piano could be heard coming from the terrace just below where they were all seated. A few of the guests murmured in excitement, "That's Lang Lang on the piano!" Next, a man dressed in a linen tunic shirt and matching trousers wandered out of the glade of high trees near the piano, barefoot and holding an accordion, and together he and Lang Lang launched into the most beautiful duet of Luis Bacalov's theme from *Il Postino.* Half a dozen bridesmaids standing at the top of the steps began their procession as Isabel emerged through the majestic front door on the arm of her father, and together they descended the steps and glided gracefully down the spiral aisle.

"How ingenious, Dedes! She did this so that she would pass by every single guest, and everyone can admire her dress!" Paloma Ortiz whispered to her sister.

"But what *is* she wearing? It looks like a potato sack!" Mercedes grumbled.

From where she was sitting, Lucie could not have disagreed more. Isabel looked absolutely exquisite in a white duchesse satin strapless gown with delicate pleats just below the bodice, mirrored by pleats at the back that flared dramatically into a long, billowing train. She recognized it immediately from the black-and-white magazine photo Isabel had pinned to her dressing mirror back in her childhood days at the Park Avenue apartment—it was a picture of Audrey Hepburn in the exact same dress by Givenchy, taken in 1955. She wondered if the dress was vintage or who might have re-created the gown for Isabel.

Lucie felt that Isabel had made a brilliant choice by staying so simple—she wore her hair pulled up into a high chignon, minimal makeup that showed off her natural glow from a week in the sun, and not a drop of jewelry aside from the heirloom Asscher-cut emerald engagement ring that had been Dolfi's grandmother's, and she clutched a simple bouquet of white peonies. Amid the grandeur of the villa, the profusion of colorful flowers, and all the guests dressed in their fanciest outfits, the bride stood out in all her unencumbered elegance.

Isabel's preference for simplicity was also reflected in the ceremony. After Auden delivered a brief homily about twin flames being the halves of one soul, he told a moving story of how he had witnessed the flame that was Dolfi and Isabel's growing over the last few years, "not at glamorous red-carpet events or A-list parties, but in the quiet, everyday moments of partner yoga, juice fasts, and plant medicine circles."

The couple then exchanged vows and rings, and a gospel choir emerged onto the steps of the villa and began to sing Peter Gabriel's "In Your Eyes," accompanied by a band of drummers. Isabel and Dolfi held hands and gazed into each other's eyes throughout the entire song as tears streamed silently down their faces, which in turn made most of the crowd well up. Lucie thought it was the most romantic thing she had ever witnessed.

As the singing ended, the drummers continued to play, and Auden loudly proclaimed, "I now pronounce you man and wife!" Everyone cheered as the newlyweds proceeded to dance down the aisle to the beat of the drums, joined by the rest of the bridal party. The Sultanah of Penang jumped out of her seat and joined the impromptu conga line, along with members of Dolfi's family. The bride and groom danced all the way to an antique horsedrawn carriage waiting at the foot of the steps. Before getting in, Dolfi turned around, grinned roguishly at the crowd, and said, "Okay, wedding's over. Let's paaaaaarty!"

XIV

Villa Jovis

CAPRI, ITALY

"I must admit that I found it all quite moving, didn't you?" Charlotte said to Lucie as they sat in the golf cart that was whizzing them up the mountain after the ceremony.

"It was too beautiful for words. The flowers, the music, the vows, everything!" Lucie said with a half sigh.

"Now, don't go fantasizing that you'll have a wedding that's anything like this—your mother would have a heart attack!"

"Don't worry, this isn't what I want at all. I'd much rather have a simple ceremony on the dock at Dorset,* maybe arriving by water on an old Chris-Craft driven by Freddie."

"That sounds lovely. I've always thought that Dorset would be the perfect place for—*Holy Mother of Joanna Gaines, what have we here?!*" Charlotte gasped.

Appearing before them was a towering arch of vines and flowers made entirely of Venetian blown glass framing the approach to Villa

---

* The private yacht club in the Hamptons that Lucie's family belongs to.

Jovis, the great palace that Caesar Augustus had built himself on one of the highest points of Capri.

"Just when I thought things couldn't get any crazier. This arch must be at least twenty feet tall!" Charlotte whispered to Lucie in awe as they got out of the golf cart. Standing under the fantastical arch was the bridal party, and Charlotte marveled for the hundredth time how Isabel had planned every moment so brilliantly. The sun was just beginning to set over the island, bathing the ruins in a shimmering golden light, but the bridal party went one step further—everyone under the arch, especially the bride, was cast in an iridescent glow from the reflected crystalline colors of the Venetian glass. The cousins noticed immediately that Issie had added a striking blue Paraíba tourmaline-and-diamond necklace by Doris Hangartner to her wedding ensemble.

"Issie, you look so exquisite! And that was the most beautiful ceremony ever!" Lucie exclaimed as she gave both the bride and groom tight hugs.

"Wasn't it? I can't believe it's really happened!" Isabel beamed with joy.

Charlotte leaned in to give Isabel a peck on the cheek. "Congratulations, both of you! Now, Isabel, you *must* tell me who designed your dress! Lucie swears it's vintage Givenchy."

"She's partially right. The design is from his haute couture line in 1955, but I managed to lure Monsieur de Givenchy himself out of retirement just this once to re-create it for me."

"Stop it!" The cousins squealed in unison.

"Yep, I had to go to Le Jonchet* for all the fittings."

Lucie and Charlotte shook their heads in awe before moving down the receiving line to congratulate the newlyweds' families. Entering the grounds of the villa afterward, they were handed delicate flutes

---

* After selling his business to Louis Vuitton Moët Hennessy in 1988 and retiring in 1995, Hubert de Givenchy spent most of his time at Le Jonchet, his beautiful Renaissance castle from the early seventeenth century. #goals

of prosecco laced with elderflower syrup as they strolled around the palace ruins. Almost all the original decorations—including once magnificent frescos that must surely have outshone the best of Pompeii—had been lost to time and looters, but the structures still retained the impression of the majestic complex that had once stood here.

As they walked toward the cliff to look out at the view, they came upon Olivia and Rosemary staring intently into a monitor held up by one of the younger drone operators.

"What are you all staring at with such fascination?" Charlotte asked, ever the busybody, as she peered into the high-definition screen.

"Oh, this man is showing us a rather curious spot that he's making the drone fly over," Olivia said.

"We are standing right above Salto di Tiberio—Tiberius's Leap. This is where the emperor would make all the subjects and servants that he didn't like jump to their deaths," the young man explained as he piloted his drone to fly sharply off the edge of the cliff toward the rocks hundreds of meters below.

"Well, that's a view to die for!" Olivia quipped.

"There are a few servants of mine I wouldn't mind doing that to," Rosemary said.

Charlotte glared at her in horror.

"Hee hee hee—joking! I *love* all my servants." Rosemary giggled. "Except maybe Princess. Princess has gotten rather lazy, which I guess goes along with her name."

"Come, Lucie, we forgot to deliver our congratulations to the Count and Countess," Charlotte said, pulling at Lucie's arm.

As they pretended to walk in the direction of the receiving line, Charlotte fumed. "Ugh, that woman! I couldn't take one more second of her. I know there are vast cultural differences between us, but I'm sorry, I find everything about her to be offensive. Her jokes, her snobbery, her inability to accessorize with any semblance of restraint."

"I get it, Charlotte," Lucie said quietly, feeling quite exasperated with Rosemary herself.

"With any luck, we'll never have to cross paths with her again after this weekend," Charlotte said as they passed the table where little cards embossed with each guest's name had been carefully laid out in circles in preparation for the wedding banquet. "Ah, the seating chart! Let's see where they've put me. If that woman is seated at my table, I will simply change the cards. Oh thank God, she's nowhere near me."

Scanning the cards, Lucie saw that she was assigned to table 3. Almost reflexively, she found herself searching for George's card and saw that he was at table 8. Damn, was this going to be yet another night where they wouldn't have the chance to talk at all? Did she dare to quickly swap cards when Charlotte wasn't looking so that she would be at table 8 too?

Bending down to peer more closely at the cards, Charlotte said, "You know, I do love looking at seating charts. They're always a fascinating indicator of who's considered important at any event. See, you're at table three, which is a prime spot as one of the tables orbiting the bridal couple. I'm at table nineteen, which is most certainly Siberia. Last night I was seated in between the second wife of the De Vecchis' tax lawyer and Isabel's dog psychic from Ojai."

"I would have preferred them any day over Mordecai von Ephrussí," Lucie replied, annoyed that Charlotte was so attentive to where she was sitting. How could she possibly change her table now? They wandered through the villa's inner chambers for a while, and when Charlotte became engrossed in a discussion with Auden on the benefits of intermittent fasting, Lucie saw her chance to slip away. She rushed back to the seating chart table, thinking that the best thing to do was swap out George's seat so that he would be at her table.

Arriving there, she discovered to her dismay other guests swarming around the table in search of their own seating cards. The cocktail hour was about to end, and guests were making their way toward the fleet of golf carts to head back down to Villa Lysis for the banquet. By the time the crowd had dispersed, Lucie saw that she was too late. George's seating card was missing, so he must have already come by and taken it.

Returning to Villa Lysis, the wedding guests were greeted by a battalion of footmen holding lit torches, dressed in costumes straight out of nineteenth-century Sicily. Entering the villa, the guests gasped in delight to discover interiors that had been utterly transformed since the wedding ceremony an hour ago. "I was inspired by Visconti's *Il Gattopardo*," Isabel told everyone after she made her grand entrance, sweeping down the vine-entwined staircase in a Valentino couture ball gown that looked as if it was constructed entirely of silk rosettes and billowing white ruffles, reminiscent of the gown Claudia Cardinale wore in the legendary film.

It was the understatement of the year. Studio Peregalli, the famed Milanese design atelier, had been commissioned to re-create the set of the film inside the villa, and when the guests entered the banquet room, they were treated to a magnificent space draped from floor to ceiling in yellow moire silk, towering antique tulipieres bursting with apricot peonies, and tables set with heirloom china from the royal house of Bourbon-Two Sicilies. The entire space seemed to sparkle, lit only by thousands of tapered candles hung from the ceiling in crystal lanterns.

Lucie took her seat at table 3, feeling giddy as she admired the voluptuous surroundings and watched the waiters crisscrossing the room in nineteenth-century livery and powdered wigs. The decadence of it all was almost too much to bear, and she felt as if she had suddenly been transported into the pages of her favorite childhood fairy tale, "The Twelve Dancing Princesses."

"Hey there," said a voice to her right. Lucie turned and saw George taking the seat beside her.

She glanced at the place card in the silver holder, and sure enough, it read MR. GEORGE ZAO.

"Wait a minute! Did you change seats?" Lucie asked in surprise.

"Er . . . would you like me to?" George asked.

"No, no, I meant . . . I just thought someone else was sitting next to me."

"Sorry to disappoint."

"That's not what I meant," Lucie said, getting flustered.

"I know," George said, suddenly flashing a disarming smile.

"Oh." Lucie felt like a fool.

"How are you today?"

"I'm good," Lucie replied automatically, before wondering what exactly he meant. Did the addition of the word "today" mean that he was checking if she was hungover? What exactly was he implying? Oh God, she was never, ever going to get drunk ever again. Fed up with the never-ending cycle of doubt she seemed to have trapped herself in, she decided it was time to rip off the bandage, hard. She took a deep breath and looked him in the eye. "Okay, I just have to ask . . . were you on the yacht last night?"

George grinned. "You don't remember?"

"I do . . . kinda . . . Weren't you wearing some strange furry costume?"

"Says the girl who was dressed like Madonna."

"I know what I wore. I'm asking what *you* came as."

"Myself."

"Did anything, you know . . . happen?"

"What do you think . . . *happened*?" George asked, clearly amused by her apparent amnesia.

Lucie gave him an exasperated look, and he decided to put her out of her misery. "Lucie, nothing of significance happened that I can think of. I went home pretty early. You were dancing with the girls when I left."

Lucie let out a quick sigh. Thank God she didn't make a fool of herself with him, at least. She wondered if what she was feeling was relief or regret. Then she remembered the Neruda poem. Just as she was about to ask if he had slipped the poem under her door, a pretty blond girl in her thirties sat down in the chair to George's right.

"Hallo! I am Petra [Munich International School / London School of Economics / Barbara Brennan School of Healing / Omega Institute / Esalen]," she said with a German accent.

"Hi, Petra, I'm George."

"Are you from Australia?"

"I'm from Hong Kong, but I went to school in Australia."

"*Ja*, I could hear the Aussie in your voice!"

"Where are you from?" George asked politely.

"Originally Munich, but I am really just a nomad. I've lived in Bali, Ibiza, Fort Lauderdale, Rhinebeck, Big Sur—wherever the spirit guides me."

Lucie wanted to roll her eyes. This girl was obviously one of the trustafarian, New Agey friends Issie had met since moving to LA. Not wanting George to get hijacked for the rest of the dinner, she impulsively did something she knew her grandmother would never approve of. She leaned over George, stuck out her hand, and said, "Hi, Petra, I'm Lucie!"

"Hallo, Lucie! Are you from Malibu?"

Lucie laughed. "No. I'm from New York."

"Ah, I thought I met you once at a drum circle in Topanga. I know Issie and Dolfi from Malibu."

"Of course you do," Lucie said with a smile.

Turning back to George, Petra continued. "I looove Australia, especially Byron Bay! I go there a lot because there is this really great *hoshindo* sensei there. Have you ever done *hoshindo*?"

"I haven't. Is it like ayahuasca?"

"No, no, no, nothing like that. Ayahuasca is so last year! *Hoshindo* is Japanese for 'bee-venom therapy.' It's like acupuncture in some ways, but it predates acupuncture by one thousand years. It was invented before the Bronze Age, in the time before they had needles, you see, so they used bee venom to treat the meridians and heal your body."

"Bee venom? Are they live bees?" Lucie jumped in.

"No, unfortunately the bees have to sacrifice themselves for your healing. And you don't get stung—they remove the stingers from the bees and just brush them lightly against your skin, to stimulate an immune response. That's all it takes. I always do a ceremony for the bees after I have a session. I think that's very important to honor their gift. I'm an empath, you see. I do energy healing work, so I am very sensitive to all animals, to the land, to places. Like this villa, for example. It has terrible energy."

"Really, you can sense it?" Lucie asked, genuinely curious.

"Absolutely. Look at my arms! All these goose bumps! If it weren't for you nice people distracting me right now, I would be *miserable* here. I would have cramps and be in the toilet making non-stop diarrhea."

"Oh my. I'm glad we're here for you," Lucie said, trying her hardest not to giggle.

"What is it about this house that creates the bad energy for you? Is it because of how it's sited on the land?" George probed.

Petra stared at George and Lucie in surprise. "*Ja,* the feng shui is very unfortunate, but that's not the only reason. You don't know the story? The owner died here. Jacques Fersen. I can sense his spirit in the house, even among us right now, and he is very restless."

Lucie looked at her dubiously. "Really?"

Petra took a deep breath, closing her eyes for a moment. "*Ja,* Fersen was a French baron.* He was very handsome and rich, but he got kicked out of Paris because he was having affairs with all the scions of the French aristocracy. It was a big scandal, because these were the sons of top politicians and noblemen. So they wanted to throw him in jail, but instead he fled to Rome. There he fell in love with another schoolboy, Nino, and he brought Nino here to this island, where they built this villa and threw the most amazing drug parties.

---

* His full name was Baron Jacques d'Adelswärd-Fersen, the Swedish French heir to a huge steel fortune. Interestingly, he was related to Axel von Fersen, rumored to be Marie Antoinette's lover. (In the exquisite Sofia Coppola film *Marie Antoinette,* the character of Axel von Fersen is played by Jamie Dornan, aka Christian Grey.)

If you go downstairs, there's a sunken opium den where Fersen and Nino would get high and have orgies with the most famous artists and writers of their day."

"Really?" George remarked.

"*Ja,* this place was like the Studio 54 of Capri in its day."

Lucie wasn't sure whether to believe this woman, but she was fascinated all the same. "So how did Fersen die?"

"They say it was suicide, that he drank a lethal cocktail of champagne and cocaine in his opium den. But you know, I don't believe that. His spirit is telling me that he wouldn't kill himself like that."

Lucie and George contemplated her words for a moment, and when George looked up, he saw his mother waving at him from a few tables down, trying to get his attention. "Excuse me for a moment," he said, getting up from the table.

Lucie smiled at Petra, deciding that she liked this girl in spite of her strange stories and all her talk of spirits. Petra returned Lucie's smile and said, "You know there's a full moon tonight. Anything can happen. I'm so glad I changed the place cards for us."

Lucie's jaw dropped. "*You* changed the place cards?"

"Yes. I was staring at the seating chart up at Villa Jovis, and the name card beside us said 'Joshua,' and I thought, *No, no, that's not right. There isn't supposed to be a Joshua sitting between me and you. The energy is all wrong.* So I looked around and something made me pick up George's card. And when I placed the card next to us, I could feel the flow. I thought, *Lucie and George and Petra.* We three were meant to be together tonight."

Lucie looked at her with a mixture of surprise and confusion.

Petra caught her look and gave a throaty laugh. "I hope you didn't think I meant a three-way! No, thank you, I'm not into three-ways. I did it for you and George."

"I'm not sure why," Lucie said stiffly.

"Oh, come on. The chemistry between you two is crazy. All my chakras are opening just thinking of you two!"

"But I don't really know him."

Petra laughed again and shook her head. "You two have known each other over many lifetimes. You just don't realize it yet."

. . .

You two have known each other over many lifetimes. The words echoed in Lucie's mind all through the five-course dinner, the toasts made by various Chius and De Vecchis, the cutting of the wedding cake, the handing out of *bomboniere,* and Isabel's first dance with Dolfi while some guy named Eros[*] serenaded them and all the Italians went nuts, and even now, as she wandered the grounds of Villa Jovis, Lucie couldn't shake off Petra's words no matter how hard she tried.

Isabel and Dolfi had invited their closest friends to the wedding after-party back up at Villa Jovis, where the palace's ruins had been luxuriously outfitted with velvet ottomans and sofas, fur throws, and painted silk lanterns. This being Italy, everyone lingering about the villa's grand chamber seemed to be smoking either cigarettes or joints, and Lucie opted to get some fresh air instead. Besides, George hadn't paid her any attention since dinner, and now he seemed all too happy to be curled up in the corner, deep in conversation with Daniella and Sophie.

Taking the lit pathway around the side of the palace's outer wall, Lucie walked by Tiberius's Leap again and spotted a glowing stairway that she hadn't noticed earlier in the day. Curious, she went down the steps and through a heavy rusted metal door and discovered a narrow candlelit chamber. The chamber was built into the cliffside, its ceiling eroded away by time and open to the stars. A seating area had been carved out of the rocks, and at the far end, a small window faced the sea.

---

[*] That would be Eros Ramazzotti, who might have been unknown to Lucie but in Italy is pretty much as famous as one gets, having sold more than sixty million records in a career that's spanned three decades.

Lucie went up and peered out at the view. The waters looked almost phosphorescent tonight under the gigantic moon, and Lucie wished she could go swimming in the moonlight. She wondered what it must be like inside the fabled Blue Grotto during a full moon, and she decided that no matter what happened, she *had* to see the grotto tomorrow. It would be their last day on Capri.

She suddenly realized how silly she had been, nursing this strange fascination with George, when after tomorrow she would in all likelihood never see him again. Petra was dead wrong—George had no interest in her; he had made it abundantly clear all week long. *She* was the one who fainted in the square, *she* was the one who slobbered like a little girl on his shoulder, *she* was the one who had thrown herself at him in Positano.

While he had been polite to a fault, he had for all intents and purposes ignored her after that. He had ignored her at the monastery, he had ignored her on the yacht, and he was ignoring her right now. Why did she even entertain the notion that someone like him could possibly be interested in her, when up at the villa there was a bevy of beautiful, sophisticated women clinging to his every word. She must have been swept up in wedding fever, in the waxing moon, in the romance of Capri.

As she was about to leave the chamber, she heard the sound of someone coming down the steps, and a moment later George appeared at the threshold.

For some reason, she knew it was going to be him.

"Are you stalking me?" she joked, trying to sound nonchalant, although she could hear her voice quivering.

"Yes, actually."

"Really. Why?"

"Because I need to give you this," George said, as he suddenly leaned forward and kissed her. Taken by surprise, she lurched backward for a moment, before reaching around, grabbing his head, pulling him closer, and kissing him hungrily.

"Isabel told everyone last night that you were her little angel, you were off-limits. That's why I went home," George whispered as he kissed the area right below her ear.

"Fuck Isabel. I was off-limits to everyone but you," Lucie muttered, surprised by her own words as she realized at that moment how much she wanted him, from the first moment she had set eyes on him in the lunchroom of the hotel to the vision of him as a godlike Apollo diving off the rock at Da Luigi, she had wanted him so desperately she could hardly breathe, gasping deeply while he shoved the heavy door closed with his foot, pressed her body against the ancient stone wall, kissing her throat, her neck, letting his mouth linger, as she reached for him urgently. They lay on the bench and he kissed her for what seemed like an eternity, but Lucie didn't want it to ever stop, and as his fingers and lips found her breasts and tortured her so exquisitely, she found herself pushing his head down, down, down, until her diaphanous skirt pooled around his head and she could feel his stubble graze her inner thigh, his searing tongue on her skin, hearing him murmur, *"Are you sure it's okay?"* as she answered with a moan, opening herself to him, closing her eyes as time collapsed and she submitted in a way she never had before, letting herself get lost in a pleasure so intense she thought she was going to pass out, holding her breath, biting her lip trying not to scream as his warm sweat beaded down her legs, her heart pounding in her chest, pounding as if it would explode, pounding louder and louder until a scream filled her ears and she realized it wasn't coming from her and wasn't coming from George, but from Charlotte.

Charlotte was pounding on the door, screaming, "Stop it! Stop it, you two! The drone! The drone can see you! The damn drone is filming everything!"

Lucie opened her eyes and saw a drone hovering above them, a tiny point of light flashing, flashing. Flashing red.

XV

Hotel Bertolucci

CAPRI, ITALY

Lucie sat in the bathtub, knees curled up to her chin, the shower turned on to its highest, trying to drown out her headache. Even with the full force of the water beating down on her, her head felt like it had been put into a vise that was tightening by the second. Any moment now it would explode, and nothing would be left but a big, messy splatter against the blue-and-white painted tiles. Her one contribution to this planet: a Jackson Pollock in the bathtub. And not a good one at that. *Too much red*, the critics would say. *What a waste*, her mother would say. What would her mother actually say? She couldn't bear to even think of it.

She had fucked up, she knew it. She had tried to be someone she wasn't. She tried to do something daring, unpredictable, and carefree, and look what happened. Isabel was right. She was far too innocent, far too much of an angel, to try playing in the deep end. How would she ever face it? The embarrassment. The utter humiliation of being caught with George Zao, of all the boys in the world. Caught and exposed *like that*. All her life she had been so responsible, so virtuous, so perfect, and the one time she had tried pretending to be the sophisticate, the bad girl, it had all gone up in flames.

The moment Charlotte started banging on the door at Villa Jovis, everything entered this strange liminal space where it all seemed to happen in slow motion but somehow also sped up. They scrambled to untangle from each other. George opened the door to a shrieking Charlotte, bolted out of the chamber, and started chasing after the two guys who had been controlling the drone. The guys ran into the woods, and George disappeared after them. Lucie stumbled out and began running herself, but in the opposite direction. She couldn't face Charlotte. Not now, maybe never.

At some point, Lucie willed herself somehow to get out of the tub. The steam had helped, maybe. She threw on the plush white bathrobe and padded out into her bedroom, letting out a quick gasp when she found Charlotte sitting in her armchair.

"You left the door half open. I just wanted to make sure you're okay."

Lucie caught her breath, her fists still clenched. "I'm okay."

"Are you sure?"

"Yesss!" Lucie hissed.

"Okay, okay. I just wanted to be sure, that's all. You don't have to be so defensive. I'm on your side, Lucie," Charlotte said, trying to sound calm, even though she was boiling with panic.

"I'm sorry, I'm a little on edge," Lucie said, sitting down on her bed.

"I can only imagine." Charlotte arched her eyebrows. She sat back in the armchair, crossed her arms, and all pretense of caring gave way to the old Charlotte that Lucie had been dreading. "Oh, Lucie, my poor Lucia. What *were* you thinking? I don't mean to overreact, but this is bad. This is very, very bad."

"I know very well how bad it is. You can stop saying it."

Charlotte got up from the armchair and began pacing the room. "I think I'm still in shock. There I was, stumbling around Villa Jovis in the dark, getting a contact high from all that pot everyone was smoking, and then I saw those two drone operators huddled over a monitor, giggling like schoolboys. I went up to them and peered at the screen, and at first I thought they were watching some sort of porno. And then, when they zoomed in on the poor girl's face, I thought I was hallucinating. I thought, *Why does that girl look so much like Lucie? And what in God's name is she letting that guy do to her under her—*"

"All right, all right, enough. Please stop!" Lucie jammed her hands up to her ears.

"I just *knew* that drone operator was into you, that little pervert! I could tell just by the way he always had that damn drone hovering over you at every event throughout the week! Now, if George wasn't able to intercept them and destroy the footage, we should go to plan B: we should go straight to Isabel."

"Come on, it's her wedding night!" Lucie protested.

"I don't care! Your future is at stake, Lucie, and she needs to know exactly what happened with her staff. Her people can do all the damage control—that Gillian lady looks like she could direct a covert SEAL team assassination if she had to, doesn't she? I want her to make sure all the footage gets locked up and destroyed, along with those creeps they hired!"

Lucie's heart sank. She couldn't imagine the further embarrassment of having to tell Isabel about this.

"Where is George? Don't you think we should have heard from him by now?" Charlotte fretted as she kept going from the door to the window.

"Can you please stop pacing? You're giving me a headache!" Lucie moaned.

"Well, pardon me if I'm giving you a headache. I'm sorry I have to worry that your reputation, your future, your whole life, is in his hands right now!"

"My whole life?" Lucie stared at Charlotte dubiously.

"Do you understand the ramifications of what could happen if that footage ever went public? Let's start with grad schools—you can forget about getting into any of the Ivys. And then you'll never be hired by a Fortune 100 company. You'll never get into any of the good clubs. You'll never marry into a good family. And let's not forget, you'll never be president!"

"I hate to break it to you, Charlotte, but I'm not going to be president. It's never been a goal of mine."

"You say that now, but you never know. I mean, do you think Michelle Obama ever dreamed she would be president one day?"

"What are you talking about? Michelle Obama isn't even running."

"Nonsense, she'll run after Hillary runs, and she will surely win. We will have two kickass female presidents in a row beginning in 2016, just wait and see. But *you*—you might have jeopardized your chances forever. And do you want to know the most terrible thing of all?"

"What?"

"Your name will no longer be *in the book*," Charlotte said ominously.

"What book?"

"Ugh, don't be dense, Lucie. There's only one *book*, and that's *The Social Register*. It would be a tragedy if you were struck out of the book!"

Lucie rolled her eyes. "I could give two fucks about *The Social Register*."

"Language, Lucie! You might not feel like it's important now, but just wait and see how you feel when the next edition comes out, and your mother and Freddie are listed but your name is conspicuously absent. I've had friends who were excised in this way, after marriage, divorce, or murder, and they all felt like they no longer existed. Like they were *dead*."

Lucie lay back on the bed wearily. She wished Charlotte would just get out of her room.

"I don't understand it, Lucie. I just don't know how you could let this happen. In all these years you've never, ever put a wrong foot forward! I didn't see this coming from even a mile away. You and George Zao? How is that even possible? I thought you detested him!"

Lucie remained silent.

Charlotte let out a deep sigh. "On some level, I can understand it. After all, he is Chinese. I mean, it's in your blood, your recessive genes. I always wondered when it might happen for you. You've always been caught between two cultures. No matter how or where you've been brought up, you would be predisposed toward someone like him."

Lucie felt like she had been punched in the gut. Of all the many hurtful, insensitive things Charlotte had said to her over the years, this was the worst. She should have been furious at her cousin, but instead she felt nothing but shame—a numbing shame buried deep within her that had always been there, the sort of shame only a family member could inflict that rendered her helpless, unable to defend herself. Suddenly, a chorus of voices began to crowd her head. The voices of her relatives, her neighbors, her college friends, her classmates back at Brearley . . .

"You'll never guess what Lucie was caught doing in Capri."

"Who would have imagined that Lucie Churchill, who only dated the preppiest guys and wouldn't even give Stavros Theodoracopulos the time of day, would end up falling for a Chinese boy from Hong Kong?"

"A Chinese boy who goes to Berkeley, of all places."

"He wears a Speedo and Birkenstocks. Together."

"Ewww!"

*"Have you seen that mother of his? NOCD."**

"I suppose it's fine that she's fallen for someone like him, since Lucie's never cared about joining Piping Rock."

"Have you fallen for him?" Suddenly Lucie realized Charlotte had been speaking to her all along. "Answer me, Lucie, so I can best help you clean up this mess."

* "Not Our Class, Darling."

Lucie shook her head vehemently. "I haven't fallen for him, Charlotte. I'm not even attracted to him! It was all a mistake! I just had a wild moment."

Charlotte let out a deep sigh that Lucie interpreted as relief. "You've been such an angel all these years, something was bound to crack. Your mother always had a bit of a wild streak, which I actually found rather refreshing in our family, and I guess you've inherited a bit of that after all."

There it is, Lucie thought. That backhanded compliment toward her mother all the Churchills were so good at delivering. Even after all these years, there was always this politely veiled implication that Marian Tang, the hippieish Asian girl from the Pacific Northwest, was never supposed to marry their darling Reggie. She wanted to defend her mother, but she knew she wasn't even in a position to defend herself.

"This has nothing to do with Mom. It's this wedding . . . I got caught up in everything that's been happening on this island, that's all." It was the best Lucie could muster up.

"Yes, Capri is rather intoxicating, isn't it? It lulls your inhibitions, seduces you, and makes you do crazy, impulsive things. Look at me—I never in my life thought I'd eat this many carbs in one week! Just think, what would have happened if I hadn't come looking for you? What if I hadn't arrived at the moment I did and saw what those boys were up to?"

"What's there to say? You *did* come looking for me." Lucie sighed.

"I don't even dare imagine what might have happened if I had not. The footage would be streaming twenty-four-seven on TMZ already!"

"I'm not famous, Charlotte. No one would care."

"You are a Churchill! Our ancestors were some of the earliest settlers of America and count two signers of the Declaration of Independence! Our great-great-great-grandfather practically invented Wall Street! The press loves this kind of stuff, whenever our kind are caught doing naughty things. They would label you something nasty like 'Park Avenue Princess' or 'Churchill Heiress,' and it would be all over Page Six!"

"Well, I've always wanted to be in Page Six," Lucie said facetiously.

"Don't even joke about such a thing, Lucie! Our family has survived unsullied by scandal for generations, and I'm not going to let you be the one who ruins it all! A scandal like this would give Granny a stroke! And mind you, even if we do succeed in destroying the footage forever, what are we going to do about George?"

"What do you mean?"

"How do we contain him?"

"I don't understand. George doesn't need any 'containing.'"

"Oh, you don't think he's going to go bragging about tonight?"

"God, no."

Charlotte glared at Lucie pitifully. "I don't think you really know what men are like. You are a big notch in his belt, and he's going to want to broadcast it to all the other guys."

"He's not that kind of guy, trust me. And things have changed since your time, Charlotte. Everyone's past is out there online, it's really not that big a deal," Lucie tried to say dismissively, even though, in her heart of hearts, it was a big deal.

Charlotte shook her head in dismay. She knew Lucie might not care as much as she did about such proprieties, but she still had their family to answer to. She pondered for a moment and then let out a deep sigh. "I suppose you see me as a has-been. Yes, I'm a Luddite, I'm too old-fashioned for your generation. God help me, I've never been on a dating app, and maybe I'm placing too much importance on protecting your virtue, your reputation, but this was what I was here to do, Lucie. It was the only reason I was invited to Capri and you know it. On that score I have totally failed our family. And your mother—your poor mother—will be blamed by Granny."

Lucie wanted to scream—her cousin was so good at playing this particular guilt card. "Why should Mom ever find out?"

"Well, if the footage leaks, she's bound to find out. And even if it doesn't . . . don't you always tell her everything anyway?"

"You think I'm going to tell her about *this*?"

"Well, the two of you are like sisters. You three have this special free-spirited intimacy that I've always found a little disconcerting—I remember how Freddie confessed to your mother that some girl had given him a hand job under the table at Serafina when he was in the ninth grade."

"Charlotte, that's Freddie! I don't tell my mom everything like he does. If anything, I tell as little as possible these days—she worries about every single thing I do."

"That's not how it seems to me," Charlotte said, turning toward the window. The moonlight on the water was astonishing. It was such a lovely view, a view that had gotten them into all this trouble in the first place. She wished she could turn back the clock and that they had never accepted the Zaos' rooms.

"What do you want, Charlotte? Do you want me to swear never to say anything, so neither of us disappoints her?"

Charlotte turned slowly to face Lucie. "You know, that wasn't my intention at all. But since you bring it up, I do think it would be in the best interests of everyone to take an oath of *omertà* and keep this incident completely to ourselves."

"Fine with me."

"Let's swear that we'll tell absolutely no one."

"It will never leave this room," Lucie swore.

"And we should leave Capri first thing in the morning."

"What do you mean? We can't leave in the morning—there's still the post-wedding brunch on board Issie's godfather's yacht!"

"Lucie, I could give a rat's ass about the brunch on a yacht right now. It's imperative that we leave tomorrow. Don't you see? For the sake of your reputation, our family's reputation, we just can't risk any hint of gossip getting out."

"But that makes no sense! Don't you think it will look more suspicious if we suddenly left without saying goodbye? No one but the three of us knows what happened and . . ."

Just then, Charlotte heard the elevator doors opening. She ran to the door and saw George coming down the hallway, looking a bit out of breath.

"What happened?" Charlotte asked anxiously.

"I caught up with them. I had to chase them all the way down to Via le Botteghe, but I got to them."

"Oh dear, did you get into a fight?"

"We managed to negotiate. It was all very civilized. We went to the nearest ATM, I got them some cash, and they gave me the drone."

"Where is it?"

"It's all destroyed, the hard drive, everything. I crushed it with a rock and threw it off a cliff. That's why it took me so long."

"Oh, thank God. Thank God, thank God, thank God." Charlotte sighed in relief. "How much did you have to pay them?"

"Don't worry about it." George peeked in at Lucie leaning by the archway to her bedroom. He was about to say something to her when Charlotte cut him off.

"George, will you please come with me for a moment to my room? There are a few things we need to discuss," Charlotte said, suddenly taking on a no-nonsense tone.

George nodded wearily.

"Charlotte! What are you doing?" Lucie asked suspiciously.

"Pack your bags, Lucie."

"Charlotte, no!" Lucie cried out in alarm.

Charlotte ignored Lucie, closing the door firmly behind her as she marched George Zao down the hallway toward her room.

New York

· 2018 ·

The Metropolitan Museum of Art

UPPER EAST SIDE

"Tell me what you see. Tell me why you like it," Marian Churchill (Seattle Country Day / Lakeside / Harvard / Columbia PhD) said to her son, Freddie, as they stood in front of Balthus's immense painting *Summertime* in the contemporary wing of the Met.

"I see innocence, I see subversion, I see a horny couple," Freddie (All Souls / Saint David's / Saint Paul's / Princeton, Class of '20) said.

Marian smacked her son on the arm with her rolled-up museum guide. "Be serious! You were the one who dragged me all the way here from my favorite Vermeers to see this painting."

"The girl in the middle of the painting is actually Balthus's re-imagining of Narcissus. Just look at all the different perspectives, the hidden figures and all their various agendas. The creepy guy smoking the pipe, the sleeping girl, that mysterious couple wandering in the distance. There's so much intrigue in the picture, you could write a whole novel about it!"

"Then you should write it! And you know what? You're right . . .

I think that couple is looking for someplace private to get it on," Marian said, squinting at the figures huddled in the background. The two of them began giggling, which soon exploded into fits of uncontrollable laughter as several museum patrons cast dirty looks in their direction.

Marian, still heaving from laughter, turned away from the painting in an effort to collect herself. "Oh, look, Grant Wood! *The Midnight Ride of Paul Revere*. I love Grant Wood."

"I'm getting a grant wood just looking at it!" Freddie said, as the two of them burst into laughter again.

Freddie glanced at his watch and gasped. "Oh, shit, three twenty-two p.m., we're going to be late!"

He grabbed his mother's hand, and the two of them began racing through the galleries, past the Rockefeller wing, down a flight of stairs, and out the little-used exit that opened onto the street level of the museum, facing Fifth Avenue.

"Cecil said to cross Fifth and stand on the steps outside Adolfo's old building to get the best view. And try to look inconspicuous," Freddie said.

"I blend in everywhere, dear. I just look like another Asian tourist. But you shouldn't have worn that coat," Marian said, scrutinizing his dapper navy-and-green-striped rowing blazer.

The two of them stood under the awning of the red-and-white stone Beaux-Arts mansion, staring in anticipation at the iconic steps of the museum, crowded like any other Saturday with visitors meeting friends, lounging in the sun, having snacks, and posing for selfies. To the casual observer, Marian and Freddie could have fit in perfectly with the rest of the crowd—they looked like two college-aged friends hanging out.

Marian's skin was preternaturally unlined, and between her petite frame and gamine pixie-cut hair, she retained such a youthful look and demeanor that people often assumed she was in her mid-twenties and not twice that age. When Freddie was a child, she was always mistaken for his au pair, since his more Caucasian-dominant features and dark blond curls bore little resemblance to her classically Chinese face. These days, one could see more of a resemblance to his mother in his perfect Cupid's bow and his refined, high cheekbones, though his hair had evolved into a floppy rich chestnut mop that every girl in the 10021 zip code (and many in the 10010) found irresistible.

"Didn't Cecil say it would start at three thirty p.m.? It's already three forty and nothing's happening," Marian observed.

"Blair Waldorf better appear and start doing parkour on those steps or I want my money back," Freddie quipped. "This is typical Cecil, don't you think?"

"What do you mean?"

"He's the master of hyperbole. Everything's always the 'best in the world,' the 'most exclusive' or 'one of a kind' with him. Today he said, 'Freddie, don't you think you'll be the luckiest guy in the world to have me as a brother-in-law?' "

"Oh, jeez, he actually said that?" Marian cackled. "What did you say back?"

"I said, 'Not really.' "

"You did not!"

"I sure did. I asked, 'How exactly does that make me the luckiest guy in the world?' And he said, 'You'll have access to my houses, the yacht, the plane, all my clubs, and now that we're related, *Town & Country* has no choice but to put you on its "Most Eligible Bachelors" list next year. You stand to benefit the most from the Cecil Pike halo effect.' "

"Ha! That's priceless. As if you'll ever need his help. The girls have been banging down our door since you were five!"

"I hate to break it to you, but Cecil already wants us all to spend New Year's Eve in Saint Barth's."

"Yuck, no thank you! What are we going to do? Hang out on that obscenely large boat of his with Russian oligarchs and Beyoncé? We always spend New Year's in East Hampton."

"I warned him you wouldn't be happy. He said you would change your mind the moment you see the new villa."

Marian rolled her eyes.

"Peter . . . Peter Submarina or something like that designed it. The guy who only designs houses for billionaires and kings, or so Cecil claims."

"Peter Marino, you mean. Oh, look, there's Cecil!" Marian said excitedly.

"Hush, Mama! Stop jumping up and down or you'll ruin everything!"

Cecil (Kiddie Kollege Preschool* / South Elementary / Kinkaid / Aiglon / Oriel College, Oxford) could be spotted emerging from a gleaming Meteor over Fountain Blue Bentley Mulsanne† in a sharply tailored navy suit and pink shirt. He was what one would describe as Armie Hammer Handsome™—he had the perfect swoop of sandy-blond hair and the perfect glacier-blue eyes accentuated by his perfectly square jaw and aquiline nose, the sort of jaw and nose that on Cecil could have been crafted only by a very pricey Wilshire Corridor surgeon. Cecil held Lucie's hand affectionately to help her out of the car, and the two of them proceeded up the steps of the museum looking like they were just having a Sunday stroll.

But then Cecil turned abruptly and gestured toward the hot dog cart parked in front of the museum. Lucie looked confused but followed him down the steps toward the row of food vendors. Suddenly out of nowhere, Shawn Mendes and Camila Cabello's "Señorita" started booming onto the street from hidden speakers. The "random strangers" milling about the steps stood up in unison and began a complicated choreographed routine to the tune as Lucie's jaw dropped.

"Boo! Flash mobs are so lame. Didn't they stop doing them around 2010?" Freddie remarked, before realizing that the spectacle

---

* A preschool in Odessa, Texas.

† Yes, that's really what they call the body paint combination at Bentley. I personally prefer the "Silver Tempest over Damson," but I figured no one would know what the hell that meant.

was turning out to be much more than a flash mob. A troupe of street dancers emerged from a passing tour bus to join the party, throwing themselves into the air in unison from the four corners of the steps and executing improbably precarious somersaults before landing safely in the arms of the other dancers, while dozens of ballerinas in pink tutus appeared from the front entrance and began pirouetting around the plaza as if they were doing a scene from *Swan Lake*.

"Jeeeesus, what did he do, hire the New York City Ballet?" Marian exclaimed.

"And from the looks of it the Big Apple Circus as well! Check out the rooftop!" Freddie said excitedly. At the roofline of the museum's imposing facade, a row of acrobats in gold-sequined bodysuits appeared and began shimmying down the front of the building on long silk cords. Flicking back the wispy golden-wheat hair from his forehead, Cecil grabbed a hot dog from the vendor, joined the dancers in the middle of the steps, and started singing into the bun as if it were a microphone:

I love it when you call me señorita,
I wish I could pretend I didn't need ya.

Marian frowned slowly. "Wait a minute . . . is Cecil actually singing that he loves it when she calls *him* señorita?"

Freddie grimaced a little. "Ye-aah, apparently. Wouldn't have been my first choice for a proposal song, and I'm not sure the wiener mic was the right move either."

Marian chortled in agreement. "Can you see Lucie's face? That damn umbrella on the bulgogi cart is blocking my view."

"Lucie's freaking out! Her face has turned bright red." Freddie laughed.

"She's mortified, isn't she?" Marian said.

"Sooooo mortified. I love it!"

As if the spectacle of a hundred dancers on the steps of the Met wasn't enough, a marching band in full regalia suddenly emerged from the Central Park entrance off Fifth Avenue, backing up the tune with its enormous brass instruments as it snaked around the dancers in front of the museum. Hundreds of tourists were now on the scene filming excitedly with their phones as the song ended and six gold-sequined dancers carried the tall yet surprisingly slight Cecil aloft and twirled him down the steps Esther Williams–style right to where Lucie was standing.

While Cecil was still propped horizontal in the air by the dancers, he reached into the breast pocket of his bespoke Attolini suit, fished out a blue velvet box, jammed it right under Lucie's nose with one hand, grabbed a real microphone with his other hand, and announced in his distinctive accent—a vaguely Central Texas meets Draco Malfoy meets pretentious French auctioneer accent that he claimed came naturally from having gone to high school at Aiglon—"Lucie, *mon ange, innamorata mia,* would you do me the greatest honor of becoming my señorita—Mrs. Cecil Pike?"

"Goddamn it, I should have worn my Bottega boots! I can't see a thing! What's Lucie doing?"

"Her hands are on her face, but she's nodding. She looks . . . stunned."

"Ha! I'll bet she does!" Marian said.

The crowd roared in approval, as Cecil took a bow and announced, "I'd like to thank everyone who helped make this spectacular moment possible. The president of the Met, the chairman of the board of trustees, everyone on the board—especially my mother—the mayor, everyone at the mayor's office, the board of the New York City Ballet, including Sarah Jessica Parker, the executive director of the Alvin Ailey Dance Foundation, choreographer Yanira Castro, Telsey and Company for casting, Great Performances for catering, and, of course, Laurence Graff of Graff jewelers. Thank you all!"

"Um, did he thank any of the performers or the band?" Freddie wondered out loud.

"He's probably too nervous. I'll give him a pass on that," Marian said, as they crossed the avenue toward the newly engaged couple.

"You didn't cry, Mama. I thought you'd be bawling your eyes out."

"Well, it wasn't exactly a Mr.-Darcy-getting-down-on-his-knees-in-a-muddy-field kind of moment," Marian remarked, although she was rather moved by the whole spectacle. Who would have imagined that her Lucie would be proposed to in such a grand manner by the man that *Vulture, BuzzFeed,* and *The Skimm* had proclaimed "The Most Eligible Gentleman on the Planet." She almost teared up at the thought. If only Reggie could have been here to witness this day—maybe now her mother-in-law and all those Churchills would finally stop judging her parenting choices.

"Mom! Freddie! Were you here the whole time?" Lucie shrieked excitedly as she hugged her mother and brother.

"Of course they were. I arranged everything so that they wouldn't miss a second of our special moment," Cecil said, beaming proudly.

"Is your mom here too?" Lucie asked, looking around.

"Very funny, Lucie. You know she's at her couture fittings in Paris."

"Yes, how could I forget?" Lucie said apologetically.

Breaking the awkward silence, Marian announced, "I promised Freddie his favorite apfelstrudel at Café Sabarsky. Won't you both join us?"

"I have another idea . . . why don't we all celebrate with champagne and scones at the Carlyle? It's Lucie's favorite," Cecil suggested.

"Sure!" Marian and Freddie gamely agreed.

The four of them strolled over to Madison Avenue together, and before long they were seated at what Cecil insisted was the "prime table" in the jewel-box-like gallery of the Carlyle Hotel.

"My bride deserves the best seat in the house! We can see absolutely everyone entering and exiting from here, and, more importantly, they can see us. Are you comfortable, Mrs. Churchill?" Cecil said as he tried to fluff up the silk pillow behind Marian with a series of needless karate chops.

"Very comfortable, thank you. You can stop hitting the pillow, Cecil," Marian replied.

"Don't you love this room and its superb stenciled walls? You know it's all inspired by the sultan's dining room at Topkapi Palace in Constantinople. Mongiardino at his best. You know my mother tried to get him to design the interiors of our first plane, but then he died. I'm so glad those Chinese owners knew well enough to leave the gallery alone when they bought the place . . ."

Cecil paused for a split second, as if it had just dawned on him that his future mother-in-law was Chinese and his bride half Chinese, and maybe his statement could be perceived as a tad offensive. If the notion momentarily disturbed him, it was forgotten as soon as the waiter arrived and Cecil held court over the table, ordering afternoon tea with a smorgasbord of finger sandwiches, scones, and petits fours for everyone, selecting the right vintage of champagne from the wine list, and, most important, making sure everything was served on his approved china. "Please take away these dishes with the blue-and-gold pattern you use for regular guests. Talk to Stephanie—she knows where the hand-painted Limoges that have been put on reserve for me is kept."

"Cecil has his own set of teacups stored here," Lucie explained to her brother.

"Seriously? What's wrong with the ones they have?" Freddie probed.

"Freddie, tea always tastes much better served in Second Empire French porcelain," Cecil began to lecture. "But more importantly, look at your sister's ravishing lips! They're like a hybrid between Andie MacDowell's and Charlotte Gainsbourg's. I simply cannot allow these precious lips to touch a teacup unless it has a rim thinner than 1.3 millimeters!"

"What would happen if they did?" Freddie stared at his sister's lips, wide-eyed.

"It would simply never happen. I wouldn't permit it! From now on, Freddie, your sister is going to be treated like the divine empress she was born to be," Cecil declared.

"Got that, Freddie?" Lucie said with a little giggle.

Cecil turned to Marian. "Mrs. Churchill, you deserve a special prize for your patience today!"

"What do you mean?" Marian asked.

"I know you're only being polite, but I cannot *believe* that you haven't asked to see the engagement ring yet!"

"Oh, yeah, let's see the ring, Lucie," Marian remembered, trying to summon up enough enthusiasm to impress her future son-in-law. Lucie shyly extended her hand across the table and caught her mother recoiling almost imperceptibly. "Oh, wow, Lucie. Oh, wow," was all Marian could muster up.

Freddie whistled. "Look at the size of that thing! It looks like a tumor on her finger. Where's Dr. Pimple Popper when you need her?"

"Very funny, Freddie," Cecil said a little crossly. He looked up and suddenly his frown transformed into a look that a penitent might reserve for the apparition of the Virgin Mary, as a trio of exceedingly chic women entered the room with a cute young girl dressed in riding breeches.

"Why, it's Jackie, Martha, Alicia, and Helena! Hot damn, *everyone's* here today!" Cecil sprang up from his seat to give double-cheeked air-kisses to the ladies, before patting little Helena on her head as if he were dribbling a basketball. "Ladies, may I present my new fiancée, Lucy Churchill? You know, her father was Reggie Churchill, and she's the granddaughter of Consuelo Barclay Churchill."

"Yes, Cecil, we know. And don't forget she's also the daughter of one of our country's pioneering geneticists, Dr. Marian Tang Churchill," Jackie said graciously, giving Marian a wink.

"Yes, yes, of course," Cecil stammered, realizing his faux pas. He hadn't realized Marian would know this particularly glamorous set of ladies.

"It's hard to believe our town's most eligible playboy is now officially off the market," Martha wryly remarked.

"He sure is. And here's the proof!" Cecil grabbed Lucie's wrist and thrust it at the ladies, who gasped in unison.

"Stunning! Is it Verdura?" Martha asked.

"What a compliment, Martha. No, it is an original Cecil Pike! The cabochon emerald is forty-nine carats and belonged to the Nizam of Hyderabad. The accent rubies are from my mother, bought from the Patiño auction many years ago, and then I had Laurence Graff personally select these twelve brilliant-cut diamonds to go around the band. All D flawless, of course."

"It looks like something one of the infantas might have worn in a Velázquez," Alicia, an art historian, observed.

"You know, that's *precisely* what I was going for! I was channeling the Duchess of Alba when I designed the piece, if you really want to know," Cecil said, his eyes misting a little.

"You did good, Cecil! I'm sure Cayetana would have approved!" Jackie declared.*

After the ladies had been escorted into the adjacent dining room where the more discreet crowd liked to be seated, Cecil sank contentedly into his antique kilim embroidered chair. "Between those ladies, everyone who's anyone will know the news before the sun sets on the island. Which reminds me . . ." He fished his phone out from his jacket pocket and began scrolling through his Instagram. "*Holy Moira Rose!* It's trending! The proposal video is trending! 27,084 likes already! Cornelia Guest just liked it! Prince Joachim of Lichtenberg just re-grammed it! Oh, excuse me, I *must* show this to the ladies. Lucie, come. Quickly, Lucie!" Cecil leaped out of his seat, dragging Lucie along with him.

"Well, I guess Cecil is part of the family now," Marian said with a shrug.

---

* That would be the late María del Rosario Cayetana Paloma Alfonsa Victoria Eugenia Fernanda Teresa Francisca de Paula Lourdes Antonia Josefa Fausta Rita Castor Dorotea Santa Esperanza Fitz-James Stuart, Silva, Falcó y Gurtubay, the Most Excellent Eighteenth Duchess of Alba. As the world's most titled aristocrat, she was five times a duchess, eighteen times a marchioness, eighteen times a countess, fourteen times a Spanish grandee, once a viscountess, and the twenty-ninth Lady of Moguer. She also took part in a bullfight in Seville. Olé!

Freddie gave his mother a look. "Yeah. I think we're gonna have to stop using those coffee mugs from Zabar's."

"SOCIAL GRACES"

by Geoffrey Madison Columbus

If you were anywhere near the Upper East Side yesterday, you might be forgiven for thinking that some hotshot director was filming a movie on location at the Metropolitan Museum of Art. There were ballerinas and daredevil acrobats, there were Broadway dancers, there was a marching band. However, this was no film that brought Fifth Avenue traffic to a standstill but **Cecil Pike** in the midst of a Marvel-budget-sized wedding proposal to **Lucie Churchill.** Cecil, no stranger to this column, is the dashing charmer who has been proclaimed the biggest catch in the universe by every magazine, blog and social media outlet that matters. He's the *GQ*-handsome bon vivant and heir to the ginormous Pike billions, first gushed in the oil fields of Central Texas and then multiplied exponentially thanks to the genius of his force-of-nature mamacita, **Renée Mouton Pike,** one of the world's leading investors, who never misses a brilliant start-up opportunity or a chic party anywhere in the universe, thanks to her private **India Mahdavi**–designed Boeing 757. The less socially attentive might recognize Cecil from his cameo appearances on *Antiques Roadshow,* where he schools the experts with his encyclopedic knowledge of 16th- to 18th-century European antiquities. This, after all, is a guy who goes deep-sea diving in search of Spanish shipwrecks and has a classics degree from Oxford. Pike *mère et fils* are esthetes extraordinaire, having restored Buckley House in London to its former glory with the help of **Jacques Garcia** at the whispered cost of more than half a billion (pounds, not dollars!), and are said to be doing the same to an ancient fort in northern Rajasthan. The lucky lass Lucie, a rising art consultant who's on the speed-dial of every wannabe Mugrabi these days, is the exotically beautiful daughter of **Dr. Marian Tang** and the late **Reginald Churchill,** a true blue-blooded New Yorker descended from generations of Churchills, Barclays and other Knickerbocker Club types. We haven't seen such a classy union of old money and new money in a while, and this will be one beautiful power couple to put on your radar, not to mention a power wedding. You heard it here first: the nuptials are rumored to be taking place this autumn at a little dive in the Persian Gulf called the Louvre Abu Dhabi.

821 Fifth Avenue

UPPER EAST SIDE

Even in the thin air inhabited by Manhattan's stratospherically high-end property agents—where no one bats an eyelash at a $35 million listing—821 Fifth Avenue was considered hallowed ground. It was built in 1918 to the most exacting standards of luxury, and each apartment in the twenty-one-story building occupied an entire floor, creating sumptuous mansions in the sky. But it wasn't the size of these residences that made the building so renowned; rather, it was the plain fact that 821 was considered to be one of the top five most exclusive buildings in Manhattan. Two ambassadors, one retired Supreme Court justice, a Pulitzer Prize winner, and even a deposed European monarch were politely turned down from purchasing by its notoriously difficult co-op board.

Much of this was due to the fact that a majority of its apartments were still held by the original families who had owned since 1918, and few units ever changed hands. To paraphrase the Patek Philippe slogan, it could be said that one never actually owned an apartment in 821—one merely looked after it for the next generation. So the building remained, well into the twenty-first century, a bastion of privacy for some of the East Coast's most rarefied and discreetly influential families, among them Lucie's grandmother, Mrs. John L. Churchill, or as she was known to everyone in her exclusive circle, Consuelo Barclay Churchill (privately tutored / Miss Porter's / Institut Villa Pierrefeu).

Consuelo's pedigree was unimpeachable. Born a Barclay, one of America's landed gentry families whose storied history went back to the Virginia land grants of King James I, she was on her maternal side the last surviving granddaughter of the Industrial Age tycoon who built the Northeast Atlantic railroads. Her marriage to John L. Churchill, scion to a Gilded Age fortune and president of Churchill Brothers Averill & Co., one of the oldest private banks in the United States, cemented her pole position within New York's Old Guard, but she had neither the interest nor inclination to follow in the footsteps of Bunny, Jayne, or Brooke and become a society doyenne. Intensely private and cosseted since birth, she never felt the need to make much of an effort. While she once presided over the Fifth Avenue residence, an estate in Southampton, and an *hôtel particulier* on Paris's Right Bank, these days she preferred to spend most of the year at her "winter home" in Hobe Sound, Florida, coming to New York only during the fall ballet season.

Tonight, however, Consuelo had made the exception of traveling to the city and opening up the apartment for her granddaughter's engagement party, which is how Lucie found herself standing in the middle of her grandmother's drawing room in a pretty Zimmermann white eyelet dress, receiving the relatives and friends on her father's side who had gathered from all over the country on a beautiful late-spring evening and who, truth be told, were mystified by how Lucie had pulled off the feat of becoming engaged to a man they had all read so much about.

"So how did you meet him again?" Teddy Barclay (Rippowam / Phillips Exeter / Harvard) asked his cousin pointedly as he grabbed another pig in a blanket from the *istoriato* Italian Renaissance platter being held by a uniformed maid.

"We met in Rome five years ago, Teddy. Charlotte and I were touring the Palazzo Doria Pamphilj, and Cecil came walking down the hallway with the owner of the palazzo and saw that we were admiring a particularly beautiful painting of Saint Sebastian. So he started telling us about it—even educating the prince about his own art collection. He's incredibly knowledgeable about Italian art."

Teddy twitched his nose, unimpressed. "So what precisely does Cecil do these days?"

"Cecil's the busiest man I know. He's got dozens of projects. He's funding about thirty start-ups, he's on the International Council of the Louvre, he started a nonprofit that restores frescoes in Naples, and he's—"

"None of those sound like real jobs to me," Teddy remarked, as he chewed openmouthed on a pig in a blanket.

"Teddy, give it a rest," his wife, Annafred (Rippowam / Deerfield / Benenden / Saint Catharine's, Cambridge), cut in.

"But this was only my third piggy!" Teddy protested.

"I'm not talking about the piggy! Stop harassing Lucie. What does it matter what Cecil's job is?" Annafred said.

Charlie Spencer Houghton (Rippowam / Phillips Exeter / Harvard), an uncle on the Churchill side, jumped into the conversation. "Cecil Pike doesn't need a job. Billennials* these days don't bother putting in time at the office for appearances' sake. They just jet around the world with their laptops. Do you know how much that father of Cecil's personally pocketed when he sold Midland Gas to Texaco? Seven billion. That was in the *eighties*, Ted, and that was before his widow decided to invest all the money in a little start-up called Google."

Teddy raised his eyebrows. Now that he had heard it from Charlie, he was finally a little bit impressed.

"Speaking of the widow, Lucie, is it true that Cecil's mother couldn't get into 740 Park or 1040 Fifth, so she bought up half a

* Billionaire + millennials = billennials

block's worth of town houses and turned it into a behemoth that dwarfs the mansion that the Qataris built?" Lucie's preternaturally poised cousin from Boston, Caroline Cabot Churchill Reed (Brimmer & May / Miss Porter's / Wellesley), who went by Cacky, asked provocatively.

"Um, I don't know about that, but Cecil's mother does have a beautiful house," Lucie replied, trying to be diplomatic and discreet.

"Oh, come now, Lucie, spill the dirt! Are you going to be moving into the Texas embassy? I hear it's got its own hair salon and an underground pool bigger than the one at the University Club."

Lucie tried to laugh it off casually. "I have no plans to move in with my mother-in-law—Cecil's in the process of finishing up our own place in the West Village."

"The West Village, how *quaint*! I remember once going to some cute little theater down there to see a Eugene O'Neill play, and we had dinner at the most adorable art deco restaurant decorated with this big socialist mural.* Now, isn't Renée Pike supposed to be more royal than the Queen? Do we have to bow when we meet her?"

"I don't know how you got that impression, Cacky."

"Charlotte told me she was very grand."

"Charlotte? She's never even met Renée!"

"Really? She spoke as if they were BFFs. Pray tell, where is Charlotte tonight? I would have thought she of all people would be here, since she was the yenta responsible for all this."

"Charlotte moved to London last year, didn't you know? She's very bummed to be missing tonight, but after *Amuse Bouche* folded she got this fantastic job working on special projects for Mary Berry, you know, who used to be a judge on *The Great British Baking Show,* and they're filming something right now. Anyway, I think you'll find Renée to be very friendly. She's not grand at all, is she, Mom?" Lucie said, turning to her mother.

---

* She would be referring to Grange Hall, the much-missed restaurant at the corner of Bedford and Commerce Streets.

he finally just put on his oldest navy pin-striped suit, the first one he ever had made at Huntsman, with his simplest Argenio tie. He didn't want the men in Lucie's family thinking he was making too much of an effort, and besides, he knew they wouldn't understand the Rubinacci.

Why was it that he and his mother felt far more comfortable among their international jet-set friends than a bunch of WASPs? Was it because even the Texas WASP contingent had turned their noses up at them all those years ago, when they tried living in that house on Lazy Lane? Oh well, it was all ancient history as far as he was concerned. For heaven's sake, he had more than three hundred thousand followers among all his social media platforms, they had just dined with the King and Queen of Jordan two nights before, and his mother had the pope on speed dial. They could handle cocktails with the Churchills. The Bentley pulled up in front of the building again.

"Ready, Mother?"

Renée gave Cecil a wink. "Let's slay 'em!"

The Seventeenth Floor

821 FIFTH AVENUE

The chauffeur opened the door, and Renée and Cecil stepped from the Bentley onto the burgundy carpeting, passed through the revolving doors of 821 Fifth Avenue, and found themselves in the hushed, elegant Belgian Art Nouveau lobby. A pair of doormen dressed like deserters from the Franco-Prussian War gave them the once-over.

"We're going up to Consuelo Barclay Churchill's. I'm Cecil Pike," Cecil announced.

The older doorman checked a list in a leather-bound logbook before giving them a curt nod. "Seventeenth floor, Mr. Pike. Ivan will show you the way."

Even the doormen are snooty, Renée thought, as they were shown to the elevator by the younger doorman. She remembered walking past the building years ago when she first began house hunting in New York and admiring its splendid facade.

Danielle, her property agent, had shaken her head and declared, "Don't even think about this one. It's a good building."

Renée was confused. "If it's a good building, why can't we consider it?"

"Sorry, let me explain . . . A 'good' building is realtor code for the few buildings left in Manhattan with co-op boards that will never allow people of a certain, ahem, background in."

Renée's jaw tightened. "What do you mean by 'background'? I have an MBA from Harvard and letters of reference from the governor of New York, Cardinal O'Connor, *and* Barbara Walters. Are you telling me we aren't qualified?"

"It has nothing to do with your qualifications or references, Mrs. Pike, which I can assure you are sterling."

"Then what is the problem?"

Danielle lowered her voice to a whisper. "No Jews, Mrs. Pike. And that means no one with a drop of Hispanic blood either. You need to have come over on the *Mayflower* to get into this building."

Now, Renée scrutinized herself one last time in the inlaid mirror of the elevator. With her expertly balayaged hair and her expensively sculpted nose, did she still look like she had any Hispanic blood coursing through her veins?

"I can't wait to see this place," Cecil whispered in his mother's ear. "How much do you want to bet it's decorated like Frank E. Campbell's?"

The elevator opened onto an entrance hall, and both Renée and Cecil were taken aback by the sight of the enormous pair of Assyrian sphinxes that were at least ten feet tall flanking a faux *marbré* set of doors in vibrant malachite and turquoise. They could hear the murmur of the crowd just beyond the doors. This wasn't the typical Sister Parish meets Mark Hampton decor they had been expecting; the place had a sumptuous, exotic flair that exuded a relaxed grandeur.

"Can you believe it? Old money with actual style," Cecil whispered to his mother.

Renée scanned the room quickly, quietly impressed, as Cecil wondered if he had time to sneak a few pictures. "Stand there, Mother. I'm going to take a picture of you before anyone sees us."

Cecil took a few covert shots on his phone before clearing his throat and asking in a loud voice, "Now, where's everyone?"

"There they are!" Lucie said, the relief evident in her voice as she caught sight of Cecil poking his head into the drawing room. She steered Cecil and his mother to the corner where her grand-mother was perched on the edge of a deep-buttoned ottoman, chatting animatedly with her friends Jeannette and Alex. "Granny, here are Cecil and his mother, Renée Pike," Lucie proudly announced.

Lucie's grandmother stood up quickly, her posture still ramrod straight after more than eight decades. "Howdoyoudo?" *Good, good, Cecil is taller than I would have thought. And the mama's wearing Oscar from one of his last couture collections for Balmain. I almost bought that suit. She's much prettier in person than her pictures. No wonder she hooked her pike.*

Renée flashed her signature million-watt smile and said in her unabashed Texan drawl, "Mrs. Churchill, it's such a pleasure, at long last! I've been wanting to thank you in person for over fifteen years now, for rescuing the Württemberg tapestries and giving them to the Cloisters." *Grandma looks like Vanessa Redgrave! And she's wearing an Yves Saint Laurent dress with . . . holy moly . . . are those Tina Chow rock crystal cuff bracelets? Not what I was expecting—this is one cool dame.*

"You are much too well informed, Renée. That was supposed to be a secret," Consuelo said, a bit taken aback. *I'm going to get everyone fired at the Met tomorrow.*

Cecil bowed ceremoniously. "Mrs. Churchill, I can finally see where Lucie gets her artistic flair. *Just. Look. At. This. Room!* I'm dying for these moss-green stamped velvet walls! And those Giacometti end tables! May I ask if Geoffrey Bennison was somehow involved in this mise-en-scène?"

"Stéphane* did the original work for me, but, yes, Geoffrey gave

---

* Stéphane Boudin, one of the most influential interior designers of the twentieth century. As president of the Paris-based interior decorating firm Maison Jansen, he was the mastermind behind the restoration of the White House for Jacqueline Kennedy in 1961 and was also known for designing interiors for the Duke and Duchess of Windsor, C. Z. Guest, the Agnellis, and the royal families of Belgium and Iran.

it a bit of a refresh in the late seventies," Consuelo replied, eyeing him curiously.

"He really did a marvelous job—it holds up beautifully. Tell me, that portrait of you over the fireplace, is that by Magritte?" Cecil asked in amazement, staring at the painting of Consuelo's face half obscured by clouds.

"Indeed it is. It was the last portrait he did, so I'm told," Consuelo said in the blasé tone of someone who'd uttered that statement a thousand times. Despite this, Cecil was genuinely awed. He couldn't quite believe he was engaged to the granddaughter of a woman so fabulous.

He was about to ask Consuelo if she wouldn't mind posing with her Magritte portrait and him for an Instagram shot when a portly man with a bushy silver mustache cut in front of him and gave Consuelo a hug.

"Ah, Harry! Come meet Lucie's beau, Cecil Pike. Cecil, this is Harry Stuyvesant Fish, a dear family friend. He's about to become our ambassador to Norway."

"Congratulations, young man! I knew your grandfather!" the illustrious ambassador-to-be (Rippowam / Groton / Harvard) said to Cecil as he pumped his hand jovially.

"Really? On which side?" Cecil asked in astonishment.

"The Pike side, of course. My family had a camp up in the Adirondacks too, on Upper Saranac."

"I'm sorry, my grandfather to my knowledge was never in the Adirondacks."

"He wasn't? Aren't you Cecil Pike IV?"

"I'm afraid not."

"Where did your family summer?"

"Usually in Europe. For a few summers my parents rented a villa in the South of—"

Harry cut him off. "You're not one of the Pikes who married into the Livingstons?"

"No," Cecil said, reddening a little.

"Ah. Well then." Harry turned away abruptly and reached out to a passing lady, grabbing her by the shoulder. "Helen! I haven't seen you since Michael Korda's talk at the Century! Where's Frank tonight?"

Recovering himself, Cecil realized that Consuelo was still standing there, eyeing him like a hawk. Before he could say anything, she turned to the assembled crowd, picked up a flute of champagne, and began knocking the glass with her Elie Top intaglio ring.

"Everyone . . . quiet! I'm going to make a toast." Consuelo turned to Lucie with a smile and began. "Now, when I first set eyes on Lucie a week after she was born, she was in her crib, and I must confess, with her peachy-white cheeks and delicate black eyelashes, I thought she looked like the most adorable, exquisite little china doll! So ever since, she has been my little china doll. She would never, ever cry, she was so quiet and well mannered, and I would dress her up in the finest silk costumes from the Orient, sent to me by my dear friend Han Suyin, and I would take her to lunch at La Grenouille, where everyone would fuss over her, or to tea at Madame Chiang Kai-shek's. Funnily enough, Madame Chiang always argued with me and told me that my little china doll didn't look Chinese *enough*! 'Look at those freckles,' she would say. 'That's no Chinese baby!' 'Well, she's half Churchill,' I would reply, 'but thank God she didn't inherit the Churchill nose!' Oh, how we had so many laughs back then, and how I wish those days would last forever. But babies do grow up, and Lucie became a scholar, graduating magna cum laude in biology from Brown, which was only to be expected since she clearly gets all her brains from her mother's side. And now she's so quickly made a name for herself in the art world as one of New York's top contemporary advisers. She continues to surprise us all, and I know her father would be so proud if he could see her today. Now Lucie has met her match in Cecil, who I'm told was proclaimed one of the most eligible bachelors in the country and hails from *such* an impressive family, one that has become *so* synonymous with diversity and the philanthropic spirit of this country. Why, every museum I go to these days, I see Mrs. Pike's name carved into the wall! Cecil, I've only just met you, but I can tell you possess the refinement of a Rothschild, and I trust you will know exactly how to treat my precious, precious china doll. To Lucie and Cecil—I wish you both a lifetime of joy and happiness."

Everyone in the room raised their glasses as Freddie cheered, "Here! Here!" Renée beamed proudly at her son, thinking, *My boy did good. Those fuckers at Saint James School in Houston wouldn't accept him, but look at him now—marrying into the elite of the elite, the kind of people who have never even* heard *of Saint James!*

Lucie blinked back a few tears, though no one in the room—with perhaps the exception of her mother—would have ever suspected the real reason. After making a few rounds of the drawing room, Cecil and Lucie managed to duck out to the building's roof garden for a little fresh air.

Cecil gave Lucie a dead-eyed stare. "Fucking hell. I have half a mind to get out my cell phone and call for a helicopter evac right now."

Lucie burst out laughing. "I did warn you . . ."

"Baby, I don't think you prepared me adequately. I thought Charlotte was bad enough, but I've never in my life met such *dreadful* people. So stultifyingly boring, so shabbily costumed, they might as well be wax figures. How could you possibly be related to them? I just don't see it! You are the swan in a field of squawking geese, the rare lotus growing in a swamp . . ."

"Oh, you're too sweet. I'm the weird-looking one in my family, you know. Cacky's considered the beautiful one. She was a Ford model back in her Wellesley years."

"Cacky? She sure looks like a Ford, and I'm talking about a Bronco! Thank God for your mother or you'd have the same unfortunate, inbred features!"

"You're too funny. You sound like my Tang grandparents, my

mom's folks. Whenever they saw me, they would always praise my 'features.' To them, Freddie and I were the most beautiful creatures in the world, and they were always so proud to show me off to their friends that it made me a little embarrassed. But to some of the people downstairs, it was the polar opposite. It was always, 'Hmm, what can we do to fix Lucie?' "

Cecil shook his head in disgust. "Well, in my opinion you're the only person downstairs who doesn't need fixing! That Annafred, there's no excuse for her name—did she escape from an order of lesbian Mennonites? Fess up, Annafred and Teddy are really brother and sister, aren't they? They can't possibly be married to each other."

Lucie was doubled over in laughter. "I always thought Teddy and Annafred look exactly alike, but you're the first person to ever say it! She's actually Annafred *the Ninth*. Her family goes all the way back to the landing at Plymouth Rock."

"Oh dear God, Pilgrims! You're related to Pilgrims! No wonder you needed me to rescue you from this pathetic lot."

"You have no idea. Freddie can do no wrong in their eyes, but I've always felt like I'm on probation—I'm only part of the family if I don't embarrass them."

"Ha! I think you've got it mixed up—you should be embarrassed of *them*!"

Lucie grinned, delighting in Cecil's dissection of her kin. It was as if she had found a kindred spirit at last, like they were the two outsiders at the back of the classroom making snide remarks about the popular kids.

"And that friend of your grandmother's—Ambassador Harry Stuyvesant Fish—what century is he from? Did anyone inform him that we won the War of Independence?"

"Oh, Harry's the *worst*. When I was at Brown, he could never stop making disparaging remarks about it. He called it 'a repository for ne'er-do-wells and the dregs of deposed European royalty.' "

"I don't understand how this man is going to be an ambassador.

He wouldn't know what diplomacy was if it hit him on his fat head. At first he snubbed me when he realized I wasn't descended from some posh Pikes he knew, but then when he was introduced to my mother and realized I was *that* Pike, you should have seen how quickly he did a one-eighty and began to grovel in her presence! He reminded me of a truffle hog, especially with that red face and that distended belly. That is one man who should never go near a pair of suspenders, and yet there he was in his Brooks Brothers braces. He looked like . . . What was the name of the guy who used to do those ghastly Quaker Oats commercials when we were little kids? Wilfred Ross?"

"Wilford Brimley!" Lucie cackled. Cecil could really be so funny sometimes, especially when he was feeling affronted.

"Harry was going on and on in that *pretentious* accent about how he was due to begin his posting in Oslo and still didn't have tenants for his estate in East Hampton because he couldn't find 'the right sort of people.' It seems the ones who are rich enough to afford the place don't meet his standards—no private equity, oil, or tech money; no one from New Jersey, Southern California, or southern anywhere; and 'no Latins because they like to dance.' He said this in front of my mother, mind you. He said they would ruin the eighteenth-century mahogany floors of his Cissinghurst, which is on the National Register of Historic Places. Who is he kidding? I've seen the place, and it looks like a Victorian bordello on mushrooms. All those turrets and Tiffany glass windows? It's an abomination! He should put it on Craigslist and rent it out by the hour. More importantly, how dare he name it Cissinghurst? It's an insult to Vita and Harold."

"It was his mother's house—Cissie van Degan Fish. She was apparently the mother from hell. Hmm . . . perhaps Harry would take the Ortiz sisters. They just emailed me asking if I knew of a good house to rent in the Hamptons," Lucie wondered.

"Who are the Ortiz sisters? Are they anything like the Borromeo sisters, the Miller sisters, the Bograd sisters, or the Yeoh sisters? Should I know them?"

"You might enjoy them. I got to know them at Isabel De Vecchi's wedding."

"Ah yes, they were part of that strange crew you met in Capri, before destiny caused our paths to cross in Rome."

"They were these rather proper but very charming sisters, Paloma and Mercedes. And they weren't the strange ones," Lucie said, suddenly getting a faraway look in her face.

"Don't Filipinos like to dance? I doubt the honorable ambassador would approve of these party animals."

"They're in their seventies, Cecil. And they come from one of the oldest and most revered families in the Philippines."

"Well then, don't let me stop you from fulfilling Harry Stuyvesant Fish's social wet dreams. In the meantime, can't I please call in a helicopter and let's head straight to Daniel?"

"I would love nothing more than to leave this miserable party, but I don't think there's enough landing room among these azaleas, and we need to make at least one more round and rescue your mother! Besides, I really think my great-aunt Cushing has taken a fancy to you."

"I swear I saw Great-Aunt Cushing squirrel some of those mini quiches from William Poll into that big wicker tote bag of hers. I think she's begun stocking up for winter."

"Oh dear. She's always the first to attack the leftovers after dinner. Last year, I heard she brought a huge nylon fold-out bag to the Casita Maria Fiesta Gala to take home as many of the centerpieces as she could fit."

"Of course she did. Baby, *pleeeease* don't make me go back down there. Everyone's *so* wretched! Now that we've done this, do we need to invite any of them to the wedding? Would any of them even want to go to Abu Dhabi? The only one who's fabulous is your grandmother. She's absolutely magnificent, and the apartment exceeded all my expectations. Tell me, who do you think she's going to leave the Magritte to?"

"Don't go getting any ideas, Cecil, I can assure you it won't be me. Cacky's my grandmother's favorite because she looks like a young Charlotte Rampling and lets her win at bridge."

"Cacky was another one who was so far up my mother's ass. She was name-dropping a mile a minute—Mandela, Macron, Marie-Josée."

Lucie shook her head in amused disgust. "I'm glad you see Cacky for who she is. All my life, I've felt like I've had to try to live up to her goddess-like perfection."

Cecil scrunched his face up like a bad smell had wafted past. "What would ever possess you to think that Cacky was worth competing against?"

"I'm not even sure anymore . . . I guess, growing up, we were like the wretched orphans, especially after Dad died and Mom got sick. I felt responsible for keeping our family together, and that meant always striving to be perfect in Granny's eyes."

"You are perfect exactly the way you are, baby," Cecil said, stroking her cheek affectionately. "You were the most exquisite thing in that room tonight, and even if your grandmother has poor judgment, at least she made a marvelous toast. Anyone who can mention Han Suyin, Madame Chiang Kai-shek, and the Rothschilds in the same toast deserves a prize. Didn't you think it was fabulous?"

"It was," Lucie said softly. She didn't have the heart to tell him how she truly felt. Every word of her grandmother's toast carried a veiled insult. It was an insult to her mother, it was an insult to Cecil and Renée, and it was a dagger in her heart. To Granny, no matter how graciously she behaved, no matter what she accomplished, she would always only ever be the poor little china doll. But, thankfully, none of that mattered anymore. Commiserating with Cecil on the roof garden above her grandmother's apartment, she was more convinced than ever that she had made the right decision in choosing him as her spouse. Yes, he had his eccentricities, but she was well prepared to handle them. Despite everything that had just happened at the party, she knew that tonight, she was sending a subtle, elegant message to everyone downstairs who had ever pitied her, judged her, or underestimated her: *I'm going to be Mrs. Cecil Pike, and I don't give a damn what you think anymore.*

Auden smiled. "We knew a George with an Aussie accent, didn't we? A lovely chap we met in Capri. George Zao."

"That's it! That's his name!" Freddie exclaimed.

Auden gave Lucie a look. "It can't be. Can it?"

Lucie froze in her seat for a moment. It had to be a coincidence. How many George Zaos were there on the planet? Probably thousands. "Freddie's hallucinating. There's no way it can be the George we knew, because the Ortiz sisters have the house."

"Oh, wait, why don't you ask Cecil? He's friends with George," Freddie offered.

"*Cecil?*" Lucie looked even more confused.

"Yeah, that's what he told me. Sorry, I just remembered. When I'm hungry you know my brain goes to mush," Freddie said as he reached for one of the brownies. "Mama, do we have any more of that Sant Ambroeus gelato?"

"I finished all the chocolate last night when I was binging on *The OA*, but I think there's some pistachio left," Marian answered. "Do you want some?"

"How does Cecil know George?" Lucie demanded, as she became more alarmed by the second.

"I have no idea. We were playing tennis, Lucie. It wasn't social hour."

Marian turned to Lucie. "What a royal screwup! Where's Cecil now?"

"Still in Venice," Lucie said.

"Well, call him if you want to get to the bottom of this mess," Marian suggested.

"Please excuse me," Lucie said, getting up from her chair and walking toward the house. Freddie yelled after her, "Grab the pistachio gelato from the fridge, will you?"

Lucie sat down on the wicker chair overlooking the terrace and dialed Cecil's number. It rang for a few moments before he picked up. "Baby! I've just been to the most transcendent show at the Palazzo Fortuny. It's a retrospective of this Korean artist I've never heard of until now, Yun Hyong-Keun. He sort of does what you do, paints on raw canvases, and his paintings are simply marvelous. They remind me of early Rothkos. I think you'd love them."

"Text me his name and I'll check him out."

"I bought you the monograph. I'm about to have dinner with the Pinaults and some fabulous people from Mexico City. Check my Insta in half an hour and you'll see all the pictures."

"Cecil, please enlighten me . . . Who exactly is George Zao?"

"George *who?*"

"Zao! Zao! He's apparently taken Harry Stuyvesant Fish's house for the summer?"

"Oh yes! Ha ha. Lucie, you're going to love this. You know how much I can't stand Harry, that pretentious fuck with his mandate to only rent his house to 'the right sort of people' who can trace their lineage back to the exact spot where their ancestors stood in Mrs. Astor's ballroom on Fifth Avenue. So I decided to play a little trick on him. I recommended this fellow George Zao to Harry. And I must have really impressed him, because his Bordello di Cissinghurst will now play host to exactly the type of people he disapproves of. They're the most peculiar pair I've ever met."

"What do you mean by 'peculiar'?"

"George isn't really that bad, but wait till you meet his mother. She's the most vulgar thing that ever walked the planet. She dresses like she's about to lip-synch for her life on *RuPaul's Drag Race.*"

Lucie could feel a chill go up her spine. *It* was *them.*

"And how do you know these people?" Lucie asked. She hadn't seen George since that fateful night in Capri five years ago, and she could feel her stomach begin to tighten.

"Well, here's the real laugh—they're complete strangers! I met them at the Frick Collection, in the fountain room when I was searching for that Modigliani portrait they're always moving around. Rosemary's feet were sore from walking, and she was sitting on one of the stone benches rubbing some awful ointment onto her heels and stinking up the place to high heaven! But we began talking because I couldn't help but remark on her turban—it was so full-on Liz Taylor batshit fabulous I had to say something—and she asked me if I knew of a house to rent in the Hamptons. Her son's working in the city now for some B-list architect, and she actually wondered if Grey Gardens could be rented, if you can believe it. She's obsessed with the film, and fascinated by the Beales and the Kennedys, of course. So I told them of an even *better* house, and I texted Harry immediately. I told him that the Zaos were 'Asian royalty,' that they were friends of my mother's and direct descendants of the last emperor who fled to Hong Kong. He bought it hook, line, and sinker. Can you believe how gullible he is? Thank God he's been assigned to Norway and not some country where we actually need someone on the ground with half a brain stem. I hope Rosemary starts filling up Cissinghurst with stray cats. Hundreds of them. It'll teach that Harry Fish a lesson! Elitist shits like him deserve to be punished."

"But, Cecil, you're friends with the most elitist people I know!"

"Please don't confuse elitism with brilliant, self-made billionaires, baby. My friends have every right to be snobbish, but they aren't. Like my father, who grew up without a proper pair of shoes in Terlingua, Texas, and worked his ass off till he dropped dead of a cerebral hemorrhage at sixty. People like Harry treated my dad with nothing but contempt, even when he could finally afford to wear John Lobbs."

Lucie groaned, not wishing to drag herself deeper into arguing over this. "Cecil, you *know* I arranged for the Ortiz sisters to rent the place from Harry. I went to all that trouble helping two extremely high-maintenance parties negotiate their terms. The Ortiz sisters even wanted the water quality tested in the pipes, because apparently they can only bathe in water that's a certain pH. I did it all without complaint, but now you've sabotaged my plans completely over some absurd vendetta you have against Harry. And to make matters worse, I know these Zaos, and the Ortiz sisters know them, which makes things doubly embarrassing."

"Oh, the Zaos were part of that wacko Capri crowd?"

"Yes. They're related to Isabel."

"I might have guessed. Those rich Asians all seem to be related, don't they?"

"Why didn't you tell me you were cooking up this scheme? I'm going to be your wife, Cecil. Why didn't you at least warn me?"

Cecil went quiet for a moment as the enormity of his screwup finally began sinking in. "Baby, I'm sorry. I didn't want to ruin the joke for you."

Lucie exhaled deeply, trying to control her anger. "I really don't understand you sometimes, Cecil. I feel very betrayed."

"I thought you'd be happy!" Cecil sputtered.

"Yeah, real happy," Lucie said, hanging up.

V

The Preppie Guru Lounge

AMAGANSETT, LONG ISLAND

The new Preppie Guru Lounge just outside Amagansett boasted a circular yoga room with floor-to-ceiling windows that afforded spectacular views of the serene wetlands leading down to Napeague Bay. The Saturday morning Master Level Puppy Yoga class that Auden led was the most popular one by far, with a two-year waiting list, as his groupies flocked from all over the world to sun salutate their carb-deprived bodies at the feet of their impossibly photogenic guru.

Lucie had been a devotee of Auden's classes for several years now, since he had opened his first pop-up class in East Hampton four summers ago. She was used to the rigors he imposed and the way he would coax her into pushing her body further than she ever imagined, but today's class was kicking her ass. He was putting them through the most merciless poses, and it didn't help that it was a particularly humid morning, causing the sweat to drip off Lucie like a broken water sprinkler, and that the class was also welcoming a rowdy new batch of shelter puppies who obviously didn't get the memo about keeping things Zen.

As Ajeet Kaur and Trevor Hall's "Akaal" played softly in the background, Lucie struggled to hold her *pungu mayurasana*—one-arm wounded peacock pose—while a French bulldog puppy tried to nuzzle into her sweaty armpit. And when she began transitioning from wounded peacock into *sirsa padasana*—head-to-foot back-bend—a corgi-Chihuahua mix started playing tug-of-war with her tank top. *Get off me, you little shit! I mean, focus, breathe, om gam ganapataye namaha,* Lucie chanted silently. On several occasions, as she stretched into a new pose, she noticed in her peripheral vision some hippie dude behind her who seemed to be executing each pose effortlessly. How was he tuning out these vicious beasts?

Everyone sighed in relief when Auden finally allowed them to relax into *shavasana,* as his voice transformed from taskmaster into his trademark laconic drawl. "And now, just ground into the earth. Feel Mother Earth's gentle embrace. Let your body melt into the soft grass, into the nurturing rich soil, grounding deeper into the earth, deeper and deeper, sending roots into the core, connecting to the giant magical tree at the center of the universe. Feel your breath flow in through the soles of your feet all the way to your crown chakra, flooding oxygen into every cell in your body, every strand of DNA, and as you exhale, think of your breath sending precious life force back through the roots into the tree, the tree of life, Mother Gaia, the tree that connects us all. Innnnn and ouuuut, innnnn and ouuuut. Feel the life force flowing through your body, carrying you home; feel your third eye pulsating . . ."

At that moment, the corgi-Chihuahua decided to bite the heel of the girl next to Lucie, causing her to squeal and let out a loud fart at the same time. A few people burst into giggles, but Lucie bit her lip, feeling embarrassed for the girl, thinking, *Oh gosh, what if the people behind thought that it was me who farted?* Auden gave the closing blessing as the class finally came to an end, and as Lucie opened her eyes and sat up on her mat, she turned around and glanced at the hippie guy behind her. He was kneeling on the ground, his back to her as he rolled up his yoga mat, and Lucie couldn't help but notice the taut, muscular perfection of his ass through the thin, shiny fabric of his faded orange workout shorts. Suddenly the guy turned around, their eyes catching at the same moment, and Lucie did a quick inhale. It wasn't a hippie; it was George. George with long surfer-dude hair. No wonder she hadn't recognized him.

"Hey," he said with what appeared to be a little smirk.

"H-hi," Lucie stammered. *He definitely thinks I'm the one who farted.*

"*George!*" Auden yelled from the front of the room as he came bounding over and gave him a big hug. "So great to see you again! I ran into your mother last week at Nick & Toni's and she told me you'd come to the lounge one day soon. Lucie, how great is this? It's a Capri reunion!"

"Um, yeah, great," Lucie replied, trying to collect herself.

"Can I treat you both to a drink at our Ayurvedic juice bar? It would be such fun to catch up," Auden offered.

"Sure!" George said brightly.

"I, um, have to run. I have a lunch date with my mom," Lucie said.

"Pity. Well, say hi to your mom for me," Auden said, as he put his arm around George's shoulders and steered him toward the door. As they strode off, Lucie could overhear Auden saying, "Your form is insane! *You* should be teaching my class!"

"Oh yeah? I've been practicing yoga ever since you turned me on to it in Capri," George replied.

Lucie felt a pang of regret. Why hadn't she joined them? What harm would there be in grabbing a juice with Auden and George after class? After all, it had been five years since they'd seen each other. She debated whether to follow after them but decided it would look a little pathetic to join them now. Besides, she really did need to get home to her mom. As she walked past the wall of mirrors outside the yoga room, she caught sight of herself and cringed. Her new dove-gray yoga pants were drenched with sweat stains all the way from her crotch to halfway down her thighs. *Oh, how perfect. I just stood in front of George looking like I farted* and *peed my pants.*

Driving home along Old Montauk Highway with the top down on her MINI Cooper, Lucie felt more relaxed as the ocean sparkled in the bright sun and the breeze enveloped her like a cool blanket. The fresh air cleared her mind, and she could finally think rationally again now that she was out of her post-yoga fog. She knew she would run into George sooner or later, but she had always imagined it would be at an opportune moment—courtside at the Dorset Yacht Club tennis matches, for instance, or at the Watermill Center's Summer Benefit party—when she would be dressed to kill. Bumping into him like this had been a complete surprise. She was caught off guard; that's the only reason she reacted like a tween with backstage passes at a BTS concert. If she hadn't just been tortured by Auden for seventy-five minutes straight, if she hadn't looked like she had just peed herself in these damn useless yoga pants that she was about to throw in the garbage, she would not have been so nervous. There was no reason in the world to be nervous. George was just some kid she had met one summer a long time ago. They had known each other for only a week, and they were both victims of Capri, yes, victims swept up by all that beauty and history and achingly romantic, Instagrammable moments of Issie's wedding. Yeah, that entire hedonistic occasion was designed to seduce. She was so much older and wiser now. She was a Brown graduate, she had made Artcom's "Thirty Under Thirty" list of the art world's leading young professionals, and, for Chrissakes, she was engaged to Cecil Pike. Who was George Zao compared with him? Who cares if even after sweaty puppy yoga he still looked like the ultimate thirst trap while she looked like a wet hamster? George Zao was nothing to her.

Lucie pulled up their gravel driveway, parked behind her mom's twenty-year-old Oldsmobile Bravada, and ran up the steps to the front door, wondering where she and her mom would go for lunch today. She was suddenly craving the egg-white omelet at Babette's.

She opened the front door and a distinct odor hit her like a gale-force wind. Chinese fermented fish sauce. She had known this smell only to exist at her Tang grandmother's house in Seattle.

"Mom, are you there?" she called out as she crept down the hallway. Entering the kitchen, she was met by a sight she had not witnessed in years: her mother at the stove stirring furiously at something in a saucepan. Mary, their cook, was standing next to her, peering over Marian's shoulder with a mixture of curiosity and alarm, ready to intervene on a second's notice.

"See, you have to keep stirring so the egg whites turn into flowers," Marian was saying.

"What's happening, Mom?" Lucie asked, almost alarmed.

"Lucie!" a voice called out.

Lucie spun around and saw Rosemary Zao coming toward her, arms outstretched. She felt herself smothered in a charmeuse hug as Rosemary continued tittering away. "Look at you! Even prettier than I remember! You've put on weight, haven't you? Good, good, I thought you were much too skinny before."

"Mrs. Zao!" Lucie sputtered. What was this woman doing in their kitchen?

Marian turned to her. "Lucie! Isn't this fun? I ran into Mrs. Zao at High Tits this morning after my run and decided to introduce myself. We started chatting about how you couldn't find any decent Chinese food in the Hamptons, and before you know it, I decided to make lunch. Believe it or not, Mama's gonna cook! I got out Po Po's* recipe book and I'm making corn egg drop soup and crispy flounder fillets in garlic sauce, and Mrs. Zao is going to make fried stinky tofu and noodles with beef and egg gravy, Cantonese style! Remember how you and Freddie used to love that dish when we went to Hong Kong?"

"We're using fresh linguini, since we couldn't find rice noodles

---

* "Grandmother" in Cantonese.

at Stop & Shop," Rosemary interjected. "And, Marian, please stop calling me Mrs. Zao or you'll make me feel like I'm a thousand years old. It's Rosemary!"

"I need to take a shower," Lucie said, backing out of the kitchen slowly. Two Zaos in one day was too much for her to process.

Her mother called after her, "I'm almost done cooking, and Chinese food has to be eaten scalding hot! So don't be a slowpoke!"

"Yes, don't be a slowpoke! I just texted George, and he's going to join us for lunch. I can't wait for his reaction when he sees you again," Rosemary added.

Too late, Lucie thought.

VI

Outlook Avenue

EAST HAMPTON, NY

Lucie emerged from her shower refreshed and with a plan in place. Anticipating that George would be downstairs by now, she would pull her wet hair up into a high ballerina bun, and then she would put on her sleeveless white jumpsuit from The Row, the one she wore to big power meetings that always made heads swivel. It would look like she hadn't put much effort into it, and the outfit was conservative yet alluring. It would erase the hot-mess image of this morning from George's memory forever.

She got dressed quickly, put on her favorite sandals from Capri, and ran down the stairs, slowing down only when she reached the dining room. There he was, wearing the same loose black tank over orange shorts that he had worn to yoga. It annoyed her that he didn't even have the courtesy to change into something proper for lunch, as any other guest coming to her mother's would have.

"Lucie! Remember Lucie?" Rosemary called out excitedly the moment she saw her.

"Of course, Mom. I already saw her this morning," George said matter-of-factly.

"You did?" Rosemary turned to Lucie with a surprised look.

"Yep, we were at puppy yoga together."

"Well, now that Princess Lucie is finally here, let's *mangia!*" Freddie said, grabbing a serving spoon and digging into the platter of beef noodles in egg gravy.

"Freddie, remember in the Chinese custom, one must always serve the honored guest first," Marian chided.

Freddie's spoonful of noodles was already almost on his plate, but he smoothly pivoted toward Rosemary and deposited the food onto her plate with a flourish. "Exactly what I was gonna do, Mama."

"Good save!" George said, winking at Freddie.

"*M sai haak hei,** Marian. Everyone serve yourselves while it's hot!" Rosemary said, before turning to Lucie. "Now, Lucie, you need to catch us up on the last five years since we saw you."

"Well, I graduated from Brown—" Lucie began.

"Magna cum laude, I might add," Marian cut in.

"—and for the past two years I've been working for an art consultancy."

"The top art consultancy in world," Marian added.

"Art consultancy—what exactly does that mean?" Rosemary asked.

"Lucie's got the most important job in the world. She tells rich social climbers what art to buy," Freddie said, chewing on his noodles.

"That's not accurate at all, Freddie. I help collectors acquire and build their art collections in a meaningful way."

"By telling them what to buy, they'll get photos of their houses into all the right magazines, hang out with the right crowd, get into all the right clubs, so their kids can go to the right schools, work for the right companies, marry the right people, have the right sort of babies, and repeat the cycle," Freddie added.

---

* "No need to be polite" in Cantonese.

"That's a very cynical view of the world, Freddie," Lucie said.

"It's your world, Lucie."

"And it isn't yours? How many eating clubs do you belong to at Princeton again?"

"Stop it, you two! Freddie's just being a provocateur as usual. Freddie, I know you don't care about the right crowd, but there *is* a right way to behave," Marian said as she dished a couple pieces of stinky tofu onto Freddie's plate.

"What the . . ." Freddie paused, holding his fork and knife in midair. He breathed in the pungent aroma of the tofu and tried to stifle a grimace.

"Just try it, Freddie. You'll love it," Marian said.

"I'm not sure about that," Freddie replied, scrunching up his nose.

Marian cast Rosemary a shamed look. "I'm sorry, I raised my children too white. They don't know how to appreciate authentic Chinese food."

"*Hiyah,* you're telling me! George refuses to eat chicken feet. Don't worry, Freddie, you don't have to eat my cooking. But if you want to be adventurous, try dipping the tofu in this sweet chili sauce."

Freddie gamely dipped a piece in the sauce and put it in his mouth, his dubious expression transforming into one of delight. "For something that smells like stinky feet, it sure tastes good."

Marian flashed him a triumphant look. "See, what did I tell you? Now, back to Lucie. Lucie's also become an amazing artist in her own right, Rosemary. She should be selling her own work."

"Not really," Lucie said, a bit mortified that her mother was morphing into a braggy Asian mother right before her eyes.

Marian let out a little squeal. "Lucie, you're forgetting the most important news. She's engaged!"

Rosemary beamed at Lucie. "Yes, we heard. Congratulations! But where's your ring?"

"Oh, I don't have it on at the moment," Lucie said a little sheepishly.

"How could she possibly wear it? It's the size of a rhino's testicle," Freddie said.

"Freddie, stop!" Marian scolded, before turning to Rosemary. "It's a beautiful ring."

Rosemary cleared her throat. "I'm sure. I would expect nothing less from Cecil. Such a nice man. You know he helped us rent Shittinghurst."

Lucie, Freddie, and Marian burst out laughing.

Rosemary frowned. "What's wrong?"

"It's Cissinghurst, Mom, *Cissing*," George said patiently.

"Oh, sorry. You know English isn't my mother tongue," Rosemary said.

"Don't apologize, Rosemary. Your English is perfectly good. It's absolutely charming," Marian said.

"Mrs. Churchill, this flounder in spicy garlic sauce is amazing. I haven't tasted anything this good since moving to New York," George said.

Marian beamed at the compliment. "Thank you, George. It's so easy to make, I'll give you the recipe. It's actually one of the few things I know how to cook, but I'm inspired to try my hand at more Chinese dishes now."

Rosemary had brought an incredible array of fruits specially flown in for her from Asia for dessert, and as they began cutting up the Thai mangoes, Japanese white strawberries, Korean pears, and honeydew melons, Marian looked around the table happily. "It's been years since I hosted a real Chinese lunch like this. I feel like I'm in the midst of a Wong Kar-wai film."

Rosemary's jaw dropped. "Waaah! You know Wong Kar-wai? I love his movies!"

"*Who* is this?" Freddie inquired.

"He's a Hong Kong director, one of the great auteurs of Asian cinema," George informed Freddie.

"Oh my goodness, I watched every one of his movies in the cinema the moment they came out in Hong Kong. I was obsessed. I wanted to be Faye Wong." Rosemary sighed as she popped a strawberry into her mouth.

"Me too!" Marian said. "I discovered his work when I moved here to do my residency at Saint Vincent's. I was always on call at the oddest hours, and I lived way up in Morningside Heights, so instead of trying to go home during my breaks, I would relax by going to the movies at Film Forum."

Rosemary nodded in approval. "*Days of Being Wild*. I could have watched that movie a million times. Leslie Cheung was so amazing, how I miss him.* Which one is your favorite?"

Marian paused in the middle of sucking on a mango seed. "Oh, come on, you can't make me choose! *Chungking Express* I can watch every night of the week. *In the Mood for Love* is an absolute masterpiece. But I have a soft spot for *Fallen Angels* because of Takeshi."

Rosemary banged her hand on the table dramatically. "Oh! My! God! Takeshi! I wanted to have his babies!"

"Get in line, sister, you would have to fight me over him!" Marian cackled.

"*Who* is this?" Freddie asked again.

"Takeshi Kaneshiro! He was the star in a few of Wong Kar-wai's movies, the dreamiest of all dreamboats.† Actually, don't you think George looks quite a bit like him?" Marian raised an eyebrow.

"My George? No way! George is handsome, but not *that kind of handsome!*"

"Hmm . . . I don't know about that," Marian retorted.

"But Takeshi was a bad boy, a sex god! Are you saying my son looks like a sex god?" Rosemary demanded.

George squirmed in his seat. "This is getting a bit awkward . . ."

---

* A brilliantly talented singer, songwriter, and actor who went from being a teen heartthrob to a pop icon in Asia, Leslie starred in Wong Kar-wei's *Days of Being Wild* and *Ashes of Time*, winning best actor awards for both performances. He committed suicide in 2003.

† Actually, Takeshi Kaneshiro appeared only in Wong's *Fallen Angels* and *Chungking Express*.

"No shit. I never realized Mama was a cougar." Freddie chuckled.

Marian turned to Lucie with a smile. "Why don't you show George your artwork?"

Lucie looked at her mom awkwardly. "Um, I'm not sure he really wants to see it now . . ."

"Actually, I'd love to see your work." George jumped up from the table, eager to escape.

The two of them headed out the French doors and took the winding, moss-covered path past the pool house. As they arrived at the art studio at the bottom of the garden, Lucie paused for a moment. "You should lower your expectations. My mom was talking things up way too much."

"I have no expectations," George said.

Lucie slid open the barn door, revealing a room flooded with natural light from the skylights in the roof. In front of them was a five-foot-square canvas Lucie had recently finished.

"This is my latest painting, and behind here is—"

"Wait," George said, putting a hand on her arm.

"Oh, sorry."

George took a few paces back and contemplated the painting for a few minutes, while Lucie stood next to the canvas uncomfortably.

"Okay, ready for the next one," he finally said.

Lucie shifted the painting aside to reveal the next canvas underneath, and after a few minutes, she brought out another and then another. As George stood in front of each painting, she wondered why he was studying the work so intently, scrutinizing every brushstroke from corner to corner. Was this all just an act of his? Was he just trying to humor her?

She studied him quietly as he studied her paintings, taking in all the changes that time had wrought—his chiseled features even more pronounced than before, his ripped triceps, the hard line of his pecs glimpsed under his loose tank top. The nut-brown tan of his youth had faded into marble white, and his lanky swimmer's body had transformed over the years into the sculpted physique of a committed athlete. She thought for a moment how she might paint his portrait.

"How long have you been working in this style?" George asked.

"Oh . . . probably since my freshman year of college," Lucie replied, a bit startled. Did he notice her staring at him?

"I really love this one," George said, pointing to one of the smaller paintings. Lucie walked over next to him to assess the work from his vantage point. They stood there in complete silence, so silent she could hear him breathing. She could smell the dry sweat on him from this morning's yoga, feel the heat radiating from his body. She found it unexpectedly alluring, and for a moment, as their shoulders touched, the sensation of his bare skin brushing against hers sent a faint shock wave all the way down to her toes. She stepped aside skittishly.

"Yeah, I think it's the best of the lot." George nodded, seemingly oblivious to what had just happened.

Recovering herself, Lucie stuttered, "It's, um, it's a bit unresolved, I think. It's an unfinished work."

"Well, how could it ever be finished? Grief never truly leaves us, does it?" George said softly.

Lucie froze in surprise. She knew he would be staring at her in that way of his, and she wasn't sure how she would feel if she looked back at him. She walked up to the canvas and began to put it away.

There was a knock on the barn door as Freddie came strolling in. "Fancy a sail, George? It's the perfect weather to take the boat out."

"Sure," George replied.

"Join us, Lucie?" Freddie asked.

"No, I think I'll stay here and straighten things up a bit," Lucie said.

"Suit yourself," Freddie said, as he put his arm around George's shoulders and led him out of the barn.

Lucie removed the painting from its easel and placed it in a stack. She was about to put another painting in front of it when she stopped, sank down onto the floor, and stared at the piece for a while. In the chaos of white-on-white brushstrokes, it all came flooding back for the very first time since she was eight years old . . .

All of a sudden, she found herself standing in the hallway of their apartment on Park Avenue as the paramedics hovered over her daddy, lying on the cold white marble floor, forcing the defibrillator against his chest.

"Stand by . . . one! Stay with me, there. Okay, stand by, shocking again, two!" the paramedic said calmly.

"Reggie, please don't leave me, please God," her mother wailed on the floor as another EMT tried to hold her back.

"Someone get the kid out of here," another voice said.

Before Lucie knew what was happening, a man grabbed her by the armpits and pulled her up, up, and away from the hallway, away from her father forever.

Lucie lay on the floor of the barn, gazing at her painting as tears rolled silently down her cheeks. She understood, for the first time, why she had bolted that afternoon in Capri when the man was having a heart attack in the piazzetta. George had been there that day. He was the only one who had witnessed her panic, her grief, as she saw that man dying, just like he was the only one who had ever looked into her paintings and saw what she saw.

VII

Ditch Plains

MONTAUK, LONG ISLAND

Every Sunday, Lucie's ritual was to jog along the coast just as the sun was rising and end up at Ditch Plains beach, a sandy stretch where dramatic moorlands rose up close to the shoreline. She would grab a coffee from Ditch Witch—the food truck in the parking lot—and sit on the rocks watching the early-morning surfers and locals out walking their dogs. Today, she had been admiring a surfer who looked far more skilled on the waves than many of the kooks out there. As he came ashore, she realized that it was George, his hair pulled back into a tight ponytail.

Why does he have to be so damn good at everything? Lucie thought, as she decided to give a friendly wave.

George came over, unzipped the top of his wetsuit, and began toweling off his torso. "Morning," he said, still panting a little.

"Did you catch any good waves?" Lucie made a concerted effort not to stare at the beads of water trickling down his abs.

"Nah." George plopped himself down on the sand beside her.

"I guess compared with Bondi Beach the waves out here must be pretty pathetic."

"Compared with just about anywhere. I needed a good swell, but beggars can't be choosers." George shrugged.

Lucie rolled her eyes. "Well, I'm sorry our beach doesn't meet your standards!"

"I never said that. You asked a question, I answered honestly."

Ugh. Why did I overreact like that? Lucie kicked herself, as she tried to extend an olive branch. "I guess you must miss the beaches in California . . ."

"I didn't actually surf much when I was up at Berkeley. No time. But I do miss the Sydney beaches, and the North Shore."

"Oahu?"

"Yeah, we have a house there."

"I remember your mom telling me. How often do you get back there?"

"These days about once a year if I'm lucky."

"So why'd you move to New York in the first place? Surely you could have worked somewhere with better beaches."

"I've always wanted to work with this firm. They're committed to creating consciously designed, affordable, sustainable spaces for working-class communities. I know that's something you might not understand."

Lucie frowned. "Why would you say that? Because you think I only work with rich people?"

George gave a half smirk. "You said it, not me."

"Look, many of my clients may be wealthy, but artists need to make a living. Most of the work I do is to connect collectors to young emerging artists who need all the support they can get. Especially female artists and minority artists—I'm on *their* side, I do everything I can to help boost their careers. I try to get their work placed with the most worthy, thoughtful collectors I know, so that hopefully their art will get the sort of notice it deserves."

"Sorry if I misunderstood. Freddie might have given me the wrong impression at lunch the other day," George offered contritely.

"Well, Freddie does a great job trivializing what I do. He's such an armchair socialist. It'll be interesting to see what he ends up doing with his life."

"Why do you say that?"

"Because he benefits from all sorts of privileges I'll never have."

"What do you mean?"

"Well, he's a man, for starters, and his genetic lottery numbers came in the day he was born. With his floppy Keanu Reeves hair and my dad's features, most people don't even realize he's got a drop of Chinese blood in him. He's grown up with all the privileges of being a male Churchill. This entire town caters to men like him. He's a legacy at Princeton and he's a shoo-in for any of the private men's clubs he wants to join."

"Are there still private clubs in New York that don't allow women in?"

"You better believe it! You know, there's an old exclusive men's club that was finally forced to let women in. Do you know what they did? They sneakily changed the menu so that the dishes that appealed to women would be awful. They made all the salads, the fish, the chicken—all lighter fare—purposely disgusting, hoping it would turn off the ladies and discourage them from joining. They kept the steaks and the burgers good, for the guys."

"Ha! That's evil. Still, Freddie's a good bloke. If he's a member of all these old stuffy clubs, I think he'll be a great advocate for change."

"Of course he will. I adore my brother, but still, it's not easy being related to that charmer. You know what happened once? We were in our elevator, coming home from the gym. I was in my workout clothes, holding a big paper sack with takeout. Some lady got into the elevator with us, obviously a visitor, and she smiled at me and asked, "Do you get good tips?""

George stared blankly at Lucie. "What did she mean?"

"Well, I had no clue either, but when Freddie started laughing hysterically, I finally figured it out. The lady thought I was delivering food. Like I was some Chinese delivery girl. That's always the story with me, but no one would ever mistake Freddie for the help."

George shook his head, appalled. Suddenly an idea occurred to him. "Hey, do you know any artists who might want to create a big outdoor mural? We're redoing this children's park up in the Bronx, and I think it could use a mural that maybe starts on a wall but extends along the ground and onto the skate ramp. We don't have a huge budget, but I think it could be good exposure for the artist."

"Are you kidding? I know about a hundred artists who would leap at the opportunity," Lucie said excitedly.

"All right then. I'll have my people call your people."

They both stared out at the ocean for a few moments, until Lucie decided to speak up again. "I think it's my turn to apologize. I'm sorry if I seemed a little prickly earlier . . . it's just that Ditch Plains is a pretty special place to me. My father used to take me out here all the time when I was little. He was friends with the owner of East Deck Motel, this wonderful old place that used to be across from the parking lot, and so he'd bring me out here to this beach all the time. It's where he taught me how to swim in the ocean . . ."

"I'm sorry if I insulted your beach. My pa taught me how to swim in the ocean too, at Coogee."

Lucie took a deep breath and ventured to say something that had been on her mind all week. "You know, when you were in my art studio, you said something about a painting that really struck me."

"The white one?"

"Yes, the white painting. Looking at it afterward gave me a vivid flashback to how my father had died. He had a heart attack at home, right in front of me, and I guess it was something I had completely erased from my memory until the other day."

George stared deeply into her eyes. "How old were you?"

"Eight."

"My father died when I was sixteen. He'd been ill a long time, but it was still terrible to see him fading away at the end. It took me years to get over it, not that one really gets over it. I can't imagine what it must have been like for you at that age."

"I completely blocked it out. I mean, I knew he'd had a heart attack, but until the other day I hadn't realized I was actually there."

George pondered her words and then looked her in the face. "Gosh, and then what happened on the piazzetta in Capri. No wonder you had to run . . ."

Lucie closed her eyes for a moment, saying nothing. They sat quietly like this for a few minutes, and as Lucie looked out at the undulating waves of the ocean, slate gray against the stark blue sky, she casually remarked, "This isn't quite the view from Casa Malaparte, but I've always loved it. It's where I learned to surf."

George turned to Lucie in surprise. "Wait a minute, you surf?"

"Of course I do."

"Really? Why haven't I ever seen you surfing out here?"

Lucie looked up at George. "Are you kidding me? I wouldn't waste my time. It's flatter than the duck pond in Central Park. You'd have to be Malibu Barbie to catch waves out here."

George let out a laugh.

"Speaking of which . . . ," Lucie said, as she tilted her head toward a statuesque blond girl paddling back to the shore.

The girl emerged from the water as if she were doing her best imitation of a James Bond girl and sauntered up to them with her surfboard just as George got up, planted a quick kiss on her cheek, and handed her his towel.

"Lucie, this is Viv."

"Hi," Lucie greeted her in surprise, staring at the intricate dragon tattoo on her arm.

"Hallo," Viv said in a gravelly Swedish accent.

"How do you know each other?" Lucie inquired.

"Oh, we met a few weeks ago. Viv was doing a shoot for *Harper's Bazaar* out at the Point," George answered.

"Resort-wear bikinis," Viv added.

"Of course." Lucie smirked.

"Um . . . Lucie's an old friend," George said to Viv.

"How nice to have old friends," Viv said to Lucie, before turning to George. "Come home for breakfast?"

"Sure," George replied, as he nodded goodbye to Lucie, picked up his surfboard, and walked off with the girl.

Saint Luke's Place

GREENWICH VILLAGE

Overheard in the canal room . . .

"You, Cecil Pike, are a visionary. This is Venice in the twenty-second century, that's what this is! If Carlos de Beistegui were alive, he would be foaming at the mouth with jealousy!"

"A canal flowing through a West Village town house! Only you could have imagined this, Cecil! When I saw the gondola floating across your living room out to the garden, I thought for sure I was tripping on mushrooms."

"Cecil! This is the most fabulous housewarming party I've ever been to. Is that Samin Nosrat cooking in the kitchen? OMG, I'm about to fangirl all over her!"

"*Comme cette maison est illustre, Cecil. C'est exquis! Le summum du chic! J'emménage immédiatement.*"

"*Mon dieu, quell compliment venant de vous, chère comtesse. J'en suis profondément honoré!*"

"I'll tell you one thing, I haven't seen anything this original since the Hilma show at the Guggenheim."

"Cecil, I hope you're not planning on raising your kids here.

Because I can just picture my future nephew or niece crawling off that mezzanine with no railing and falling headfirst into the canal."

"Freddie, that's why I hired the gondoliers to be full-time. They will double as lifeguards."

"A Yayoi Kusama Infinity Mirror powder room! How in the world did you pull that off, Cecil?"

"Are you Lucie? Cecil told me you're responsible for curating all the art here. To place the Kehinde Wiley and the Lucian Freud facing each other in the library—genius, pure genius. Here, let's follow each other on Instagram!"

"Cecil, what will it take for you to let us do a feature on the house?"

"You're too kind, Martina. But you know how private my family is. We don't ever let our houses be photographed."

. . .

Overheard in the mezzanine screening room . . .

"Oh my God, Lucie, guess what? Martina wants to feature the house in *Cabana*!"

"Really? How cool."

"I'm playing hard to get. I'll let her feature the house, but I want to make sure she puts *me* on the cover!"

"If that's what it takes to get the story, I'm sure she'll oblige you."

"Actually, it should be the both of us on the cover together. In this room. Sitting on the gondola."

"Um, we can talk about that later."

"Lucie, is that your mother over there talking to Hanya Yanagihara?"

"Yes."

"Do me the favor of removing her, please, before she says something stupid. Do you know what I heard her say to Bruce Weber? She said, 'Oh, I looove the photo you took of Lucie! I put it up on my fridge!' "

"I don't see what harm there was in that, Cecil. She was only try-ing to pay him a compliment."

"Lucie, that's like saying to Michelangelo, 'Oh, I put your little sculpture in the garden next to my plastic gnomes!' "

"Cecil, be nice."

"I *am* being nice. I'm saving your mother from embarrassing herself."

. . .

Overheard in the library . . .

"You know what I love about new money? They serve superb wine at their parties, because they are always trying to impress. And you know my policy: I only drink if it's very, very expensive wine and somebody else is paying."

"Ho ho ho! Mordecai, you're terrible! All the same, this is a lovely d'Yquem."

"Not as lovely as this little Vuillard. It sits so perfectly on this broken easel."

"But why is the easel broken?"

"Well, Robert broke it, of course. You know how he is. Every room he's done must look like it's *not* done, as if it had been aban-doned half a century ago by some consumptive aristocrats who could no longer afford firewood."

"Don't tell me the coffee stains on this Oushak aren't real?"

"Oh, Robert has the best coffee spiller anywhere. Diego, an abso-lute genius. Makes every stain look like it's been there for genera-tions. He's particularly good at faking dog stains on old chintz. You know, so it looks like your Rhodesian ridgeback has drooled all over that chaise longue for years and years."

"Hmm . . . I didn't realize Robert had a hand in all this. I thought Axel did it."

"Axel did the kitchens, the spa, and the glorious canal room; Francois did the screening room and the bedrooms; and Robert did the drawing room and the library."

"Cecil had *three* of the most expensive designers in the world on retainer?"

"Four, including yours truly. I helped with everything from the Cycladic period, of course."

"Well, I hope you made out like a bandit. Cheers to you, Mordecai!"

"And cheers to Lucie Churchill, that lucky girl. I knew from the moment I laid eyes on her in Capri she'd make a terrific match, although it turns out I failed to bet on the winning horse."

"Oooh. Pray tell?"

. . .

Overheard in the kitchen . . .

"Cecil, tell me, where are the appliances? Your kitchen looks like a Zen rock garden."

"Marian, first of all this is the *show* kitchen, not the real kitchen in the basement where the real cooking is done. Everything here is centered on the principles of *wabi-sabi,* about a oneness with things. See this black river rock from Wajima? You just wave your hand over the diagonal slit in the rock, and voilà!"

"Sweet Jesus, what's that coming out of the floor? Is that the dishwasher?"

"No, it's a truffle vault. Axel put the dishwashers in the china room."

"Holy moly! Wait till Charlotte sees this! Can I please bring her over when she's here?"

"God help us—Charlotte is coming back to New York?"

"She's back for a visit next month, didn't you know?"

"Marian, please don't tell me she's staying with you in East Hampton."

"Of course she is."

"Well, I shall make myself very scarce."

"Mom, does Charlotte really have to stay with us? You know how Cecil gets around her. When we were in London he broke out in hives the day she tried to take us to some hot new restaurant in Maida Vale."

"Was it really Charlotte that caused his hives, or was he having an allergic reaction to something he ate?"

"Well, I do get a migraine whenever I'm forced to go outside of Zone 1, but I think it's safe to say I have a Charlotte Barclay allergy. It's not as bad as my allergy to South African wines, but it's an allergy nonetheless."

.　.　.

Overheard in the china room . . .

"Wah! Three separate dishwashers for different types of china. What a house!"

"It's actually three town houses put together, Mrs. Zao."

"I suspected as much. It must be the biggest house in New York, yes?"

"It's big, but I'm sure there's something bigger. The thing about the superrich is that they always need more space with no people in it."

"You always know everything, Freddie. Three dishwashers! Three town houses! And here I can't even find a simple flat for myself in New York."

"I didn't know you were looking for a place in the city, Mrs. Zao."

"Now that George got a promotion at his firm and will be designing this new apartment complex in Queens that's made only of recycled trash, it looks like he will be staying for a while. So I think I must get a place in the city for myself. I don't want to be in that big Shittinghurst in the winter, and I can't keep on staying with him at his apartment . . . How will he ever find a girlfriend if his mother is there all the time?"

"You're a wise woman, Mrs. Zao. Sometimes it gets a bit tricky when I bring girls home. They all end up wanting to chat with my mom! What sort of place are you looking for?"

"Well, I like the older buildings here, like the Dakota one where John Lennon lived. What do you call them? Pre-bomb?"

"Prewar, Mrs. Zao."

"Yes. I don't need anything too big for myself—just four or five bedrooms will do."

"You know there's an apartment that's about to go on sale in our building? The old lady who owned it had lived there since the thirties but preferred to spend the last twenty-five years living in Beth Israel Hospital, even though she was in perfect health. It's beautiful, like a time capsule with all the period details intact—I got a chance to sneak in and see it last week when the realtors were taking photos."

"Really? I love your building!"

"In fact, I have the realtor's card in my wallet right here . . ."

"Freddie, you really need to get a new wallet. That thing is falling apart."

"I know. But I can't bear to change it. It was my father's."

. . .

Overheard in the pool room . . .

"It's entirely eco-friendly and organic, George. It's a self-sustaining system: the fish droppings in the koi pond fertilize the aquatic plants in the reflecting pool, which in turn create biological filters that clean the water in the lap pool."

"Yeah, I've seen natural swimming pools like this before."

"Why do I get the sense that you're not impressed?"

"It's very impressive, Lucie. I've never seen a trilevel infinity pool of such scale, two stories underground."

"Cecil's very proud of it. He spent a year obsessing over every detail of the pool—it was his idea to make it glass-bottomed so you could see right into the wine cellar."

"It's very clever. He can stare at all his pinot noirs while he's swimming the butterfly."

"Or maybe we can invite *Viv* over and you can stare at her tattoos while she does the backstroke."

"Viv was on the Swedish national swim team. I'm sure she'd love to use this pool."

"It wasn't a real invitation, George. I was just responding to your snide remark. I know you don't care for this house."

"How have I given you that impression?"

"I see the way you're staring at everything in disapproval."

"Lucie, you're being absurd. I'm staring because I've never seen anything like this before. There's a Venetian canal in the living room!"

"So you like the house?"

"Lucie, you're the one who has to live here. Do *you* like the house?"

"I like it, I like it a lot. So . . . how long have you and Viv been dating?"

"We're not dating. She's just a surf buddy."

"Uh-huh."

. . .

Overheard in the warming room . . .

"This is my favorite room, Cecil. I love the scent of oud and the fire pit and all these velvet chaise longues placed in a sunburst. What exactly do you use this space for—séances?"

"It's where you relax and warm up before going into the infrared sauna or the cold plunge pool or one of the spa treatment rooms, Mother."

"How lovely! I want to warm myself up here sometime. This party is *such* a success, darling. Everyone is wowed by the house, as they should be. Do you know what Mordecai von Ephrussí told me? He was so impressed by your vision that he's going to nominate you for the Rome Prize."

"Mon dieu!"

"And Lucie's been brilliant tonight. Absolutely brilliant! You know, to be honest, I was a little doubtful when you said she would rise to the occasion. She's soooo WASPy in some ways, it was hard for me to picture her without her collection of old canvas tote bags or that little black scrunchie she uses for her ponytail. But seeing her tonight in the Valentino and the Carnet earrings I lent her, I thought, *That girl cleans up gooooood!* She's absolutely precious, and she's beginning to remind me of myself."

"I told you, Mother, she's more like you than you think. Did you hear the raves she got for curating my new art collection? Jeffrey Deitch tried to hire her on the spot, and the Spraggs want her to redo all the art at their family foundation."

"Yes, yes, Lucie's a true gem. She's like the Koh-i-Noor, a diamond that only gets discovered once a millennium. Natural and unspoiled in so many ways, but with the most polished pedigree."

"She's got the blood of Ming emperors flowing through her veins, mingling with the blood of Old New York and British aristocracy," Cecil declared. "Can you imagine what our children will look like? Quarter Asians are the most beautiful species in the world—just look at Prince Nikolai of Denmark, who's modeling for all the top fashion houses now, or that blond kid on *Saved by the Bell*, or Phoebe Cates, who still looks like she's twenty-five! Our children will never age!"*

"Oh, Cecil, should we move up the wedding? I can't wait to have my quarter-Asian grandchildren who will never age!"

.   .   .

---

* Prince Nikolai of Denmark has a Danish father and a mother who's actually of English, Czech, Austrian, and Chinese ancestry. Mark-Paul Gosselaar, aka Zack Morris on *Saved by the Bell*, has a German father and a Dutch Indonesian mother. Phoebe Cates has a Jewish father and a mother who's half Chinese and half Russian. And yes, she still looks twenty-five.

After all the guests had left, Lucie took the elevator up to the fifth-floor master suite, annoyed with herself that she was still fixating over her exchange with George in the pool room. Why had she offered to give him a tour? Why did she press him about the house? Why did she feel like she was being judged? Why the hell did she ask him about Viv? Would he think she was jealous or something? Ugh, why did she even care at all? She wondered if she was being overly sensitive to everything because she was simply fatigued. Social gatherings like this really took it out of her, in contrast to Cecil, who seemed to be energized by them. She entered the bedroom to find Cecil sprawled on the bed, eagerly scrolling through all the Instagram posts that his friends had made from the party.

"Whitney posted a pic of himself on the gondola. And I love this picture Rozi posted on the roof garden with the both of us next to the Richard Serra. Poor thing, she doesn't have that many followers—she only got thirty-five hundred likes."

Lucie reached around, trying to take off her gown. "This dress is impossible! Will you help unbutton me, Cecil?"

"Of course. Right after I check if Patrick's photos are up on his website," Cecil said.[*] "Son of a bitch! Nothing yet. Patrick, get off your lazy ass and upload your pics!" Cecil ranted at the screen as he got up from the bed and headed over to where Lucie was standing. He began fastidiously undoing the tiny buttons along the back of her gown. "I know you had your heart set on wearing that little black Mouret, but thank you for wearing this dress my mother bought you."

"You're welcome, and you were absolutely right, Cecil. It matched the red in the Richter perfectly. I got so many compliments. I'm just not used to wearing such a bold color."

---

[*] That would be legendary party photographer Patrick McMullan, of course, who has chronicled New York's nightlife for over four decades. If Patrick wasn't snapping away at your party, it might as well not have happened.

"You looked stunning, everyone said so. Mother wants you to come with her to the couture shows next January."

"Oh, Cecil, I'm not sure I would ever be comfortable spending that kind of money on clothes . . ."

"Don't worry, my pet, Mother will pay for everything. She's just dying to introduce you to all her designers and spoil you rotten. By the way, do you have a family tiara?"

"A tiara? Actually, believe it or not, I think my grandmother has one. It's an old heirloom with mine-cut diamonds. I've never seen it in real life, only in pictures, but I hear it's in her vault."

"Oh, goody."

"Cecil, I told you, Cacky's going to get everything of Granny's. You know what she's already done? She's gone around putting Post-it notes with her name behind every painting she wants in the apartment."

"The nerve of that woman! Don't worry, I'll work on your grandmother, and until that Magritte and the tiara become yours, Mother thinks you need your own. She'll take you to get one at Mellerio in Paris. Hmm, maybe we can find one that has some Chinese provenance, maybe something with jade!"

"Cecil, when am I ever going to need a tiara?"

"Baby, you're going to need it for the wedding! Besides, Mother and I get invited to court dinners all the time when we're in Europe. The von Habsburgs, von Auerspergs, von Hohenlohes—all the vons dress formally for dinner. You're going to need a tiara like you need oxygen."

Lucie's gown fell to the floor as soon as Cecil unfastened the hook, and she bent down to pick it up.

"Those Ludovic de Saint Sernin panties should be illegal. I just went from six to midnight. Why did you have to bend down in front of me like that?"

"Why did you let the dress fall to the floor?" Lucie retorted with a chuckle.

Cecil pulled her toward him and began kissing her neck, reaching that sweet spot right below her ear. Lucie sighed softly in languorous pleasure.

"Er . . . will you do Lady Mary, please?"

"Okay." Lucie nodded, clearing her throat and breaking out her best British accent: "What on God's earth are you doing here? I really don't think it's appropriate for you to be in my bedchamber, sir."

"I couldn't resist, I had to see you! Please, let me worship you in my seraglio and bring you to the gates of paradise," Cecil said in a vaguely Omar Sharif–esque accent.

"But my lady's maid could discover us at any minute."

"Don't worry, I gave Anna a very generous tip to disappear. Besides, she's too busy schtupping that gimp Bates in the servants' quarters to notice your cries of pleasure tonight."

"No, you're wrong. Anna is always watching over me."

"Well, let me watch over this," Cecil said as he slowly unhooked Lucie's bra from behind. As she turned to face him, he stared at her with his mouth agape.

"Don't move!" he whispered, utterly transfixed by the sight of her body. As he traced the curve of her breasts with his finger, he muttered, "I can't believe you're mine. You're absolutely perfect! You're more exquisite than the Venus de Milo!"

He buried his face into her chest as she began to unzip his perfectly pressed Dormeuil trousers.

"Mr. Pamuk!" Lucie let out an exaggerated gasp. "My goodness, is this what happens to boys who eat too much Turkish delight?"

"Sorry, Lady Mary isn't doing it for me tonight. Can we transition to Alexandra?"

Lucie almost wanted to roll her eyes. She was enjoying the Lady Mary pantomime, but she knew this was going to happen—Cecil always ended up wanting Alexandra.

As if sensing her reticence, Cecil pleaded, "I promise this is the only time I'll ask you for the rest of the month."

"Well, in that case . . ." Lucie gave him a mischievous smile and took a deep breath, raised her arm, and slapped him clear across the face.

Cecil gasped loudly, grinning. "The beef Wellington is fully baked now!"

"Nikolai Alexandrovich, you have behaved very badly," Lucie scolded, her Agent Amasova impersonation spot-on.*

"What have I done to disappoint you this time, Alexandra Feodorovna? Is the new Fabergé cigarette case not to your liking?"

"Why would you ever give me a cigarette case? First of all, smoking causes cancer, and those vulgar diamonds on the case . . ."

"Wait—there aren't any diamonds on the Fabergé case, baby. Remember, it's jeweled silver gilt and lavender guilloche enamel."

"Don't interrupt me, you miserable serf! The enameled cigarette case looks so common, like something Prince Felix Yusupov would give to one of his lesser servants."

"I'm truly sorry, my empress. I have failed you."

"Let's see . . . how should you be properly punished today?"

"Check out my royal scepter, baby," Cecil said eagerly.

"You peasant! How dare you insult me with your . . . your filthy Rasputin?" Lucie roared with outrage.

"Ooohh! Ooohh!!!" Cecil moaned in delight. "Scold me more, my queen!"

"I am not your queen. I am your imperial majesty! Pathetic excuse of a man! How will you ever defend us against the revolutionaries? Do you not hear them chanting for our heads outside the gates of Tsarskoe Selo?"

"I'm a contemptible fool, Your Imperial Majesty!"

Lucie bit her lip so she wouldn't laugh at the ridiculousness of it all. She couldn't believe how much he was enjoying this. "The revo-

---

* My favorite Bond girl from the Roger Moore era, Major Anya Amasova (aka Agent XXX) was a Russian KGB agent played by the incomparable Barbara Bach in *The Spy Who Loved Me*.

lutionaries are at the gates of the palace! And here all you have is this jeweled heirloom dagger to defend yourself . . ."

"Tell me about the heirloom dagger! Tell me more about it, baby," Cecil grunted, his jaw clenched and his breath quickening.

"It's a scimitar with a gold filigree handle studded with ancient Burmese jade and a scabbard crafted of lapis lazuli and inlaid amber. The razor-sharp blade is hand-forged of meteoric iron, hardened and hardened by centuries of pounding against the jagged steppes of the Caucasus."

"Agggrrrhhhh!" Cecil shuddered in ecstasy, hugging Lucie tightly as he began sobbing against her shoulder like a little boy. "Alexandra Feodorovna, I love you."

"I love you too, Nikolai," Lucie murmured softly.

"Call me Alexei," Cecil whimpered.

"Alexei, Alexei Nikolaevich," Lucie whispered as she held him, wondering why he always wanted to be called by the name of a tragic young hemophiliac prince. As her fingers ran through the soft hair on the back of Cecil's head, she suddenly imagined she was stroking George's silky hair while he kissed her. Wildly, slowly, as the memory of his mouth all over her came rushing back so vividly.

IX

Dorset Yacht Club

SAG HARBOR

The laminated sign on the brass stand discreetly placed by the members' door read:

HOUSE RULES REMINDER

**PLEASE DISCOURAGE YOUR GUESTS FROM
ARRIVING IN IMPROPER ATTIRE WITH THE
NOTION OF DRESSING AT THE CHECK ROOM.**

The Club Committee

Cecil and Lucie pulled up to the valet of the club in his recently acquired 1973 Ferrari Dino 246 GTS.* The paintwork on the car was

---

* Named after Enzo Ferrari's late son, Alfredo "Dino," the 2.0-liter, V-6-powered mid-engine open-top sports car was designed by the great Pininfarina, with original, unmolested specimens going for upward of $400,000.

done in an exceedingly rare "Bianco Polo Park," so Cecil insisted that Lucie wear the white Schiaparelli couture shift dress that his mother had also recently acquired for her, and he had outfitted himself in matching white sea island cotton trousers, a snow-white cashmere sweater, and his bespoke Corthay Cannes suede loafers.

Dorset was arguably the snootiest private yacht club on the Eastern Seaboard, with a membership descended from the oldest Hamptons families, and the style of the club was conspicuously shabby and its members went to great lengths to amplify this aesthetic. Dorset members might have an Aston hiding in their garages on Further Lane or Captains Neck Lane, but they drove to the club in dusty Wagoneers with towels covered in dog hair over the back seats or thirty-year-old Land Rovers with cracked rear windows and faded Mondale-Ferraro bumper stickers. The men took great care to wear only the most threadbare of their Peter Elliot seersucker blazers and faded Vineyard Vines reds, while many of the usually chic womenfolk kept special "for Dorset only" wardrobes consisting of only their frumpiest dresses from the likes of J. McLaughlin or Lilly Pulitzer and hand-me-down Jacques Cohen espadrilles.

Lucie would normally have been embarrassed to show up at the club in such a fancy car, but she was used to Cecil's ways by now and saw no point in challenging him. Cecil, who took great pride in his sartorial efforts, would always say, "My father was a WASP, but it skipped a generation." He emerged from behind the wheel and handed the valet his keys, patted away the wrinkles on his trousers, and walked jauntily around to escort his beautiful fiancée into the clubhouse. He couldn't wait to take pictures of the both of them dressed so *après-beach* on the Insta-worthy private dock. As they entered the foyer and Lucie approached the check-in desk to sign them in, a ruddy-faced female attendant gave Cecil's outfit a once-over and said, "He can't go in like this, Ms. Churchill. No collar."

"Oh, shit, I forgot. Men have to wear collared shirts in the dining room, Cecil," Lucie said sheepishly.

Cecil stared at Lucie and the attendant incredulously. "But

that's absurd. This is a *very* dressy outfit, especially for an al fresco luncheon."

"Sorry, it's the dress code, sir. Your top doesn't have a collar."

"This isn't a *top*. It's a V-neck Henley designed by one of the greatest and most elusive Belgian designers, a man who hasn't been photographed in thirty years. It's made of the finest cashmere harvested from baby Zalaa Jinst white goats that roam free on the Mongolian steppes,* and it's hand-knotted in Lake Como by old Italian women with arthritis and varicose veins in a beautiful atelier within spitting distance of George and Amal Clooney's villa."

"And it doesn't have a collar," the attendant said simply.

"This is ridiculous! I've been to dinners at royal palaces more casually attired than this! I am looking into your dining room right now and I can clearly see little boys in shorts and flip-flops."

"Wearing collared shirts," the attendant repeated.

"Do you mean to tell me that the little boy in that shirt with the creepy snowman is more appropriately dressed than me?"

"That's not a snowman, that's Olaf from *Frozen*," the attendant corrected.

"I don't care if it's Olafur Eliasson, it looks putrid."

"Cecil, please, let's not argue . . . ," Lucie began.

Cecil ignored her and continued on his rant. "How much do you make working here? I bet you my outfit costs at least ten times more than your monthly salary. I'm wearing about twenty thousand dollars' worth of clothing right as I stand! If you want to include my Nautilus, it's a hundred and fifty thousand dollars' worth. You're telling me that's not appropriate enough for this godforsaken club?"

Lucie's face reddened in embarrassment. She could not believe Cecil just said that to the attendant.

---

* No baby Zalaa Jinst white goats were harmed in the making of this novel. Cecil's sweater was actually made from adult goats that grow long, fine fibers in the winter to protect themselves, and herders hand comb the fibers from the goats since shearing them can be too stressful for the animals. An average-sized Zalaa Jinst cashmere sweater requires the wool from approximately four adult goats.

The woman sighed. "Sir, I make fifteen dollars an hour, and I don't make the rules here. You can go home and change into a collared shirt, or you can buy this polo tee here. If you read the sign at the entrance, I'm not supposed to let you change into this shirt at the club, but tell you what, I'll look away this time."

She reached under the glass counter and got out a light blue collared knit polo with the club's rope-and-anchor insignia sewn at the breast.

"Where's it made?"

"I have no idea." The woman checked the label. "Myanmar."

"Over my cold, dead bod—"

"We'll take it!" Lucie said quickly. "Charge it to my account."

"I can't believe you're making me do this," Cecil said in dismay. "I don't want to change into a shirt from Myanmar in that sad toilet with the peeling walls and the rotting wood floors!"

"I'll have you know our rotting wood floors are very coveted, sir. Every week some fancy decorator comes in wanting to buy up all our floors," the attendant said indignantly.

Lucie pushed him toward the men's room. "Please just go change, dear, and I'll see you in the dining room. I'm sure my mother and Freddie are already on desserts by now."

As Cecil went reluctantly to change, Lucie sprinted into the dining room and found her mother and brother seated on the outdoor terrace overlooking the club's private marina.

"Where have you been?" Marian asked.

"Sorry, wardrobe malfunction. Whatever you do, don't say anything about Cecil's shirt, *pleeeease,*" Lucie warned as she sank wearily into one of the canvas deck chairs.

Two minutes later, Cecil sauntered onto the terrace in his Dorset Yacht Club polo tee, worn untucked over his cotton trousers.

Freddie couldn't resist. "Cool polo, brah."

Cecil, observing Freddie's faded old Lacoste tennis shirt disdainfully, replied, "Thanks, I rather like it. Don't you think it shows off my biceps, Lucie?"

"It sure does, Cecil."

"Cecil, how smart you look!" Marian said, genuinely thinking that he looked handsomer than usual. The shirt was a breath of fresh air after all his fussy designer duds.

"Now, are we all going to do the lobster lunch buffet today?" Lucie said.

"Well, I just got a text from Charlotte. Her plane got in early so she's coming straight from the Jitney to join us."

"First the collared shirt nazi, and now the Charlotte has landed," Cecil muttered under his breath, as everyone else at the table pretended not to hear him.

Minutes later, Charlotte appeared at the table all flustered and laden with shopping bags. Everyone except Cecil got up from the table to give her hugs.

"Marian, I'm so sorry, I took a cab here, and I only have pounds on me. Do you have some cash for me to tip the driver? He's waiting."

"Um, let me see . . . ," Marian said, digging into her purse. "I'm sorry, I only have a few quarters."

"Does anyone else . . . ?" Charlotte looked around the table.

Everyone shook their heads.

"Sorry, who uses cash anymore?" Freddie said. "Wait a minute, let me see if Frankie has any change."

"Why didn't you just add the tip to your credit card charge?" Lucie asked.

"I'm so jetlagged, I forgot. Plus, if I left the tip on my credit card, wouldn't that make the tax amount higher by a few dollars?"

Marian simply shook her head, not wanting to think how much Charlotte's trust fund must be worth at this point. The Barclay family office was even moving into swanky new digs at Hudson Yards next year.

Freddie came back from the maître d' with a twenty.

"Oh, that's too much of a tip for the driver, don't you think?" Charlotte wondered. "Can we see if anyone can break that into smaller bills?"

"Freddie, just give it to the driver," Marian commanded.

"Classic Madam Buzzkill," Freddie muttered under his breath as he ran off.

Charlotte was still standing, looking rather preposterous with half a dozen shopping bags across each arm. "I checked my luggage with the nice lady but thought I'd better not check all these precious duty-free gifts—wouldn't want them to accidentally go missing," she said breathlessly as she began distributing her bags. "Marian, here's that hand cream you wanted from Boots. And, Lucie, some of your favorite royal blend tea and salted caramel biscuits from Fortnum & Mason. Freddie, thank you for taking care of the driver. I thought you might like these English chocolates." She handed him an oversize bar of chocolate from a brand that was available at every deli along Lexington. "And Cecil, let's see, I got you a signed copy of Mary Berry's new book . . . Now, where did I put it?"

"Charlotte, please sit down. We can do presents later. Now, shall we all do the lobster buffet or order off the menu?" Marian said.

"I don't care as long as I can steal some coconut macaroons from the dessert table," Freddie said.

"Oh, before we order, I should wash my hands. I haven't washed since JFK," Charlotte said, getting up again.

"For fuck's sake!" Cecil muttered, throwing his napkin on the table. "Arcadia Mueffling has the Duke and Duchess of Ravenscourt over this weekend, and I could be at her stunning Atelier AM–designed house on Gin Lane drinking decent champagne and enjoying a special luncheon cooked by José Andrés right now!"

Lucie, Freddie, and Marian gaped at Cecil, not sure how to react to his outburst.

"Cecil, I'm very sorry you have to endure this. But Charlotte did just arrive straight from London, and naturally she's a bit out of it. If you'd prefer to go to your royal luncheon, please don't let us keep you," Marian said calmly.

Cecil, realizing that he had crossed the line, forced a smile and said, "It's fine, Marian. I'm sorry if I was being rude. I think I'm just faint with hunger."

"Why don't you go ahead to Arcadia's and I'll join you in a little bit?" Lucie gingerly proposed.

"No, no, I'll wait for you, baby."

. . .

Charlotte was in the process of hovering over the toilet seat when she heard the door fling open and someone enter the next stall. From the force of the stream hitting the water, she knew it had to be a man.

"Excuse me, this is the ladies' room," she said in a loud voice.

"Oh, sorry, I thought this was the men's. It had a picture of a sail on the door," the man in the next stall replied.

"Yes, it's rather confusing if you're not a member. The sails are for the ladies. The men's has the drawing of the rope on the door," Charlotte said, feeling a little awkward as she tried to minimize the sound of her peeing. She came out of her stall and headed for the sink. A few moments later the man also emerged and they caught sight of each other at the same moment in the big wicker mirror.

"George Zao!" Charlotte gasped as though she had seen a ghost.

"Oh, hi." George smiled back, looking far less surprised.

"What are you doing here?"

"I have a tennis match with Freddie."

"What! You know Freddie? Does Lucie know you're here?"

George frowned. "I dunno. Maybe."

"What are you doing in Sag Harbor?"

Taking his turn to wash his hands, George explained, "I work in the city. We took a summer house here."

"Who is 'we'? Are you married?"

"No, I spend weekends here with my mother," George replied, rather amused by Charlotte's apparent confusion. As he headed out the door, he said, "I believe we'll be seeing you later. My mother has invited everyone over for dinner tonight. She's having her new chef who's just arrived from Vancouver make Peking duck."

"Oh," Charlotte said, as her mind began spinning into overdrive. She walked slowly back to the table with a strained expression on her face and said nothing as she sat down.

"Okay, we've taken a vote and we're all doing the buffet," Marian announced, as she and Freddie leaped up from their seats and made a beeline for the lobsters.

Lucie was about to get up when Charlotte gripped her arm forcefully and stared into her eyes. "*I saw him*. In the ladies' room."

"Who?"

"George Zao!"

"George was in the ladies' room?"

"He came in by mistake. Why didn't you tell me that man was here?"

"What is there to tell? He lives in New York and East Hampton now."

"East Hampton! But that's too close! I thought maybe he'd be in Hampton Bays or Quogue with all the summer riffraff. And that ghastly mother of his is here too?"

"Yes. Mom's become friendly with her."

"How typical. She's trying to cultivate your mother! Does it make things awkward? Where are they in East Hampton?"

"Cecil got him to rent Cissinghurst."

"*Cecil?* How do they know each other?"

"It's a long story . . ."

"Oh dear God. Has George been stalking you? Is that why he came to East Hampton?"

"It's nothing like that, Charlotte," Lucie said, exasperated.

"Does Cecil know about you and George?"

"Of course not."

"Oh, Lucie, my poor Lucie. How mortifying for you! I hope it doesn't bring back too many awful memories. Remember, you were just a teenager then! You were so young and impressionable, and swept up by your first summer romance with an exotic foreigner!"

Lucie shook her head in frustration, annoyed at Charlotte's over-reaction. At the same time, a tide of shame suddenly came seeping into her mind.

"You should have told me he had resurfaced! I could have helped."

"Charlotte, don't start with all that again. Capri is ancient history. I'm about to be happily married and George couldn't care less about me. He's got this Swedish model girlfriend with blond hair like an Afghan hound's and legs that go up to her throat."

"Really?" Charlotte paused. "But what would happen if—"

Lucie stood up abruptly. "Charlotte, I don't want to hear it. I want my lobster. Coming or not?"

X

Cissinghurst

EAST HAMPTON

The chef was presenting a pair of glistening roasted Peking ducks to everyone at the table just as Cecil arrived for Rosemary's dinner party. He came bearing a case of Dugat-Py Mazis-Chambertin Burgundy for Rosemary and a profusion of flowers.

"I'm sorry I was in such a foul mood this morning." Cecil smiled sheepishly as he presented Marian and Charlotte with enormous bouquets.

"What beautiful peonies!" Marian remarked.

"And that's not all," Cecil said, as he whipped out two boxes of chocolate truffles and handed one each to Marian and Charlotte.

"Ooh! Truffles from Maison du Chocolat! My favorite! You're absolutely forgiven, Cecil," Marian exclaimed, as Freddie leaned over and swiped a truffle with stealth speed and popped it into his mouth.

"Thank you, Cecil. I'm not even sure what we're forgiving you for," Charlotte gushed, as she began to think of whom she could regift the expensive chocolates to.

"What happened this morning?" Auden whispered to Freddie.

"Cecil was just being Cecil," Freddie whispered back, his front teeth all brown from the chocolate.

"Darling, could you come with me for a moment?" Cecil asked Lucie.

"Of course," she said, getting up from the table. The two of them went into the cavernous oak-paneled living room, which was dominated by three huge Tiffany glass chandeliers and Venetian revival furniture. Cecil and Lucie sat down together on the Knole sofa and, clearing his throat, Cecil began:

"Darling, I have to explain about this morning. When my family first moved from Midland to Houston, we were invited to lunch at the local country club by these business associates of my dad's. This couple was trying to do Dad a favor and get us into one of Houston's most exclusive clubs. We got all dressed up—my father put on a new suit he had bought at Barneys New York in the Galleria, my mother bought a dress from the Yves Saint Laurent boutique at the Pavillion and took me shopping for my outfit at Neiman's. I was seven and thought I looked supercool in a new striped dress shirt and dress pants from some Italian brand I couldn't pronounce.* We got to the country club and my mother immediately realized that everything about our outfits was wrong. *Everything.* My father's suit looked too shiny, her Yves Saint Laurent cocktail dress was too flashy for Sunday brunch, and, worst of all, I wasn't wearing a jacket and tie, which was required. I was seven years old, for fuck's sake. Who knew that all the men, no matter what age, were required to wear a jacket and tie? The coat check man at the club tried to be helpful and lent me a jacket and tie. I was very small for my age, and even the kid's-size jacket was so large it looked like an overcoat on me. And the tie was this horrendous pickle-green thing from the seventies that smelled of mothballs. But I had no choice, I was forced to wear it, and I felt so humiliated. I remember all the other boys in their smart navy Brooks Brothers jackets and chinos staring at me like I was some freak."

* Ermenegildo Zegna. Go ahead, see how fast you can say it.

"Oh, Cecil . . . ," Lucie began, feeling guilty.

"We weren't accepted into the club, of course, and I realize now it had little to do with how we dressed. At the end of the day, our money was just too new, my dad hadn't gone to the same schools as all the other fellows, and my mother looked a little too exotic for their tastes."

Lucie gave him a confused look. "Too exotic? But your mother looks like Robin Wright."

"You didn't know my mother before she changed her hair and had all her work done. She looked like Salma Hayek. She was very pretty, but it didn't matter to those people. My mother swore that day that she would make it her mission to become one of the best dressed women in the world, and by God, did she ever."

Lucie nodded. "Your mom is the chicest lady I know."

"I know it sounds silly, but this morning at Dorset triggered me, and it brought me back to that moment when I was seven. I felt like a complete outsider back then, and I felt like one again today. It made me realize that no matter how much money you have, no matter what you've accomplished, these people will just find new ways to make you feel excluded."

"Cecil, I understand, really I do. You've seen firsthand that among my father's family, I don't really feel like I belong. They'll never truly see me as one of them."

"I know, Lucie. That's why we're meant for each other. You are a thousand times more beautiful than anyone in that family of yours, and you know what? They're just jealous. I could see it in all their eyes at our engagement party. You and I, we're a threat to them. I thank God every day for my little bit of Latin and royal French-Cajun blood. We are marvelously photogenic, we have exquisite style and taste, we're famous to only the right people, and we live fabulous lives they will never begin to understand. Still, that doesn't excuse my behavior this morning. I was a complete ass. Will you forgive me?"

"Of course, Cecil," Lucie said, as she embraced him on the sofa.

"I'm sorry I made you go through all that. We should have left, really."

Cecil reached into his pocket and took out a velvet box. *Oh God, not another ring,* Lucie couldn't help thinking.

"Here's a little present for you. I saw it on Newtown Lane and just couldn't resist."

Lucie opened the box and in it was a strange-looking key fob. "What's this?"

"Come outside with me," Cecil said.

They walked to the front door of the house, and parked in the circular driveway was a brand-new platinum-white Aston Martin DB11 Volante convertible with a big pink-and-silver bow on its hood.

"Your MINI Cooper's almost ten years old now. It's high time you were driving something newer, safer, and befitting your status," Cecil commented.

"Oh, Cecil, you shouldn't have!" Lucie sighed, wondering how she would get over the embarrassment of driving such a flashy car.

At this point, everyone had come outside to see what the commotion was, and Cecil proudly showed off his new gift to Lucie.

Freddie whistled. "That's a nice set of wheels. The two of you should get into fights more often."

"My goodness" was all Marian could say.

"You're very blessed, Lucie," Auden said, checking out the instrument panel of the car.

"I know," Lucie replied, trying to sound grateful.

George remained silent, but Rosemary hugged Lucie excitedly. "Lucky girl! Cecil, how much did you pay for this?"

"Er . . . it was a little over 225k."

"Wah, so cheap! In Hong Kong, this car would cost at least half a mil."

"Well, you should get one then, Mrs. Zao," Cecil remarked.

"I just might. But how can I drive such a car to garage sales? I won't be able to get any bargains if they see me pull up in this thing!" Rosemary said.

"We really should go back in before the Peking duck gets cold," Marian warned.

"Oh, shit!" Freddie exclaimed, as he rushed back into the dining room ahead of the others.

"Wait! We need to take some pictures of me and Lucie by her new car. George, would you do us the honor?" Cecil asked.

"Sure." George grabbed Cecil's phone while Cecil draped himself over the hood of the car, raising his arms and propping his head up with his hands as if he were Ferris Bueller, all the while directing Lucie. "Now, Lucie, just stand a little to your right and lean back onto me. Legs apart, like you're a Bond girl. Twist yourself into an S shape. No, Lucie, S shape, not L."

Lucie contorted herself against the cold metallic hood, mortified by the ridiculousness of the pose. She wondered if this was how *Sports Illustrated* swimsuit models must feel when they were trying to look sexy balancing on sand dunes. Did these poses just come effortlessly to someone like Viv?

"Where's your surf buddy Viv tonight?" Lucie asked George with a wink.

"She's in Miami."

"Another bikini shoot?"

"Probably," George answered.

"George, could you put it on beauty mode and raise the phone really high? That's the best angle," Cecil called out.

"Sure."

"Smile, Lucie," George called out.

"Don't smile too much, babe, it won't look sexy," Cecil said as he tilted his head ever so slightly.

Lucie stopped smiling abruptly. She felt her face get hot as she tried not to look at George, more out of embarrassment for Cecil than for herself.

After the impromptu photo shoot, the three of them went back into the house, and as everyone began tucking into the aromatic crispy duck drizzled with sweet bean sauce and wrapped in delicate rice-flour pancakes, Cecil looked at his plate in dismay. "My tortilla is filled with nothing but duck skin."

"It's not a tortilla, it's a Chinese pancake," Freddie said with a laugh.

"The skin is the delicacy in Peking duck," Marian explained. "It's air-dried for seventy-two hours and glazed with spices before it's specially roasted to produce this perfect golden crispy skin."

"Sorry, I can't eat the skin of any animal, not even if it's a delicacy," Cecil said.

"*Hiyah,* have some of the noodles with duck meat, then," Rosemary said, heaping a portion of the braised e-fu noodles with duck onto his plate. "Don't tell me you're just like that model lesbian friend of George's! She won't eat any animal skin because she thinks it's too fattening."

Freddie's curiosity was piqued. "Is she a model lesbian or a lesbian who's a model?"

"I'm not sure. Both, I think. But haven't you met her? Viv?" Rosemary said.

"I haven't had the pleasure," Freddie said, glancing across the table at George and noticing that his sister was also looking at him strangely.

Cecil checked his phone and let out a gasp. "Over sixteen thousand likes on the Aston pic already. See, whenever you're in pictures with me, our likes go through the roof!"

"I'm glad it makes you happy," Lucie said.

Cecil cleared his throat to make another announcement. "One more surprise: I managed to get tickets to a very special screening of a new movie tomorrow night. The duke and duchess were executive producers on the film, and they are hosting an exclusive sneak preview screening at the East Hampton Cinema before the film officially premieres at the Toronto International Film Festival. A few of the actors will even be there."

"How cool! What's the movie called?" Lucie asked.

"*Glimpses of the Moon* or something like that."

"*Glimpses of the Moon*—is it an adaptation of the Edith Wharton novel?" Auden asked.

"I'm not sure," Cecil said. "I think it's supposed to be quite groundbreaking. It's by an avant-garde British director, but the two lead actors are Indian."

"Indian? Really?" Lucie said curiously.

"Well, unfortunately I'm going into the city to do a live interview with Nima Elbagir on CNN International tomorrow, or I would have loved to come," Auden said.

"Oh, what's the interview about?" Charlotte inquired.

"I'm going to speak about the role of mindfulness in resolving global conflict."

"Well, Rosemary, Charlotte, and I are going to have a Korean-themed spa night, but why don't you kids all go?" Marian said.

"Sounds like a bit of a snorefest. George and I were thinking of seeing the new *Jurassic World* movie," Freddie said.

"Let's go see this. We can see *Jurassic World* any night," George said.

. . .

CBC Originals

and

ITV Studios

in association with

Channel Four Films

and

Canal+

presents

a Ravenswood Pictures

and

Smart Tomato

production of

GLIMPSES OF MOONLIGHT
a film by Olivia Lavistock

"Oh my God! Olivia Lavistock! I know her!" Lucie whispered excitedly to Cecil as the film titles flashed across the screen at the East Hampton Cinema on Main Street.

"How do you know her?" Cecil asked.

"She was at the Capri wedding! She made a doc about Dolfi's polo team."

"Milk Duds?" Freddie offered, passing his box to George, who passed it along to Lucie, sitting to his right. His arm casually grazed against hers, and Lucie quickly jerked her arm away.

"No thanks," Lucie said, pausing for a moment before saying to George in a quiet voice, "I guess Viv really was just a surf buddy?"

"As I told you," George replied.

As the movie unfolded, it soon became clear to the audience that the film was a Bollywood musical meets Italian neorealist cinema mash-up set in Tuscany in which Merle, a ravishingly pretty half-British, half-Indian girl (played by Naomi Scott) meets Devendra, a dashing young Indian prince and son of a Maharajah (played by Avan Jogia) at the wedding of their mutual friends, the fabulously wealthy Kundaris. Because Merle is not a full Indian and of a different caste, a romance between her and Devendra is strictly forbidden by his disapproving older cousin, Princess Gayatri (played by Mindy Kaling), and the two of them spend the first half of the film making eyes at each other over a decadent, weeklong wedding set in one jaw-droppingly luscious Tuscan villa after another. As the star-crossed couple struggle to resist their feelings for each other, a dance number featuring hundreds of Indian and Italian dancers in full regalia takes place in Siena's glorious Piazza del Campo during the famous Palio horse race.

Cecil giggled into Lucie's ear. "A dance-off between the Indians and the Italians! This is so fabulously silly, I'm loving it!"

Lucie stared at the screen, mesmerized by the spectacular dance sequence and a bit unnerved at the same time. The film was the sort of fun and frothy romantic comedy she usually loved, but something about it was making her feel uneasy. In the next scene, she realized what it was. Merle and Devendra escape from the wedding banquet while everyone is dancing and climb to the top of one of San Gimignano's fabled towers. The week of flirting and unbearable tension has led to this explosive moment, as fireworks literally explode in the distance and the young lovers kiss for the first time. Things get more and more heated, as Devendra reaches under Merle's ball gown, rips off her panties, and pokes his head under her skirt. Suddenly, a drone appears in the night sky and begins to film their furtive lovemaking. Suddenly, there is a loud banging on the door as the prince's aunt screams from the other side, "Stop it, you two! You're being filmed!"

"Oh, for fuck's sake! Mindy to the rescue!" Cecil roared with laughter.

Lucie froze in her seat, not daring to breathe, not daring to look at George. Out of the corner of her eye, she could see him in profile, staring expressionless at the screen. She felt her belly tighten into knots as a strange sensation came over her body—some combination of shock, panic, and desire. She took deep breaths, trying to quell the panic. The rest of the movie was a blur to her, and when the lights came up and the audience rose to give the producers a standing ovation, Lucie whispered to Cecil, "I need to go to the ladies' room."

As she stood up and made her way out of the row, her eyes caught George's for a split second. Instead of going to the toilet, Lucie headed down a back hallway to the fire exit that led outside. She needed fresh air. She needed to think. *Oh my God, oh my God, oh my God. How can I face George? I can't see him, I can't see him, I can't see him. Should I just leave? Should I get an Uber right now and go straight home? Should I say something to Cecil? Should I pretend that nothing's wrong?*

The heavy metal door opened behind her, and George stepped out.

Oh fuck oh fuck oh fuck oh fuck.

Lucie glanced at him for a moment and turned away, not saying anything. They were standing in an alley behind the theater, facing an empty back lane and some clipped hedges. George leaned against the wall, silent as usual.

Finally, Lucie summoned up the courage and blurted out, "I had nothing to do with that. I told Olivia nothing!"

"I know," George said.

"Then how did Olivia know every single detail about that night? Did *you* tell her? Did you tell your mother?" Lucie demanded.

George gave her a look like she was crazy.

"Who else knew?" Lucie asked accusingly.

"I told no one."

"It must've been Charlotte then, that hypocrite! She swore me to secrecy, and look what she ends up doing," Lucie said angrily.

"We'd better go back inside," George said as he turned to open the door, but Lucie suddenly grabbed his arm, stopping him.

"Wait."

"What?" George asked.

Lucie paused for a moment, unsure of what she wanted to say. She could feel the tension between them and the deafening throb in her eardrums as she held his gaze. *Don't don't don't don't don't.* Almost in slow motion, George pushed her against the wall and kissed her.

"Stop!" Lucie cried, pushing him away.

George stepped back, startled. "Sorry, I thought . . ."

"You thought wrong!" Lucie huffed, as she stepped through the door and slammed it firmly closed.

George stood in the alley, a little dazed. Suddenly the door swung open again and Lucie was pulling him toward her, kissing him deeply, frantically, as his soft lips melded into hers and his tongue sent shock waves through her entire body. Why did his kisses feel like nothing else in the world? Her desire was so insatiable, she felt like she was about to burst into flames, and in a flash it was as if she were back in the candlelit ruins of Villa Jovis, and the stars above were spinning, spinning as she arched her back and surrendered to his touch. She pressed herself against him, feeling his hardness. She shoved her hand down the front of his jeans as a desperate longing overtook her. All she wanted to do right now was pull him into the dark corner behind the hedges, tear off his clothing, and climb up his impossibly godlike body, feeling all of him in her. "Oh God, just fuck me right here!" she heard herself moan. *Stop it,* a voice in her head suddenly said. *Stop it,* Charlotte's voice said. *Shame on you,* the voice said, as she broke away from his arms and ran down the side alley that led to the front of the cinema.

Cecil and Freddie were standing under the little marquee outside the building, looking around.

"There you are!" Freddie said. "Let's get ice cream."

"It got too crowded inside so I went out the other door," Lucie said, flushed and breathless.

A couple minutes later, George emerged from the front doors of the cinema, drying his hands on a paper towel.

Cecil stared at Lucie and George curiously. "So? Were you both swept up in the romance?"

Lucie could feel her heart pounding out of her chest. *Oh my God, he knows. He can see it all over my face.*

Cecil rolled his eyes impatiently. "What did you think of your friend's movie?"

"Oh." Lucie's shoulders dropped in relief. "It was okay, I guess. It had its moments."

"I give it a B minus," Cecil declared. "Tuscany looked amazing, and the actors were pretty enough, but the costumes were godawful—whoever the costume designer was should be fired. It's a wedding with nothing but crazy rich Indians and all the jewelry looked *so fake!*"

Lucie nodded, giggling nervously, and Cecil continued his rant. "Indians are known for having the most fabulous jewels in the world! What a missed opportunity! But with the dance numbers and the terrible acting, it's bound to be a camp classic. The plot was too ridiculous for words."

Freddie nodded in agreement. "The whole drone subplot with the wedding videographers trying to blackmail the couple? That was so ridiculous. But what was even more ridiculous was that sex scene—they're like two virgins, and when they finally get it on in the tower, the first thing he does is drop to his knees and eat her out? Sorry, that would never happen in real life—dudes always need to get off first. So unbelievable! What did you think, George?"

"Yeah, it was pretty unbelievable," George said.

XI

Outlook Avenue

EAST HAMPTON

I feel the earth move under my feet,
I feel the sky tumbling down, a'tumbling down . . .

Lucie, Freddie, and Cecil returned to the house to find three ladies with an array of Korean facial masks plastered on their faces, singing and dancing around the living room as Carole King's *Tapestry* blasted on the old McIntosh turntable. Cecil took one look at Charlotte and Marian shimmying on the sofa in bathrobes and wordlessly turned around, heading straight up to Lucie's bedroom.

"Well, I see you kids are having quite the party without our permission! Mama, isn't it past your bedtime? And what's *this* here?" Freddie said in a mock angry tone, holding up an empty bottle of the 2016 Mazis-Chambertin Grand Cru.

"It's *very* good wine. I googled it and it's 859 dollars a bottle. And we've finished three bottles so far!" Rosemary giggled like a schoolgirl from the wing chair, where she sat with her restorative donkey-milk facial mask* on, soaking her feet in a wooden tub filled with a hot dark brown liquid that smelled like Robitussin. A Korean masseuse in a pale pink smock stood behind Rosemary, kneading her shoulders forcefully with her sharp, bony elbows.

"Oww, oww, yes, right there!" Rosemary moaned.

Marian stopped dancing and grinned through her cracked twenty-four-karat gold foil hydrating mask. "Oh my God, we're having the best slumber party spa night! Are you still hungry, Freddie? What did you have for dinner? There's so much leftover Korean barbecue, you should have some."

"Is there any kimchi?" Freddie asked.

"Of course."

"Is it spicy? You know I can't eat Korean barbecue unless there's good kimchi to go with it."

"The kimchi is so spicy it will burn a hole in your pants, Freddie. There's some leftover mandoo as well. I think Mary's gone to bed already, but you can just stick some of the barbecue in the microwave for forty-five seconds and it will taste like it's fresh off the broiler."

"Forget about it." Freddie plopped down on the sofa.

"Lazy boy! Here, come with me, I'll do it for you," Marian said, shuffling toward the kitchen with Freddie in tow.

Lucie felt a huge sense of relief as she saw them go. Now the only one left to get rid of was Rosemary. She needed to steel herself to confront Charlotte privately. She felt like her mind was spinning out of control with . . . what? Shame? Desire? Contempt? She wasn't sure what it was exactly, but she knew one thing—it was all Charlotte's fault. She never would have inhaled George's face outside the theater tonight if Charlotte hadn't blabbed to Olivia about what happened at Villa Jovis, if Olivia hadn't betrayed them all by showcasing the whole affair in her movie.

---

* Donkey milk abounds with vitamin C, proteins, and fatty acids, conferring a multitude of antiaging benefits for your skin. Cleopatra was known to bathe in donkey milk to maintain her renowned beauty and youthfulness, so if it's good enough for the Queen of the Nile, isn't it good enough for you?

"How was the film?" Charlotte asked, as she took a careful nibble of chocolate truffle, not wanting to open her mouth too wide for fear of cracking her snail-slime-and-bee-venom mask.

"Funny you should ask, Charlotte. It turns out the movie was directed by *your dear friend Olivia Lavistock,*" Lucie said.

"OH-livia! That English girl who only wore black all week long in Capri?" Rosemary asked in surprise.

"The very one," Lucie said mock cheerily.

"Really, they showed Olivia's film? I wish I'd known, I would have come. Last thing I heard she was still editing it," Charlotte mumbled through her mask, placing her feet into one of the wooden buckets as another attendant poured more of the mysterious hot brown liquid in.

Lucie was incensed. "You *knew* Olivia was making a film?"

"Of course. She's been slaving away at it for the past two years," Charlotte said.

"The film was shot *two years ago?*"

"Possibly more. Apparently the cinematographer was this Indian fellow who was an absolute nightmare to work with. He stole some of the footage and kept it hostage for a while."

"Well, you wouldn't know it by looking at the movie. The cinematography was spectacular, especially this one rather curious scene where the two main characters—a half-Indian girl and an Indian prince—make love in a castle tower in Italy *while a sinister drone hovers above them and captures every moment of their lovemaking,*" Lucie said as she glared into Charlotte's eyes.

"A drone? Like the ones that were all over Issie's wedding? He he he . . . how fun!" Rosemary laughed.

Charlotte's jaw dropped and the snail slime began to crack around her mouth.

"Well, I think I'm going to have me some of that *treacherously* spicy kimchi," Lucie said archly as she stormed out of the room, knowing Charlotte was bound to follow.

Sure enough, Charlotte, her face freshly washed, came into the kitchen a few minutes later and nonchalantly sidled up to the wooden counter where Freddie sat with Marian and Lucie, gobbling down his beef galbi as he recounted the movie to his mother.

"And then these Italian dudes are trying to blackmail the young maharajah with the drone footage! Meanwhile, there's a dance sequence on the rooftop of a villa, where these pretty girls start twirling and whipping the shirtless buff Italian dudes with their long saris."

Marian slapped her knee, howling with laughter.

"Lucie, if you aren't going to eat, you should come with me. You've got to try this foot-soaking tub. It's *so* relaxing," Charlotte said gingerly.

Lucie got up from her barstool and marched Charlotte into the library, closing the door behind them tightly. "So thoughtful of you to suggest a relaxing soak, Charlotte. After all, I don't think I'll ever get to relax again once this film premieres next month at the Toronto International Film Festival."

Charlotte sank down on the buttoned leather sofa. "I can't believe it! I just can't believe it!"

"Believe it. It's all there in high definition!" Lucie seethed, as she sat in the club chair directly across from Charlotte, as though she were staging an interrogation. "How *could you*, Charlotte? How could you tell Olivia everything, after you made me swear never to breathe a word to anyone?"

"But I didn't tell her!"

"What then, Olivia Lavistock is psychic?"

"I mean, I only told Olivia about the drone thing right after I'd discovered you and George at the villa. After you had both run off into the woods, I went back to the party in utter panic! I didn't know what to do, I needed her help," Charlotte sputtered.

"You told me you had told no one!"

"I haven't told a soul since that night, I swear. The only person I confided in was Olivia, who I thought was my friend. How in the world was I supposed to know she would use it in her goddamn movie!"

"Well, clearly Olivia doesn't have an ounce of imagination. She stole every bit of our story and put it in her film."

"Oh my poor girl, I'm so sorry!"

Lucie snorted. "You always say that, but are you ever really sorry?"

Charlotte began to tear up. "I truly am! I'll never speak to Olivia again!"

"Well, you shouldn't have spoken to her in the first place."

"What was she thinking?!" Charlotte moaned, shaking her head. "At least she made her characters Indian."

Lucie rolled her eyes. "Yes, it's a fine example of cultural appropriation."

"What I mean is, I don't think anyone would ever link you and George to this film."

"Anyone except the four hundred people who attended Issie's wedding. Just think what Mordecai von Ephrussí's going to say when he sees the film! You know he'll see it!"

"Ugh, that insufferable toady!"

"And that's not the worst of it, Charlotte! George was right there!"

"Christ Almighty, I forgot he was at the screening!"

"I had to sit through that god-awful movie with George on one side of me and Cecil on the other!"

Charlotte stared at Lucie fearfully. "What did George do?"

"What he did, Charlotte, was he followed me outside when the movie was over, pushed me against a wall, and shoved his tongue down my throat!" Lucie said melodramatically.

Charlotte put her hands to her face. "Oh my God, Lucie! Are you okay?"

"I'm fine. I got away from him fast."

"What is it with that boy? It's the second time he's tried to seduce you. He's never gotten over you, has he?"

"He humiliated me! He clearly hasn't gotten the message that I'm about to become Mrs. Cecil Pike," Lucie huffed, trying to sound indignant.

"Did you tell Cecil?"

"Are you mad? Of course I didn't."

"Thank God! Knowing Cecil, he'd probably try to challenge George to a duel!"

Lucie didn't respond, but she suddenly had a vision of Cecil dressed up in a crisp white fencing uniform and helmet, saber in hand. *It's not a saber, Lucie, it's called an épée,* she could hear him already correcting her, as he assumed the proper fencing stance opposite George, who stood before him in his standard black tank top and surfer shorts. Cecil waved his épée threateningly in the air with great flourish, while George, in one swift Jean-Claude Van Damme move, raised his leg and kicked Cecil in the head, knocking him out cold.

"Where is George now?" Charlotte asked, snapping Lucie out of her daydream.

"He hightailed it back to Manhattan after the movie."

"With his tail between his legs, I should hope!"

Suddenly, all Lucie could think of was George between her legs, ravishing her with his hands, with his tongue, with his deliciously hard . . . *Stop, stop, stop it!* Why was she thinking such obscene, shameful things? Wasn't fantasizing about another man the same as cheating on Cecil? She couldn't do this to Cecil; she couldn't do this to herself. She couldn't ruin her whole life because of some inexplicable obsession with George Zao. Yes, that's what it was. She could admit it to herself now. She was obsessed, utterly obsessed with him, and it just wasn't right. She had been torturing herself since the day she had found out he rented Cissinghurst, and it had tormented her to the edge of insanity. It had turned her life upside down. She had lost her appetite, she felt sick and anxious all the time, she was having the most intense dreams about reenacting pagan love rituals in cliffside caverns with George. It wasn't natural to have these kinds of dreams, to feel such things for a man whom she didn't even like. George was the polar opposite of the kind of guys she liked. He didn't grow up in New York. He wasn't suave and sophisticated. He didn't dress properly. He didn't in any way resemble Cary Elwes in *The Princess Bride*. He was nothing like the husband she had always envisioned for herself. He had driven her crazy and done nothing but mess up her life and mess with her head since the moment she had first set eyes on him in the lunchroom of the Bertolucci, and the one thing she hated more than anything was messy. Her life, her image, her whole being up till this point, had been a study in perfection. She had gone to Brearley and had always been popular as Lucie Tang Churchill, the cool half-Asian girl. She had graduated from Brown with honors. She had landed her dream job with the coolest company in town, and she was about to marry a dashing, erudite gentleman whom even *Esquire* proclaimed "The Most Desired Dude on the Planet." They would live in an exquisitely original town house in the West Village, summer in East Hampton, and maybe even get a place in Provence. They would both serve on the boards of the Brooklyn Museum of Art and PS1 and maybe even the Dia. They would in precisely four and a half years start to have beautiful, gifted children (a boy, then a girl) who would attend Saint Bernard's and Brearley, followed by Harvard or Brown or Bard—actually, no, not Bard, Brearley girls didn't go to Bard—and be adored by everyone, adored by Granny, adored by all the Churchills. And if all went as planned, she would see Cecil and her children's names appear alongside hers in *The Social Register*, and it would be the happiest day of Cecil's life. There was no way in hell she was going to let George ruin this magnificent life she had planned out for herself since she was eight years old. All the happiness in her future, her family's future, her children's future, depended on the removal of George from her life.

Lucie got up and turned to Charlotte decisively. "First thing tomorrow, you're coming on a drive with me, Charlotte. We're going to the city and we're going to find George Zao. You were responsible for this mess, so you're going to help me end it. Once and for all."

XII

Three Lives & Company

WEST VILLAGE

"Why are we meeting him at a bookshop?" Charlotte asked, as they approached the red French doors of Three Lives & Company on Waverly Place.

"His office is at South Street Seaport, and I didn't want to meet him way down there. And I didn't want to be spotted with him anywhere on the Upper East Side either, so I thought this would be neutral territory where no one will know us," Lucie explained, as they entered the quaint little bookshop filled with green shaded reading lamps that cast a cozy warm glow over the space.

Lucie walked to the back of the shop to check if he was there. Perched against a shelf, flipping through a copy of Alan Hollinghurst's *The Stranger's Child* was Cecil's mother.

"Lucie! I didn't know you'd be coming into the city today!"

"Yes . . . er . . . I'm on my way to meet with a client," Lucie blurted out as she attempted to hide her shock. It was the first thing she could think to say.

"Oh, look, here's your cousin," Renée said cheerily, as Charlotte peeked around the corner. "I suppose she must be coming to meet your client too."

Lucie looked at her like a deer trapped in headlights.

Charlotte came to the rescue. "Mrs. Pike! What a divine jacket you're wearing! Off-White?"

"Alexander McQueen couture."

"Of course it is. Now, what brings you so far south, Mrs. Pike?"

"Please call me Renée. I'm on the board of God's Love We Deliver. I'm killing a little time before a board meeting and thought I'd come in here to take a browse."

"God's Love—what a wonderful organization! I volunteered at their kitchen one Thanksgiving. Now, Lucie, have you found the book you wanted to get for Cecil? We're going to be very late!" Charlotte announced.

"What book are you getting for Cecil?" Renée asked.

"Er . . . I already looked, and they don't have it," Lucie said, irritated that Charlotte had dug her into a deeper hole.

"Well, perhaps Toby can help you find it? Who is the author?" Renée prodded.

"Um, Maira Kalman," Lucie said, spying one of her books on the shelf behind Renée.

"Oh, I love Maira! But has Robert approved the book yet?"

"Approved?" Lucie looked at her, confused.

"Well, you know Robert only allows books with distressed spines in Cecil's library. One shiny new spine could throw the whole look off."

"Oh yes, I forgot."

"Excuse us, we really are very late!" Charlotte interjected.

As they walked toward the exit, the door suddenly opened and a blond lady in a chic camel driving coat entered with a little tow-headed boy.

"Lucie Tang Churchill! Long time no see!" the lady said.

"Lief! What are you doing here?" Lucie gasped.

"A good friend of mine lives in the Village, so every time I come down to visit him, I pop in here to grab the latest children's books for William."

"And who is this now?" Charlotte asked grimly.

"Oh, sorry, Lief, meet my cousin Charlotte. Lief was my tennis partner a few summers ago at Dorset," Lucie explained.

Renée poked her head around. "Lief, is that you?"

"Renée! What are you doing here?" Lief squealed. Turning to Lucie and Charlotte, she explained, "I just saw Renée this morning at qigong class. We must be on the same vibration!"

"Yes, unfortunately we need to vibrate straight out the door!" Charlotte declared, taking Lucie firmly by the shoulder and steering her outside. Ducking around the corner, Charlotte let out an exasperated sigh. "What in the world possessed you to pick that dangerously adorable bookshop? Everyone you know in the whole wide world is in there today! What if Renée sees you with George? I think we should abort the mission!"

"Too late," Lucie said grimly as she saw George walking up West Tenth Street toward them.

"Hey," he said. "Did you want to go inside?"

"Noooo!" the ladies said in unison.

George frowned. "So why did you want to meet here?"

"Oh, for fuck's sake," Charlotte said, as she marched Lucie and George down the street, turned right on Greenwich Avenue, and herded them into Jefferson Market Garden. Finding a bench hidden deep in the lush foliage next to the lily pond, Charlotte sat down and looked from Lucie to George. "Well, here we all are."

Lucie folded her arms pensively, summoning the courage to say what she had come to say.

George gazed at her calmly. "I suppose you want to talk about Olivia's film?"

Lucie shook her head. "I want to talk about what happened *after* the film. Actually, I don't. I just want you to promise that you'll never set foot in my house in East Hampton ever again."

"I can't do that."

"Why not?"

"Well, isn't it your brother's house? He invited me over for poker night next Saturday."

"It may technically be Freddie's house, but it is my childhood home and I still spend the summers there. And I don't ever wish to see you again."

"Why?"

"Because you have crossed a line. You insulted me within twenty feet of my future husband by trying to kiss me last night."

"You thought that was insulting?"

"What is wrong with you, you monster? You forced yourself on her! You're lucky that we're not reporting this to anyone!" Charlotte exploded.

George gazed at Charlotte in shock. "Is that what she told you?" He turned back to Lucie, looking mystified.

"I think you have a problem, George. You don't seem to understand that your advances toward Lucie have been inappropriate and unwanted," Charlotte said in a gentler tone.

George snorted. "Inappropriate and unwanted? Lucie, in case I'm remembering incorrectly, *you* kissed me first in Positano. *You* shoved your hands down my pants last night and begged me to fuck you."

Charlotte stared at Lucie for confirmation.

Lucie's face turned bright red. Ignoring Charlotte, she took the opportunity to double down on her words. "You have offended me gravely, and you have offended my future husband. You need to realize that your proximity, your mother's proximity, to my family, is making me very uncomfortable in light of all that's happened."

"All that's happened? We made out, Lucie. You're making it sound like it was some tragedy."

"It wasn't a tragedy, but it was a mistake, George. A big mistake. I was young and foolish in Capri, but there was no excuse for what happened last night. Do you not care that I'm about to marry Cecil?"

George sighed deeply. "If Cecil were anyone else, you know I would never have kissed you. I would never do anything to disrespect the both of you. But you can't really be serious about marrying him."

"Why not?"

"Because he doesn't love you!"

"How dare you say that! How could you possibly know how he feels?"

"Because of who Cecil is. He doesn't even *know* you! He doesn't have a clue who you really are, or the fact that you'd never be caught dead driving an Aston Martin. He loves the idea of you, the image of you; he just wants to post beautiful, hot pictures of you and him and see how many likes he gets. He's in love with the social media impression of you, how you enhance his brand. It's all about sex and vanity to him, nothing else! He can't possibly love you in the way you deserve to be loved because he's incapable of seeing you as a real person, a real woman. But *I* see you. I see the beauty inside you, and also your sadness, your fears, your flaws. I see exactly who you are and I love you for all those things, Lucie. I've loved you since the moment we met. I love your family, I love your mind, and I love your art. I want to be there to support your passions and dreams, whatever they are, and I want to know you more so I can love you more."

Lucie was stunned speechless. Her throat felt like it was closing up, but she stubbornly stood her ground. "There's only one problem. I don't want all that from you."

George stood stock-still for a moment, and then gazed at her fiercely. "I don't believe you."

"I don't care what you believe!" Lucie shrieked, throwing up her hands.

Charlotte placed a hand on Lucie's shoulder, trying to calm her down. "Lucie, please . . ."

"Stop it, Charlotte! Haven't you done enough?" Lucie turned back to George. "I'm in love with someone else and I'm going to be his wife in September. So will you please just . . . just go. Just leave us alone."

"Can you hear yourself? You can't even say his name!" George groaned, looking to Charlotte in frustration. "Do you believe her? Do you really want to see her married to someone like Cecil?"

"I . . . I'm here to support Lucie, and I think right now you both just need to stop fighting and calm down," Charlotte sputtered.

George placed his hands on Lucie's shoulders, staring into her face. "Look me in the eyes and tell me the truth. Tell me you really don't love me."

Lucie's eyes darted away from his as she fought back her tears. She couldn't ruin everything, not even for him. "I don't love you."

An ocean of hurt flashed across George's face. Then he turned abruptly and walked off without another word.

"George! Stop, George!" Charlotte cried out.

Lucie glared at her cousin as if to say, *Get a hold of yourself!*

Charlotte sat there with tears in her eyes. She knew now—hearing George's words and looking into his face today—that she had made a huge mistake. She had been wrong about him today. She had been wrong about him from the very beginning.

XIII

Doubles

FIFTH AVENUE

The handsomely appointed lobby of the Sherry-Netherland hotel was a haven of tranquility just steps away from the hustle and bustle of Fifth Avenue, with its discreetly watchful uniformed attendants, dignified Louis XV bergère chairs, and barrel-vault ceilings painted with neoclassical scenes. Ten feet into the lobby was a velvet panel on the left that looked like it was part of the wall, but when the select crowd who knew of its existence pushed against it, the hidden panel would swing open smoothly, revealing a narrow red carpeted stairway that was like a secret passage to one of New York's most legendary hideouts.

One flight down was Doubles, a private dining club that was one perpetual, elegant, raucous party from the moment it opened for lunch till the last scented votive candle was snuffed out late into the evening. Every surface of the exclusive subterranean playground was bordello red, from the red floors to the red ceiling, and mirrored walls only amplified this empire of scarlet. With founding members ranging from Rockefellers and Whitneys to society icons like Nan

Kempner and the much-missed comedienne Joan Rivers, one ceased to notice the red after a minute or two because the club was always packed elbow to elbow with the sort of crowd that added the true color to the place.

Lucie had been coming here since she was a young girl—Doubles was a regular haunt for the Churchills in the same way that TGI Fridays might be for a different set, the local standby when they couldn't be bothered to think of anywhere else to go. Today, as Lucie navigated through the festive crowd to their table, she wasn't in much of a celebratory mood. It had been only a few days since the big confrontation with George, and though she hated to admit it, she was still a complete wreck. She had decimated several boxes of chocolate truffles and hadn't slept a wink in the past few nights, as she lay in bed replaying the encounter over and over again in her head.

It didn't help that everything Cecil did seemed to annoy her today. He had been the one to suggest lunch at Doubles, which had become one of his favorite eateries, and he had made her change outfits twice, finally producing a Chanel couture dress that was yet another gift from his mother. Now she was irritated by Cecil's insistence on stopping at practically every table along the way to greet yet another society doyenne. Fed up, Lucie decided to let Cecil work the tables at his leisure and went on ahead of him.

"Here you go, Ms. Churchill," the hostess said, showing Lucie to the corner table where Charlotte sat pensively waiting.

"It's absolutely *packed* today! What is going on?" Charlotte asked.

"Mom isn't here yet?"

"No sight of her," Charlotte replied.

Lucie frowned. It wasn't like her mom to be late to anything. "Where's Cecil?"

"He's making the rounds."

"Quite the mocialite, isn't he?"

"Ugh, I hate that term, Charlotte! *Please* don't call Cecil that!"

"You don't think it fits him perfectly? He's the quintessential male socialite—he doesn't really seem to work, he spends most of his time jetting around the world to parties, and he's far more popular here than you'll ever be."

"So is Freddie, and you wouldn't call *him* a mocialite," Lucie countered as she observed the sea of humanity parting to allow Freddie to cross the room diagonally from the dessert buffet, holding his plate high above his head. Every few feet, he would cast his winsome smile onto some girl he knew and she would come rushing up to him to plant a kiss on his cheek.

"Freddie's not trying to climb any ladders or get on any boards. He's just the rascal next door that every girl wants to shag," Charlotte said.

Lucie rolled her eyes. "Listen to you, Charlotte! One year in London and you're sounding just like one of them."

Freddie arrived at their table with several lipstick marks on his face. He sat across from Charlotte, putting down a plate piled with the biggest heap of chocolate mousse and fresh whipped cream that she'd ever seen.

"You're starting with dessert?" Charlotte asked.

"Why not? I'm starving. Where's Mom?"

"Right behind you," Lucie said, as Marian came rushing up to the table.

"So sorry, I was dealing with a little crisis. Freddie, please don't tell me you're going to eat all that mousse before your lunch."

"This *is* my lunch."

Marian shook her head in dismay. "I weep for your kidneys."

"Did one of your researchers screw up at the lab again?" Lucie inquired.

"No, I wish. That I can fix easily." Marian sighed. "You know this year is the twenty-fifth anniversary of the Animal Rescue Fund of Long Island, and we were planning our biggest summer gala yet. Jane Goodall was our special honoree, and everyone was so excited about that. But we just heard that she's had to drop out because of some chimpanzee emergency back in Tanzania."

"Oh dear, I hope the chimps are going to be okay," Charlotte remarked.

Marian let out a deep sigh. "So now who are we going to get to take her place less than a week before the gala?"

"Leo," Freddie volunteered.

"Ha! Fat chance!" Marian said.

Just then, Cecil arrived at the table. "Fat chance what?" he asked.

"Jane Goodall had to drop out as the honoree at Mom's charity benefit, and Freddie suggested trying to get Leonardo DiCaprio," Lucie explained.

"Ha! Fat chance!" Cecil said. "Lucie, would you come with me for a moment? I'd like to introduce you to Princess Marie-Laure de Polignac, who's lunching with Elizabeth Merchant and Lord Ivory today."

"Can we order first?" Lucie asked.

"Marie-Laure needs to see your engagement ring," Cecil added.

"But I'm not wearing it today," Lucie said.

"What? I specifically told you to wear it to lunch!" Cecil groaned in dismay.

"Cecil, I have to go down to Soho Art Materials after this to get supplies. I can't be schlepping canvases and stuff wearing that ring."

"Why do you need to be schlepping anything in the first place? I've told you so many times I have a multitude of underlings from Pike Projects ready to wait on you hand and foot. They can get you whatever you want, whenever you want, and deliver it right to the door of your barn in East Hampton."

"But I need to choose the materials myself, Cecil. The brushes, the paints, everything."

"Well then, where is your ring? I'll have one of my three personal assistants go to the apartment and bring it here to you. It can be done within fifteen minutes." Cecil took out his phone and began texting away furiously.

"Are you sure you want one of your assistants to go to all that trouble?" Lucie asked.

"Of course. What's the point of being a billionaire if you can't have an army of slaves at your beck and call to do whatever you want? My mother has one girl who does nothing but fly around the world doing all her returns for her."

"But is it so crucial for her to see the ring right now?"

"Absolutely. Everyone's been talking about my ring, and Marie-Laure has one of the most legendary *joaillier* collections on the planet. If Marie-Laure approves of the ring, she might actually come to the wedding!"

"*Who* is she again?" Lucie cocked her head.

"Baby, her family owns the Imperial Hotel in Gstaad and she's a dear friend of my mother's. We're going to be seeing her every February from now on when we do the season in Gstaad."

Freddie looked up from his plate. "I didn't know you skied, Cecil."

"I don't. I go to Gstaad for *the season*."

Lucie finally gave in, knowing Cecil wouldn't stop fixating on this till he got what he wanted. "The ring is in the top-left drawer of my highboy, behind all my sunglass cases. Mom, could you please call Tony and tell him someone's coming by?"

Marian gave her a weary look. "Mary's got the day off—there's no one at home right now. Are you sure we want a total stranger up there?"

Charlotte leaned in. "Do you trust your assistant, Cecil?"

"Of course I do!" Cecil insisted.

Marian reached into her thirty-year-old Coach handbag and got out her phone. "What's the name of your assistant? I need to tell Tony to let them up."

"I don't know," Cecil answered.

Marian looked up at Cecil incredulously. "Uh . . . you don't know the name of the assistant you're going to be sending to rummage through my home looking for a multimillion-dollar ring?"

"Marian, they change so frequently, I can't be bothered to keep track of their names. Rose, Kirk, Lili, Emile, who the hell knows?

But I can ensure you not a single one of them would ever be stupid enough to risk being fired for screwing up this errand. We only hire kids from the Ivys, and they are all grossly overpaid if you ask me. Besides, the ring is insured, and trust me, there's really nothing in your apartment that anyone would want to steal."

Freddie projectile spat his mouthful of chocolate mousse all over his plate as he burst out in laughter.

"What's so funny?" Cecil asked angrily.

"Nothing," Freddie answered lightly. "Where's the waiter? Don't we need to order?"

Lucie fumed as Marian and Charlotte sat in uncomfortable silence, not sure how to resolve this matter.

"You know what? If you don't trust one of my Ivy League minions, *I* will go and get the ring myself," Cecil announced, rising from the table and rushing off just as the waiter arrived to take their orders.

"Oh well, let's go ahead and order first. I'm not waiting for Cecil," Marian said decisively.

After everyone had placed their lunch orders, Charlotte suggested, "Let's google some famous animal activists and find the perfect person to honor at your benefit, Marian."

"Yes, who should we try for?" Marian wondered.

Charlotte scrolled through her phone. "Okay . . . here's a good list of celebs. Let's see . . . Paul McCartney . . . we'll never get him either. How about Penélope Cruz? She was so good in the latest Almodóvar film."

"Hmm . . . I'm not sure she's quite right for this crowd," Marian assessed.

"Jared Leto."

"Love him, but not right for this crowd either," Lucie assessed.

"Oh, how about Bea Arthur?"

"She's dead," Freddie said.

"When did she die?!" Charlotte cried.

"Like, years ago," Freddie replied.

"How sad! I must have missed that news cycle. Wait, here's a good one for the Long Island crowd—Wendy Williams."

"That's a good possibility. Any others?"

Charlotte gasped. "I've got it! I've got it! Cornelia Guest!"

"Oh, she'd be terrific!" Marian agreed.

Charlotte held up a PETA ad featuring Cornelia with an incredible mane of blond hair cleverly covering up her voluptuous nude body, accompanied by the slogan I'D RATHER GO NAKED THAN WEAR FUR.

"She's a babe!" Freddie said.

"She's so much more than a babe, Freddie. She's an actress, she's a cruelty-free fashion connoisseur who designed a line of vegan handbags, she runs her own vegan catering company and animal rescue operation, *and* she's actually from Long Island!" Charlotte read out loud from the web page.

"Even more perfect!" Marian clapped her hands together excitedly.

"You know, I think Cecil might actually know her," Lucie said.

"Really? Then this will be a piece of cake! Making the connection is the hardest part. Usually I have to spend months going through all these awful PR reps, agents, and managers to get to anyone famous."

When Cecil returned to the table, everyone looked at him in anticipation.

Lucie grabbed his arm eagerly. "Cecil, we solved Mom's problem while you were away. Cornelia Guest!"

"What about her?"

"Mom wants to honor her at the summer gala for the Animal Rescue Fund of Long Island!"

"She'll never do it."

Lucie was confused. "But isn't she your friend?"

"Of course she is . . . but I wouldn't dare ask her."

"Why not?" Lucie asked.

Cecil paused for a moment. "I just know she'll say no."

"Why?" Marian prodded.

"I hate to say this, but I think it would be too low class an affair for her."

"Low class!" Marian looked taken aback.

Charlotte was indignant. "But Cornelia's a huge champion of animal rights, *and* she grew up on Long Island!"

"Not *that* part of Long Island. She's from Old Westbury, which as you well know is haute WASP country. Besides, I think she's mostly in LA these days, busy with acting projects."

"But our crowd would adore her. They would open up their pockets even more at the gala. Come on, Cecil, pleeeeease? Do you want me to get down on my knees and beg?" Marian said with a little laugh.

"Oh, Cecil, won't you please just ask her? What's the harm in just asking, for Mom's sake?" Lucie pleaded.

"Lucie, Cornelia Guest was the Debutante of the Decade in the eighties. She was BFFs with Andy Warhol, and the Duke and Duchess of Windsor were her godparents. She's the daughter of polo legend Winston Guest and C. Z. Guest, who was the swan of all swans, and she's the closest thing we have to royalty in this country. Trust me, we will *never* get her to come to your mother's dinky fund-raiser, and I wouldn't *dream* of wasting my social currency to ask her."

Everyone was stunned speechless. After an awkward pause, Charlotte cleared her throat and offered encouragingly, "Well, let me see how I can connect the dots to Wendy Williams. I think someone on my PR team in London will know how to get to her."

Cecil nodded. "Yes, Wendy Williams, whoever she is, will be a much better choice. Now, Lucie, please put on this 26.5-million-dollar ring I bought for you—and designed myself—and come with me to meet the princess!"

Lucie could feel her jaw grinding in rage. She forced the ring on to her finger and got up from the banquette.

"Wait—where's the jacket Mother gave you?" Cecil asked.

"It's draped behind Freddie's seat."

"Well, put it on! It's Chanel couture, and Marie-Laure is very close to Karl. She'll be so touched to see you in it."

Freddie, Marian, and Charlotte watched in silence as Lucie put on her black-and-white bouclé jacket and walked slowly behind Cecil as he weaved expertly through the crowded room.

XIV

Rockefeller Center

MIDTOWN MANHATTAN

After lunch, everyone dispersed in various directions—Marian had to get back to her lab at Columbia; Charlotte was off to her dermatologist for a "mole check," which everyone knew meant that she was getting Botox; Freddie was going to meet a friend for tea at Cha-An; and Cecil had his weekly appointment with his wealth psychologist.

Lucie, who was headed to Christie's to look at some Hockneys coming up for auction for a client, decided to walk the ten blocks or so to Rockefeller Center since it was such a pleasant summer afternoon. Freddie, who was on his way to the East Village, decided to stroll down Fifth Avenue with his sister for a while.

They walked in perfect sync, keeping the same pace the way siblings often did, Freddie texting away at warp speed, barely looking up while expertly dodging the multitude of tourists, dogs on leashes, babies in strollers, and other sidewalk obstacles that got in his way as only a native of this island knew how, while Lucie stared straight ahead, never making eye contact with passersby.

"Ha ha—mission accomplished! Only took four texts," Freddie proudly announced.

"What mission?" Lucie asked distractedly.

"Cornelia Guest said yes to Mom's gala!"

Lucie stopped dead in her tracks and stared at her brother. "How on earth did you pull that off?"

An office lady walking a few paces behind them swerved around them and cussed loudly, "Fuckin' Asian tourist," yet the siblings didn't seem to notice.

"I texted my friend Sloane, who texted her friend Chai who went to Brearley with Penelope, who as it turns out is related to Cornelia. And Cornelia just texted me right back. Look: 'I am honored and thrilled!!!' "

Lucie looked at the text, shaking her head in wonder as they started walking again. "It didn't even occur to me to use the Brearley connection. Everything just happens so easily for you!"

"It may look easy to you, but I was formulating a plan all through lunch. Remember the theory of six degrees of separation, where anyone on the planet can be connected to anyone else through no more than six different people? Like I could be connected to Cornelia if I just found the right six people to connect me to her? I looked at her Instagram and noticed that along with animals, she's into art and fashion, so who of my WASPy fashion friends might know her? Well, Sloane interns in the *Vogue* fashion closet* and knows everyone. I remember this story about how a big fashion shoot at the Armory fell through at the last minute and Sloane texted her mom, who made one call and was able to shut down the MoMA Sculpture Garden for a whole day so they could do the shoot. So I started with her and just got lucky, I guess."

"See, you've always had that luck. I feel like I've never had a fraction of the kind of luck that you were born with."

"Me? Born lucky?" Freddie snorted.

---

* Not to be confused with the accessories closet intern or the beauty closet intern.

"Oh my God, Freddie, look in the mirror! Actually, look at your reflection in this window!"

Freddie glanced quickly at the Bergdorf window. "Ooh, I like that linen jacket with the bamboo print. Think that'll look good on me?"

"Everything looks good on you, Freddie! That's my point. You're the perfect mix of Asian and WASP, and that's why Granny adores you."

"She adores you too."

"That's not true at all. She has come to 'appreciate me.' Her actual words, not mine. You know, when I was a little girl, Dad and Mom would send me down to Florida to spend summers with her, and she would spend all her time trying to fix me? I was subjected to hours of etiquette lessons, speech lessons, bizarre Victorian-era posture exercises. She would get her maids to poke and prod me till I looked acceptable enough to accompany her to one of her clubs. This frightful maid, Oonagh, would spend hours brushing out my hair till my scalp bled. Everyone thought I was having such a good time in Hobe Sound, but it was torture."

"Fuuuck! I had no idea. Although I remember Granny would occasionally say things to me like, 'I'm so glad you got your father's eyes, not your mother's.' I remember thinking that sounded totally whack. But look who's laughing now. You have the prettiest hair, Lucie, everyone says so."

"Thanks, but it takes a lot of work to make it look like this, while you just roll out of bed every morning and your hair looks like it's straight out of an Aveda ad. And besides, you were born at just the right time. You don't remember Mom being depressed, do you? Like, not just saying she was depressed, but actually being so depressed she couldn't even get out of bed."

Freddie shook his head.

"You were barely four when Dad died. I had to deal with it all—I took care of you, I shielded you from everything, and by the time you were fully conscious Mom had already adjusted to all her meds, so you've only ever known 'Happy Mom.' You have no idea how lucky you are."

"I guess I don't." Freddie suddenly stopped and gave Lucie a big bear hug.

"What was that for?" Lucie asked.

"For being so lucky to have you as a big sister."

Lucie smiled. "Look, I'm sorry if I'm going on and on about this. I guess I was just a bit blown away by how effortlessly you charmed Cornelia into coming to Mom's fund-raiser."

They walked in silence until they reached Forty-Ninth Street.

"Okay, I'm going this way," Lucie said.

"Wait a minute." Freddie paused for a moment, gathering his thoughts. "You know, you say you're unlucky, but I've never seen it that way. I've always seen you as the lucky one."

"Oh yeah? Name three ways that I'm luckier than you."

"That's easy. You got to have time with Dad. I have his things, but I have barely any memory of him at all. And you're an amazing artist. I can't even draw a straight line with a ruler."

"Okay, that's two. What's the third thing that makes me luckier than you?"

"Hmm . . . let's see . . . You're going to become Mrs. Cecil Pike," Freddie said.

"Ew," Lucie blurted out before she could stop herself.

Brother and sister stared at each other for a split second, and then they both burst out laughing. The two of them stood on the corner of Forty-Ninth and Fifth for a few minutes, leaning against the gray limestone wall outside Michael Kors, doubled over in laughter. When they had recovered enough, Freddie turned and continued down Fifth Avenue, while Lucie began walking along Forty-Ninth Street toward Christie's auction house. In the middle of the block, right outside NBC Studios, she stopped, got out her phone, and sent Cecil a text, her fingers shaking uncontrollably.

XV

Tea & Sympathy

WEST VILLAGE

"Why did you want to meet here? If you wanted afternoon tea, we could have met up someplace more glam like the St. Regis or the Mandarin."

"I like this place, Cecil. I love their scones, and this room reminds me of those little country cafés my dad used to take me to the year we lived in England. Plus, it's near your house."

"Oh."

A waitress with a Cockney accent approached their corner table by the window to take their order.

"I'll have the cream tea with the Assam, please. And could I get an extra side of clotted cream for my scones?"

"Of course. What will you have, sir?"

"Nothing, I'm not hungry."

"House rules, sir, you have to order something if you want to stay here."

"I'll have a macchiato."

"Sorry, sir, we have coffee or thirty-seven types of tea."

"For fuck's sake. I'll have a Darjeeling tea. And the sticky toffee pudding."

"You didn't have to be rude to her, Cecil. She's only doing her job."

"Was I being rude? I thought she was being so condescending. Why are you laughing?"

"Never mind, Cecil."

"Look at that woman outside. Do you think she let her roots grow out like that on purpose? Or is she just too cheap to get her color done properly?"

"Maybe she likes it like that, Cecil."

"How could anyone possibly like their hair like that? I'd be ashamed to leave the house. Why are you handing me your ring?"

"I'm returning it to you, Cecil."

"Ahhh! You don't like it, do you? Mother was right. She had a feeling it might be too avant-garde for you."

"I think it's a very original design, Cecil, but I just can't wear it."

"You have such slender, delicate fingers. I'll admit, the cabochon emerald might not be the most flattering look for them. But the stone is so special. Why don't we turn this emerald into a necklace, and I'll get you something more classic for your engagement ring. Admit it, you've always wanted a diamond from Tiffany, haven't you? You've been brainwashed by decades of Audrey Hepburn propaganda."

"Cecil, I'm returning the ring to you be . . . because I . . . I can't marry you."

"Oh please, we can go to Tiffany if you really want. Although maybe we should go to Paris and I can get Joel to design something more classic for you."

"Cecil, listen to me. I cannot marry you."

"You're not joking?"

"No, Cecil."

The waitress returned with a bowl of sticky toffee pudding with warm custard oozing over it, a plate of freshly baked scones, two small ramekins of clotted cream, and one small ramekin with house-made jam. She also put down two unmatched teacups, a teapot in the shape of a double-decker bus, and another teapot with a photo of Prince William and Kate Middleton printed on the side.

"Excuse me, would you happen to have a teacup with a slightly thinner rim? Maybe that floral one up there on the end?" Lucie asked.

"Um, sure."

The waitress retrieved another teacup from the shelf and swapped it out with Cecil's teacup.

"Thank you for requesting this teacup, Lucie. You're so thoughtful, which makes me all the more confused. Why are you breaking off our engagement?"

"I'm sorry, Cecil. I . . . I just realized that we're really not suited to each other, and I think we won't be happy together in the long run."

"Not suited? Are you crazy? We're so perfectly suited. Everyone says so. Even *Town & Country*—they want to do a cover story on our wedding!"

"If you really knew me, you'd know that's the last thing I'd ever want."

"Okay, we don't have to do *Town & Country* if you don't want to, but we at least have to do the Vows section of the *Times*."

"See? You're not even listening to me."

"But I adore you! You're the most precious thing in the whole world to me."

"That's what I mean, Cecil. You see me as a thing, a possession. Like your yacht, or one of your Rothkos."

"That's not true. You are more than a thing to me. So much more. You're the light of my life. You're the only person who truly understands me, Lucie."

"But you don't understand *me*."

"How can you say that? After all we've been through these last five years? I understand and appreciate you like no one else does."

"If you truly did, Cecil, you wouldn't always be trying to change me—how I live, how I wear my hair, how I dress."

"I thought you loved fashion."

"I do love fashion. But my style is completely different from your mom's. I don't have any interest in wearing couture, and I really don't care for the sort of statement jewelry your mom loves."

"Listen, you don't ever have to wear anything you don't want to. I'll get you the smallest diamond in the world if that makes you happy. Is three carats small enough for you? And I won't care if you never make the International Best Dressed List. I just didn't want you to feel left out, since Mother and I are both in the Best Dressed Hall of Fame."

"Here's the other thing, Cecil. You are so close to your mother, and I have no issue with that. I think it's one of the most redeeming qualities about you, actually. But have you ever considered how close I am to my family? And that when you hurt them, you're also hurting me?"

"How have I ever hurt your family? They've hurt you, those nasty snobs."

"I'm not talking about the Churchills and the Barclays. I'm talking about my immediate family. Mom and Freddie."

"How have I hurt them?"

"Cecil, you wouldn't even make a phone call to your friend today, when my mother practically got on her hands and knees and begged you to. That really hurt her."

"Lucie, I didn't want your mother to be disappointed. I knew Cornelia would never say yes. I was sparing her the humiliation."

"But she did, Cecil. She said yes."

"What do you mean?"

"Freddie contacted her. Freddie got her to say yes."

"I don't believe it! How the hell did he manage that?"

"All he did was ask nicely. Don't believe me, but she's coming to the gala."

"That brother of yours! I wonder what lies he must have told her . . ."

"He didn't lie, Cecil. Freddie never lies. I was right there when it happened. He simply sent her a text and she said yes. Here's the other thing, Cecil—you've never really liked Freddie, and you've never cared much for my mom either. Don't try to argue with me, I know how you feel. I know you've tried your best to get along with them over the years, but I can see that it doesn't make you happy. And I really *do* want you to be happy, Cecil. My family is always going to be an essential part of my life. We've always been so close, and that will never change. I don't want to spend New Year's in Saint Barth's or summers on your yacht in Saint-Tropez. I want to be with my family in East Hampton during the summer and in the city during the holidays. I want to go to All Souls Church on Christmas Eve and celebrate Chinese New Year at Congee Village like we always do. You can't stand Chinese food, Cecil. Don't pretend you do."

"I like that appetizer . . . crab rangoon."

"That's not real Chinese food, Cecil. My point is we actually have so little in common when you really break it down. And I know you think it's wrong of me to say this now, but I know you'll be miserable being married to me in the long run. You deserve someone who actually has an Instagram account with more than eight posts. You deserve someone who loves sitting in the front row at the haute couture shows in Paris, who loves wearing huge emeralds while sunbathing on your super yacht. Someone who likes tying you up in the gondola in your town house and reenacting the wrestling scene from *Death in Venice*. I know there's someone out there who's perfect for you, who will love you for exactly who you are, Cecil."

"But I thought . . . I thought that person . . . was you."

"For a while, I thought I was that person too, but I've come to realize that I'm not."

The waitress approached the table with a pot of boiling-hot water.

"Would you like me to freshen up your teas? Are you all right, sir? Do you need some tissues?"

"No. I mean, yes, thanks."

"I'm sorry, Cecil. Truly."

"Can we stay friends?"

"Of course we can. I want to stay friends. I really do care for you.

That's why I'm doing this today, as difficult as it is for me to see you so hurt right now. But I just know you'll be thanking me down the line. I know you'll find your perfect soul mate, your twin flame, a lot sooner than you might think."

"You seem so different suddenly, like a new woman."

"A new woman?"

"I can't quite explain it. It's like your whole energy has changed, your voice has been transformed. There's a new clarity, a fiery quality to it. Like someone who's been transfigured."

"What do you mean? I hope you don't think I'm in love with someone else."

"I didn't mean that at all."

"Or maybe you think I'm cheating on you or something . . ."

"That never crossed my mind."

"But you said I seem transfigured, like you're implying that I've been swept up by some new passion."

"Lucie, relax, I wasn't implying anything."

XVI

Jacqueline Kennedy Onassis Reservoir

CENTRAL PARK

Lucie thought a morning run around the reservoir would help clear her head, but it didn't. She managed to sleep about four hours the night before, which was a victory compared with the previous days, but her head still felt like it was in a fog and she could not shake off this sensation deep within her bones that she couldn't quite put into words. What was it? Anxiety? Dread? Guilt? Regret? None of those feelings quite described how she truly felt.

After twice running around the track that encircled the reservoir and showcased spectacular views of the Manhattan skyline, Lucie cooled off by jogging along the path behind the Metropolitan Museum of Art. As she passed a group of Tibetan monks in gold-and-maroon robes gathering by the grove of cherry blossom trees, she noticed someone waving at her. Squinting a bit to get her vision in focus, she realized it was Auden, dressed in light gray robes that set off his piercing blue eyes.

"Sorry, didn't mean to stop you," Auden said.

"It's okay. I'm just cooling down from my run," Lucie said, bending forward with her hands on her knees as she caught her breath. "What are you doing here?"

"I've just been showing this delegation around the park, before our breakfast with the Dalai Lama."

"You're going to meet the Dalai Lama?"

"Yes. We always meet up when he's in town."

"Oh," Lucie said, a little awed.

"Which reminds me, I got the most amusing email from Paloma Ortiz last night. You know the sisters are going to be in town next week?"

"Oh, really?"

Auden fished his phone out from his knitted hemp satchel. "Indeed they are! Paloma writes:

Mercedes and I have been luxuriating in Spain for the past two months. After Cissinghurst fell through, we were fortunate enough to rent the most wonderful villa in Tossa de Mar, on the Costa Brava, where we had a constant invasion of children and grandchildren. A big villa by the sea with the temptations of Barcelona nearby made for the perfect grandchild trap! So while it was not as relaxing as we would have liked, it was great fun nonetheless. Next week, we fly from Barcelona to New York, where we will be stocking up on provisions for our expedition to Mongolia! Yes, Mercedes and I are checking off a bucket-list dream of visiting Mongolia, where we intend to spend time with the eagle hunters, known as the burkitshi, *and the reindeer people, also known as the* Dukha. *It is a four-day trek on horseback to the summer herding grounds of the* Dukha, *and I pray our old bones will be able to manage so much time in the saddle. (I'm told if all else fails we can charter a few helicopters and Cessnas to help.) We will be in Mongolia for three weeks, and if all goes well, we intend to fly from Ulaanbaatar to Urumqi in China, where our plan is to buy a big, comfortable Land Rover and drive along the Silk Route, journeying to such fabled cities as Tashkent, Samarkand, and Bukhara, following in the footsteps of Marco Polo.*

"Can you believe it? The sisters are going to do Mongolia on horse-back, and then they are going to attempt driving four thousand miles along the Silk Road, across five countries! I really think they might make it all the way to Venice just like Marco Polo did!" Auden laughed.

"How fabulous! I hope I have as much of an adventurous spirit when I'm their age." Lucie smiled.

"I trust you will, especially now that you've shaken things up."

Lucie gave Auden a wary look. "What do you mean by that?"

Auden paused, realizing that he had perhaps said too much. "I hope I haven't overstepped, but Freddie did tell me the news ... about you and Cecil."

"Did he tell you at your gong bath last night?" Lucie asked, rather annoyed.

"No, I ran into him at Serendipity. He was sharing this humon-gous banana split with a very pretty redhead."

"So he was high on sugar and gossiping with everyone."

"No, he told me in the strictest of confidence because he's a bit worried about you. He feels you've been going through a great deal lately."

"Really? Freddie said that?"

"Lucie, any ending of a relationship—no matter how right the decision might feel—is still extremely soul-wounding."

Lucie bristled. "My soul feels fine. Never better, actually."

"Fantastic! All the same, I would be glad to gift you a breath work and guided meditation session any time you want, Lucie. Just say the word. Your breath is an incredibly powerful healing tool, and mov-ing the breath through your body is an amazing way to open up your chakras, clear blocks, and resolve any inner conflicts that you have."

"Thank you so much, Auden, but I can tell you this is the first time in my life where I've truly felt like I am absolutely free of inner conflict. Breaking up with Cecil cleared up all the conflict in my life."

Auden smiled. "It makes me so happy to hear that. And now you can start afresh with George!"

Lucie glared at Auden. "*George?* What does George have to do with any of this?"

"I'm sorry, I thought that you ended things with Cecil because—"

Lucie cut him off before he could finish. "Well, you thought wrong."

Saying goodbye hastily, Lucie jogged off. What would possess Auden Beebe to think that she had any interest in George? She ran in a fury down to the Seventy-Ninth Street exit and headed straight back to the apartment, eager to scold Freddie. Entering the stately lobby of 999 Fifth Avenue, she barely nodded at the doormen and stewed in front of the slow elevator, jabbing the button repeatedly.

The left elevator door opened, and out stepped a woman with a perfect blond blowout accompanying a stylish Asian lady.

"Hi, Lucie!" the lady smiled warmly.

"Hello?" Lucie replied politely, not quite placing her.

"It's me, Rosemary!"

Lucie's eyes widened. Rosemary was unrecognizable. Her usual gigantic Elizabeth Taylor perm* was pulled into a discreet low bun, and she was impeccably dressed in a cream Carolina Herrera suit, a single strand of pearls, and barely a hint of makeup.

"Ha ha! You didn't recognize me, did you?"

"I didn't. You look . . . transformed, Mrs. Zao."

"This is Dolly, my broker. We just came from the co-op board interview."

"Interview?" Lucie was confused.

"Yes! Don't you know? I put an offer on apartment 9A!"

A chill ran up Lucie's spine. *No, no, no, this can't be happening.*

"Ahem, knock on wood, Mrs. Zao," Dolly said, as she rapped her knuckles against the wooden marquetry of the elevator door.

"Yes, yes, knock on wood. I just have to pass the co-op board interview, and they have to read all my letters of recommendation,

* See the White Diamonds perfume commercials for the specific era of Elizabeth Taylor's hair.

but I think it went very well, didn't it? Dolly advised me exactly how to dress and what to say."

"They loved her. Especially your board president, Ms. Ferrer, who has notoriously high standards."

"Really? Ms. Ferrer liked her?" Lucie said, getting even more alarmed.

"Yes! She told me how much she admired my father's writings."

"Your father?"

"Yes, he was a poet."

"Come on, Mrs. Zao! She's being so modest. Her father was one of the most revered poets in China. They teach a class on his works at Yale," Dolly bragged to Lucie.

"Oooh, I just can't wait for all of us to be neighbors!" Rosemary squealed, giving Lucie a little hug as she breezed along with her agent out of the lobby.

Lucie took the elevator up alone, feeling shell-shocked. When the elevator doors opened, the first person she saw was Charlotte, who was in the foyer misting the orchids with a plastic spritzer bottle.

"I think Mary's gotten quite lazy. She doesn't dust or spritz your orchids quite enough. This one here looks like it should be sent to palliative care."

Lucie grabbed Charlotte firmly by the arm and forced her down the hallway into her bedroom.

"What's the matter now?" Charlotte said in a hushed whisper, even though no one was about.

Lucie shut the door firmly behind her and gave Charlotte a look of frustration. "Did you know that Rosemary Zao's attempting to buy an apartment in this building?"

"She is?"

"Yes! I just saw her in the lobby with her agent."

"I wouldn't worry too much about that. She'll never get past the board, especially in one of her crazy caftans. Doesn't that Ferrer lady on the third floor rule this building like Catherine the Great?"

"Mrs. Zao was stripped bare of makeup and dressed like a Scandinavian royal when I saw her in the lobby. And Ms. Ferrer is a huge fan of her father's work. Apparently he's some famous classical poet."

"Why on earth is she choosing to move into *this* building? I would have thought she would want to buy in one of those ghastly glass skyscrapers along Fifty-Seventh, where all the other international gazillionaires live," Charlotte wondered.

"Charlotte, get a clue! Now that I've broken things off with Cecil, she's trying to force George on me, and she obviously thinks her moving into this building is going to help! From the very beginning in Capri, she's been trying to get us together."

Charlotte almost cracked a smile. "Well, my dear, she can't force you to do anything. We all know that. But you know, I've come to see that she's really not that bad. She's awfully generous with your mother and me. She treated us to that lovely Korean spa night."

"I didn't realize you were that easy to buy off."

"That's not it. She's actually quite amusing. She was telling us the most hilarious stories about her dating days in Hong Kong. She certainly is an authentic soul, that's for sure."

Lucie stood by her window, staring out onto Central Park pensively. "Why does everyone seem to think that I've broken up with Cecil because of George? First Auden Beebe accosts me in the park about it, and then Mrs. Zao actually has the audacity to try to invade my home! God knows what everyone will think when the news truly gets out that I've broken things off with Cecil, if it hasn't already— Freddie's been gossiping up and down Madison Avenue. I'm sure even the three guys at 3 Guys Restaurant know by now."*

"Lucie, don't you think you're overreacting a little?"

"Absolutely not! You know what? I think I should go away. The Ortiz sisters are going to Mongolia to visit the reindeer people on horseback, and then they're going to drive the Silk Road all the way

---

* A diner on Madison Avenue between Seventy-Fifth and Seventy-Sixth Streets, 3 Guys Restaurant has been called New York's "Most Powerful Diner" because it's a popular haunt for many of the city's biggest business titans like Michael Bloomberg, Lloyd Blankfein, Jamie Dimon, and, of course, Freddie Churchill.

from China to Italy, tracing the route of Marco Polo. I'm sure they'd love another driver. I can even call it a work trip. I mean, you never know what emerging artists I might discover along the way."

"I really don't think escaping to Mongolia is going to solve anything," Charlotte gently suggested, worried by how worked up Lucie seemed to be getting.

Lucie paced her room. "Actually, it's going to solve everything. Don't you see I must go away for a long while until this all blows over?"

"I don't understand. Why is this such a secret? Why are you acting like it's the nineteenth century and you're some cad who's going to ruin a girl's life by breaking off your engagement? You dumped Cecil. And I'm sure there's going to be a thousand girls swarming around trying to land him the minute the news gets out."

"I don't want to give George or his mother any ideas. And I certainly don't want our family to ever think that I'm interested in George Zao!"

"But what would it matter if you did?"

Lucie stared at her incredulously. "I can't believe I need to spell things out for you. Don't you see? It was already bad enough when I was engaged to Cecil. Can you imagine what would happen if I brought someone like George home? I can already hear the snide comments coming out of Teddy's and Cacky's mouths."

"Oh my goodness, who cares about them?"

"Charlotte, you of all people were against my fraternizing with George when we first met him in Capri, or don't you remember?"

Charlotte paused for a moment, trying to find the most delicate way to answer Lucie without spooking her. "You know, Capri seems like another lifetime. I hope you realize I have nothing against George. I mean, when you were nineteen and there was a risk of a drone sex video going viral, I had my concerns, but nothing about George concerns me anymore."

"But you tried to shame me! You said I couldn't help being attracted to him because of my recessive genes!"

Charlotte looked horrified. "Did I really say that? Oh dear, it was so long ago . . ."

"Are you really changing your tune now? All my life, all you Barclays and Churchills have made me feel like I wasn't really part of the family, like I was some little troll in the attic."

"What are you talking about? We've done no such thing!"

"Why is it that every time you introduce me to someone new, you have to explain to them exactly how we're related? Our racist grandmother does the exact same thing, as if no one would ever believe from looking at my face that I was really a Churchill, a bona fide *Mayflower* Knickerbocker *Social Register* Churchill!"

"Lucie, our grandmother is many things, but the one thing she is *not* is racist. She is an insufferable snob and a creature of her background, and she has many limitations that I myself have been victim to."

Lucie shook her head vehemently. "I'm sorry, but Granny *is* a racist."

"But Granny loves you!" Charlotte insisted.

"Don't you see it's possible to love someone without realizing you're being racist toward them? How can you not see it? Especially after the way Granny treated you over your Jewish boyfriend?"

Charlotte sank onto Lucie's bed, visibly conflicted. Within her cocoon of privilege, it never even occurred to her to equate her own tribulations with those of her cousin. "You know, Lucie, shortly after your father passed, Granny called a few of us together for a special lunch. We were all quite aware there would be snotty, close-minded people out there, particularly among our crowd, and your father was no longer here to guide you through this maze. Granny wanted to rally the family and circle the wagons, as it was our duty now to protect you and your brother, and that's all we've ever tried to do."

"But protecting me is precisely what's made me feel like a total freak my whole life!" Lucie cried.

Charlotte sighed deeply. "That's the last thing any of us ever wanted to happen. I don't know how you could ever think of your-self as a freak. I mean, jeez, what I would do for your skin! I'm only forty-two, but I'm already beginning to resemble an alligator Birkin."

"Charlotte, you're forty-nine."

"Oh, hush! The point is, if you ever felt I was being insensitive, I am truly sorry. You know I have always adored you. You know you've always been my favorite cousin. I mean, hell would freeze over before I would travel anywhere with Cacky!"

"Help me, then, if I'm really your favorite. I'm going to call the Ortiz sisters right now about Mongolia, and I expect your full sup-port if Mom makes a fuss about it. Now, I just need to deal with Fred-die, before he hits the R&T* this afternoon," Lucie said.

She walked down the hallway toward Freddie's bedroom, passing her mother's study along the way. Peeking in, she noticed a white envelope sitting in the wire tray by the door that her obsessively organized mother always used for outgoing mail. It was marked *To the Co-op Board* in her mother's handwriting on the front. Curious, she carefully opened the half-sealed envelope and confirmed her suspicion. It was a letter of recommendation for Rosemary Zao that her mother had written to the board of their building, a particularly glowing letter that Lucie knew would go a very long way with the board.

No, no, no, she simply couldn't bear the thought of Rosemary liv-ing in the building, just floors away from her, and having to run into her and George all the time in the elevator. She didn't want Rosemary invading for more Chinese meals with her suddenly woke mother. As if she was seized by some mania, Lucie sat down at her mother's desk, opened her laptop, and began frantically composing a new let-ter, her heart pounding in tandem with the words she was pounding

---

* The Racquet and Tennis Club, a private social and athletic club on Park Avenue that boasts an exquisite cigar lounge and one of the handsomest locker rooms this side of the Atlantic. It is also one of the few private clubs in New York that has retained its men-only membership policy.

on the keyboard. When she was finished, she printed the new version on her mother's letterhead, forged her signature quickly, and placed the resealed envelope back in her mom's outgoing tray.

DR. MARIAN TANG CHURCHILL

999 FIFTH AVENUE, APT 12B

NEW YORK, NEW YORK 10028

(212) 358-9880

July 14, 2018

To the Board of Directors of 999 Fifth Avenue:

It gives me great pleasure to highly recommend Rosemary Zao to our building. I met Rosemary earlier this summer, as she is renting the house of a family friend, Harry Stuyvesant Fish, in East Hampton. Though I have not known Rosemary for very long, we have become good friends and have shared many fascinating experiences in a very short time.

Over the months, my respect for Rosemary has grown as I have watched her tirelessly pursue her special gift as the consummate hostess. She is *very* social, and her theme parties in East Hampton, thrown on a weekly basis, have already become legendary for their originality. Especially memorable was the Beasts of Burden S&M-themed party that she threw last month, complete with thirteen boa constrictors, a lemur, a cheetah, and dominatrix twins from Berlin. (You should have *seen* what those twins could do with those snakes!) Rosemary took great effort to line all the hallways leading all the way up to the attic of this National Register Victorian wooden house with tens of thousands of long-tapered medieval candles, flickering away freely, and it was such a success that she has promised to host a similar soiree at her new Manhattan apartment on a bimonthly basis with the same type of candles.

Rosemary is above all a very considerate and polite person, and I have learned from people who have known her far longer about her extraordinary humanitarian work. She has consistently provided a haven to those in need, and her homes around the world have always had an "open door" policy. She has looked after Islamic dissidents released from Guantánamo Bay and homeless Appalachian teenagers addicted to opioids, and after meeting two pregnant Syrian refugees at a UN action alert party, Rosemary invited both women to stay at her home for the duration of their final trimesters and even financed their home births.

Such generosity and sensitivity is a hallmark of Rosemary's. As she painstakingly sought to create a well-appointed home out of her Hong Kong apartment several years ago, I was told how conscientiously considerate she was to her neighbors during the renovations and the sixty-nine applications of aubergine-colored lacquer to her drawing room. She even rented special trucks with ventilation units to ease the fumes from the building for the fortnight that it took to dry the layers of lacquer. (The effect was *stunning*. Very much like what Mario Buatta did for the Langerford apartment, before their tragic double suicide.) I am certain Rosemary will do the same in her new home and that she will become a treasured addition to the building.

Sincerely,

Marian Tang Churchill

XVII

The Animal Rescue Fund Summer Gala

SOUTHAMPTON

Marian, Freddie, Lucie, Charlotte, the board of the fund-raising committee, and all the staff and volunteers of the Animal Rescue Shelter of Long Island formed a receiving line at the entrance courtyard of the spectacular thirty-acre oceanfront equestrian estate in Southampton. At 5:40 p.m., a Chevy Suburban could be spotted turning onto the long gravel driveway from the majestic gated entrance, and when it came to a stop outside the front door of the main house, Cornelia Guest (Green Vale School / Foxcroft / Wheatley / Professional Children's School), who was at the wheel, stepped out looking like a no-nonsense country girl in a faded yellow T-shirt, Lilly Pulitzer shorts, a pair of flip-flops, and a cardigan slung over her shoulders.

She walked around the SUV and opened the back door, and out tumbled a Great Dane, an equally gigantic Newfoundland, a Great Pyrenees, a Jack Russell terrier, a white West Highland terrier, a Chihuahua, two rescue dogs of indeterminate breed, and an inquisitive black duck. "I thought it'd be fun to bring all my dogs!" Cornelia called out.

Everyone gasped at the delightful menagerie, as the board member who had generously opened up her hundred-million-dollar property for the gala and Marian—already dressed in her heirloom purple silk cheongsam—walked up to greet their VIP. "Ms. Guest, it is such a great honor to have you here with us. Our little fund-raiser has become the hottest ticket in town tonight because of you. I can't thank you enough for your tremendous help!" Marian gushed.

"Oh please, you guys are doing all the work, I'm just coming to a party. I'm so happy to help this worthy cause."

"May I ask, why is the duck here?" Marian inquired.

"This is Lucky. He thinks he's a dog and goes everywhere with the pack. Now, where can I change?" Cornelia asked as she took her luggage out of the truck.

Freddie came forward in his dapper new bamboo-print Etro linen blazer and matching linen slacks. "Here, let me help you with your bags."

"Are you the cutie who roped me into doing this?" Cornelia asked as she handed him her bags.

"Sure am!"

"Yes, this is my son, Frederick, and here's my daughter, Lucie," Marian said.

Lucie, in a pink ruffled Alexandre Vauthier cocktail dress cinched at the waist with a black satin bow, came forward and shook Cornelia's hand, slightly awed.

"What a gorgeous family you are!" Cornelia said, as she was escorted upstairs to a guest suite to get ready.

By 6:30 p.m., the party was in full swing. Marian had decided on a Chinese theme this year, and guests dressed in their festive summer finery wandered around the meticulously manicured grounds just as it was transforming into the golden hour, sipping on mai tais and munching on delectable dim sum appetizers. The central courtyard had been transformed into an ice sculpture fantasyland straight out of Harbin, China, and massive pavilions carved out of ice and lit in a spectrum of colors had been generously flown in for the occasion courtesy of Isabel and Dolfi De Vecchi, who unfortunately could not attend the gala, as they were at an intimacy retreat at Lake Titicaca. Meanwhile, towering arrangements of rare flowers encased in blocks of ice by Japanese artist Makoto Azuma stood melting in the late-afternoon sun.

Despite the jaw-dropping decor, the most popular attractions were the rescue animals, of course, and each of them was show-cased in one of the luxurious stables—each state-of-the-art, climate-controlled stable boasted its own chandelier. Everyone oohed and ahhed over the adorable dogs, cats, and even a few miniature horses, trying to decide which ones to adopt and bid for in the charity auction later in the evening.

Cornelia had morphed in less than half an hour from country girl to fashion goddess, making her entrance into the central courtyard in a shimmering silver off-the-shoulder Oscar de la Renta gown and mingling happily with all the guests as a band of Chinese musicians dapperly outfitted in white silk tuxedos played 1930s Shanghainese jazz standards.

Lucie approached Cornelia, shyly handing her a mai tai. "I thought you could use one of the signature cocktails. You've been talking to so many people nonstop."

"How sweet of you. Thanks!"

"So I understand you were friends with Andy Warhol?" Lucie began, a little intimidated, knowing that Cornelia had been good friends with Keith Haring and Jean-Michel Basquiat as well.

"Yes, he was an absolute doll to me."

"I hope you don't mind my asking, but I went to see the Warhol retrospective at the Whitney, and I couldn't help but notice that out of all the iconic silk-screen portraits he did of famous people, yours was the only one that had a bit of . . . um . . . nudity," Lucy asked delicately.

"I was topless," Cornelia said matter-of-factly.

"Yes. Was that his intention or yours?"

"I was nineteen. It was my intention to piss off my mother," Cornelia answered.

They both broke out in laughter.

Freddie came rushing up, looking a little disheveled. "Lucie, can I steal you for a moment?"

"Can you give me a sec? Cornelia and I were just chatting—"

"Actually, I *really* need you now," Freddie said through gritted teeth.

"Everything okay?" Cornelia asked.

"Perfect!" Freddie flashed her his megawatt smile as he rushed off with Lucie.

"What's the deal?" Lucie asked, suddenly alarmed.

Freddie took her into the kitchen, where several of the kitchen staff appeared to be hugging Cornelia's humongous dogs.

"The animals somehow got into the kitchen, and now half the Wagyu beef sliders we were going to serve the guests have disappeared."

"Oh, shit!" Lucie exclaimed as she burst into giggles.

"Stop laughing! I need your help getting these beasts to the smaller riding ring. Mom and Charlotte have already taken the Westie, the Chihuahua, and the duck."

Lucie gamely helped to wrangle the big dogs, and when they had been safely ensconced in their plush indoor riding ring, she went to the ladies' powder room in the main house to tidy up. As she stood in front of the large mirror over the sink, trying to brush off what seemed like a million dog hairs from her party dress, a tall patrician lady in her seventies entered the powder room.

"Hello, Lucie," the lady greeted her warmly.

Lucie looked up, surprised to see her neighbor from 999 Fifth Avenue. "Hi, Ms. Ferrer."

"My God, what have you been doing, wrestling a polar bear?"

"Actually, he was a Great Pyrenees."

"Here, let me help you. Don't use your hands—one of these dry towels would be far better," Ms. Ferrer said, as she expertly began brushing off the fur caught on Lucie's ruffles.

"Oh, wow. How did you know that would work?"

"I was a photo editor at *Life* magazine for more than a decade, my dear. We had to deal with every conceivable issue on our shoots."

"It's so nice of you to come to Mom's fund-raiser. I didn't realize Mom even told anyone in the building about her event."

"She didn't. It was Mrs. Zao who did such a good job of convincing me to come out for the gala."

"Rosemary's here tonight?" Lucie said, quietly alarmed.

"I haven't seen her yet, but I assume she's coming."

"How is her application to live in the building coming along?" Lucie knew she shouldn't be asking, but she couldn't help herself.

"Oh, I can't talk about that. These applications are strictly confidential."

"Sorry."

Ms. Ferrer leaned in. "But I will tell you—*entre nous*—your mother really surprised us."

"How so?" Lucie asked, getting a bit nervous.

"She submitted a grossly inappropriate recommendation letter."

"Really?" Lucie felt a sudden pang of fear.

"Yes, it was the most hilarious letter, a brilliant practical joke. I almost lost my mind reading it! Everyone on the board was rolling on the floor! Who knew your mother could be so funny? Which reminds me, I still need to thank her for it."

Suddenly overcome with the panic of not only her mother discovering her fake co-op letter, but her whole plan misfiring, Lucie found herself blurting out, "Ms. Ferrer, there are some things I think you ought to know about Rosemary Zao!"

"Oh, and what might that be?"

"She's not the woman you think she is."

"What do you mean? Aren't your families very close?"

"I wouldn't exactly call it that. Rosemary has been trying to cultivate my mother all summer, and as you know, Mom just tries to be polite to everyone."

"She does, doesn't she? Your mother is very polite."

"If you must know, Mrs. Zao is *very social*—when I first met her in Italy, she told me about all the wild parties she used to go to in Lan Kwai Fong," Lucie said, taking her own liberties with the truth.

"What's Lan Kwai Fong?"

"It's the red-light district of Hong Kong."*

"My goodness! Was Rosemary one of those Suzie Wong party girls?"

"I don't know what that is, but she did party. She partied very hard."

"I can't even imagine. She seems so fastidious and well put together. I love her understated elegance."

"Let me show you something, Ms. Ferrer." Lucie took out her phone and found a group photo she had taken at the Peking duck dinner. She zoomed in on Rosemary striking a flamboyant pose in one of her signature rainbow-colored sequined caftans.

"That's Mrs. Zao?" Ms. Ferrer stared at the screen in disbelief.

"Uh-huh."

"Why is she wearing kabuki makeup?"

"She's not. That's how she normally looks."

"You don't say! And those Christmas ornaments around her neck . . . this wasn't some theme party?"

"It was just a family dinner, and those aren't Christmas ornaments, Ms. Ferrer. Those are real rubies and diamonds, and that's how Rosemary dresses when she's not attending co-op board interviews."

"How *interesting* . . ."

Just then, a flush could be heard in one of the toilets connected to the powder room, and Cornelia Guest emerged from behind the door. Acknowledging Lucie and Ms. Ferrer with the briefest of smiles, she quickly washed her hands and left the powder room.

Ms. Ferrer continued. "Well, Lucie, I am quite astonished. Thank you for letting me know all this."

---

* Lucie's completely mistaken. Lan Kwai Fong is an upscale entertainment district popular with expats and tourists and is unconnected in any way with Wan Chai, the decidedly wilder neighborhood that's home to bars, brothels, and nightclubs that are equally as popular with expats and tourists.

"You're quite welcome. Ms. Ferrer, can we keep this conversation totally between us?"

"Absolutely. I take my duties very seriously. Any information provided to the board president shall remain private."

"Even from my mother?"

"Of course." Ms. Ferrer patted Lucie's hand as she left the room.

Lucie leaned against the sink, letting out a groan. *Fuck. Fuck. Fuck. How much did Cornelia overhear? What would she think now?*

Collecting herself, Lucie left the powder room in search of the guest of honor. She had to do as much damage control as she could. She couldn't let Cornelia, of all people, get the wrong impression of her. Entering the drawing room of the manor house, she found herself face-to-face with Rosemary Zao, who stood chatting with Ms. Ferrer.

Fuck me again, Lucie moaned to herself.

"Lucie! We were just talking about you," Rosemary said in her usual excitable tone.

"You—you were?" Lucie stammered, noticing that Rosemary was still sporting her new look in a sophisticated but subdued champagne-colored Akris pantsuit accessorized with a stunningly simple amber bead necklace.

"Yes, we were. Actually, Ms. Ferrer, could you excuse us for a minute? I have something important to discuss with Lucie."

"Certainly," Ms. Ferrer said, arching an eyebrow.

Rosemary and Lucie went into the adjoining sitting room, and taking a seat on one of the armchairs, Rosemary gave Lucie a sad look. "So, I need you to be very honest with me . . ."

Lucie took a deep breath, steeling herself. "Okay?"

"Are Freddie and George fighting?"

Oh thank God, I thought Ms. Ferrer ratted on me. "Freddie and George? Not that I know of. Why?"

"George refused to come with me to this gala tonight. In fact, he hasn't been out to East Hampton two weekends in a row. Normally he can't wait to drive out the moment he gets off work on Fridays. He said he has too much work, but I don't believe it."

"Well, maybe he does have too much work." *She doesn't know. She doesn't know one thing that happened between me and George.*

"But it's so strange that he would miss this weekend, especially because he's been so excited for your mom's charity gala all summer. Do you know he found the jazz band for your mom? They are the band from the Peace Hotel in Shanghai, and he flew all of them here to New York first class and paid for them to perform tonight."*

"I had no idea . . ." *Why would he do all that for Mom?*

"He's been even more quiet than usual. I can sense that something's wrong but I don't know what. So I thought maybe it had something to do with Freddie. They have become such good friends. They even went skinny-dipping in some pond the other day with Auden Beebe."

"I wish I could help you, Mrs. Zao, but I'm as much in the dark as you are."

"Well, if you get the chance to talk to George, can you try to find out for me what's bothering him?"

"Mrs. Zao, I'd like to help, but you know I'm going to Mongolia next week. I might not be back till Christmas."

"Not back till Christmas! Is Cecil going with you?" Rosemary asked in surprise.

"Excuse me, but I need to take care of something for my mother before the dinner starts," Lucie said awkwardly, as she got up from her armchair and rushed off.

She couldn't find Cornelia anywhere as she wandered through the various rooms, inner courtyards, and the stables, her panic growing

---

* The jazz band at Shanghai's Peace Hotel is one of the city's most beloved institutions. Often described as "the oldest jazz band on the planet," its dapper musicians range from their late sixties to their ninety-nine-year-old former trumpeter Zhou Wanrong. Xiao Xueqiang, saxophonist and manager of the band, reports, "He still comes around to perform with us once in a while, but now he shakes the maracas instead."

with every minute. She knew she needed to get to her before the dinner began. Finally, she found Cornelia in the indoor ring, crouched down on the floor playing with her dogs.

"Hi, Cornelia!" Lucie chirped.

"Oh, hi," Cornelia answered as she gave Olive, her Westie, a big kiss. "I'm sorry you've been banished here, but you've all been naughty dogs tonight!"

"I, um, just wanted to . . . to explain . . . ," Lucie stammered.

Cornelia looked up with a diplomatic smile. "Lucie, it was none of my business. There's nothing you need to tell me."

"Oh. Okay. But I just wanted to say, in case you might have heard some things out of context, it really isn't what it looks like."

"It's fine, Lucie. Shall we go in to dinner?"

"Yes, of course."

"I'm told the dining tent is down by the ocean."

"Yes, I'll show you the way. But I just wanted you to know that I was actually trying to help my mother in there. I'm just trying to protect her from this woman who's . . ."

Cornelia put down her terrier, stood up, and looked Lucie straight in the face. "Lucie, I'm really trying to stay out of your business, but it seems like you won't let it go. Who are we kidding here? You were in the middle of a takedown, a total smear campaign. Now, I don't live in your building, I don't know any of these people, and this really doesn't concern me, but please have some self-respect and stop trying to bullshit me. Because the only person you're deceiving is yourself. And from the looks of it the only thing you'll succeed in doing is pissing off *your* mother."

Cornelia turned and walked out of the room, leaving Lucie red-faced and speechless.

XVIII

Montauk Highway

THE HAMPTONS

"I hate to admit it, but the one good thing you got out of Cecil was this car," Marian said to Lucie from the driver's seat of the Aston Martin as she sped along Montauk Highway. They had spent the day in Manhattan, meeting up with the Ortiz sisters at the Colony Club for lunch and running last-minute errands before Lucie's big trip.

"I'm glad someone's driving it. I just never thought it would be you," Lucie remarked distractedly. The full enormity of all her decisions over the past few weeks was finally crashing down on her. *Why did I tell George I never wanted to see him again? Why did I break his heart?*

"Yeah, I never imagined myself in a car like this either, but it really drives like a dream. And if we were anywhere but the Hamptons, I'd be too embarrassed. But you know, life is short. Why the hell shouldn't I drive a sports car if I want to? Am I not entitled to my own midlife crisis?"

"You deserve a nice car, Mom," Lucie said. *Why did I fake that co-op letter? Why did I lie to Ms. Ferrer? Why did I lie to Rosemary?*

"Are you sure Cecil doesn't want it back? I'm really getting quite attached to Chad."

"You've named the car *Chad*?"

"Don't you think he looks like a Chad? I had a mad crush on this guy back in high school named Chad. He was on the basketball team."

Ew. Why is Mom telling me about her high school crushes? Why can't I get George out of my mind? "I dunno . . . I've always found it weird when people anthropomorphize machines."

"Weird or not, I hope Cecil's not taking Chad back."

"For the eleventh time, Mom, I told you he won't take Chad . . . *it* . . . back. He said to consider it a breakup gift."

"Ha! Chad's a mighty generous breakup gift."

"The cost of this car to someone like Cecil is like the cost of a bag of Cheetos to you and me."

"Yes, I gather that's why the Ortiz sisters had a hard time believing Cecil wouldn't be dropping in to visit you during the grand expedition, especially when he's got his own jet. I don't get why you won't tell them about your breakup. I'm sure they already suspect. I could see it in Mercedes's face. She doesn't say as much as Paloma, but she's very astute."

"I'll tell them after we've left New York, Mom," Lucie said. *Why am I going to spend four months traveling through Central Asia with two nice ladies I've just lied to? Why the hell can't I get Cornelia Guest's words out of my head?* "The only person you're deceiving is yourself."

"What's the big secret? You finally dumped Cecil and we should all be celebrating. I always thought you were too young to be getting married anyway."

"Well, that's what I realized too. I *am* too young, and I want to enjoy the rest of my twenties. As you know, I'm going to be twenty-five next year, and that's when the Churchill trust kicks in. Maybe I'll use that money and get a place in LA." *The only person you're deceiving is yourself.*

"LA? You want to move to LA? Why would you want to move to a place that's devoid of culture and has no seasons?"

"It's not devoid of culture. The food scene's exploding and so is the art scene.* So many artists I know have moved out there, and they're all loving it. I can't wait to try it out." *The only person you're deceiving is yourself.*

"You want to use your trust fund to buy a house in a city that's full of wildfires and earthquakes? Really smart, Lucie. But I suppose your moving there and having your house burn to the ground is the price we'll have to pay for getting rid of Cecil." Marian sighed.

"Mom, tell me, why in all the years that I was dating Cecil did you never express to me how much you hated him?"

"I never hated him, Lucie. He irritated me to no end, but I could see that he was a wounded bird, so I felt sorry for him. That father of his clearly did a number on him while he was around. Besides, what would have been the point of my saying anything? You seemed to like him, and he worshipped the ground you walked on. I didn't want to come between the both of you."

"But you're a Chinese mother. Isn't it your job to come between us?"

"Ha! I've gone out of my way not to be a Chinese mother, you know that!"

"Why is that, Mom?"

"What? Would you prefer me to be some sort of Tiger Mom and drag you down to Chinatown every Saturday for Mandarin classes and force you to take classical Chinese dance? Not allow you to have sleepovers or have a phone or date any white boys until you were thirty? Because that's how I grew to resent my mother."

"Wow. Sounds like Freddie and I dodged a bullet."

"You sure did. You guys hit the jackpot when you got me as your bad mama."

---

* Even the *New York Times* had to concede in 2018 that Los Angeles had become "America's best and most exciting food city."

Driving down Main Street in East Hampton, Marian suddenly made a right turn on Dunemere Lane.

"Where are you going?"

"Oh, Charlotte texted as we were leaving the city. She was at the Maidstone meeting up with a friend, and she wanted to catch a ride back with us."

"There's no room, Mom."

"Well, you could squeeze into the bucket seat in the back for a few minutes, can't you?"

"Why can't Charlotte just take a cab like everyone else? She's so cheap! And of course she's richer than all of us put together."

"Stop complaining. We're almost there and I did promise her."

"Can you put the top down if I'm going to have to squeeze in the back?" Lucie asked.

"If you can figure out how to get the top down, you can have the top down," Marian replied.

"How many PhDs do you have? See, it's this button right here," Lucie said, reaching for a switch on the center console. The convertible roof of the car began to retract in the most elegant manner. As the view opened up around them, they drove passed Cissinghurst, and through the hedges Lucie glimpsed several moving trucks parked in the driveway and men carrying Goyard suitcases out the front door. Lucie said nothing, but a sudden panic washed over her.

The car pulled up to the quietly dignified entrance of the Maidstone Club. "Go get Charlotte, please," Marian said. Lucie hopped out of the car and ran into the clubhouse. A minute later, she reappeared.

"No sign of Charlotte, Mom. There's hardly anybody inside the club right now. They're in the midst of switching over to dinner."

"Well, this is annoying. Where could she be?" Marian asked as she began texting Charlotte.

"Maybe her friend gave her a ride home?"

"She would have texted me if she had. You know, she probably walked over to Cissinghurst to say hi to Rosemary and poke around.

You know what a busybody she is," Marian surmised. "Let's head over there."

"No, no, I think we should stay right here. Maybe Charlotte is in the ladies' room or something," Lucie said nervously. The last thing in the world she wanted to do was run into Rosemary right now.

"Well, why don't you go check the toilet and I'll run over to Cissinghurst to see if she's there?"

Trapped by her own suggestion, Lucie could say nothing. She got out of the car again as Marian drove down the block to Cissinghurst. A few minutes later, Marian returned with a frown on her face. "No Charlotte, but it's the oddest thing, Lucie. There were movers at the house, packing up all of Rosemary's belongings. They couldn't tell me much, except that she was moving out."

"Rosemary's moving?" Lucie pretended to be surprised.

"Yes, but I thought she had taken a one-year lease on the house. It's so strange. No sign of Charlotte?"

"Nope."

"Then let's go. I'm done waiting."

As they drove past Cissinghurst for the second time, Marian said, "I hope nothing bad has happened. Why would Rosemary suddenly give up the house? She said nothing to me Saturday night at the gala. I hope she's not having to leave New York for good. I would be so sad. She's become a good friend, and for the first time in ages I feel like I'm reconnecting to my Chinese roots."

Lucie pondered her mother's words, feeling a piercing sense of guilt. Her mother's phone let out two chirps.

"I'm sure that's Charlotte. Will you check it?" Marian asked.

Lucie picked up her mother's phone and read it in annoyance. "You're not going to believe this. For some reason Charlotte found her way to Auden's Preppie Guru Lounge in Amagansett, and she's requested that we pick her up there."

"Oh, for Chrissakes! Classic Charlotte Barclay!" Marian sighed.

XIX

The Preppie Guru Lounge

AMAGANSETT, LONG ISLAND

Lucie wandered through the healing center, peeking into the various spaces. There was an afternoon Ashtanga class in the big lotus lounge, a five elements acupuncture session in the chakra lounge, and no sign of Charlotte in the juice bar. Where could she be? Lucie walked to the back where the staff offices were and heard some voices coming from Auden's private lounge. She poked her head in and saw Charlotte relaxing on the Flag Halyard chair facing the door.

"Lucie! Come in," Charlotte said with a little wave.

Lucie entered the room, expecting to see Auden seated at his usual place on the sofa against the wall, but in his place sat Rosemary.

"Oh! Hi," Lucie said, recoiling a little.

"Rosemary is here seeking temporary refuge from her movers. I took an Uber here when I found out where she was."

"I hope I'm not interrupting you two."

"Not at all, Lucie. Not at all," Charlotte said with a strange look on her face.

"Um . . . Mom's outside waiting."

"Yes, I'm sure she is." Charlotte got up from her comfy perch reluctantly and said, "I shall go to your mother."

Lucie attempted to make a quick break for the door, but Charlotte blocked her way. "No, no, you stay."

"What?" Lucie said in shock.

"Yes, be a dear and keep Rosemary company for a while," Charlotte said with a smirk as she left the room.

As she arrived at the car, Marian sighed in relief. "Oh, good, Lucie found you!"

"Yes, thank you so much for coming all the way here to pick me up!" Charlotte said as she got into the convertible.

"But where's Lucie?"

"Lucie won't be joining us. We'd best head home first."

"Huh? What is the girl doing now?"

"Don't worry, she's going to be quite occupied for a while."

"I don't get it. What's Lucie up to? If she thinks I'm driving back here to pick her up, she's out of her mind."

"You're quite right. She has been out of her mind, but I think she's going to be fine now. Rosemary will set her straight."

"Rosemary? Rosemary is here at the Preppie Guru Lounge?"

"Just drive, Marian, and I'll explain."

After Charlotte had left the room, Lucie turned to Rosemary with a sense of dread. She had known she would have to face the music eventually for all her machinations, but she didn't expect it would happen now. She assumed Charlotte and Rosemary had talked, and all hell would break loose now.

But instead of being angry, Rosemary gazed at her mournfully. "Lucie, this is very hard for me to say, but I am sorry. Very, very sorry. I truly am ashamed."

Lucie was baffled. "Ashamed of what?"

"I'm ashamed for my son. He finally told me everything, on Sunday morning. How he loves you. How he hurt you and embarrassed you. I'm sorry, I never knew a thing, dear. I didn't know you two had a little romance in Capri, and I certainly didn't know about the terrible drone thing until Charlotte just told me. Oh my, what you've been through all because of my silly son!"

"It's okay, Mrs. Zao. It was a long time ago," Lucie said, rather surprised at Rosemary's words.

"And then for George to try to win your love again in East Hampton, when you are already engaged. *Aye yie yie,* my son has no shame. I know how he must have offended you and Cecil. As his mother, I am ashamed too. Because it's all my fault."

"How is any of this your fault?"

"I have always encouraged George to pursue his passions, to always seek out his truth and follow his heart. I just didn't know he would go so far following his heart that he would end up hurting you like this. That's why I have to leave."

"You're leaving?"

"I moved out of Shittinghurst today and I've also retracted my offer on the cute little apartment in your building. Who was I kidding? I would have never been accepted by that board anyway. It's such a nice building, I'm sure they don't want more than one Chinese family."

Lucie sank down on the Wegner chair, not sure what to say. She had succeeded beyond her wildest imagination in getting rid of the Zaos, and now she was flooded with guilt.

"But where will you live?"

"Don't worry about me. I have so many houses. I think I want to go back to Hong Kong for a while, and then I'll see where George lands."

"What do you mean 'where George lands'?" Lucie asked.

"George resigned from his job this morning."

"Noooo!"

"Yes, he's going to look for a job in another city. He says it's too painful to be here."

"No, no, no. Can you stop him? He really shouldn't have to give up his job." Lucie rose from her chair in alarm.

"He wanted to quit his job."

"But he was doing so well there! Isn't he about to start a big new project in Queens? The apartments made out of trash?"

"It's out of the question now, Lucie. Come on, how can my son be here, after all he's done to you?"

"But I don't mind, Mrs. Zao. Really, I don't. Besides, I'm going to be away. I'm going to be traveling for the next four or five months at least with the Ortiz sisters. I'm going to Mongolia, and then I'll be driving along the Silk Road from China to Italy. George doesn't need to give up his job. He shouldn't give up his job!" Lucie found herself pacing the room, hyperventilating. She was overwhelmed and angry with herself. She couldn't stand thinking that she might have ruined George's career.

"I don't understand why you're driving from China to Italy. Doesn't Cecil have his own plane? Don't you have to plan your big wedding?"

"There isn't going to be a wedding, Mrs. Zao."

"Why? Are you going to elope in Vegas?"

"Cecil and I aren't getting married," Lucie blurted out before she could help herself.

"Whaaaat?!"

"Yes, I ended things with Cecil last week," Lucie confessed.

Rosemary's jaw dropped, and then she said almost in a whisper, *"Last week?"*

"Yes."

"Now I know why Cecil didn't show up to your mom's gala. I thought it was because he was scared of Cornelia Guest!"

"Well, I'm scared of her too, but that wasn't the reason."

"Then I'm confused. Why did you break up with Cecil? I thought you were so excited to have that big lavish wedding in Abu Dhabi." Lucie could see Rosemary's mind going into overdrive.

"I realized I didn't love Cecil. I realized that I would never be the perfect trophy wife. I want a chance at a new life. I want to travel and move to Los Angeles to become an art dealer. And that's why George should stay here. You both should stay here, Mrs. Zao. You shouldn't have to leave your comfortable house in East Hampton. My mother would miss you so much," Lucie pleaded, fighting back tears.

"I would miss her too. But we've done enough damage, Lucie. It would be too awkward for you to have to be around me and my son all the time."

"No, it wouldn't, Mrs. Zao. It wouldn't at all!"

"Really? Then why did you tell him you never wanted to see him again? Why did you make him promise to leave you alone?"

"He told you that?"

"Yes, he said you commanded him never to set foot in any of your houses again. And so he won't."

"But I didn't really mean it that way . . ."

"What did you mean then? Because he took you at your word, dear. That's the kind of boy he is. He is true to his word, and the last thing he would ever do is hurt anyone. He would never wish to hurt you. He still loves you so much, the poor boy. I can see how he's suffering every day."

Lucie suddenly burst into uncontrollable sobs.

"*Hiyah!* Now you're crying. Why are you crying?"

Lucie couldn't answer through her heaving sobs.

Rosemary narrowed her eyes. "Is it because there's some tiny part of you that actually has feelings for my son?"

"Of course I do."

"What, you're feeling sorry for him now?"

"I don't feel sorry for him. I love him," Lucie cried.

Rosemary tilted her head dubiously. "You really love my son?"

"I've always loved him!" As much as it hurt, Lucie felt an intense relief to finally say it.

"So why did you tell him you didn't? Why did you have to go and break my boy's heart?"

Lucie crumbled onto the sofa. "I don't know. I was confused, I was ashamed. I was afraid of what my family would say . . ."

"Your family? Do you mean your mother?"

"My mother, yes, but also my extended family. You don't know what it's like for me. Ever since I was little, it's always seemed like my mother's only wanted me to be around my dad's family. It's as though Mom's ashamed of her Chinese roots—I hardly ever see my Chinese grandparents. I know she rebelled against her parents by marrying my dad, and I didn't think she'd ever want me to fall in love with a Chinese boy either. And I thought my father's family would be disappointed in me if I didn't marry some billionaire prince. I've been in a no-win situation all my life. My Chinese relatives treat me like I'm some sort of precious unicorn, too good to be one of them, and my WASP relatives treat me like I'm not good enough for them," Lucie cried.

Rosemary put her arms around Lucie as her tears kept falling. "You poor muddled girl! You've been deluded into being racist toward yourself! You don't even know how strong your mother is. She's not ashamed of her Asian roots at all! Do you want to know what she told me a few weeks ago? We had a long talk late one night on the beach, and she told me she made a decision to sacrifice her own family so that you and Freddie could spend as much time as you could with your Churchill family. Because she felt that you got plenty of Chinese influence with her at home, she wanted the both of you to maintain as strong of a link as possible to your father. She was so sad that you lost him at such a young age, and she felt terrible that she got so sick she couldn't help you deal with it properly at the time."

Lucie was stunned. "Why did she never tell me this?"

"I don't know." Rosemary sighed. "Why do mothers and their children never tell each other the most important things?"

They sat silently next to each other for a long while. As she dried her tears, Lucie spoke up again.

"Mrs. Zao, it's my turn to say sorry. I'm so sorry for all I put you and George through. I never wanted to hurt him either, and I hope he'll be able to forgive me."

"I know he will."

"I love your son, and I don't give a fuck what anyone thinks anymore!"

"No one will think anything, dear. They will keep loving you, and I know they will love my son. It makes me so sad that you've wasted so much time deceiving yourself thinking that it would be any different."

Lucie broke into a smile. Cornelia was right. Lucie had done nothing but deceive herself, and the deception hadn't just begun this summer. It had started all those years ago in Capri, at the moment she had been caught with George at Villa Jovis. That moment had changed everything. It had threatened to explode her whole world, and it sent her into a tailspin. It had forced her unconsciously to lock up her body and soul, and it made her seek out safe harbor with Cecil Pike, a man who she knew could never break her heart.

"I don't know what came over me, Mrs. Zao. It's like I've been trapped in a bubble for so long . . . since Capri, actually . . . It's like I've been sleepwalking through my life ever since."

"I understand. Something fateful happened in Capri that changed you and George. It changed the both of you forever."

Lucie sat up properly and gave Rosemary an awkward look. "There's something else I really need to apologize for, Mrs. Zao . . ."

"If it's about the co-op thing, I already know."

"You do?"

"Yes, Ms. Ferrer sat next to me at your mother's party. We had a very long talk. She wanted to know all about my years as a prostitute in Lan Kwai Fong."

Capri

· MAY 2019 ·

From: Charlotte Barclay
To: lucietangchurchill@gmail.com
Subject: Catching up!

Dear Lucie,

Thank you for the lovely postcard. It's filling me with wanderlust and making me wish I had more time to travel! Speaking of which, guess what I've managed to convince your mother to do? After the huge success of her Chinese cooking classes with Rosemary at the Preppie Guru Lounge last fall, we are bringing their classes to London this summer! Yes, it's high time Londoners experience some truly authentic Chinese home cooking, and I've already found the most wonderful venue for them, thanks to the generosity of my friend Yotam Ottolenghi, and I can't wait for everyone here to experience their double act.

I don't know how much you've been keeping up with the news since you have been so busy, but I think you'll be amused to know that Cecil's torrid romance/international incident has been filling up tabloid space both in the U.S. and here in the UK. He helped this beautiful Middle Eastern princess, HRH Sheika Kiza,* whom he met at the Paris couture shows, escape her awful husband. Apparently she was so taken by Cecil's knowledge of Judy Chicago and feminist art that she decided to reclaim her divine feminine power, fled in the dead of night, and was taken aboard Cecil's super yacht, which was secretly anchored in the Gulf of Aden. They are now safely ensconced in London, where she is suing her husband for divorce

---

* Before marrying one of the richest royals in the world, converting to Islam, and taking on her Arabic name, Her Royal Highness Sheika Kiza was married to two of the wealthiest men in Asia. Kiza in Arabic, by the way, means "kitty."

and seeking full custody of their child, the little prince. No doubt she will be well protected by Cecil and his mother's lawyers! Mordecai told me that Cecil's tapped him to oversee a new decorating team to make his mansion fit for the princess, and Olivia is in talks with them to do a documentary about the whole situation. BTW, how is her film project going with George?

Meanwhile, the new Preppie Guru Lounge in Shoreditch is progressing nicely. Auden and I hope we can open by September (fingers crossed!) and I'll be able to transition from full-time with Mary Berry to a project-by-project basis as I help Auden launch in London. He's back in New York teaching a flower essence therapy class at the moment, and as much as I adore him, to tell you the truth it's nice to have the flat to myself for a few days (the towel alignment training is still under way). We'll know before the end of the month whether we can visit you in July. I know I sound like a broken record, but I'm trying to work around some deadlines.

I saved the best for last . . . I saw Cacky at the Central Park Conservancy Luncheon (wearing the most ridiculous hat!), and of course she couldn't wait to casually drop that she has been given an audience with the pope this summer—thanks to the intercession of her new BFF Renée Pike—and she's bringing Granny along to the Vatican. After Rome, they want to visit you and Prince George in Capri. Believe it or not, Granny wants to spend more time getting to know George, because some Norwegian countess who's part of her bridge club in Hobe Sound told her that he's a direct descendant of Qing dynasty emperors! You've been warned.

Love,
Charlotte

From: Lucie Churchill
To: charlotte@preppieguru.com
Subject: Re: Catching up!

Dear Charlotte,

I can't believe that silly story that Cecil made up about George is still making the rounds. Is Harry Stuyvesant Fish spending my tax dollars bragging about his precious tenants over lavish diplomatic dinners at the U.S. Consulate in Norway? If Cacky and Granny do end up coming to Capri, I'm sure George will be gracious enough to give them the royal treatment. (Not sure about me.)

Thanks for all the updates! As you know, George and I decided to quit social media as an experiment, and since I'm so rarely online now, I really haven't kept up with any news. The days seem to fly past because most of my time is spent in a joyous painting frenzy. You'll probably be shocked to know that my new canvases are full of color. George calls it my "rose period."

Living here on Capri has inspired and rewarded me in so many astonishing, unexpected ways, and I'm so grateful that George and I seized this opportunity and threw caution to the wind. Of course, it was easier for him since he'd already quit his job, but for me it seemed so irresponsible to drop everything and move to a tiny island in the Mediterranean for a couple of years without a clue what I was going to do. But I keep thinking of that little framed quote from Auden's friend Gemma Rose that hangs on his office wall in Amagansett: "When we align with the truth of who we are, all things are possible."

George's renovation of Issie and Dolfi's villa is coming along splendidly and will hopefully be done well before her second baby arrives. It's already looking so exquisite, and I'm told it will be the first LEED green-certified house on the island! Meanwhile, the top-secret project that Dolfi's parents commissioned George to design in Rome is shaping up to be something that will be a game changer for the city. Olivia has been doing a marvelous job documenting his work, though I have to wonder what kind of Jedi-level guilt trip you must have laid on her. She's been so sweet to us, and I think she still feels like she has to atone for her ghastly film. It will be so exciting to see what she's creating for this new project of George's. I'm more impressed every day by George's talent and how aligned he is with nature. I don't think I've ever seen him this happy.

Speaking of happy, did you see those pictures Freddie sent? I cannot believe that after driving the Ortiz sisters all the way from China to Italy, he would deposit them at the Aman Venice and head straight back to Mongolia to go live with the eagle hunters! Those amazing pictures of him in that crazy beautiful outfit training his eagle on horseback remind me of a cross between Jon Snow and Genghis Khan! I miss him terribly, but I'm glad he's found his true passion and seems to have found love with Paloma's lovely granddaughter Bella Ortiz. (She's lasted five months, a record for him. And it can't be easy living with Freddie in a yurt!)

Oh, I almost forgot to tell you the biggest news . . . A gallery in Florence wants to give me a solo show in September. Can you believe it? I'm so excited but super nervous at the same time—I'm going to have to produce quite a few more works in time for the show. If you speak to Mordecai, can you ask if he has any recommendations for a good pensione in Florence? Preferably one with a view of the Arno.

Really hoping you and Auden can make it in July when Mom and Rosemary visit. The island will be at its most beautiful. It's finally warm enough to swim in the sea. Guess where George is taking me tomorrow at the crack of dawn?

xoxo,
Lucie

≋

La Grotta Azzurra

ANACAPRI

It was still pitch dark when they arrived at the steps leading down the cliffside to the entrance of the grotto. George held a flashlight, illuminating the path down to the water as they climbed quietly down the steps.

"This is crazy," Lucie said, breaking the silence. "Tell me why we're doing this so early again?"

"You'll see," George said with a little smile. "Okay, we're at the water's edge. I'll dive in first. Hold the flashlight."

George dove in, gasping at the icy water.

"How cold is it?" Lucie called out.

"Not too bad. Now, hand me the flashlight and dive in over here."

Lucie braced herself, took a deep breath, and dove in.

"Jesus Christ, it's freezing!" she cursed through her chattering teeth.

"Come on, it's not that bad. I'm warming up already," George said, as he swam up to her. "Okay, now follow my light."

George put the flashlight in his mouth and glided through the darkness, while Lucie swam behind, following the bobbing light.

Soon, they were at the mouth of the grotto, which was only about one meter high.

"This is the entrance where the rowboats go in?"

"It's the one and only entrance," George said, as he began swimming through the short tunnel. Soon, they were both inside the grotto, its towering limestone walls dimly lit by the weak flashes of light from George's torch.

"So this is the Blue Grotto. I'm impressed." Lucie laughed. "This is so silly, I feel like we're spelunking in the dark."

"Just wait a few minutes," George murmured, checking his watch. His timing had been perfect, and it was now exactly 5:45 a.m. Sunrise would come at 5:53 a.m. He turned off his flashlight, and now they were in complete darkness.

"Was this place always here?" Lucie called out.

"It was a cave that formed over millions of years, and the sea level rose up to what it is now," George replied. "In Roman times, it was the emperor's private nymphaeum, his bathing temple. I'm sure he got up to all sorts of nasty business here."

They swam around the grotto for a few minutes, and without warning, there was a sudden flash as the sunlight broke across the horizon, refracting against the deep underwater cavern and transforming the water around them into the most intense azure blue. It was as if Poseidon had flicked on a vast lamp at the bottom of the ocean, flooding the grotto with the purest light.

Lucie gasped in disbelief. She had never seen waters so blue, so bright, so inexplicably beautiful. She felt as though she were suspended in the liquid center of a sparkling aquamarine, as though she were having an out-of-body experience. How was such a place possible? The towering walls of the grotto now glowed in shades of cerulean, and she realized that the cave they were in was far larger than she had imagined. She was overcome with gratitude that she had waited till now, and it was George who had finally brought her here. Tears flowed down her face, mingling with the salty sea as she gazed at everything around her like a newborn, wanting to remember every sight, wanting to remember everything about this moment.

She lazed on her back, feeling absolutely weightless as the waters caressed her skin. She thought of Tiberius, of Caesar Augustus, of all the emperors who had swum these same waters, and she let her mind drift further back in time to commune with all the mythical gods that she knew had a hand in creating this paradise, hoping that they would inspire and heal her.

After a while, she swam over to George as if in a trance. He looked to her like an otherworldly silver merman, and she noticed for the first time that both their bodies shimmered and glowed under the silvery surface of the water. Lucie simply stared into his eyes, too moved to say anything. George stared back at her in that unbearably alluring way of his, and then he broke into a grin, filled with an intense happiness at the sight of her joy. He took her in his arms, and they kissed passionately.

"I love you," Lucie declared, kissing him again and holding him even more tightly.

"I love you too," George replied, thinking, *We're going to do this again, and next time I'm bringing a ring.*

They kissed for a few more minutes, lingering against each other, and then Lucie let go of George. She drifted with the current for a few moments, and then she raised her arms, kicked against the water with her powerful legs, and began to swim out of the grotto, into the bright new day.

Acknowledgments

Grazie mille to these wonderful souls, who in their uniquely magical ways were instrumental in helping me to create this book:

Ettore Castelli

Ryan Chan

Judy Chicago

Gianluca D'Esposito

Todd Doughty

David Elliott

Ilana Fayon

John Fontana

Simone Gers

Aaron Goldberg

Cornelia Guest

Suzanne Herz

Jenny Jackson

Alicia Lubowski

Alexandra Machinist

Acknowledgments

Gillian Longworth McGuire
John Penotti
August Railey
Gemma Rose
David Sangalli
Holly Star
Lief Anne Stiles
Bill Thomas
Chai Vasarhelyi
Jimmy O. Yang
Jacqueline Zirkman

Kevin Kwan (Far Eastern Kindergarten / ACS / Clear Lake High / UHCL / Parsons School of Design) is the author of the international bestsellers *Crazy Rich Asians, China Rich Girlfriend,* and *Rich People Problems. Crazy Rich Asians* was a #1 *New York Times* bestseller, was adapted into a major motion picture, and has been translated into more than thirty languages. He lives in Los Angeles and is trying to eat less pasta.

A NOTE ON THE TYPE

Pierre Simon Fournier *le jeune* (1712–1768), who designed
the type used in this book, was both an originator and a
collector of types. His services to the art of printing were
his design of letters, his creation of ornaments and initials, and his standardization of type sizes. His types are
old style in character and sharply cut.

Composed by North Market Street Graphics,
Lancaster, Pennsylvania

Printed and bound by Berryville Graphics,
Berryville, Virginia

Designed by Anna B. Knighton